D1468541

OTHER BOOKS BY JILL WINTERS

Plum Girl

Blushing Pink

Raspberry Crush

Just Peachy

Lime Ricky

JILL WINTERS

 NEW AMERICAN LIBRARY

New American Library
Published by New American Library, a division of
Penguin Group (USA) Inc., 375 Hudson Street,
New York, New York 10014, USA
Penguin Group (Canada), 90 Eglinton Avenue East, Suite 700, Toronto,
Ontario M4P 2Y3, Canada (a division of Pearson Penguin Canada Inc.)
Penguin Books Ltd., 80 Strand, London WC2R 0RL, England
Penguin Ireland, 25 St. Stephen's Green, Dublin 2,
Ireland (a division of Penguin Books Ltd.)
Penguin Group (Australia), 250 Camberwell Road, Camberwell, Victoria 3124,
Australia (a division of Pearson Australia Group Pty. Ltd.)
Penguin Books India Pvt. Ltd., 11 Community Centre, Panchsheel Park,
New Delhi - 110 017, India
Penguin Group (NZ), cnr Airborne and Rosedale Roads, Albany,
Auckland 1310, New Zealand (a division of Pearson New Zealand Ltd.)
Penguin Books (South Africa) (Pty.) Ltd., 24 Sturdee Avenue,
Rosebank, Johannesburg 2196, South Africa

Penguin Books Ltd., Registered Offices:
80 Strand, London WC2R 0RL, England

First published by New American Library,
a division of Penguin Group (USA) Inc.

First Printing, May 2006
10 9 8 7 6 5 4 3 2 1

 REGISTERED TRADEMARK—MARCA REGISTRADA

LIBRARY OF CONGRESS CATALOGING-IN-PUBLICATION DATA:

Winters, Jill.
  Lime ricky / Jill Winters.
    p. cm.
  ISBN 0-451-21836-1
1. Women cooks—Fiction. 2. Fire fighters—Fiction. 3. New York (N.Y.)—Fiction.   I. Title.
PS3623.I675L56 2006
813'.6—dc22   2005029686

Set in Adobe Garamond
Designed by Daniel Lagin

Printed in the United States of America

PUBLISHER'S NOTE
This is a work of fiction. Names, characters, places, and incidents either are the product of the author's imagination or are used fictitiously, and any resemblance to actual persons, living or dead, business establishments,
events, or locales is entirely coincidental.
  The publisher does not have any control over and does not assume any responsibility for author or third-
party Web sites or their content.

This book is for Aaron.

ACKNOWLEDGMENTS

Thank you, Mom, for reading the five-hundred-page version of this book and for giving me great feedback. Your insights were invaluable—proving yet again that you are more than just a blond bombshell and a pretty face. And thanks to Laura, my incisive and very cool editor, who is a gem to work with and who anxiously awaits my ferret subplot in a future book—right?

Part One

CHAPTER ONE

*G*retchen woke up to her apartment on fire. It was strange the way you could fly out of bed—burst up from a cocoon of comforters, your head still heavy with sleep but your body jolted awake and thrumming with fear. How, in the murky depths of your mind, you could believe you were still dreaming, even as pure instinct sent you racing out of your room and into the acrid stench of burning plastic.

Gretchen slapped hard on the wall switch and flooded the hall with light.

"Oh God!" she yelped as panic seized her chest. Billows of smoke slid between the cracks of Dana's door, then expanded, puffing up into listless clouds that evaporated into the ceiling. *Is she okay? Oh God—please let her be okay!*

With her heart slamming against her ribs, her mind sharpened quickly, and she bolted across the hall to her cousin's bedroom.

Grasping at her neck, Gretchen felt herself choke—on smoke or on fear—and without thinking of the heat of the brass door handle, she turned it and flung the door open. A bright orange glow in the corner by the window illuminated the rest of the room.

A thick fog of smoke was rushing toward her, gray and smothering, and through it she saw Dana's bed, still made. The mustard-colored quilt was pulled tightly across it; the long, spiral pillow rested at the head of the bed like a plump golden rod with fringe. Gretchen's eyes stung. The smoke burned into them, made them water like diluted acid and clogged her throat like a rough piece of bark. She struggled to cough—to breathe—as she blinked away tears.

Then, like an electric shock, a bolt of relief struck her chest:

Dana was out tonight. She'd said something earlier about crashing at her friend's place so she could make an early audition the next morning. *Thank you, God,* Gretchen thought frantically, exhaling a shaky sigh. *Thank you, thank you, thank you.*

Inching over the threshold of the room, she tried to move past the smoke, but it didn't seem possible; it was rising furiously, but from where—from what? From that orange glow in the corner, of course. Squinting, Gretchen tried to make it out, to make sense of it, as the pungent smell got stronger with each step she took toward Dana's window. She'd gotten only halfway across the room when suddenly, the frilly yellow curtains exploded into flames.

"Aaah!" she screamed, leaping back.

Startled and terrified, she pressed her hand to her pounding heart. Her mouth dropped open and her eyes shot wide, watching as the curtains were devoured by fire.

She turned and ran from the room. Hooking a sharp right, she almost skidded in her wool socks on the hardwood floor as she raced away from the smoke, from the stench, from the flames, and toward the front door.

Then she stopped. She couldn't just leave. What about her neighbors? What should she do? Think fast. Call 911, or simply flee the scene in her nightgown and socks, hitting the fire alarm in the hallway on her frantic way to the stairs?

Wait—was there even an alarm in the hallway? Now she couldn't remember. She'd moved to New York only two weeks ago and had spent none of that time exploring the building, which had a distinctly elegant charm but would be a lot less charming if it burned to the ground. If her cousin kept a fire extinguisher around here, she'd never mentioned it.

Suddenly something crashed in the other room. Startled, Gretchen jumped. She scurried into the living room and fumbled in the darkness for the end table beside the couch and the brass lamp that sat on top of it. Once she had some light she could find her cell phone, which was tossed God-knows-where.

Her knee banged into the table. Hurriedly, she reached out, registering the cool, sleek metal against her fingers as she slid her hand up the lamp and yanked hard on the chain. More choking coughs. Each one spread a hot blast of pain across her chest. Smoke from the other room was still stuck inside her, gagging her. *Shit!* she thought, panicked, as she raced around the room. *Where is that damn phone!* She thought she'd find it tucked within the soft curves of the red sofa or buried in the bulk of the cream-and-floral armchairs. Nothing. Climbing over the side of the sofa, she jammed her fingers between the cushions, then all but tumbled onto the hardwood floor, running her hand underneath.

Bang, bang! Bang, bang, bang!

Startled, Gretchen yelped, nearly dropping the phone from her trembling fingers. Someone banged on the door again. She hopped to her feet just as she heard a man's voice shout: "Open up—fire department!"

The voice was deep and loud, though a little muffled, and Gretchen was suddenly, inexplicably, frozen in place. Terror closed up her throat as she clutched her chest with her palms, feeling her heart thud hard beneath her breasts; reality was barely sinking in, her reason and judgment suddenly scattered, uncomprehending, paralyzing her, even as she willed herself, *Do something already—fucking move!*

The door burst open. Big and faceless, a man in black barged into the apartment, moving past Gretchen without seeming to notice her at all, went down the hall, straight into the fire, when Gretchen had run from it.

The floor nearly shook as his boots thumped across it. Gretchen had barely taken in any details about him other than his tall, broad frame, the gas mask on his face, the hard hat on his head, the big metal canister strapped to his back. Now she heard a ferocious gush of spray coming from Dana's room, and she edged closer, waiting on the border between the living room and the hallway. Waiting for him to come out, to tell her everything was okay, waiting for him to explain, or rather for a chance to explain to *him,* not that she even could.

Her mind buzzed with a scrambled mess of indiscernible thoughts when suddenly—abruptly—all sound stopped.

Except for the sound of her own breathing, which was short and choppy and barely calm even as she realized: *The fire is out.* It was over, solved, no thanks to her, but still over. Relief seeped like warm liquid into her skin. Gingerly, she walked toward Dana's room, but just as she started down the hall, she heard a loud, hoarse voice call from behind. "Hey, Pellucci!" Gretchen whipped around. "You okay?"

A second man was standing in the doorway now, wearing the same heavy black garb, only he was much shorter than the first. He had his gas mask pulled up so it was resting on his head almost like a visor, and she could see deep wrinkles creasing the flesh below his eyes, like spiderwebs woven above his cheeks.

"Yeah," the first firefighter called back as he exited Dana's room, pulling off his hat and mask. Again he walked right past Gretchen in the hall like he didn't notice her. Hey, maybe he truly *didn't* notice her; and that would actually be a good thing. "Just a girlie fire," he added, expelling what sounded like a tired sigh.

Girlie fire, Gretchen thought speculatively. *What does that mean?*

"Scented candles?" the shorter one said.

"Yup."

Oh.

Wait . . . suddenly Gretchen realized. Dana and her inane relaxation rituals—that was how this mess started. Before an audition, Dana did the whole scented candles and meditation bit—apparently trying to get into deep concentration about a character, or so she'd mentioned a few times when she'd shut the door on Gretchen, apologizing but telling her she needed to be alone for it. She should've known her cousin wouldn't be completely innocent in all this.

Meanwhile, the firefighter called Pellucci was no less intimidating without his mask on. Gretchen eyed him as she drew closer. Tall and broad-shouldered, he had blackish hair that was messy and disheveled from his hat and a strong jaw darkened by stubble. She bit her lip, feeling her heart kick up again. He still wasn't looking at her and it was making her nervous. "Jesus Christ," he muttered savagely. He sounded exhausted and angry—especially angry.

"Ma'am," the shorter one said, nodding politely at Gretchen. "You all right?"

"Yes," she said tenuously, like a mute speaking for the first time.

She cleared her throat to get all of her voice back. "I'm fine," she added. "Thank you."

Then Pellucci slanted his gaze at her. It was narrow, assessing, almost squinting; she'd say he appeared . . . annoyed? Disgusted? Or maybe he was just shy?

Yeah, right. A sudden shiver rippled up her spine; the aftermath of the fire had left her starkly cold. Or maybe she was just realizing now that she was cold. After all, she was hardly dressed for a night in the middle of January. Her black nightgown was long and slinky with spaghetti straps and a plunging V that barely covered her breasts. Definitely too skimpy when you were standing in a lit room with two strange men, but it was perfect for the way Gretchen liked to sleep—snuggled in a bed thick with pillows and blankets, buried under a heap of covers, where she could feel completely safe and warm.

She crossed her arms, partly for warmth, partly to cover her breasts, and was about to say something to Pellucci when he averted his eyes. "I'll call the boys off," he said, then muttered, "Goddamn those fucking girlie candles." The other man chuckled as Pellucci put some kind of walkie-talkie up to his mouth. "Class A, Code four," he said, his voice firm and authoritative. He glanced back at Gretchen briefly before adding, "Possible HBD."

Huh? She flashed him a tremulous smile, wondering if "HBD" was a bad thing, and then there was some mumbling on the other end, followed by a long, low-pitched beep. With that, Pellucci shoved the radio back underneath his coat somewhere and looked again at his coworker (or was it colleague? What did firefighters call each other anyway?). "I'll give the place one last look; then we can get the fuck outta here," Pellucci said.

"Oh, I'm flattered," Gretchen said sarcastically, bizarrely trying to lighten the mood, because he just seemed so . . . *annoyed*. But if Pellucci heard her, he didn't show it. Instead he kept his eyes on his partner.

"Tell the others, I'll be right down," he said, his voice gruff and commanding, and the shorter one simply nodded—first at Pellucci, then at Gretchen. Putting his hand to the gas-mask visor on his head, as though tipping his hat, he smiled briefly. "Ma'am," he said, and turned to go. Gretchen had never been thrilled with the term "ma'am," but still, at least *this* guy had some manners. The surly one,

Pellucci, could definitely learn a thing. And why was he still here? Why would he be "right down"?

Once they were alone, Gretchen's breathing became shallow, labored. Somehow the older, friendlier fireman had sucked much of the air out with him. Why had Pellucci stayed behind? Why had he sent his partner off? What did he want?

He turned to look at her. There was an intensity in his gaze, in the way his light blue eyes studied her, and his assessing glance lingered before he spoke.

In turn, Gretchen assessed him, too. He stood tall above her. She'd guess he was around six-two, and there was a kind of heat that vibrated off him—or maybe it was just anger. As his gaze pored over her, Gretchen swallowed a bit tremulously but kept her head up. There was definitely something powerful about him. Maybe it was the height, or maybe it was just the thumping boots. In any case, he was making her nervous. With her fingers locked around the cool, soft flesh of her upper arms, she was still trying to conceal her cleavage and waiting for whatever he was going to say, whatever reason he had for staying behind.

"Have we been drinking tonight?" he said finally, his voice flat and cold. It came out somewhere between a question and a statement.

"No!" Gretchen nearly exclaimed, taken aback by the question. It was a reasonable one, but she just hadn't been expecting it. More calmly, she added, "I mean, no . . . I was asleep. Well, I had some wine with my steak earlier . . ."

With a perfunctory nod, he said, "Yeah, right." But he didn't sound overly convinced. At this point, it was pretty clear he was a jerk, but he'd saved her life, so she wouldn't nitpick.

Then it clicked: *HBD,* as in *Has Been Drinking.* So he thought she was a clueless drunk. Oh, whatever—she just wanted to make nice and put this whole night behind her. "Look, I'm really sorry about all this," she said. "I just woke up and I . . . well, thank God you came when you did."

Wordlessly, he moved past her again. He went down the hall, but before he disappeared, she could've sworn she saw him roll his eyes. "Where are you going?" she called after him. No response; he had this maddening tendency of ignoring her. She followed a few steps behind. First he checked Dana's room, then glanced across into Gretchen's, which was dark; then he stuck his head in the bathroom doorway, flicked on the wall switch, gave it a glance, and went back down the short hallway toward the living room.

"So about those scented candles," Gretchen said again, though she wasn't sure why she was bothering to explain to him; she supposed she just wanted it on the record somehow. "They weren't mine," she threw in, but he just ignored her and continued to the front door.

Stopping just two feet in front of her, he turned around. As he pulled off his heavy black gloves, he shook his head and gave humorless laugh. "You know, people like you have real fucking nerve." Whoa—people like her? She hadn't expected open hostility; the simmering attitude up to now had been just fine. "Fucking unbelievable," he added, looking at her dead-on, his blue eyes drilling into her like ice picks.

"Wait a minute," Gretchen said, holding up one hand. "The candles weren't mine," she repeated. "My cousin must've left them burning before she left tonight. I had no idea. I mean, I know there's no excuse, but—"

"You're right. There is no excuse," he stated bluntly. "None of those candles were insulated; you had papers and folders stacked up all around. What the hell were you thinking?"

She expelled a frustrated breath and tried again to explain. "I wasn't *thinking* anything; I already told you, it wasn't my room. I didn't even realize—"

"Didn't *realize*? You couldn't smell that shit before half the room caught on fire?"

Oh, *now* it was half the room—a minute ago, it was a "girlie fire."

"No, of course I smelled it," she protested. "Eventually."

"I smelled it all the way downstairs," he said, his shadowy, stubbled face screwed up at her like she was a moron. "And if you can't even work a goddamn fire extinguisher, you could at least call 911— do *something* for chrissake. You could've burned down the whole building!"

"I was *about* to call the fire department! Anyway, what's the difference now? You're *here*, right?"

The black-haired, blue-eyed savage was practically sneering at her. In his heavy black coat with fat yellow stripes across the sleeves, he was a hot-tempered and gigantic bee. "What's your name?" he demanded.

That threw her. Oh, jeez, did he really need her name now? Was there going to be an official report or something? This was ridiculous. "Gretchen," she replied in spite of her reservations. "Gretchen Darrow." She supposed she had to answer—and she supposed he wasn't the type to find humor in a response like "Ura Prick."

"You live here alone?" he said, then roved his eyes around the luxurious living room.

"No," she said, her voice edged with impatience. "I already told you my cousin lives with me." Wait, had she told him that yet? He had her so flustered, she wasn't even sure. "And for the record, I'm a really deep sleeper." Now, that was just lame. But true. In fact, once Gretchen climbed into bed, buried herself under one of her thick cover heaps, once her head hit one of her many pillows, she was pretty much out of commission until the shrill blaring of her alarm clock the next morning.

"And where's your cousin right now?" he asked flatly.

"She's at a friend's tonight. The fire was in her bedroom," Gretchen explained. She released a sigh and relaxed her posture. She needed to calm down; the worst was over—namely, the fire—she supposed the fireman was still just keyed up about it. And also, as she'd already noted, the guy was a jerk.

He slanted his cold blue gaze at her. "You get along with your cousin, Gretchen?"

She paused, thrown by the question, which sounded suspicious, suggestive—though she couldn't begin to guess what he was suggesting.

"Yes, of course we get along. I love her, why?" Gretchen stopped short of blathering on about how Dana was the closest thing she'd ever had to a sister, how she'd invited Gretchen to stay with her as long as she wanted until she found her own place, how she could always be counted on to brighten any occasion—okay granted, she didn't usually use actual fire. But instead of blathering, Gretchen cut right to the chase. "Why are you asking me that? What does it have to do with anything?"

Pellucci paused, tilted his head, as though he knew something. Now his face changed. Instead of anger, there was something smug in his expression. A moment of silence stretched between them and Gretchen sucked in a breath. She had to admit he had a decent face. Though it might be improved with a little smiling.

Honestly, she couldn't believe she was even finding him attractive at all! Yes, he was . . . well . . . ruggedly eye-catching. Not just his height or his dark scruff, but his overpowering presence—the confidence he exuded, the critical cool blue eyes, the way he seemed to consume most of the space and air and energy in the room. But still, did any of that make up for his bullying personality?

And confidence was one thing, but Pellucci seemed to radiate arrogance—a whole other effect and much less appealing.

Why she was even analyzing any of this, she didn't know. It wasn't like he was asking her out. More like he was thinking of filing some kind of complaint against her.

"No problems with your cousin?" he pressed. "Like maybe you two had a fight this evening? Maybe you went a couple of rounds over a guy or something?"

Now it was Gretchen's turn to grimace. "No, of course not! And if we did ever fight—which we don't—I can guarantee it would never be over something as insignificant as a guy." Should she break out the Gloria Gaynor to punctuate her point? No, that seemed a little desperate. Then, suddenly, she realized: "Wait a minute . . . Are you saying . . . Oh my God!" she yelped. "Are you trying to imply that I set Dana's stuff on fire?"

He just looked at her.

Her jaw dropped even lower as her eyes grew wider with feeling, with shock, with outrage . . . with fear. Was she in some kind of trouble? "That's what you're saying, that I caused a raging inferno in there on purpose."

He shrugged. "Fine, so maybe it was an accident. You never meant for it to get so out of control."

Heat crawled up her neck and spread across her cheeks as frustration and anger bubbled up inside her. "That's crazy! I didn't even do anything!"

"Exactly. You didn't call the fire department because you thought you could handle it? But of course, being a rich, useless princess, you couldn't." His vitriolic tone was like acid and seared a hole through the last shred of civility in their fabric of conversation. Stunned, Gretchen didn't know whether to counter his misperception of her as rich and useless, or simply to punch him in the tightly locked jaw.

What a psycho!

Finally, shaking her head, mouth agape, she pressed a palm to her forehead as the other slid to her hip. "God, this is insane. Do you treat all your damsels in distress like this—or just the ones who want to rip your face off?"

In her state of agitation, she'd forgotten about her low-cut nightgown and full, jiggling breasts. When Pellucci's eyes dropped down, though, she quickly remembered. As he eyed her nearly naked breasts, his expression changed, his face became unreadable.

Gretchen's breath caught in her throat. Her pulse soared. God, he made her nervous. Swallowing hard, she crossed her arms again. But why? What was done was done. When Pellucci's gaze slid up from her breasts, it seemed to linger on her lips. As he studied her mouth, a different kind of tension climbed into the space between them. It strung tight and stretched on with more than anger. Attraction. No, but that couldn't be right . . .

Her fingertips dug into the soft flesh of her upper arms as her face flamed hotter. It wasn't like her to feel so suddenly flustered, so rattled, so disconcerted. But she supposed everything that had happened was just crashing down on her.

Pellucci stepped closer to her then, and Gretchen stepped back, though not as quickly as she should have, and when their eyes locked, her heart pounded harder—faster—and she became powerfully aware of how near he was, of the seconds ticking and the tension thrumming between them, and before she could speak, Pellucci's blue eyes drifted down to her mouth again. Then slowly, wordlessly, he raised his arm, brought his hand to her face. Taking Gretchen by surprise, his fingertips grazed her cheek; they were warm and gentle as they moved lightly over her skin.

Her breath caught in her throat, her heart jumped beneath her breasts, and she was suddenly speechless. Maybe not so suddenly.

When he pulled back, his fingertips were tinged with smoky black. "Ash," he said, bringing his hand back to his side. "Lock up behind me," he added, and then he was gone.

CHAPTER TWO

*L*ater that night Broderick "Rick" Pellucci sat at the Firing Squad, a rundown bar a few blocks from Engine 88. Most of the guys on third watch tonight were there, too, filling up a couple of tables in the back. The last call of the night had been the hot woman on East 81st Street. Or rather, a neighbor had placed the call—the woman had been a surprise.

Tonight was supposed to be some kind of send-off for Rick, who had a week's worth of vacation starting tomorrow. In truth, taking the vacation hadn't been his idea, but more of a stern invitation from his captain. It had been more than a year since Rick had taken any time off and, as he'd observed in the five years he'd been with the New York Fire Department, people in civil service didn't like it when you pissed off the benefits of working for the state, the generous vacation package being one of them.

He didn't plan to do anything in the next week except spend time at his late father's house in Maine. He would do some fishing, watch some sports, maybe read—hell, there was a thought. How long had it been since he'd actually read a book? A *whole* book? In the not so distant corner of his mind Rick wondered how much longer they'd have the cabin. He and Brett had inherited the place earlier that year, but they were still divided on what to do with it. Of course, Brett wanted to sell. With some fixing up, he'd said, they could get a quick score—as if Brett needed a score, quick or otherwise. Rick's younger brother was rolling in money, but like most people who had it, Brett always seemed driven by any chance to have more—and more. *Tack on a sauna, cut down half an acre of pine.* Rick could still hear his brother's voice, trying to persuade him to expand the place and put it on the market.

Now, as Rick glanced around the Firing Squad, nursing his beer, he realized that his so-called send-off was really just an excuse for the guys he worked with to stay out later than usual and get a little drunker. He took another swallow and thought back to the four-alarm that had blazed nearly half a block a few hours earlier. With a shake of his head, he tried to dismiss the images that still tormented him—so violent, so vivid still. It was an electrical fire, for sure. What else would light up a whole building so savagely, so goddamn fast?

His mind kept echoing back to the little girl who'd been crying out, screaming for someone to help her. Rick and DeMarco had climbed their way higher, rushing up the claustrophobic interior of the high-rise apartment building, hearing one high-pitched voice still calling out. At first she had been crying "mommy"; then they were cries to anyone. As he'd run to find her, Rick had heard his boots thundering up the stairs, through the old building, and the pounding of his heart in his ears. He'd felt the sweat running down, dripping from his hair to his forehead, the heat and anxiety baking him, but driving him on, and abruptly, the screams stopped.

Then he found her. So small, buried under a chunk of burning ceiling beam, which had fallen on top of her. She was tiny, couldn't be older than six, and was losing consciousness, no longer able to speak. It had taken Rick less than five seconds to get her out from under the beam and to cradle her in his arms while he darted back toward the stairs.

After the fact, he'd found out that her name was Tara Goldstein. She was asleep when the fire broke out. Her nineteen-year-old babysitter, some spoiled brat who also lived in the building, had apparently "panicked" and fled the scene to save herself, leaving Tara behind. Thinking about it now almost made Rick's chest shudder—with relief, with anger—and he expelled another sigh and toyed with his bottle of beer.

"What a night, huh?"

It was Charlie Spire, one of the EMTs who'd been on duty tonight, flashing his usual thrilled, dopey smile after a shift of total chaos. Most of the time Rick couldn't stand the asshole; any major catastrophe made him giddy.

"Yeah, what a night," Rick grumbled in return.

"Major rager on Lex, huh? Gotta love it!" When Rick shot him a look, Charlie clapped him on the shoulder and gave him a half-apologetic grin. "Oh, come on, the rush—that's what it's all about, man. And it's not like anybody died."

"Yeah." But Tara Goldstein had come damn close.

"So don't look so miserable."

"What can I say. I'm not a trauma junkie like you," Rick replied, managing a dry smile, one that belied the darkness of his mood.

"Pellucci always looks like that," Jon DeMarco said, sliding into the other side of the booth and setting his beer mug down with a clunk. "This guy's always fuckin' serious. And brooding . . . always fuckin' brooding." He picked up his glass and took a drink, then said, "Buddy, you're on vacation. You're supposed to be celebrating. Hey, look. The captain's even doing a special hula dance for you and everything."

When they glanced over, Charlie burst out laughing, stomping his foot on the floor like he could barely control himself, and Rick chuckled in spite of himself. The captain, a chubby, cheery guy who everyone simply called "Clip," looked ridiculous.

"That's better," DeMarco said with a nod.

Leaning back against the booth's torn red upholstery, Rick took in the noisy, rowdy antics and thought that while he loved these guys, he was getting too old for this shit. He was only thirty-two, but still, he couldn't shake the thought—especially when he watched his fifty-five-year-old captain trying to belly dance on top of his chair with his eyes sealed shut and a paper napkin hat. Instead of Rick thinking, *I hope I have that kind of kick in me at fifty-five,* Rick found himself simply thinking, *Jesus, that's pathetic.*

Suddenly Clip noticed Rick across the room and called out, "Pellucci! Come over here, son!"

Rick got up and crossed over, taking his bottle of beer with him. "What's up?" he said, smiling and coming closer as Clip jumped from his chair back to the floor, immediately becoming surrounded by a bunch of guys. Included among them was Don Bennet, who some called the Wall, not for his size or strength but because he was solid, sturdy, and always steady. Bennet had been polite to Ms. Gretchen Darrow, the last call of the night, while Rick had pretty much acted like a jackass.

Now Rick towered over Clip, who stood only about five feet, six inches tall. "We're gonna miss you next week," Clip said, reaching up to put his arm around Rick's shoulders, and Rick humored him by bending down a little. "First vacation in—what? Over a year? How does it feel?"

"Has it been that long?" Rick said, then shrugged. "Feels fine."

"Hey, I hear you put out a fire for a naked woman tonight," Clip said.

"Naked woman?" Jake Bowen echoed, raising his eyebrows, obviously rabid for details.

"I said *half* naked," Bennet said, holding up his hand to set the record straight. "I never said naked."

"Bennet, you shmuck," Rick remarked offhandedly. He didn't feel like getting into it. Then he'd have to feel guilty about how he'd acted, putting the brunt of his frustrations onto Gretchen Darrow— his anger about Tara Goldstein and her worthless, irresponsible babysitter, his disgust, and his pissy mood in general.

"Fine, fine, half naked," Clip said. "So come on."

"Come on what?" Rick said casually. He offered another shrug. As if he'd barely noticed her body . . . How could he *not* notice? She was curvy and sexy as hell . . . with lightly tanned skin that looked soft and smooth to touch . . . and her breasts. God, those breasts were unbelievable. Big and bouncy, straining against the low-cut front of her nightgown—but still with plenty of jiggle. *Wow.*

Well, hell, he couldn't help but notice. Her nightgown might have been long, but it didn't hide all that much. *Damn,* he thought with another shake of his head. She might be a scatterbrain, and definitely a little Manhattanite princess—judging by her apartment, which had to cost at least four grand a month—but she was still smoking.

"C'mon, Pellucci, tell us about the naked woman," Jake Bowen urged desperately.

That jerked him back into the conversation. With another shrug,

Rick said simply, "I went in and put out a fire—there's nothing more to say."

Saved one little girl tonight, saved one big girl, watched Clip hula with a napkin on his head. Shaking his head, Rick laughed to himself. Helluva way to start his vacation.

The next morning Gretchen was getting dressed for her first day of work when her pillows began to ring. So *that* was where she'd left her cell. She dove across her bed, nearly sliding on the sleek satin of her red-and-gold comforter, and pulled her phone out from under one puffy pillow. Then she rolled over onto the other and propped herself on her elbow.

She flipped her cell open. "Hi, Dana."

"Hey, G. Get this. I haul ass at seven this morning and find a note on the door. The casting call was moved to four o'clock!"

"Oh, I'm sorry," Gretchen said sympathetically.

"It's just so annoying!" Dana yelped. "How am I gonna make it now? I've gotta work from twelve to eight today. I mean . . . I *think* . . ."

Rolling her eyes, Gretchen scooted her way off the bed and swung her legs around till her wool socks hit the floor. She'd been living with her cousin for only a couple of weeks and already she'd come to expect Dana's less-than-diligent attitude toward her job. But then, working as a waitress at Medieval Faire, Dining and Jousting, pretty much screamed "transitional gig"—or was that Dana who screamed it, usually after she'd been reprimanded for coming in late or for having a little too much fun with the skull mace?

Gretchen pulled out the expensive but bland power suit her parents had bought her to celebrate her new job. With a sigh, she gave it the once-over. She didn't like it any better now than when she'd first unwrapped it. It was so her parents. They had as much flair as you'd expect from a forensic psychologist and a dentist, but like she'd noted—and like her mother had written in the brief card that had come with the gift—it was very expensive and "top of the line."

"I'll just have to sneak out while I'm at work," Dana was saying.

"Really?" Gretchen said skeptically. "You can do that?"

"Eh. I'll ask Lolly to cover for me. If Al comes sniffing around,

I'll have Lolly tell him that I'm in the bathroom, sick from the food they serve. That ought to shut him up."

"Can't Lolly just tell your boss that you're on break?"

"No. The casting call could run over an hour, maybe two," Dana explained. "But I have to go or I'll die. I will literally drop dead." Meaning that Dana was not great at handling disappointment. As it was, for the past eight years she'd been juggling her love of acting with her need to make a living, and ignoring her English degree altogether. She was pretty optimistic by nature, but from what Gretchen could see, it was a tough business. Today's casting call was for a soap opera, which once upon a time Dana had said was beneath her. Now she was praying for just a chance on it. She remained hopeful about her proverbial big break, especially after it had happened to her friend Marcia Rabe, who soared into celebrity status last year with a much-hyped miniseries.

It was thanks to Marcia Rabe, in fact, that Dana and Gretchen were living like queens (by New York standards, anyway). She'd been in London filming a television show for the past three months and would be there for at least another five. Still, she wanted to keep her place in New York. Not only was it gorgeous, but this way, she'd have it whenever she was back in town. So she'd struck a deal with Dana: In exchange for keeping up the place—taking in the mail, paying the utilities, watering the plants, and dusting occasionally—Dana could stay there rent free. To Marcia, that was far better than leaving the place vacant for months, vulnerable to burglary, or subletting it to a stranger who would scour it for something to sell to the tabloids.

Like the rest of Marcia Rabe's apartment, the guest room Gretchen was staying in was meticulously stylish, with elegant, antiquey touches—like the copper and glass lantern dangling from the ceiling on a heavy black chain and the lavish grandfather clock standing regally in the corner.

Too bad Dana's scented candle fiasco had pretty much marred the beauty of her bedroom. In fact, when Gretchen had ducked her head in earlier that morning, she'd turned her nose up at the pungent smell that still lingered. Winced at the black holes that had bled through the pale yellow curtains, leaving each a charred and filthy version of its former self.

"By the way, are you nervous for your big day today?" Dana asked now.

"Yes," Gretchen admitted.

"What are you gonna wear?"

"Good question," she said, studying the suit in her hands again. Hmm . . . should she wear this? A suit would be the most professional way to go, and she *was* trying to make a great impression. Not only for Susanna Tate, her new boss, but also for the other celebrity chefs at the Cooking Channel—or TCC—and the powers-that-be at the network.

She fingered the hem of the blazer once more and deliberated. Top of the line, maybe, but it was just so damn . . . monochromatic. In dark, lifeless blue. And was it just her or were those shoulder pads kind of hard core?

"You know that suit your parents gave you?" Dana said, talking over street noise in the background and the honking of a horn; she was obviously walking and talking.

"That's so funny you mentioned that!" Gretchen began. "You're reading my mind."

"Please don't wear that. You look like the Incredible Hulk in that jacket."

With a startled laugh, Gretchen said, "Oh, thank you." So glad she'd tried the thing on once for her tactful cousin. Though Dana hadn't said much at the time—she'd been too busy suiting up in dish-washing gloves, getting ready to scrub the kitchen, with her dark red hair tied back babushka style. Now, apparently, she had the focus to be blunt.

"Sorry," Dana added with a frothy little giggle, "but I had to tell you. The Incredible Hulk is definitely not the vibe you want to be putting out when you meet Romeo Ramero."

"True. Or ever." Gretchen had to admit with her hour-and-a-half-glass figure, suits tended to make her look boxy and shapeless.

"Hey, do you think you'll meet him today? Oh my God, I would die!"

"No, you wouldn't," Gretchen replied with a grin, and pulled out her tea-length lime green dress. It was a stretchy, smooth material but fit loosely enough to be appropriate for work. Nothing was worse than when something was too tight around her breasts and people kept staring at them. Men and women alike. She didn't even think it was sexual for the most part. It was almost like people just couldn't help looking—as if they were thinking, *Huh, now those are some big jugs. I wonder if she needs a back brace.*

"Okay, I wouldn't *die*," Dana said now, "but I'd kiss him, or jump his bones, maybe."

"On your first day?" Gretchen said, squinting incredulously. "In front of everyone?" Please, her cousin was all talk. "Anyway, I have no idea if or when I'll meet him. I don't know if Susanna and he even interact; I'm sure they tape at different times, too."

"Hmm . . ." was all Dana said to that. There was no question that she, unlike Gretchen, had a major thing for Romeo Ramero, the supercute star of TCC's live cooking show *Brooklyn Boy Makes Good . . . Food!* In fact, ever since Dana learned that Gretchen would be working as set supervisor at the same network, she'd been coercing her to start some wild affair with him—as if that were up to Gretchen anyway—and for the sole purpose of giving Dana the lurid details.

So far, Dana had already asked Gretchen to find out if Romeo was a good kisser, a "generous lover" and, oh yeah, if he was well hung and could go all night. (Her cousin had reality problems.)

All savagery aside, though, Gretchen had to admit: The idea of meeting such a big celebrity in the flesh *was* exciting. He had to be one of the most well-known television personalities right now, with his cookbooks everywhere and his camera-ready face popping up in magazines beside his recipes. He saturated the daytime talk-show circuit with guest appearances. He had a charming guy-from-the-old-neighborhood way about him; one of his claims to fame was that he'd never had formal culinary training, but had learned everything he knew about cooking from his father. Undoubtedly his "star quality" came from several things. One, he was cute. Two, he was extremely fit—as evidenced by his tight black shirts and snug ribbed sweaters. Granted, his defined, circular muscles and supertrim waist were too bodybuilderlike for Gretchen—her ex-boyfriend not withstanding. She preferred a guy who wasn't so carved and sculpted. Romeo's looks plus his charisma gave his show a real dynamism, and the enthusiastic live audience only added to the verve and the energy of each episode. And that led her to another thing that gave Romeo star quality: The guy seemed to love the attention.

Now, as Gretchen was shimmying into stockings, she realized her cousin was still talking. "I can't believe the casting call was changed again, but okay, I'm over it . . . Basically, I crashed at Lolly's for no reason last night."

Last night! Of course—how had she forgotten? "Oh, speaking of last night," Gretchen interjected. "I could kill you!" She went on to tell her exactly what happened with the candles, including the part about getting yelled at by a very pissed-off fireman.

"Holy shit!" Dana exclaimed. "I can't believe I *did* that! Shit, shit, shit!"

"It's okay," Gretchen relented. "I suppose it could've happened to anyone. But you have to be more careful."

"Oh, G . . . I am so sorry," she said, her voice drenched with guilt.

"That's okay. I just felt so bad about it. The fireman seemed really put off by whole thing. Of course I tried to blame you, but he seemed less than interested."

"Why should he be put off?" Dana asked, then scoffed. "It's not like he doesn't see fire on a daily basis—oh, I just realized! Can you imagine if we'd burned down that beautiful apartment? Marcia would've killed us!"

"What's this 'we' business?"

"She could've sued me for everything I had!"

"What do you have?" Gretchen asked, confused.

"Or she could've had me blackballed in the industry!"

Gretchen rolled her eyes. "Well, maybe if she found out you'd killed your cousin in the process she would've taken pity on you."

"God, I am so sorry. . . . Please don't be mad at me."

"I'm not—really, it's okay," Gretchen said.

"I'll make it up to you, I promise. How about I make a special dinner for us tonight?"

"No, no, that's fine," Gretchen said quickly.

"No, I insist," Dana said. "I want to make dinner. I want to say I'm sorry."

"But then you'll have to you're sorry twice."

Dana laughed in spite of herself, and Gretchen laughed, too. There was no point beating it to death at this point. Then Dana remarked, "You know, I can't believe the fireman gave you a hard time. Are they even allowed to do that?"

"I guess. I mean, he thought I was a menace to everyone in the building, and I really can't say I blame him. Not that he had to be such a jerk about it. But hey, at least I never have to see him again. . . ."

"Was he cute?"

Cute. Interesting question. Well . . . Gretchen had to admit to herself that she *had* felt a strange, fleeting attraction to him. For a few crackling moments, the air between them had thickened with tension. How much was annoyance and how much was sexual was tough to say, especially now that the moments had passed and, oddly, seemed far away.

But *cute*? Somehow cute didn't fit him. Intimidating, yes. Pushy. Strong. Potent.

"I'll take that as a yes," Dana said, snapping Gretchen back to attention.

"Oh . . . well . . ."

"C'mon, how long does it take to say someone's dogmeat?" she teased.

With a surprised laugh, Gretchen said, "I never plan to find out."

"That cute, huh?" No. Gretchen just wasn't the type to call someone "dogmeat"—but of course, Dana knew that.

After Dana apologized again about the candles, they hung up. With her lime green dress waiting on the bed, Gretchen headed to the shower.

CHAPTER THREE

*T*he taxi ride to TCC was bumpy—and not as in a gravelly road, but as in bumper cars. Every few feet it seemed, the driver stopped short and sent Gretchen's upper body hurling forward, then slamming back. To gain more balance, she scooted over closer to the window and rested her hand on the door.

Gazing out the window, she felt the chill of winter air seeping through the glass, which was partially misted over. Sleet spilled sideways from the sky. Sliding onto the tops of cars, it smeared down windshields and pattered onto the slushy street.

Gretchen couldn't remember the last time she'd seen so much traffic. She'd lived in California for the past three years, at a resort in Carmel that was as much an idyllic paradise as was possible to simulate. Deluxe Resort was a sprawling six-story estate with violet-colored flowers climbing up its corners. It was surrounded by a hundred acres of rolling hills, with emerald-green grass and lush groves of pear trees and orchids. The thing Gretchen hadn't realized when she'd taken the job as a chef there, however, was that this luxury resort was also a health spa, and therefore she would be expected to prepare succulent, impressive dishes that were also low fat, low calorie, low sodium, and low whatever-else-made-things-taste-good.

And since Deluxe catered to the fabulously wealthy, the clientele expected to be comfortable. Which meant full. Sure, they wanted to be chain-smoking skinny, but they also wanted food—and lots of it. When Gretchen had begun, she'd been thrown into the pit with a bunch of other confounded cooks, trying to figure out how, exactly, Oprah's personal chef did it. It hadn't taken long, though, for Gretchen to rework her oeuvre of recipes, to experiment and create dishes of her own, which moved her quickly up to assistant head chef.

By her third year, she'd become restless with restaurant work . . . and with California. Of course, her tense breakup with Tristan, a personal trainer at the resort, hadn't helped. Shutting her eyes now, Gretchen tipped her forehead to rest lightly on the cold, dewy glass of the window. Now *that* had been awkward. But breaking up with someone wearing three plaster casts was never easy, was it?

Almost automatically, she pushed those thoughts aside. It was strange, but while the details of her relationship with Tristan— including its bitter end—were indelibly etched in her memory, that era of her life became more irrelevant all the time, and the memories taken as a whole lost their visceral weight in favor of a surreal, detached kind of awareness.

Now if only the painful individual details, broken apart like shards of glass, could lose their sting as well, Gretchen could forget about Tristan altogether and finally be able to laugh about him. Or *at* him—whichever.

Despite Gretchen's passion for cooking, there was something she'd learned about working as a chef: No matter where you were— no matter how upscale or even how serene a place might seem—the facade was dropped the minute you walked through the swinging kitchen door. It was the same everywhere: pure stress, total chaos. Yelling and dropping dishes and pointing fingers and management breathing down the head chef's neck—who, in turn, smothers his staff and makes everyone a nervous wreck half the time.

She'd just had enough of the frenetic atmosphere. Plus, she'd begun to miss the northeast, and more acutely than she'd ever realized she might. Though she'd grown up in a pretty Connecticut suburb, she hadn't lived nearby in a long time. After earning her culinary degree from Johnson & Wales in Charleston, South Carolina, she'd spent two years at a prestigious Cordon Bleu program in Minnesota, then was off to California.

It had been way too long since she'd been back in the northeast, and it was the seasons she missed the most. Especially wintertime, when the evergreens that wrapped around the house were weighed down by frosty bunches of snow. When even sunny days were bluish, and nights were spent reading under the blankets or making s'mores in the fireplace or lying in bed watching tiny flakes drift past her window. (It was funny the things she'd done to amuse herself when she was younger and alone.)

In spring, when the air in Connecticut smelled like fresh-cut grass, the dogwood trees bloomed like frilly pink umbrellas, and in the blazing hot, bright yellow of summer was the scary excitement of a coming rainstorm. And most of all, Gretchen missed the golden blanket of autumn. That lone apple tree in the backyard.

She'd had enough already of California, she'd realized. Enough with weight-conscious rich people and perennially warm weather. It was at this crossroads that Gretchen had learned about the position at the Cooking Channel in New York City and she'd known she had to go for it.

"Here," the taxi driver mumbled as he swerved to a stop in front of a nondescript, brick-front building with only the number 75 on it in small black lettering. Some of that scary excitement fluttered in her chest. *This is it,* she thought, and flung open her door.

Gretchen stepped through the front doors of the building into the warm, cavernous interior. The inside was like a long, wide corridor that stretched the length of half a block. Soft spotlights lined the red-brick walls. The air was thick with the aroma of fresh-baked bread. Gretchen's heels clicked loudly on the stone floor as she passed a bakery on her right, then a small café on her left, then a few more shops and vendor carts, until she got to a line of people waiting restlessly behind a gold rope.

To the right was a set of glass doors with T•C•C emblazoned across them in silver block letters. Gretchen offered a quick, close-mouthed smile to the people at the front of the line as she moved past them and approached the guy guarding the door, who was dressed in jeans and a navy blue T-shirt with an employee badge hanging from his belt. He turned out to be a production assistant— or "PA"—for *Brooklyn Boy Makes Good . . . Food!;* the people on line had tickets to the live taping at noon.

Once Gretchen got clearance, she entered TCC. The receptionist's desk was a wide domed white table set up high from the sea-green carpet. With her heart beating faster, Gretchen approached. Probably in her thirties, the receptionist was pretty with layered brown hair and a straight white smile like a commercial for Crest Whitestrips. "May I help you?" she said.

"Yes, I'm here to see Lila Mendal," Gretchen replied, giving her the name of the human resource director she was supposed to report to—the one who'd hired Gretchen for the job. Gretchen still hadn't met Susanna Tate, who was probably too busy and famous to spend her time interviewing candidates.

The receptionist glanced down at her appointment calendar. Then her smile widened, her face lit up, and she said, "Oh, you must be Gretchen Darrow. We've been expecting you!"

A surge of pride soared inside Gretchen. They were expecting her, like she was somebody special. In a way it made her feel like she already belonged.

"I'm Denise," the receptionist added brightly as she hopped up from her seat and came down from her perch. "May I take your coat?"

"Oh, yes, thank you." Gretchen shrugged off her long black jacket, which was glistening with the thawed rain that had streamed down it in rivulets.

She couldn't help feeling important as Denise took her coat and hung it up with alacrity, as if Gretchen was not to be kept waiting. She tried not to let it go to her head, but she couldn't help it, especially when Denise added, "We're so excited for you to join the family, so to speak."

Gretchen beamed even more. So everyone had been waiting—anticipating the arrival of little old her? And to think: Only two months ago she'd been getting bitched at for grating an onion instead of mincing it. And now here she was, at a major television network, treated like a part of the "family"—one might even say a VIP.

"Let me show you around," Denise said.

First she took her to the kitchen, which seemed an odd place to start, but maybe Denise figured that Gretchen wanted a cup of coffee to kick off the day. "So this is the kitchen," she explained, then gave a laugh. *"Obviously."* Gretchen laughed along, and Denise continued. "And . . . let's see . . . here are the two main sinks . . . and then here you see we have a lot of counter space. Two microwaves—one on that end and one over there," she said, pointing across the room to a counter by the windows. "Let's see, what else?" She thought it over.

Well, what else could there be? So this was the kitchen. Good info, Gretchen supposed, but it wasn't like she planned to spend a lot of time in here.

"Oh, and we have three trash cans that get emptied twice a day," Denise said.

Gretchen held back a confused look. Trash cans? Who cared about trash cans? Denise was probably just new at giving welcome tours to the new employees.

"Now, Lila has a sheet made up to make it easier for you . . . Let me find it," Denise said, looking around. Then she pulled a laminated sheet out from between the toaster oven and the coffeemaker. "Oh, here it is!" she said. "This will be your guide, you know, until you get your whole routine down."

"Oh, great," Gretchen said, nodding, vaguely wondering why the guidelines for her job were in the kitchen. And while they were on the subject, why had the tour of TCC still not advanced beyond this point?

"So each day is listed here and is slightly different in terms of what's needed from you," Denise began, running her eyes as well as a French-manicured nail down the laminated page. That's when Gretchen strained her eyes to try to get a look herself; the page was turned toward Denise, but even at this skewed angle, Gretchen could see it was a bullet-point list of items, and she managed to make out a few of them:

- CLEAN MICROWAVE
- EMPTY TRASH
- HOSE DOWN GARBAGE PAILS TWICE A WEEK

What the hell? There had to be some mistake here. Gretchen's pulse quickened as she debated whether or not to say anything—to question yet. But then Denise interrupted her stream of thoughts, which were fraught with panic. "Now I know your supplies are around here somewhere . . ." She bent down and opened one of the cabinets beneath the sink. "Oh, here it is!" She pulled out a long rectangular box with a handle that reached across the entire length of it. It looked exactly like something you'd see a handyman or a super carrying around. Images of Schneider from *One Day at a Time* flipped spastically through her mind. Except Schneider's box would have contents like hammers, screwdrivers, and pliers. The one Denise was holding out contained Lysol, Pledge, and Soft Scrub (holy shit, was that for *toilets*?). Just bottles of cleaning products crammed against each other.

A skinny roll of paper towels and some crunched-up black garbage bags flapping over the side did little to alleviate Gretchen's sense of doom. Eyes widening, she felt her breath come up shorter and tried to swallow down her distress. *Is this some kind of joke?*

"Here you go," Denise said, thrusting the heavy carrier into Gretchen's hands, and Gretchen stupidly took it, shaking her head, her mouth dropping, and bafflement cinching her brows together. This didn't make sense. Denise had said they'd all been expecting her. . . .

Unless . . .

Had HR misled her about the job? Or had Gretchen somehow missed the part about toilets? She'd thought she'd landed the dream job of a lifetime, one that would open up a surfeit of opportunities—making connections, getting exposure, maybe a cookbook of her own someday—and now it all started to trickle away as the reality of the situation set in. No, she hadn't been on the verge at all—she'd been hired as the cleaning lady!

CHAPTER FOUR

"**S**o this should be all you need," Denise said, smiling, but then seemed to notice Gretchen's concern. "Oh, but don't worry—we can order more of whatever you want!"

Obviously Denise had misinterpreted Gretchen's pained expression of utter horror. More Soft Scrub was the last thing on her mind. "I'm sorry," Gretchen said finally. "I'm really confused here. I thought I was working as a set supervisor for Susanna Tate's show. Not . . ." Her words drifted off, but the portable trunk of cleaning products between them said it all.

Okay, there was nothing wrong with being a cleaning lady. It was very important work. Crucial work. It was a noble profession. (Wasn't that what the right term was for all the jobs you didn't want?) But this was not what Gretchen had studied for and worked toward; she hadn't had years of culinary training so she could better clean exploded Hot Pockets from the microwave.

"Gretchen?"

Both she and Denise turned. They saw Lila Mendal, the HR director, entering the kitchen. "There you are. I was afraid that maybe you got lost on your way over. The subway system can be so confusing," Lila said with a warm smile and extended her hand.

Gretchen was so relieved to see a familiar face, she had to resist the urge to run into Lila's arms and call her "mommy." Instead, she took the handshake, smiled, and said, "Hi, Lila! It's great to see you again."

"Um, Lila, apparently there's some kind of . . . miscommunication," Denise said apprehensively. "I was just giving Gretchen the rundown," she added, holding up the laminated page from hell.

Furrowing her light eyebrows a bit, Lila reached for the sheet and looked it over. It took her less than five seconds to let out a short laugh and say, "No, no, Denise. This is for the new cleaning service worker I hired. Gretchen's going to be working with Susanna."

A *sigh* slid from Gretchen's lips as her chest eased with relief. Thank goodness! For a few moments there, the prospect of hosing down garbage pails had seemed like a particularly cruel fate, even if it *was* only twice a week.

"Oh, I'm sorry!" Denise said, color filling her cheeks.

"That's okay!" Gretchen said as a small giggle bubbled in her throat. "I figured there was just some mix-up. . . ."

"Yes, we have two new hires today, so you'll have to bear with us," Lila said amiably.

After that Gretchen got the rest of the tour. She and Lila did a quick walk-through of the first floor, past Denise's desk, revealing more of the tranquil sea green and silver decor, full of cubicles and private offices. Then they went to the second floor, where Lila pointed out the office of Marjorie Bass, producer of *Sinful Temptations,* which was next to Joel Green's office. That one had the door closed and a garbled man's voice coming from the other side. "Joel is Brett's producer," Lila explained as she continued on.

"Who's Brett?" Gretchen asked curiously. Before moving to New York, she'd thought she'd memorized every cooking show on TCC, but the name Brett didn't ring a bell.

"Oh, that's right—you probably know him as 'Romeo,' " Lila said, then grinned. "Our resident stud, Romeo Ramero. Ever seen his show?"

"Yes, many times. I just didn't realize—then Romeo's a stage name?"

"Yes . . . but a fitting one, I'd say."

Next Lila showed her where the ladies' room was and pointed out a vacant office right beside it. "Technically that's Susanna's office," she explained, "but she never uses it. If she's here, she's usually on the set or in her dressing room."

As they circled back around, Lila stopped in front of another office. An administrative assistant was working outside of it; her desk was streaked with white sunlight from the window behind her. "Hi, Nell. Is Abe in?" Lila asked pleasantly.

The sixtyish woman, Nell, stopped typing only long enough to say no, that Abe was on a conference call.

"Abe Santasierra is Susanna's producer. You'll be working with him a lot," Lila explained as she and Gretchen headed toward the main elevators, near the reception area. "The third and fourth floors, more offices. On the fifth floor is Terra Cottage, the food court. The actual shows are filmed on the sixth, eighth, ninth, tenth, and twelfth floors." Gretchen nodded with concentration, adding more details to the burgeoning cache in her mind. First days at new jobs were always like that. On the one hand, they were stress free because you weren't expected to know anything; on the other, there was so much to learn and remember. "Now I'll take you up to meet Susanna."

The elevator careened up to the eighth floor; they emerged into a narrow, butter-yellow corridor with no end in sight—because it wrapped around. And as they followed its curve, Lila said, "Here we are," stopping suddenly in front of a black door marked STAGE C. She shoved hard on it, but it was so heavy that it opened only a few inches before it started hissing closed. So Gretchen leaned her weight on it, too, and both she and Lila entered. "This is where we tape *Susanna's Kitchen*," Lila said.

It was a huge open room with a closed-off stage in the center. They crossed the floor to the stage and climbed the two steps up to get onto the actual set. Until today, Gretchen had only seen this kitchen on television; she had trouble accepting that she was really standing inside the set now. It was like stepping into a life-size diorama—a warm, homey kitchen that existed only within this finite and contrived space. Oak counters with ceramic tiles, cabinets with decorative glass doors, lacy curtains on the two square-shaped windows—and a fake brick and ivy backdrop, which was visible through them.

Wow, Gretchen thought, absorbing it all with a breath. It was both smaller and more breathtaking in real life. It was hard to explain how something could look so glaringly artificial, but so idyllic and welcoming at the same time. Opposite the kitchen was a scattered mess of cameras and spotlights. Two of the cameras were massive, standing bulkily at around eight feet tall. There were mikes hanging from the ceiling and three different monitors set high up, at different corners of the stage.

"You'll be spending most of your time here, of course. And in the supply kitchen, which is through those doors back there." A big part of Gretchen's job was making sure that the right ingredients for each show were available, fresh, prepared in whatever way necessary before taping. If substitutions had to be made, it was up to her to make them, which was where her culinary background was key. "You can get to it by Susanna's dressing room, too," Lila said, then beamed a smile at Gretchen. "Now let's go say hi to Susanna and get you two acquainted."

Behind the stage, at the far end of the room was a doorway; then down three steps to a black door with a shiny gold star painted on it. "Here we are," Lila whispered and knocked.

"Yes? Come in," Susanna called from inside. Suddenly Gretchen felt nervous again.

Gingerly, Lila opened the door, revealing a spacious room ornately decorated in Laura Ashley, fragrant with the tangy-sweet smell of flowers. There were three vases on Susanna's vanity alone. Right now Susanna was sitting on the pale pink floral settee along the wall, talking with another woman, who stood above her—a skinny, sharply dressed woman with inky black hair arranged in artful, oversized corkscrew curls.

Both looked over—first at Lila, then at Gretchen—curiously. Well, Susanna looked curious; the other one seemed a bit annoyed by the interruption. What struck Gretchen instantly was the woman's violet eyes (contacts, obviously), and her insanely high heels. They were four inches high and as brittle looking as a wishbone. "Hi, Susanna. I hope we're not interrupting you," Lila said, then gave Gretchen a light, supportive pat on the back. Or was that a nudge forward? Gretchen stepped inside a little farther as Susanna rose from her seat and came closer.

In person, Susanna Tate was short—even shorter than Gretchen, who hit about five-three without heels. Gretchen would peg her at about five-one. She was wearing one of her trademark long drapey outfits; today it was a maroon, blue, and black floral number, with wide, flowing pants and a matching overjacket that extended past her knees. Her thick, heavy blond hair was somewhere between honey colored and strawberry and fell neatly a few inches below her shoulders.

After Lila made the introductions, Gretchen reached out to shake Susanna's hand. "Hi!" she said brightly. "I'm so excited to get started!"

Who knew she could be such a kiss-ass?

Susanna smiled; with her free hand, she covered their handshake and gave it a squeeze. "Thank you. We're thrilled to have you. Has Lila given you the tour?"

"Yes," Gretchen said, still smiling. A moment passed before she realized she was still nodding. Nodding almost uncontrollably now. Lila said a generic hello to Violet Eyes, then excused herself and left. In fact, she'd seemed pretty eager to leave . . . But Gretchen had other things to focus on at the moment, like willing her head to stop bouncing.

"Oh, Gretchen, I want you to meet my agent, Misty Allbright. Misty, this is Gretchen, my new assist—ah, set supervisor."

Smiling warmly, Gretchen said hello and walked closer to Misty to extend her hand. But Misty didn't extend back. In fact, it was bizarre. She just looked at her. Dead on. Expressionless.

No, that wasn't right. Expressionless was putting too much of neutral spin on it; there had been something chilly and unreceptive in Misty's gaze. Several seconds passed before Misty finally shook Gretchen's hand, but it was a blatantly obligatory gesture—and a limp, half-assed one at that.

"Susanna, I should run," Misty said, glancing at Susanna. "I'll call you," she added with a smile. Maybe smiles were reserved for famous people, potential clients—after all, she hadn't really smiled at Lila, either.

Right before Misty left, she slanted her gaze at Gretchen one more time.

Once the door shut, Susanna smiled and linked her arm through Gretchen's elbow and said, "Gretchen, I am *so* glad you're here. We desperately need someone who actually knows what they're doing around here. You don't know how difficult it's been for me!" she added emphatically, looking up with wide, searching eyes. "I've had to fire six people this year!"

As Susanna led her around, introducing her to various people, she went over what she would need from Gretchen on a daily basis. She also mentioned that Gretchen could have use of her vacant office on the first floor. Gretchen thanked her—almost absently because she was preoccupied, noticing how the people at TCC seemed to react to Susanna. Like they wanted to keep her happy, like they were on their best behavior. Either that or they'd scurry away as soon as they saw her coming—and before she saw them. She thought of Lila, how she'd seemed eager to exit Susanna's dressing room herself. And Gretchen kept hearing the words "I've had to fire six people this year" echo through her mind. It was only January, for pete's sake—what exactly had Susanna meant by *this year* anyway?

Was Susanna Tate less likable and pleasant than she appeared on her show?

There was something else Gretchen noticed. Nobody was wearing a dress besides her. In fact, once past the fourth floor, gone were the skirts, heels, ties, and jackets. Gone, too, were the carpeting and the serene sea-green and silver surroundings of the offices.

Up here, the pace was frenetic and the dress was casual. Like the production assistant who'd been manning the line of people with tickets to Brett's show, everyone working on or around the sets wore jeans, sweatshirts, untucked T-shirts, some even torn. Some people had headpieces dangling around their necks; many had clipboards in their hands. It was hard for Gretchen not to feel overdressed, especially with each echoing click of her heels as she walked. But it was a good thing, really. Now that she knew how relaxed the dress code was, she could swap the pantyhose for blue jeans, oh, and a nice soft, comfy sweater, her Nikes and—

"I love your dress, by the way," Susanna said now, and then it was as if she'd read Gretchen's mind and preempted it. "I must tell you, it's such a relief to see *someone* around here who takes pride in their appearance, especially when working on *my* show." She flattened her palm against her chest with feeling, casting Gretchen a dramatic look that said *Is it just me?* Then she patted Gretchen's hand and added, "I have a feeling you and I are going to get along great." Okay, so much for sneakers. "Oh, there's Brett," Susanna said, squinting ahead and tugging a little harder on Gretchen's elbow to lead her forward.

Sure enough, "Romeo Ramero" was all the way at the other

end—or curve—of the hallway, walking with an older man with thick, messy gray hair and baggy pants.

Wow . . . Gretchen's pulse kicked up. She didn't even have a thing for him, but seeing him in person—getting closer with each step—was almost surreal.

As he approached them, Gretchen noticed that, though he might be larger than life, he was also a lot shorter than she would've guessed. He looked like he was about five-nine—but more important, he was smiling at her. She had to admit: He was just as cute in person as he was on-screen. He had pretty blue eyes, a chiseled but still masculine face, white (capped) teeth, and a flawless complexion. He wore a black ribbed sweater and blue jeans.

"Hi there," he said, looking right at Gretchen. Then he winked. Somehow it wasn't lecherous, but flirty, charming. She supposed he just had a way about him.

"Hi," she said, smiling back. Susanna jumped in to introduce everyone. The gray-haired one—Brett's producer, Joel Green—grunted a hello. He had a brusque, dismissive air about him, making it apparent that he was anxious to resume whatever conversation he'd been having with Brett before Susanna had run into them.

"Hey there. It's great to meet you," Brett said, smiling warmly at Gretchen and capturing her hand in his. His grip was firm, though his hand was a little cool to the touch. Killer smile. Dana would die if she were here right now.

Brett's short dark hair was styled the same way it always was on television, but up close it was shiny and stiff with gel.

"It's so exciting to meet you," Gretchen said. "I'm a big fan of your show." Not quite the truth, but close enough. "I'm sure you hear that all the time, though."

"Hey, believe me, I never get tired of hearing it. Especially when it comes from a pretty girl," he added with a grin and another wink.

Just then Joel Green gruffly interjected, "Listen, Brett, we've really gotta go over these details for the Hawaiian show. Let's talk in my office."

"Sure, sure," Brett said, nonplussed by the apparent urgency of the Hawaiian show. He flashed another winning smile at both Susanna and Gretchen. "Bye, ladies. See you later." As he sauntered off with Joel, Gretchen noted that, short or not, he definitely had charm.

*   *   *

Rick buzzed apartment 5B again. Still no answer. Damn, it was freezing out here, and he was probably stupid to come back in the first place, but for some reason, the way he'd left things with Gretchen Darrow was still bothering him. He figured the least he could do for acting like such an ass the night before was bring her a portable fire extinguisher. She obviously needed one, and hey, maybe she'd even find it charming.

And there was another reason why he'd come back: This was the first day of his vacation and already he was bored as hell. Tomorrow he was heading up to his dad's place in Maine—no, *his* place. He had to keep reminding himself that it wasn't his dad's anymore. Some days it was so quiet up there, you could stand outside and hear the wind, maybe, but nothing else. It was no wonder that his brother didn't give a damn about the place. Brett had no patience for the quiet. The silence probably scared the shit out of him.

Rick was about to buzz a final time, but then thought better of it. *Screw it.* It was only ten to five; Gretchen was obviously still at work. Assuming she worked, of course, and wasn't just living in that big apartment on her parents' dime . . . or maybe she even had a sugar daddy, for all he knew. Bad behavior of his aside, he wasn't ruling out his initial assumption that she was rich and/or spoiled.

He started to turn away, then stopped when he heard someone coming to the door. A guy pushed it open, jerking his head back as soon as the cold air hit his face. "Hey, excuse me," Rick said to him. "Do you know Gretchen?"

"Who?"

"Cute girl on the fifth floor," Rick explained.

"Oh, the redhead?" the guy said, raising his eyebrows.

"No, no. She's got long dark hair. Dark eyes." He stopped short of commenting on her voluptuous breasts and the blatant sex appeal of her body. As it was, the guy looked blankly at him.

"Ah, no," he finally said with a shrug. "Don't know her." He continued down the front steps, and Rick moved past him, catching the door in his hand before it closed. He took the steps to the fifth floor and simply left the fire extinguisher outside apartment 5B, wondering if Gretchen would realize he was the one who'd left it, or that it was even for her—or even how to use the goddamn thing. But what the hell?

On his way back down the stairs, he had to admit that he was disappointed. He hadn't realized how much he'd wanted to see her again until just now. Maybe to see what she looked like again, to see if she was as cute and as sexy as he recalled, or if his whole perception from last night had been skewed, like his mood.

When he got back onto the sidewalk, his cell phone rang. He pulled it out of his back pocket and flipped it open. "Hello?"

"Brody."

"Hey," Rick said, recognizing his brother's voice. Also, Brett was the only person who called Rick "Brody" as their parents had. "What's up, man?"

"Shit, Brody, where have you been? I've been calling you." Brett's voice sounded threaded with frustration—and relief—like he didn't know whether to smack Rick or to hug him. Fortunately, he couldn't do either through the phone.

"Yeah, sorry. I was gonna call you later," Rick said, recalling the message his brother had left him earlier. It hadn't sounded particularly urgent. Besides . . . well, he might as well admit it: He loved his brother, but he didn't really like him much. Since getting his own show on the Cooking Channel, Brett—known to his endless parade of fans as "Romeo Ramero"—had been particularly unbearable. "So what's going on?"

"Something bad," Brett muttered. "Brody, I'm scared."

"Of what?"

"Jesus," Brett went on, his voice thready and low. "I don't want to believe it. I mean, maybe it's nothing, but . . . I don't know what the hell to think at this point . . ."

"Brett, just tell me what's going on," Rick said impatiently. He didn't do well with riddles; whatever it was, he'd rather just hear it straight out.

"I've been getting these . . . threats," Brett said finally.

"Threats—from who?"

"That's a good question," Brett said with a humorless laugh. "Too bad I have no fucking clue."

"Whoa, just back up," Rick said, concentrating, now on full

alert. Since Brett was famous, he was more susceptible to crackpots, weirdos, and stalkers. It didn't necessarily mean they'd be dangerous, but still, Rick stopped walking, halting on the sidewalk and assuming a tense, protective stance as he waited for his brother to explain.

According to Brett, there had been a couple of phone calls—which he'd dismissed as cranks—but then he'd gotten an e-mail today that had him worried. But when Rick pressed him for what the threats had said specifically he said he couldn't get into it right now.

"Well, is it a fan or something?" Rick asked, trying to get some clarification.

"No. I mean . . . I don't see how it could be . . ." Brett replied evasively.

"Where are you right now?" Rick demanded.

"In my dressing room. That's why I can't really talk. But can you come over later? I'll tell you more about it."

"Brett, c'mon. What the fuck is going on? I mean, give me *something* here."

Brett exhaled a slow, shaky breath before whispering into the phone, "Death threats. Well, the phone calls were."

Jesus. Rick's gut tightened. Again, he reminded himself that it could just be a harmless, obsessive fan, but still, he needed more information. "What do the calls say?" he asked.

"It's like a muffled voice saying, 'You will die,' that kind of thing."

"Your cell phone?"

"No—my penthouse."

"How many calls?" Rick asked, gripping his phone to his ear so he could hear over the street noise, while he stepped back to clear room for some woman with shopping bags.

"Three altogether, I think. I got the first one a few days ago. But I just ignored them. Especially because the only people who know my home number—well, I just figured it was some girl I pissed off."

"Oh, Jesus, have you been banging married women again?" Rick said with a sigh.

"*No,*" Brett said defensively, then added, "not lately . . ."

An irate husband was a possibility, Rick knew, and it wouldn't be the first time. But not death threats—usually the "I'm gonna mess your face up" kind of threats that didn't end up panning out. Though threatening Brett's face was the same to Brett as threatening his life. "Then I thought maybe it was someone bigger, you know? Someone intimidated by my success—like Emeril, or something."

"Huh?"

"You know, Emeril Lagasse?"

"Oh, yeah, vaguely . . ."

"We both have live shows, but I'm younger and a lot better looking."

Rolling his eyes, Rick mentally crossed Emeril off the list. Then he asked, "So what does the caller say, just that you'll die? Anything else?"

"*Just* that I'll die?" Brett echoed, his voice cracking. "Isn't that *enough*?"

"You know what I mean. Do they want something specific from you? Is it the same muffled voice every time?"

"Yeah . . . I think so. The last one was on Sunday and I haven't gotten any calls since then." Today was Tuesday; give it a few more days without a word, and the chances of it being just a bad joke were excellent. "But then I got that e-mail today. Shit, Brody, I don't know what to do . . ."

"What e-mail?" Rick pressed. "What did it say?"

"I can't get into it right now!" Brett whispered. He sounded petulant, like a frightened teenager lashing out. Then he sighed and said, "Please, just come over tonight so we can talk. I don't know who might be listening right now . . ."

"Wait, are you saying you think it might be someone at the studio?"

"I gotta go," Brett said quickly. "Just come to penthouse tonight, okay? I'll explain more."

"Well, are you gonna be all right?" Rick asked, worried. It was a futile question, he knew.

"Yeah, I'll be okay. I've gotta tape soon, but I'll see you tonight—around nine?"

"Yup," Rick agreed.

"And, Brody?" Rick waited, poised to snap his phone closed. "Thanks."

CHAPTER FIVE

*W*hen Gretchen came home she found a fire extinguisher with a bow on it waiting for her in the foyer. "Dana?" she called out over the whirring sound of the vacuum. The whirring dissolved into a hiss and then silence, and soon Dana emerged from her bedroom.

"Hey!" she said brightly, then motioned toward the fire extinguisher. "I see you got my peace offering. That's to say I'm sorry. About the whole almost-killing-you-in-a-raging-inferno bit."

Gretchen smiled and set her purse down. "Thanks—that's sweet." She slipped off her wet heels and shook out of her heavy, velvety coat, then crossed to the living room to flop on the couch. It didn't take long to curl like an inchworm into the fetal position and let out a tired sigh.

"Tough day?" Dana asked, standing over her. She had her hair tied up in a sheer scarf; from this angle, the words *Spoiled Rotten*, which were emblazoned in white across her shirt, appeared upside down. Gretchen's eyes slid closed for just a moment as she savored the softness of the sofa.

"Mmm-hmm," she murmured. "What time is it anyway?"

"Eight," Dana said, then corrected herself. "No, closer to eight thirty, actually."

"Oh God . . ." Gretchen moaned softly and dug her head deeper into the warm red cushion. Her feet were killing her, her body was tired, her mind was flooded with new information. Then she remembered and opened her eyes again. "How was the casting call?"

"Good," Dana replied breezily. "The casting director said he'd be in touch—which could mean he'll be in touch, or it could mean 'give up, loser.' I'll find out in a few days. And I should tell you . . . the fire extinguisher's not really from me. I mean, I would've gotten you one if this one wasn't already here."

"Gotten *us* one, you mean," Gretchen said, slowly climbing up to a sitting position.

"Right, us—and if I'd thought of it."

"So where did it come from?"

"It was outside the door when I got home. There was no note or anything, but I guess it's pretty obvious that one of our neighbors is trying to make a statement without actually having a confrontation."

"Hmm. No note, but a bow?" Gretchen said. "That's weird."

"No, I put the bow on."

"Oh. Say no more," Gretchen said with a grin.

"Seriously, I hope our neighbors don't hate us," Dana said, folding her arms across her chest, thinking about it. Then she waved a hand through the air. "Eh, who cares? They're really Marcia's neighbors anyway."

"Nice," Gretchen said dryly, then had a thought. It could've been a neighbor who'd left the fire extinguisher, but . . . "You don't think . . ."

"What?"

She shook her head to get rid of the thought. "Never mind. There's no way."

"What?" Dana pressed.

"Just that . . . I was thinking maybe it was the fireman who was here last night. But no," she said again, even more firmly. "He would never come back here. I'm sure he's way too busy." Saving lives, sliding down poles, owning a spotted dog, and whatever else firemen did.

"That asshole you told me about? You think it's from him?" Dana said, surprised.

"He wasn't an asshole," Gretchen said. "Just . . . touchy . . . and rude . . . and obnoxious."

"I stand corrected. Now, come *on*"—Dana tightened her grip on her arms as if she were cold, nearly shivering with excitement, anticipation—"don't keep me in suspense. Did you meet Romeo Ramero or what?"

"Ohh," Gretchen said with a nod. "Yes, actually, I did."

"Oh my *God*! How can you be so calm about it? I would've died," she insisted, her bright green eyes huge with feeling. "Well? C'mon. Is he cute in person? What did you say to him—no, how did you meet and what happened exactly? Tell me everything. First of all, how tall is he? Oh, I bet he's a total asshole in real life, right?"

Gretchen broke the news gently that—despite being friendly and quite cute—Romeo's real name was Brett and he was only about five-nine.

Momentarily, Dana's face fell, as if this would somehow impact her decision to marry him and have his children. Then she gave her head a little jiggle and said, "I guess I can work with that."

"Oh, good."

"And what's Susanna Tate like in person? I bet she's a real bitch, huh?"

"Why do you say that?"

Dana shrugged. "I don't know, I just figured—the mask has to come off, you know?"

"No, she seems nice," Gretchen said, then, recalling the irritated glances and eye rolling going on behind Susanna's back all day, amended, "I mean . . . she was nice to *me* . . . Today, anyway . . ."

"Okay, now for my next bit," Dana said, reaching over to tug on Gretchen's arm. Gretchen looked quizzically at her. "I need to do some acting exercises tonight. To practice in case that casting director actually does call."

Rising to her feet, Gretchen said, "Oh, did you want me to leave? No problem. I'm gonna jump in the shower anyway—"

"No, no, I don't want you to leave. I want you to help me."

"Help you?" Gretchen echoed, not liking the sound of this. Not only was she bone tired, she wasn't the least bit theatrical. She didn't know what helping Dana entailed and doubted she wanted to. "How?"

"It'll be fun," Dana insisted.

"What do I have to do?"

"I'll be right back!" Dana said, and left the room, heading down the hall. Within moments, she returned with a stack of cards in her hand. As she flipped through the cards, Gretchen slunk back onto the sofa and waited. Then Dana's green eyes came alive, and she lightly slapped a card and said, "This is a good one. It's a conversation between a patient and a doctor and the doctor's giving the patient bad news."

"Yeah, you're right, that *is* fun," Gretchen remarked.

With a giggle, Dana insisted, "No, this is good, trust me. Besides, if I'm gonna be on a soap opera, I need to practice maudlin crap."

It was hard to argue. But Gretchen was a little biased because soap operas, on principle, depressed the hell out of her. She associated them most of all with back when she was little. School got out at two then, and she'd gone home and let herself into her empty house, and it had felt like there was nothing else on but soap operas. She always felt so bored and so alone, and bleak melodrama only made it worse.

"Okay, let's start. Who do you wanna be first?" Dana asked, obviously bubbling over at the prospect of either giving or receiving bad news. (Actors were bizarre people.)

"Um, you choose. I'm flexible."

"All right, you be the patient first," Dana instructed. "I'll come in while you're in the examining room waiting anxiously for your test results."

Gretchen agreed. For authenticity, she assumed, Dana darted out of the room, just around the corner to the hall; then she entered the living room, all in the mode. Looking serious, she approached Gretchen and motioned toward the armchair. "Ms. Darrow, please sit down."

"Okay," Gretchen said, though she already was sitting. Dana waited. "Oh . . . okay," Gretchen said, getting up from the couch and going over to the armchair. Once she sat down, Dana paused dramatically. "We've gotten your test results," she stated, her voice starkly serious, almost to the point of imperious. "Well, Ms. Darrow, this is going to be difficult for me to say—and difficult for you to hear."

Gretchen sat there, waiting. Then Dana sighed lightly and said, "Look more nervous than that. Jeez, you're sitting there like a stone."

"Oh, sorry . . ." Gretchen tried to follow orders by pursing her mouth a little, furrowing her eyebrows.

Apparently that wasn't cutting it. Dana grimaced speculatively, then said, "Just pretend you're at the doctor's, waiting for pregnancy-test results."

"Then I wouldn't be nervous, believe me." Depressing but true—she hadn't even made out with anyone in a year. Nice of her cousin to remind her.

"Gretchen, *hello*?" Dana urged, like a child getting frustrated.

Gretchen sat up straighter. "Sorry, sorry."

"Be serious."

She clasped her hands together prayer style and bit her lip, which was just gonna have to do for serious.

"Would you like to hear your test results now?" Dana asked, back in doctor mode.

"No—surprise me on my deathbed." That's what she *almost* said, but she didn't dare. Instead she replied, "Sure." Dana twisted her lips. "I mean—yes, please." Was that dirge worthy enough? Who knew her cousin was such a control freak?

Dana looked down at the nonexistent medical chart, then back up, her face darkening, her eyes lucent windows to abject solemnity (yes, what *fun* this was) and she said, "May I speak plainly?"

"Yes, doctor, please do," Gretchen said.

"Okay, let me put it to you this way." With a slow intake of breath, Dana paused, then exhaled gently. She leaned down to cover Gretchen's hand with her own. "The good news is: There's a sale on headstones at Home Depot. The bad news is . . . Well, you can probably figure that out for yourself."

"*What!*" Gretchen yelped with a shock of laughter. Then she tossed a pillow at Dana. "Get real!"

Dana was laughing, too. "Well, you weren't being serious!" she exclaimed. "So why should I be?"

"But this isn't my career, it's yours—"

"Just barely," she remarked.

"And you know I'm no good at this," Gretchen finished with a smile.

"Okay. Let's switch."

They traded roles: Now Dana was the patient and Gretchen was the doctor. She just hoped she could bring something heavy-handed and lugubrious to the role to appease her cousin.

Dana poised herself in the armchair now, looking pensive, expectant, anxious—just the way a patient anticipating test results might look.

"Ms. Darrow," Gretchen said, stealing Dana's opening line, but it was her last name, too. "I have your results—"

"Wait!" Dana injected. "I just thought of something . . . Maybe this scene will work better if I wrap some paper towel around me?"

"Huh?" Gretchen said, confused.

"You know, like a gown?"

"You're gonna wrap paper towel around your clothes? No, I don't think that'll be necessary."

"I mean, I could take my clothes off—"

"*No,*" Gretchen insisted, holding up her hand. "It really doesn't need to be *that* authentic, okay? Besides, doctors don't give patients bad news when they're naked. They always let them get dressed first."

"Oh. That's true," Dana conceded. And thankfully—not only would wrapping herself in paper towel be a waste of an important kitchen tool (the cook in Gretchen), but also Marcia Rabe might not be crazy about the prospect of Dana's naked butt on her expensive furniture.

"Let's continue," Gretchen said. "Ms. Darrow, I've reviewed the test results."

"Yes, doctor? What is it?" Dana said anxiously, her brows creasing, her voice cracking just enough to sound emotional but not pubescent.

"I'm very sorry," Gretchen went on, "but it seems that—"

She didn't even get to finish. Dana dropped down to the floor, to her knees, and started fake wailing. "Oh, God, NOOOO!" she bellowed. "Why, why, WHY! Oh, for the love of God, life has only just begun!" She threw her head in her hands before sinking headfirst to the floor. It resembled some kind of yoga position with her butt up toward the ceiling, her body angled with her head down, and Gretchen tossed her hands up and let out a laugh.

"Oh, why do you even bother me with this stuff? I'm going to take a shower."

"No, wait, come back!" Dana said through rapid laughter. "I was just trying to own the scene! You should've seen your face!"

Through her giggles, someone's cell phone rang. It was a salsa beat ring, which meant it was Dana's. As Gretchen made her way down the hall toward the bathroom, she heard Dana say, "Hello? Oh, hey, Mom!"

Gretchen felt a twinge of envy. It was silly, but Dana just seemed to have such a great relationship with her parents and with her two older brothers, Davin and Andrew. With a sigh, Gretchen kept going. She'd feel better—all around—once she got into a hot shower.

It wasn't that she didn't feel close to her parents, but sometimes she wished "close" could mean the same thing in her family as it meant in Dana's. It seemed like Dana's family knew each other's business, kept in touch, swapped stories about their personal lives, and Gretchen's . . . well, they'd always been so busy with work when she was growing up. And then after she'd graduated college, her parents had collaborated to write a crime thriller, combining what her mom knew about forensic psychology and what her dad knew about dentistry. Their first book, *Vicious Veneers,* featured—what else?—a dentist with a passion for forensic psychology, who gets involved in solving murders. They'd gone on to write two more books in the past three years.

Now the Dr. Culpepper thrillers were a bonafide series, and her parents were so caught up in the signings and publicity, they had even less time to check in with Gretchen—much less to "swap stories." In fact, they still hadn't called to ask how she was liking New York.

She should stop feeling sorry for herself. This was stupid; she knew her parents loved her. And she could always call them, too. She could hear her mother's voice: *The phone works both ways, Gretchen.* That's what she would say. Maybe she wasn't calling because on some level she was testing her mom to see when she called—how much she cared. *Ridiculous.* Twenty-seven years old and still testing her parents.

Just then, she overheard Dana chatting with her dad, who'd picked up the other extension, and Dana asked her parents to put Daisy, the family Labrador, on so she could tell her she loved her. In that moment, Gretchen realized that she didn't really miss her parents. She missed what she'd always wanted. She missed what Dana had.

CHAPTER SIX

*T*he next morning Rick was at TCC, still digesting what had happened the night before. He'd met Brett at his apartment on Madison Avenue, and Brett had filled him in on the e-mail he'd received yesterday. Prior to that, he'd thought one of his latest girlfriends might've been behind the calls—one who hadn't taken kindly to Brett's way of "dating," which was basically to lay it on thick for a few weeks, then blow the girl off out of nowhere. Brett didn't have to say that, of course, but Rick knew him well enough to know his pattern. Apparently there was one women he'd dropped just recently, but she wasn't even returning his calls, he said, so he had to wonder if she could really be obsessed with him enough to bother.

And then he'd gotten an e-mail at work. It was his corporate account, which he seldom used. In fact, he'd checked it yesterday only because Susanna Tate had mentioned that she'd e-mailed him an article he might find interesting. Only he'd never gotten that; instead he'd gotten an e-mail from a Yahoo address that was nothing more than a scramble of numbers and letters. The message read: *You will never make it to Hawaii. You'll die first.* What had Brett so freaked out— well, it was two things, really—was the fact that his work e-mail address was private. It wasn't "romeo@tcc.com" or some variation that anyone could easily guess; it was "b.pellucci@andersen.com"— Andersen Corp. being the parent company that owned the Cooking Channel.

The second thing was this: Brett's TV special in Hawaii, scheduled for that coming June, was not public knowledge. There hadn't been any promos about it yet. It, like Brett's TCC e-mail account, was in-house information. And all of this seemed to point to one thing—something even Brett was sharp enough to pick up on: The person who'd sent the e-mail was most likely someone at TCC. And if it was the same person who'd made the "you will die" phone calls . . . then someone at the network was either fucking with Brett's head for the hell of it, or wanted him dead. The question was who—and why?

There were a few thousand employees at TCC, but according to Brett, only about a hundred or so knew him personally. Obviously the place to start was with Brett's enemies. But the problem was, Brett couldn't think of any. He kept insisting that the only enemies he might have were disgruntled ex-flames—oh, yeah, and Emeril.

Everyone at work liked Brett, or so he'd thought before all this had happened, which was why he wanted Rick there. He'd asked him to come to the studio with him and check out the situation for himself—to watch the people at TCC closely, not just those who interacted with Brett, but any lurkers he might notice lingering in the background.

Brett wouldn't dare mess with that macho shit that he marketed so well; hiring a real bodyguard would only call attention to his fear. Cowardly wasn't the image he was going for, and to Brett, image was everything. Hell, he'd even given up his own name when his publicist convinced him to call himself "Romeo Ramero," which was apparently catchier and "easier to remember" than Brett Pellucci. *Alliteration,* he'd told Rick once, clearly parroting his publicist. *People are stupid, but they'll remember alliteration.*

So Brett was scared and he wanted Rick to watch his back, to protect him. Of course, there was always the chance that Brett was in no real danger. Still, Rick wasn't unconcerned; as always, he was approaching things cautiously and with a cool focus.

Now, as he sat in Brett's dressing room, complete with an entertainment system and a minibar, Rick thought that he might not have his brother's money or fame—okay, the money he wouldn't mind, and the fame he'd definitely skip—but he had strength, and that was something.

The guys he worked with seemed to think that he was fearless—which was hardly true but filled him with pride anyway. They de-

pended on him, they looked to him, they knew he was never shy
about going in first. Bennet called him "the wolf." Having Bennet's
respect considering the twenty-year age difference between them was
a feat in itself. Rick supposed all that made up for a lot of his regrets
about his past, about what a fuck-up he'd been was when he was
younger.

He was still waiting for Brett to emerge from the bathroom. Eyeing the collection of hairbrushes and the various spray products that
apparently went with them, Rick shook his head in bewilderment.
He tugged lightly on his tie knot; he'd forgotten to ask Brett last
night what the dress was like at this place, so he'd worn a jacket and
tie just in case. Of course, once he got there he saw his brother and
almost everyone else there in jeans. The tie he'd leave, but he'd tossed
the jacket on the couch a few minutes ago.

Now he heard the flushing of the toilet; Brett was finally done.
His private bathroom adjoined with the dressing room, a few feet
from his mirrored vanity. *Mirrored vanity,* Rick thought, twisting
his mouth, laughing darkly to himself. For some reason, that just
said it all.

The bathroom door swung open. "Okay, let's go."

"I didn't hear the water running," Rick commented as he rose
from his chair.

Rolling his eyes, Brett said, "Oh, shut up, dick." Then he ducked
back into the bathroom to wash his hands. Some things never
changed.

They left the dressing room, heading up the steps to the main
floor, passed through Brett's set, and exited to the hallway. *Brooklyn
Boy Makes Good . . . Food,* Rick thought. *Please.* The Pelluccis moved
from Brooklyn two weeks after Brett was born; Rick had been two at
the time. They'd both grown up in Newark, but according to Brett's
publicist, Newark didn't "sell". Brooklyn sold, so Brooklyn it was.

As they walked around the curved hallway toward the elevators,
Rick eyed the surroundings carefully. Even though Brett had given
him the full tour that morning, Rick was especially watchful of pockets of space, shadows, open areas that could leave someone vulnerable. Not that he was a cop, but he'd worked as a security guard for a

federal bank several years back, and a few years before that, he'd had a brief stint in the criminal investigations unit of the U.S. Air Force. Plus the fact that he was suspicious by nature.

"I've got a meeting downstairs I gotta get to," Brett said and punched his thumb on the elevator button. One sprang open instantly, and he and Rick stepped inside. "We're talking about some stuff coming up for the spring special in March, should probably be about an hour, maybe less."

"All right. You want me to wait outside?"

"No, no—just wait for me downstairs in the food court, okay? It's on the fifth floor."

"I can wait outside your meeting. It's not a problem."

"No way!" Brett said, his lip curled back. "What are you, crazy? I'm telling people you're here to tour the studio. They'll think it's weird if you're sitting outside the conference room. Jesus. I don't want anyone to suspect something's up."

"Okay, okay," Rick said. "Where in the food court?"

"Uh, the fruit smoothie place near the elevators. Yeah, that'll work. I want to get a carrot-kiwi shake anyway."

"Oh Jesus," Rick muttered. Vanities, hair spray, fruit smoothies— what next? When had his brother turned into such a pretty boy?

"What?" Brett asked, confused.

"Nothing. Okay, I'll meet you there. But isn't the whole point that I have your back? Are you sure you're not going to be alone between the time the meeting ends and the time you get down to the food court?"

"No, no, I'll be fine," Brett assured him, though for a moment he pinched his neat eyebrows—what, did he trim those things now?—then he relaxed his face along with his shoulders, which had tensed up. "I'll be fine," he said again, and it seemed to be a reassurance to himself as well as to Rick.

The elevator stopped on the twenty-second floor, which was Brett's stop. He paused, holding the "door open" button, and spoke quietly to Rick. "More than anything, Brody, I need to get your impressions of the people here. I'm no good at reading people; it's never been my thing."

"What are you talking about?" Rick said, then let out a short, dry laugh. "People fucking fall all over you. You must be doing something right."

With a shrug, Brett said, "Hey, can I help it if people pretty much eat up the same shit across the board?" Interesting point. "So, I'll see you later," Brett finished, stepping out.

The elevator doors sealed behind him, leaving Rick inside, contemplating what to do in the meantime. If he was going to be vigilant he should get a much better look around the place, especially the kind of security running throughout the building. After all, image obsessed or not, Brett was still his brother.

Gretchen sat beside Susanna in a conference room on the fourth floor, which was flooded with sunlight, even as snow floated airily past the windows. Gretchen felt a little out of place at this meeting, which hadn't begun yet, but so far consisted of producers and TV personalities (or "the talent" as they were called). Susanna had said that it was more of a brainstorming session than an actual meeting; it concerned the "Spring into Spring" week, a theme week planned for the middle of March. Apparently, TCC would be airing all new episodes, focusing centrally on springtime recipes and entertaining ideas. However, Gretchen couldn't help wondering why there were no other set supervisors or crew members there after Susanna had insisted that it was crucial for Gretchen to attend.

Also sitting at the table was Cady Angle, the pastry chef who hosted *Sinful Temptations*—a somewhat ironic title considering that Cady herself had that asexual kindergarten teacher look. Short and chubby, she looked out at the world through a thick, impenetrable wall of bangs. She wore pretty matronly clothes—apparently on and off camera, as Gretchen could see now—even though she was barely thirty. Like Brett, Cady was extremely accomplished in her field for someone her age. Her short brown hair was curled in at the bottom and only a little longer than a standard mom haircut, barely grazing the collar of her floral print dress.

Next to Cady was her producer, Marjorie Bass, who was strikingly opposite—tall and gauntly thin. She wore a crisp black business suit in what had to be a size triple zero. With her long, dangling limbs and ice-pick-sharp elbows and knees, she looked like a well-dressed grasshopper. Her wavy, auburn hair was pulled up at the sides.

Susanna had introduced Gretchen to several other people at the table, including Juan Mirando, host of *Best Dishes* and resident tool. When he shook Gretchen's hand, he said, "I'm the zany guy you always see wearing the apron," then pointed down at his apron, which read: I'M A BUTT MAN (PORK BUTT, THAT IS).

Enough said.

Brett's producer, Joel Green, sat on the far end of the shiny oval table, looking through some paperwork, being just as antisocial as he'd been yesterday when Gretchen had met him.

Now another man walked through the glass door, capturing Gretchen's attention. Probably around forty, he was lean and fit with dark hair and warm brown eyes. He smiled hello as he entered and there was just something magnetic yet subdued about him. "Abe!" Susanna said, hopping up out of her chair and gliding over to him with her billowing garb puffing out around her. Today she wore a loosely flowing red pantsuit, with both the knee-length jacket and the pants a fluttering rayon material. (When they'd entered the conference room, Juan Mirando had bellowed, "Hey, you match!" because they were both wearing red. Gretchen had smiled, but her pretty red dress had taken umbrage.)

"Hi there," Abe said, smiling. So this was Abe Santasierra, Susanna's producer. "Nell said you stopped down yesterday when I was on a conference call. Sorry I missed you."

"No problem. Was it an important call?" Susanna said suggestively, and Gretchen realized Susanna was unsubtly giving Abe the opportunity to divulge if and how the conference call pertained to her show.

But Abe just smiled amiably and said, "The usual."

"Ah," Susanna said, her smile faltering a bit. "Oh, Abe, have you met my new set supervisor, Gretchen?" Leading him closer to the table, Susanna wordlessly tried to urge him to into the chair next to hers. Gretchen, who was on Susanna's other side, stood to shake Abe's hand.

"Hi there, it's a pleasure," he said. "I'm sorry I wasn't there when you first interviewed for the job, but Lila would know better than me anyway," he added with gracious humility—and what sounded like a very mild Southern accent. It was subtle, which was why Gretchen hadn't noticed it immediately. Just the smoothest hint of a drawl that polished the edges of Abe's words.

"Speaking of away, Abe, how was your vacation?" Marjorie asked.

"Oh, it was great, thanks. Great to visit people back home."

"Where are you from?" Gretchen asked.

"North Carolina." Well, that explained it.

"Here, Abe, sit next to me," Susanna declared, motioning to the vacant chair. Suddenly, in contrast, Susanna came off as brassy and showy. "I saved you a seat."

Yes, and Gretchen recalled *how* she'd saved it. When Cady Angle had tried to sit there several minutes ago, Susanna had spoken abruptly. "Oh, Cady, would you mind? This seat's for someone else." Cady's cheeks had turned bright pink and Gretchen had all but dropped her jaw at Susanna's tactlessness. Moving quickly, she pulled out the chair to her left and motioned for Cady to take it. Which she did, after a mumbled "Sorry" to Susanna that could've been genuine or sarcastic, it was hard to tell. Unlike Susanna, Cady obviously wasn't the confrontational type; in any event, Gretchen was sandwiched between the two of them.

Next Brett Pellucci arrived. When he walked in, the table seemed to come to attention. Unlike Abe, who'd sort of poured into the room like honey, Brett lit it up, brought it to life. His blue eyes and white teeth shone in the bright sunlight, which bled through the windows. And he was smiling that devilishly cute smile he always donned for the camera. Was the guy *ever* down? Gretchen wondered. He said an affable hello to the table, winked at Gretchen, then at Marjorie, and dropped into a chair beside his producer, Joel.

"Brett, who was that guy I saw you walking around with today?" Marjorie Bass asked.

"Uh . . ." He seemed to falter for a second, then said, "That's my brother. Brody. He's got some time off work, so he wanted to come take a tour," Brett explained. "You know, see a real live television studio." (Gretchen wasn't going to point out that television studios weren't alive.)

"Oh, is he visiting from out of town?" Cady asked.

"No, he lives in New York, but . . . well, what can I say? The guy looks up to me," Brett said with a humble shrug.

Marjorie let out a playful little whistle and said, "He's a pretty big guy, huh?" By her knowing grin, it was clear that she approved of Brett's brother, who was presumably very built. But then, so was Brett. But maybe his brother was also tall?

Cinching his brows, Brett asked, "What do you mean?"

"Oh, I don't know . . . he just . . ." Marjorie looked around the table and joked, "Well, I may be married, but I can still look, right?"

Everyone chuckled and Cady added sheepishly, "I looked, too, so don't feel bad." People laughed again, but more out of obligation for a follow-up one-liner.

"There are some good genes in that family," Marjorie joked and let out another tinny little whistle. "If I weren't married, I'd make you set me up with your brother, Brett." Idly, Gretchen wondered if Marjorie's husband would appreciate this conversation.

According to Susanna, Marjorie was married to a CPA named Ronald, so the odds of him being jacked were . . . well, you didn't need to be a CPA to calculate those odds. In fairness, then, if Marjorie drooled over muscular guys, it was only natural for her to take notice of one in the vicinity.

When Gretchen glanced at Brett, he appeared less than thrilled. His smile had waned. Marjorie continued. "Don't go by me, though; I like a big man."

Well, sure, Gretchen wasn't exactly opposed to one either—or rather, that was the *old* Gretchen. The new Gretchen was done with eye candy; the new Gretchen was focusing solely on her career—at least until her biological clock started blasting music at her, which wouldn't be for at least a few more years.

"Is he married?" Cady asked casually but quietly.

"Uh, no . . . he's not married," Brett answered. Then with a short laugh, he added, "*Definitely* not married. In fact, don't even get me to go there. A *lot* of issues in that department."

"Oh . . ." Marjorie said, straightening up a bit, as though to distance herself from an uncomfortable conversation or to look like she was prying for more details. But Brett went on anyway. "Yeah, I try to be there for him, and like I said, he wanted to come to the studio because he's not working right now and his morale's pretty much in the dumper." He finished with another short but altogether humorless laugh, and Gretchen thought: *Not working?* She thought Brett had said his brother was off *from* work, not out *of* work—big difference. "And let's just say, my bro really needs this. I mean, I try to get him out of the house when I can. He's got a lot of issues and . . . well he kind of worships me, so . . ." Brett shrugged almost helplessly. "He's not all there, if you know what I mean."

Suddenly a pall fell over the table; well, that little tidbit of too much information killed the mood. Here Marjorie and Cady had been making lighthearted conversation about Brett's brother, only to find out he was mentally challenged or something. Talk about awkward.

"Now about Spring Week," Joel said gruffly, setting his papers aside, leaning forward in his chair, and shifting around like he had inchworms in his boxers. He was probably just one of those people with an edgy demeanor, always impatient. "I know the scheduling is pretty much nailed down, but how about on the last night of that week we run some kind of finale—you know, a show with all of the talent there, cooking on the set, warm banter, and all that crap. We'll use Brett's set, of course."

"Why 'of course'?" Susanna asked.

"That's a good idea," Abe said with a nod. "And we can run promos for *Dining Elegance* during the breaks." *Dining Elegance* was a new show scheduled for the summer season. It would star Susanna and begin taping this spring. It was going to be Susanna's first foray into Brett's usual terrain: prime-time TV. Of course, Susanna would still keep her daytime program, *Susanna's Kitchen,* which was a hit with the stay-at-home mom and over-fifty demographics. (It was amazing how much information Gretchen had been saturated with and it was only the start of her second day.)

"Wait, what about Ray?" Juan Mirando said then. "Shouldn't he be taking part in this? Did anyone let him know about the meeting?"

"Oh . . . well . . ." Abe faltered. "Joel, perhaps you could address that . . ."

"Ahh . . ." Joel stalled, looking uncomfortable in his own craggy, gray-stubbled, tweed-covered skin, then brought a fist up over his mouth and cleared some hoarse gurgles from his throat. All Gretchen knew was that Joel Green had been coproducer of Ray Jarian's southwestern cooking show, *Tex-Mex Teddy,* up until about a month ago, when the show got pulled from its usual lineup. Since then it hadn't aired; reruns of Cady's show had aired in its place. "Right, well, actually, it probably won't come as a big surprise, but Ray Jarian isn't going to be with the network in the new season," Joel said finally, his gravelly voice accomplishing the conciseness, if not the smoothness, of a diplomat. "He's moving on to other opportunities." He didn't elaborate further. Gretchen thought, *So it's official then—Ray Jarian's been canned.* It fit with the rumors she'd heard thus far (from Susanna, of course): (1) Ray Jarian's restaurant, also called *Tex-Mex Teddy,* had filed for bankruptcy, and (2) Ray was having trouble getting a contract for his latest cookbook. (His last had been published in 2003.)

"Poor Ray . . ." Susanna murmured, but loudly enough for everyone to hear. Still, the discussion of Ray Jarian and his spiraling decline seemed to end there.

After forty minutes of brainstorming about Spring Week and how best to maximize the theme while still aggrandizing each celebrity to the extreme, the meeting wrapped up. As people pushed their chairs away from the table, Gretchen heard Joel say to Brett, "Wanna grab a cup of coffee? We've still gotta talk about Hawaii."

"Oh, I can't, thanks, um . . . I'm meeting my brother for a fruit smoothie . . . alone." People all kind of stopped and looked, so Brett expanded. "Um, he's really not comfortable with other people around, you know. He likes me to just be with him. Basically, he really, really needs me. And I don't want to leave him alone too long anyway—he gets pretty skittish when I do."

Okay.

Everyone filed out and veered off in separate directions. On the way to the elevators, Cady spoke softly to Gretchen. "So Brett's brother sounds pretty . . . interesting. Huh?"

By the look on her face, it was clear that "interesting" wasn't synonymous with "delightfully unique." More like: *bizarre, perplexing, bring-Jane-Goodall-in-on-this-one*. Inwardly, Gretchen had to agree. With a nod, she said simply, "Yeah . . . definitely interesting." Neither wanted to voice what both were clearly thinking: The guy sounded pretty pathetic.

CHAPTER SEVEN

$\mathcal{S}$usanna's show taped shortly after the meeting. It was Gretchen's first taping, and it had been fascinating to see it all live; she'd been so close she could see the granules of makeup on Susanna cheeks and the daisy pattern on the dish towel that lay folded in the background. The most surreal part was when Gretchen had opened up the refrigerator beforehand to check on some of the ingredients. She'd actually opened up Susanna Tate's refrigerator! The one she'd seen Susanna open a hundred times before on television. (Up close, it smelled strongly of strawberries and citrus.)

Susanna had introduced Gretchen to her niece, Shawnee, who was working as an intern for the show—or rather, leaning idly on the craft table, looking surly. She was nineteen or twenty, with short dark hair parted on the side and cropped in a vintage uneven-mushroom cut. A narrow shock of blond framed her almost bullish face. Her most striking features included a bulbous nose and an eyebrow ring—and a limp, clammy handshake, to boot.

The taping had gotten off to a rocky start. Susanna had stopped a couple of times, once because the light was in her eyes, once because the prechopped scallions weren't chopped finely enough, once because she tripped over her lines and had to go to her dressing room to "clear her head." Abe was extremely patient with her, diplomatically letting her indulge her temperamental ego. But, wanting to make a good impression, Gretchen tried to do more than just that. She fixed a cold glass of pineapple juice, threw in two maraschino cherries, and brought it to Susanna's dressing room. It seemed to work; Susanna had perked up and returned to the set with minimal drama . . .

For a *few* minutes anyway . . .

Gretchen learned quickly that when she was in gear, Susanna was an exquisite professional, but when the slightest thing set her off, she changed abruptly and seemed to become deliberately uncooperative—waiting to be coaxed back to work. But after working at a health spa in California for the past three years, Gretchen was no stranger to diva behavior.

Now Gretchen was standing beside Kit, the director, who was raising her butt off her chair, motioning to the sound guy, who, in turn, inched the ceiling mike higher. There were three large, roving cameras; they towered over Gretchen liked ten-foot turkeys, their black metallic necks stretching out and back, swiveling as Susanna moved around her kitchen. Two cameramen with handheld cameras moved with precision and ease around the floor, but still, Gretchen was amazed that Susanna could be so unfazed by them.

Now Susanna was wrapping up the episode. Today's theme was "Seasonal Treats that are Good All Year," and rounding things out was Susanna's eggnog cake. As she sliced into it, she said, "And now let me just have a taste of this scrumptious cake. We have one right here that's cooled . . ." Gently, she slid a wedge onto a daisy-patterned plate. "Eggnog cake is one of my absolute *favorite* recipes," she continued. "In fact, my husband asks me to make this every year for his birthday. Oh, and it just looks perfect. Look at this." Two of the cameras moved in closer as she took a bite. "It's light and airy . . . yet . . . rickly sal—sa—and . . . *Cut!*"

She dropped her pleasant smile swiftly and sent her fork clattering against her plate. As she expelled a sigh, Gretchen got the distinct feeling it was going to be someone else's fault that Susanna had flubbed her lines.

"What does that even *say?*" she snapped. "I can't even *read* that card!"

Sounding bored, Shawnee called back, "It says, 'richly satisfying.' Last time I checked, it was in English."

With a short, humorless laugh, Susanna challenged, "That's supposed to be 'satisfying'? It looks like . . ." She shook her head, flummoxed, trying to pinpoint exactly what it looked like. "It looks like 'salsa flying' or 'salty string'—and 'richly'? That's supposed to say 'richly'? It looks like *rickly*! I don't know who here needs to learn the difference between an H and a K, but . . . uh . . . come on, I'm not crazy here, people!"

"Okay, okay," Kit said, raising her butt out of her director's chair again. She was a compact woman with frizzy auburn hair that seemed to levitate off her back; she wore a khaki vest with lots of pockets and zippers, reminding Gretchen of a Girl Scout leader or a bird watcher. "It's no big deal. We'll just roll tape again. It's almost a wrap anyway."

"No, it's not just the cue cards; it's this cake, too," Susanna said, shooting daggers down at the inanimate slice she'd just tasted.

"What do you mean?" Kit asked, then turned and threw a hapless shrug at Abe, who simply gave a nod, wordlessly telling her to be patient. He was skilled at keeping the peace, which, on Susanna's set, was obviously critical.

"Um . . . Gretchen, come here, please," Susanna said.

Suddenly all eyes shifted toward Gretchen; she was no longer a spectator. People were waiting for some kind of an explanation. As set supervisor, and the one in charge of the show's "culinary integrity," a bad cake definitely fell under her scope of responsibility. She could've sworn "the choppers," who premade food so it would be ready for Susanna to taste on camera, had followed Susanna's recipe.

Stepping forward, Gretchen moved closer to the kitchen set; Susanna waited for her to join her behind the counter. "Um, what's wrong with the cake?" Gretchen asked calmly.

"It's awful!" Susanna whispered sharply. Then she seemed to catch herself and said, "Oh, Gretchen, I didn't mean to snap at you."

That shocked Gretchen more than anything. "I need five, please," Susanna called to Kit, and pressed her hand to her forehead dramatically.

"Susanna, what is it? Is there anything I can do?" Gretchen said quietly, realizing that something was bothering her.

"It's just that cake. I hate it."

"Really, I'm sure they followed your recipe. They all seem diligent about that." And honestly, what motivation would the choppers have to go off on their own and get creative? It wasn't like they were going to get credit for being innovative.

"Oh, but that's the whole problem," Susanna explained quietly.

"I haven't made this cake in so long, and I didn't realize the recipe was so . . . *blah*. I don't want to endorse this—I can't! I *won't!*" she exclaimed dramatically.

Gretchen glanced over at the rest of the crew, who were waiting around impatiently, tiredly. Shawnee rolled her eyes and blatantly scratched her crotch. Nepotism was probably the only way one could pull off mouthing off to Susanna, who obviously had no compunction about firing people.

"Well, you said you make it every year for your husband's birthday. Is there something different you do then?" Gretchen asked, searching for a way to be helpful.

Susanna just blinked at her. Then she said, "Oh, I don't *really* make this cake every year. That's just off the cue card."

Huh. Gretchen didn't know why she was surprised by that, but she was.

"I haven't made that cake in at least five years," Susanna went on, "and now I see why." She shot her eyes to Gretchen's as though struck by something. "Gretchen, *you* taste it. Tell me what you think. It's bad enough this recipe is immortalized in my first cookbook." Would telling her that the cookbook's probably out of print make her feel better?

Probably not.

Gretchen glanced over at the rest of the crew, who all looked bored and irritated, then refocused on Susanna and her eggnog cake; she grabbed a clean fork from the drawer, broke into the soft cake, and stabbed a small piece. As she chewed it, she instantly realized that it was good—very good, in fact. But it was missing something special. The zing of the fresh nutmeg, the richness of the heavy cream, it was all there, but it just needed something else . . .

An orange glaze! That would be perfect!

And it was extremely simple to make. When she told Susanna, she didn't take offense when Susanna said, "Of course. Why didn't I think of that? It's so obvious!"

Smiling encouragingly, Gretchen patted her arm and said, "Great. I'll get the ingredients assembled on the counter right now, and should I tell Kit you're ready?"

"Oh, Gretchen would you?" Susanna said sweetly, then yelled, "Makeup! Come touch me up!"

A few minutes later, tape rolled again and Susanna said, "This orange glaze is sweet but tangy—my husband always asks me to put extra glaze on his . . ."

Linking her arm through Gretchen's elbow, Susanna walked in the direction of her dressing room and said, "Run down to the food court and get me a turkey sandwich from Lemberto's, will you? And a Perrier." She clasped her throat and made frog faces to indicate how parched she was. Earlier she'd eschewed the food on the craft table because it was "sitting out."

"Oh, sure, no problem," Gretchen said. She couldn't help thinking . . . wasn't this the kind of thing a personal assistant did? Then again, it wasn't a big deal; it was just a sandwich, and if it would keep Susanna happy . . . "Should I bring it to your dressing room?"

"Yes, that would be great. Thanks. You're the *best*." Gretchen attempted to disengage from Susanna's grip and the grip tightened. "And wait, before you go . . . there's something else I need you to do for me . . ."

This is when Susanna hit her with the pitch, the pitch that would become a running theme. Susanna wanted to get a guest spot on Brett's show—a few guest spots, actually. With her first prime-time show, *Dining Elegance,* airing in June, Susanna seemed concerned. She was obviously trying to tap into Brett's fan base early—to get the after-eight audience to know and like her. She didn't spell it out exactly like this, but it was clear even to Gretchen and it was only her second day. Gretchen supposed it made sense, though she was a little surprised that Susanna, at this point, would feel insecure about her popularity.

"What do you think?" Susanna said.

"Yeah, guest spots sound like a great idea," Gretchen said supportively. Then Susanna clutched her elbow a little tighter.

"So maybe you could suggest it when you see Brett," she added, coming to a halt.

"Me?" Gretchen said, confused. "How come? I mean, have you mentioned it to Abe?" She didn't know much about the cable network world yet, but she was still pretty sure Susanna's producer was in a better position to make this happen.

"Well . . ." Susanna began as they descended the small set of steps to get to her dressing room. Susanna let her gaze wander off to the side, up to the gold star on her door, then ultracasually back to Gretchen. "I don't want to get all *official* about it yet, you understand. But I thought if you happened to see Brett, you could bring it up."

Hmm . . . Maybe Susanna was afraid of rejection? Or was she just reluctant to clue Abe in on her niggling insecurities about the success of her new show? It made sense to want to project only confidence in this kind of business. And is that why she didn't simply mention it to Brett herself? It would certainly put him in a position to turn her down—or worse, to agree but then openly know that Susanna considered him a bigger star. She had almost twenty years on the guy and a prestigious culinary background, while "Romeo Ramero" had muscles, charisma, and a lot of talent—but no formal chef training.

Gretchen supposed if *she* suggested it, it could look like her idea—like a brainstorm she'd had—and then Susanna could act surprised and accommodating. This was assuming that she'd pegged her boss's motivations correctly, of course.

"Sure, no problem," Gretchen said finally. Again she tried subtly to extricate her strangled arm from Susanna's choke hold. No luck—at least not with the subtle method—and her other arm was powerless, cradling both a clipboard and a fat notebook with the *Susanna's Kitchen* episode log.

"Great, thanks!" Susanna said, smiling. "And *now,* if you could."

"Now?"

"Well, we're done taping till this afternoon, and I'm not going to need anything else from you until then . . . except *this,* of course . . ."

"Okay . . . but where is he?" Gretchen said.

"Just try his dressing room," she suggested, finally letting go and turning around. Then, glancing back, she added, "And use your tact and discretion, of course." She flashed a warm, grateful smile right before she shut the gold star in Gretchen's face.

Brett's set, a huge room marked "Stage B," was also on the eighth floor. Gretchen circled around the corridor and looked for him there, but the set was empty and his dressing room, which, like Susanna's, was tucked behind the set, was quiet. She knocked twice and waited. Right arm aching, she switched her overstuffed clipboard and episode log to her left.

She didn't know why the prospect of talking with Brett alone made her nervous. She supposed she wasn't yet 100 percent desensitized; in her mind, he was still a huge celebrity. Maybe it was all that winking. In any event, there was a slight fluttering in her belly as she knocked again. Nothing. Oh, well, she'd just have to try him later.

Down at Terra Cottage, Gretchen waited on line for half an hour at Lemberto's, slowly working her way around a yellow zigzagging rope. By the time it was her turn to order, she felt beaten down, tired of getting shoved, and in the mood for a drink. She was so dumb—she hadn't even thought to drop off her stuff in her office on the second floor before coming to the food court and now her arms ached, and she still hadn't gotten Susanna's dumb lunch.

"Hi, can I please have a turkey sandwich?" she said despite its dumbness (hey, she was still feeling irritable).

"Lettuce and tomato?"

"Uh, sure." Personally Gretchen didn't go for lettuce on her sandwiches, but she'd better play it safe and get it for Susanna.

"Alfalfa sprouts?"

"Yes . . . ?" Gretchen said tentatively, figuring Susanna would probably go for that.

"Bean sprouts?"

"No, no . . . just one kind of sprout is fine," Gretchen said, thinking, *Bean sprouts and turkey? Eww.*

"Mayo?"

"Um . . . mustard, I think." What had Susanna said again?

"Honey mustard, barbecue mustard, cranberry mustard, or chipotle mustard?"

Jeez, now Gretchen was really kicking herself. Here she'd waited an eternity in line and hadn't even planned any of this. She supposed she hadn't been anticipating the choices (too busy giving annoyed looks to people who'd elbowed her—which was a lot of annoyed looks). "Well, what mustard do you recommend?" she asked, then almost laughed at her own idiocy. For pete's sake! She was a trained chef, and here she was asking the minimum-wage clerk at the food court what was good in a sandwich.

That was it. If Gretchen's expertise were to be taken seriously, she'd have to make an executive decision (if you could really call mustard an executive decision). Susanna hadn't given her a million specifications for her order, that was true, but maybe that was because she trusted Gretchen to select something that was up to her standards.

"You know what, let me start all over. Here's what I want . . ."

After ordering turkey breast on lemon-sage focaccia with goat cheese and chili-Dijon sauce, she contemplated a Diet Coke and Greek salad for herself, but then realized there was no way she could juggle all that. So she paid for Susanna's lunch, added the take-out bag to her pile, and finally broke free of the yellow zigzagged prison.

As Gretchen maneuvered through the crowded food court, triceps nearly throbbing now, she suddenly spotted someone she knew. Or recognized anyway. Her eyes shot wide open and she came to an abrupt halt. Her jaw dropped. Her stomach began fluttering wildly.

No way—it couldn't be!

Squinting, though, she confirmed that it was. The arrogant fireman from two nights ago was standing only twenty feet away from her! He was on line at a hut-shaped stand with a sign overhead that read: TALL COOL ONE. But he seemed to be looking around more than not. What on earth was he doing in her office building?

And in a tie?

She was sure it was him even though he looked different from this angle, and when he wasn't being all angry and intimidating, glaring down at her with his rumpled black hair, heavy black coat and boots, and the sharpest contrast to all, those penetrating blue eyes.

He turned his head toward her and she ducked quickly behind a pillar.

Then a thought occurred to her: Could he be there to see *her*? It sounded ludicrous even in her own mind, but then again . . . he *had* seemed a little overly interested in her situation, grilling her about why she hadn't been more careful, harassing her about that whole sleeping-through-the-fire bit. Jeez, maybe he was stalking her now!

Suddenly she remembered the fire extinguisher left at her door. Was he the one who'd left it after all? Was it one of those sick valentines—like when psychos sent pig hearts in the mail? Maybe he'd formed some unnatural attachment to her, or some biding interest. She supposed stranger things could happen. Especially when she recalled the low-cut nightgown she'd worn . . . the way his eyes had wandered down, lingering there for a few smoky seconds . . .

Maybe he was just a normal, hot-blooded guy and this was a total coincidence, or maybe he was a perverted freak in addition to being an arrogant bastard. Either way, did she really have time to find out? Susanna's lunch was waiting and Gretchen's arms were about to fall off. So she tried to wiggle behind a mob of businessmen so she could make her way over to the elevators without—*what was his name, Pellucci?*—spotting her.

Looking over her shoulder for only a second was her downfall. She slammed right into someone who hadn't been looking either. The mob dispersed as Gretchen's clipboard and notebook crashed hard to the floor. The bottle of water shattered. Several sheets of paper flew out of the episode log and into the puddle of Perrier that yawned wide across the floor, spreading itself underneath the table nearby. People shifted their feet and scooted their chairs. Face flaming hot, Gretchen murmured apologies and sank to her knees to gather up her stuff.

Damn it! Heat still flooded her face as she tried to get her papers out of the water before they were ruined, and also to find Susanna's sandwich, which had rolled somewhere. It was a very human moment, of course, could happen to anyone, blah blah blah, but still, she felt degraded by her position scrambling on the floor. Her knees were sore; the only thing between them and the bare hard floor were her sheer black stockings. She'd had to hitch her dress up several inches so it wouldn't get dirty.

She'd have to get a custodian to mop up the water and pick up the broken glass. Now she was grateful she hadn't gotten herself a soda and salad.

"Is this yours?"

Gretchen turned and trailed her eyes up a man's legs to his brown belt and white shirt and blue tie and . . .

It was *him*. And he was holding out Susanna's sandwich, wrapped in cellophane.

Gretchen's heart started racing. Her mouth ran dry. He was right there, so close, and for some unknown reason, intimidating and over-powering all over again. With his pants at eye level, Rick's thighs suddenly preoccupied her. An image of them naked—strong and muscular—flashed through her mind. A picture of herself gripping them, pulling herself up enough to nuzzle him, lick him, suck him—

What? Where had that come from?

Now was hardly the time for the horny girl's slide show (unfortunately, though, it was as autonomous as any other brain activity).

"Thanks," she said quickly, not looking at him but down at the floor as she gathered items up in her arms. "Thanks very much . . . I got everything now, but thanks . . ."

He'd leave in a second, any second now. Maybe she was being absurd to think he would remember her. He had to put out dozens of fires a week, right? Then again, on the off chance he *was* stalking her, clearly he remembered her. Still, it didn't seem likely.

"Hey, it's you."

His voice was deep with a slight rusty timbre to it—it was unmistakable. He was still there and he'd recognized her.

Slowly, she turned back to face him—or his pants. *Let's not start this again.* With most of her stuff in hand, she climbed to her feet and brushed wisps of hair away from her face. He was still nearly a foot taller than she, but it was an improvement.

CHAPTER EIGHT

*R*ick was discovering quickly that Tall Cool One was Brett's favorite haunt. The first time they'd been there had been that morning right after Brett's meeting, which he hadn't said much about, and then, after a few hours of Rick shadowing him around his set and waiting for him outside a private meeting with his producer, here they were again.

Rick had heard the loud crash over his shoulder and shot his head around to see a brunette put her face in her hands, then drop to her knees. Suddenly she disappeared from view behind more people shuffling to get their lunch. He felt a stab of pity for her, but his brother had just shrugged, nonplussed, and since he hadn't wanted to lose his place on line for his second carrot-kiwi-kelp smoothie of the day, Rick had left him for a moment and crossed over to help the girl.

Now that he stood before her and saw clearly who she was, it nearly blew him anyway. *Gretchen Darrow.* Talk about a small world.

He looked at her up close and their eyes locked, stayed fixed on each other. It was like a shot of adrenaline. Jesus, she was pretty. Her light tan skin looked smooth and soft, and her dark eyes were sexy, inviting. Most of her hair was falling down her back—the rest was pulled away from her face in a messy spiky little bun. It didn't look she was wearing makeup, which was exactly what he liked, except her lips were flushed dark pink. He didn't know if that was natural or not, but he couldn't take his eyes off that mouth.

She broke the spell by looking down for a second, shifting the weight of her stuff in her arms. Her sandwich slid off the top of the notebook she was carrying and hit the floor again. Her eyes shutting for a moment, Gretchen sucked in a breath like she was barely containing her temper. Rick grinned—he couldn't help it. It was damn adorable.

He whistled. "You must some kind of walking disaster," he said and bent down to swipe it up effortlessly. "Here's your sandwich—again."

Her jaw tightened as though she was holding back a sigh or something else. "Thank you—again," she said briskly, letting him set the sandwich on top of her pile. With a cordial but perfunctory smile, she added, "Well, I guess I'll see you around—"

"Whoa," he said, touching her arm. "Going already? Seems like you've gone to a lot of trouble to get my attention here. Besides, you haven't even threatened to rip my face off yet. What's your rush?"

His smug grin was irritating; besides being the last thing she needed at the moment, it also reminded her of his arrogance the other night—the things he'd said, his bombastic sense of entitlement. "I have to get back to work," she explained simply.

"What, you work in this building?" he asked, sounding genuinely surprised.

"Obviously."

"Wow, no shit."

"You didn't know that?" she said with a touch of skepticism in her voice. The words came out before she could censor herself . . . not that she necessarily would have.

"How would I know it?" he challenged.

She shrugged. "I don't know. I thought maybe you were following me or something."

He let out a short, brusque laugh. "Following you? Wow." After a negligible pause, he added, "Actually, I'm here visiting someone . . . who also works here."

Involuntarily, Gretchen glanced around, looking for this person—she assumed it was a girl—who Rick was visiting. He'd said "someone." He hadn't said his buddy or some guy. He'd said "someone." She felt a pinch of jealousy at the thought, which was absurd and she knew it. Then she spotted the big puddle of water and shattered glass behind her that she'd somehow forgotten. "Oh, shoot—I'd better find a maintenance person to mop that up."

"Looks like he's got it," Rick said, motioning to a man in an olive-green jumpsuit who was crossing the room, pushing a mop and bucket in front of him. Even though it was his job, Gretchen felt a stab of guilt. Maybe it was because she remembered what it felt like for those few startling, horrific moments when she'd thought she was TCC's new cleaning lady.

"Oh . . . well . . . good," she said lamely, gazing up at him again. The pale blue of his tie brought out the startling blue of his eyes. She swallowed hard, having trouble looking away. He exuded cockiness—cockiness she was done with, it had been decided—but yet . . .

There was just something sexy about him—a viscerally potent quality. Maybe it was the concentrated way he looked at her, or the thickness of his deep, masculine voice. It was as though his body thrummed with a kind of heat, an energy that seeped into her space, nearly swallowed her up. Definitely stole her ability to speak like a human.

God, those eyes . . . Clear and bright like a mountain dog's, and just as watchful and intense. And she had to admit, the shirt and tie were an extremely hot touch. What man didn't look better in a tie? That's what she wanted to know.

But why did he irk her so much? He made her uncomfortable, rattled her nerves. And she still didn't get what he was doing here. Who was he "visiting"? And where were they?

"Do I make you nervous or something?" he asked. It was like he'd read her mind.

"No, of course not," she lied, refusing to look away or around or to chew on her lip, all of which would betray her. Instead she tilted her hip, leaning her weight on that side, and kept looking at him dead-on.

"Bullshit," he stated bluntly. "You're like a little bunny."

With a false, smart-ass sense of comprehension, she humored him. "Meaning what? That I'm fluffy and hop around a lot?"

He laughed at that, the corners of his eyes creasing with genuine amusement. "*Exactly*. And also . . . I scare you."

"No you don't," she nearly yelped, surprised. Then realized instantly it was another lie . . . sort of. "It's just . . . well, why are you always around when I least expect you?" Scared her? No. Threw her off, shook her defenses, sent her heart speeding inside her chest? Yes. Absolutely.

He paused for a moment, then said, "It's only been twice now." He had a point. But twice in two days? In a city of eight million people? "And one time doesn't even count," he went on casually. "When you set a building on fire, you gotta expect the fire department. You can't blame me for that one."

With a puff of a sigh, she rolled her eyes. She couldn't help it. "I hope you're not gonna yell at me again," she said, sounding weary at the prospect. At the same time, she inwardly fought the nervousness that encroached on her chest with each breath she took.

A smile tugged at the corners of his mouth. "Why? Do I have a reason to yell at you? You didn't throw one of your girlie rituals this morning, did you? Forget to blow out your candles?"

She nearly groaned. "I'm *really* not in the mood for that whole speech again." Leaning harder on her hip, tilting her head defiantly, she said, "Like I said, I've got to get back to work. Thanks for the sandwich and for . . . helping me." She motioned vaguely with her head to the mess she'd made just a couple of feet behind her. Maybe she was being too guarded, too humorless, too much a defensive dud, but she was still irritable from all the pushing and shoving at Lemberto's, then her klutzy, embarrassing debacle, and then, on top of everything, his exasperating presence that inexplicably frazzled her.

Before she turned to go, he squinted down at her a bit, studying her, and said, "Why do I get the feeling that you don't like me very much?"

His voice, low and deliberate, instantly melted her resolve. And what the hell was she so resolved about anyway? Making a fool of herself? Snapping irrationally at the man who'd first saved her life, then saved her boss's sandwich? What was her problem today anyway?

Softening her stance, she let out a small sigh and relaxed her shoulders. With a sardonic twist of her lips, she said, "If I don't even know your name, I can't very well dislike you—*yet*."

"Oh. Well, let's hurry up and get to the good stuff then. It's Rick," he said. "Rick Pellucci. I'd shake your hand, but I see they're both kind of full at the moment. And I wouldn't wanna bring on another disaster."

With a deprecating grin, she struggled to think of something snappy to say, but her mind blanked; her heart was racing too fast, her palms were beginning to sweat, feeling hot and slippery against the hard surface of the clipboard. Then Rick touched her lightly and smiled at her. It was a devastatingly sexy smile.

"You probably won't believe this, but I'm actually a really nice guy."

Gretchen's stomach fluttered at the gruff but softly spoken words. She wasn't sure if it was the boyish charm of what he'd said, or the low, smooth quality of his voice when he'd said it—or maybe it was his warm, strong hand she could still feel on her wrist even though his fingers had only briefly grazed her skin.

His face was close enough to hers for her to notice the nick along his jaw and the small curved scar on his forehead. She hadn't noticed it before; she'd been looking at his eyes.

"How about a cup of coffee?" he said.

"Huh?" That threw her. "Oh . . . no, I couldn't possibly . . . um, when?"

"Now."

"I can't," she said and glanced down at her pile by way of explanation.

"Okay, I'll have coffee; you can have your sandwich."

"No, no," she said, shaking her head, "I couldn't. Like I said, I have work, and—"

"Brody!"

Abruptly, Rick turned his head, then cursed softly. Gretchen followed his gaze and saw Brett coming toward both of them with his hands out, palms up, as if to say: *What the fuck?* "What's up, man? I thought you said you'd be only a minute." As he came closer, he took notice of Gretchen. A smile spread across his face. "Oh, hey, there." He winked. "What's up?"

She barely got out a hello—she was too stunned. *This* was the person Rick was visiting? And why was he calling him "Brody"?

"I thought you were coming back to the smoothie place! I told you I'd buy you a fruit smoothie," Brett said, his focus back on Rick. "I drank my smoothie waiting for you. What, you don't want a smoothie?"

"Not so loud, will you?" Rick muttered.

Comprehension might have been slow to set in, but when it did, it hit with a thud. Holy cow, was Rick . . . could Rick be . . . Rick and Brett . . . *brothers*?

But Rick's last name was Pellucci. If Brett's last name was Ramero . . .

Duh. If "Romeo" was fake, "Ramero" could easily be fake, too.

Winking again, Brett said to Gretchen, "I see you've met my brother. I hope he hasn't been bothering you."

Fervently, she shook her head as she took in the details. Now she could see a resemblance. The blackish hair. Although Brett's was styled and gelled, while Rick's looked soft to the touch. And the eyes. Both had crystalline blue eyes, bright and beautiful. Rick stood about five inches taller than his brother—but his face was rougher, less striking, less, well, *perfect* than Brett's.

"Sorry," Rick said to him now, "I should've come right back."

"I can't believe you two are brothers," she said, shaking her head. Yet even as she processed it, it was extremely hard to believe. Rick Pellucci was the same guy Brett had been talking about at the staff meeting that morning? *Rick* was the mentally slow or "skittish" un-employed hanger-on whom Brett had been describing in such pa-thetic detail—the one with the interminable "issues" who worshipped the ground Brett swaggered on? That must be why Brett was afraid to let him out of his sight for too long. Dear Lord . . . how unbelievably strange.

In fact, it was almost inconceivable. Rick Pellucci seemed way too confident to play second banana to anyone, much less his younger and much shorter brother. (For a shrimp herself, Gretchen was ludicrously hung up on height all of a sudden. But she'd tackle her issues some other time—right now she was preoccupied with Rick's.)

Issues. She contemplated the word. What was it Brett had said ex-actly? She remembered the crux of it was that his brother's morale was in the dumper—and then there was the part about how he wasn't "all there," whatever that meant. A thought occurred to her. If Rick was a fireman (and clearly she knew that he was), then why had Brett said he was out of work?

Instinctively, she gave Rick a supportive smile. Whatever his problems were, whatever the details of his situation, it wasn't her place to figure it out. She gave him another smile—this one spreading closemouthed across her lips, freezing meaningfully on her face, as if to say, *Chin up, Tiger, it's all gonna work out in the end.*

He just looked at her.

"Yeah, I'm just giving my bro here a tour of the studios," Brett elaborated, clapping Rick on the back. "You having fun so far, bro?"

Rick slanted him a look.

"Oh, by the way, I hope you're coming this weekend, Gretchen," Brett added.

"Coming where?"

"To my house in the Catskills," he replied. "Didn't Susanna mention it? It's my birthday bash. Everyone will be skiing. It's gonna be awesome. You gotta come."

"Oh . . . well, thank you . . ." This was the first she'd heard about it, but then this was also only her second day, which raised another point: She didn't particularly *want* to go to Brett's party. She couldn't ski to save her life. Who would she even know there? Of course, she knew the logical answer: She would meet people there and then she would know them. That was all well and good, but it sounded like a lot of effort for her first week at work. She was more the type to let relationships form naturally with those around her, not to try to force friendships too fast. Or maybe she was just being lazy about this. After all, she didn't exactly have a surfeit of close friends these days. Let's see, there was Dana and . . .

Dana and . . .

Okay, this was getting sad. She'd reverted back to the shy, solitary ways of her youth sometime when she hadn't been paying attention.

"So, Gretchen . . ." Brett continued. "How are you liking the new job so far?"

"I love it. It's great," she replied.

"Working for Susanna, I imagine that's pretty, uh, *challenging,*" he said, smiling warmly and topping off his statement with a wink. He made winking look natural and breezy. He was one of those people who could wink without contorting his face, which was sort of a skill, she supposed.

"Yeah, I've definitely learned a lot so far," Gretchen replied diplomatically. The second day seemed a bit early to vent about her boss being a diva—speaking of which, she suddenly remembered the other errand Susanna wanted her to run that afternoon. This was the perfect opportunity! She had Brett right here; she could pose the idea to him of guest spots on his show. If it would ameliorate Susanna, it was definitely on Gretchen's to-do list, because, the truth was, she really did love her job so far. "Listen, Brett, I—"

Just then someone came up behind him and tapped him on the shoulder. When he turned Gretchen got a look at the girl. She was cute and blonde, probably about twenty-five, with curly hair and an enormous smile bordering on horse teeth (yet still pulling off cute). "I'm sorry to bother you," she gushed in a giggly voice, "but I'm a huge fan of yours . . ."

She went on to ask if he'd come to her lunch table and sign autographs for her and the other girls she worked with. Apparently they worked across the street, but frequently had lunch at Terra Cottage. He excused himself, saying he'd be right back, and followed the girl to her table.

"Well, don't let me keep you from your work," Rick said casually and gave her a friendly nod. "See ya." He turned to go in Brett's direction, when Gretchen seized an opportunity.

"Wait!" He stopped and angled his head back. "About that cup of coffee," she said, shimmying the stuff in her arms to balance the weight as she came closer. "Let's do that—now." He appeared momentarily confused, but when Gretchen added eagerly, "The three of us," his quizzical expression flattened to one of bland understanding.

She didn't want to leave Rick room to say no—in case he was to tell her that he and Brett were spending the day together or whatever. And she needed this chance to talk to Brett about his show. As it was, Susanna would already be peeved about how late her lunch was, and maybe she wouldn't even like the sandwich Gretchen had had made for her. Think how thrilled she'd be, though, if Gretchen returned with a resounding "yes" from Brett on the guest-appearance question.

But Rick just looked blankly at her, so she pressed on. "I mean, I can see you and Brett are hanging out, so I'm not going to take you away from him or anything. Oh! Not that you have some kind of weird attachment, but . . . uh . . . I still can't believe you two are brothers."

When he continued to look expressionlessly at her, she suddenly felt vulnerable, naked. No, forget naked. She felt like she was vulnerable and wearing a pair of ill-fitting, period-stained underpants. That beat naked for unflattering any day of the week.

"Anyway, a cup of coffee—the three of us—sounds like fun," she finished.

Finally, he nodded slowly. "That would be fun," he said, now not really looking at her, but out in front of him, as though contemplating the idea, really nursing it, appreciating its wonder. "But I think I'll pass."

He'd stated it so bluntly that Gretchen felt the blow of rejection almost instantly. "Oh . . ."

"See ya around," he added with a brief, dismissive wave and walked away.

Just like that he left! Gretchen was left standing there, slack-jawed, confused as to what had just happened. Hot color suffused her cheeks, as the embarrassment of Rick's bland dismissal sank in. He'd dusted her—rejected her outright—abruptly and with no explanation.

Well, she couldn't very well trail after him and try to ask Brett about Susanna now. She had her pride, after all. She'd just talk to Brett some other time. Damn his stupid brother!

Turning on her heel, Gretchen sighed, shaking her head, as she moved briskly toward the elevators, hitting the button with her knuckles once she got there. This was ridiculous. Why should she feel embarrassed? *He* was the weird one; he was the one who ought to feel like an ass. And why did she care so much that he'd rejected her? What she should be frustrated about more than anything was the fact that she hadn't gotten to talk to Brett. As she slipped into the elevator, she told herself that Brett had been right about his brother after all. Hot or not, the guy had issues.

CHAPTER NINE

*A*s Rick waited for Brett to come out of his private bathroom, yet again, he thought about what had happened downstairs. It was kind of hard not to with Brett still carping at him. "I can't believe you, man," he was saying. "Here I hire you as my freaking bodyguard and you go off and leave me—"

"Hire me?" Rick said, swiveling in his chair to face the closed bathroom door. "I'm getting paid for this?"

"You know what I mean. Not *hire,* but—"

"Beg."

"Fine, whatever. The point is, I ask you to come and watch my back, and then you're off hitting on some chick. I mean, come on, man, this is my *life* we're talking about."

"I'm sorry. I'm sorry," Rick said, folding the newspaper he'd been glancing at and tapping it against his open palm. Honestly, he wished he had a good excuse. Granted, he really hadn't gone that far, and he'd been pretty much 100 percent sure nothing was going to happen to Brett in the middle of a crowded food court, anyway. Whoever was behind the threats obviously liked toying with Brett, liked being secretive, sly. It seemed unlikely, then, that he'd suddenly burst out of the shadows waving an Uzi. Assuming he was even someone who worked at TCC. And assuming it was even a "he." Rick still hadn't ruled out the possibility that one of Brett's exes was behind this; it could all be a bad joke, and God knew Brett had a boatload of exes.

That said, it was still inexcusable. The fact was, in those moments when he'd realized the girl on the floor was Gretchen, and when the shock had begun subsiding just as the kick he got from being close to her again took effect . . . he'd temporarily forgotten his brother.

God, what kind of shit am I?

"I mean, I'm gonna need to count on you better than that, bro," Brett continued. "I need protection here." He was really laying it on with this guilt trip, though Rick knew he deserved it.

"I said I was sorry. I'm sitting here guarding your bathroom door while you take a shit. Doesn't that count for anything?"

"Shut up, shmuck," Brett called back, and Rick laughed. After a pause, Brett said, "So you think she's cute? That Gretchen chick?"

Actually . . . he *had* until she'd shown the opportunist in her. The one who thought she was gonna use Rick to get to Brett. The one who'd suddenly become interested in spending more time with Rick once she'd found out that Brett—the big TV star—was his brother. He could still see her now, beaming about the prospect of "the three of us" having coffee—after she'd just turned Rick down, saying she had too much work. But her whole demeanor toward Rick had changed once Brett had come up to them. And what was up with all those fake smiles she kept giving him?

The faint scent of her perfume seemed to linger, at least in his mind. He couldn't help it—she'd smelled good. Good enough to stir his blood, to send heat right to his groin . . . and what was with the hot red dress? *Damn.* She was by far the best-looking girl he'd seen all day.

"Brody?"

"Oh," he said, snapping back into focus. "Gretchen? She's okay, I guess."

"Yeah," Brett agreed. "Actually, she is pretty cute. She's got great tits." Rick smiled grimly. He couldn't argue with that. "But she's not as fit as I like," Brett went on. "I mean, she's not fat or anything, but I dig girls who are more athletic. Tiny, tight little chicks, you know? With hot butts."

"This is a scintillating conversation," Rick remarked dryly, and tossed the newspaper back on Brett's vanity.

Hell, when had they switched gears to what Brett preferred? Who said it was all up to him? But the hell of it was . . . it was usually true. Which pissed Rick off even further. It *was* up to Brett. If he decided he wanted Gretchen Darrow, he could snap his fingers and get her. It was goddamn annoying.

"Jesus, are you almost done in there?"

Finally the toilet flushed. Water ran (surprisingly) and Brett came out. "Sorry about that. I guess something didn't agree with me."

Maybe it was the constant consumption of raw vegetables instead of real food, but Rick didn't bother saying it. Instead, he rose from the chair and asked, "And, by the way, could you have made me sound more like a lame-ass tourist down there?"

"What do you mean?" Brett asked.

"Forget it," Rick said, realizing he didn't want to get into it. Who cared how he looked to Gretchen? She was obviously more interested in his brother, so that meant Rick wasn't interested in her. Sure, he might be physically attracted to her, but that's where it ended—cold.

Besides, Brett was obviously anxious to talk about the more serious matter of his safety. "So come on, give it to me. It's almost two o'clock. You've been here for five hours now. What have you noticed so far?"

Rick drew a breath, then shook his head. "Nothing, honestly. If anyone's been lurking around you, they haven't been lurking around me. I checked out the layout of this whole place while you were in your meeting earlier. I've checked the locks to your dressing room, which are secure, but anyone can just walk onto your soundstage."

"But they'd need security clearance on the first floor," Brett countered.

"But if they work here, they already have it," Rick said.

"Oh, good point. I guess that was pretty obvious."

"Have you gotten any more e-mails?"

"I was afraid to check," Brett said.

"Let's do it now."

They booted up his laptop, accessed his corporate e-mail. There was one new message; it was from Susanna Tate. Rick opened it and found a link, followed by a short note from Susanna that read: *Thought you'd find this article interesting!* It was a piece in the *Daily News* about the growth of American cuisine in New York City.

"This must be what she'd sent me that she wanted me to see yesterday," Brett remarked.

"Maybe . . ." Rick said speculatively. Susanna's e-mail might have just arrived late in Brett's in box; it was probably coincidental that yesterday, after Susanna had told Brett to check his e-mail, he'd found an anonymous, threatening note rather than her friendly message. *Probably.* But Rick couldn't be too sure about anything at this point. As it was, so far there didn't seem to be a damn ominous thing about Brett's work life or the people who surrounded him. If anything, everyone seemed to buzz around, too busy to stop and schmooze, much less to stalk. Of course, you never knew who was nursing a secret grudge . . .

And there was no denying the calls he'd gotten or that e-mail saying he'd die before he made it to Hawaii. The Hawaii thing was the lynchpin. Brett had said that nobody knew about the upcoming Hawaiian show, except for certain people who were in the know at the network.

But then again . . .

Couldn't Brett have mentioned it, just casually, to any of the girls he was seeing? So Rick asked him that now. Brett stopped to think. "No, no, I'm not really seeing anybody right now." Rick looked at him doubtfully. "Well, except for . . . no, that doesn't count. We just screw."

Lucky girl, Rick thought sarcastically. "Who is it?"

Brett waved his hand to dismiss the point and stood, shutting his laptop with a click as he rose to his feet. "No, it's not her. Believe me. We fuck around, but it's a casual thing. For both of us." Brett tilted his head, as though thinking about it more, then added, "Even though you wouldn't think she'd be the type, but . . ."

"But she knows about the Hawaii trip?"

"I can't remember if I mentioned it or not. But it doesn't matter."

"Still, you should tell me who it is," Rick said.

Brett shook his head. "Trust me, it's not her. She has no reason. Besides . . . she likes to keep me happy."

"Sorry I smell."

"I'm going to kill you if you tell me that again," Gretchen said.

"For the tenth time, you don't smell." Dana shot her a disbelieving look. "Okay, yes, I can smell it. But I like it. That's what I'm trying to tell you."

"G, I spilled half a bottle of Tommy Girl on me, and if I want to lash out at the world, the least you could do is sit there and take it—"

"I thought I was—"

"With grace and dignity."

"Oh, I apologize," Gretchen said with a giggle. "Go for it. You were saying?"

"Well, forget it now," Dana said, grinning. She held the door open for Gretchen, who stepped inside Starbucks first.

"Think of it this way," Gretchen remarked, glancing over her shoulder as Dana followed her in. "You always said you wanted to bring Tommy Girl back to its heyday; maybe this will help."

Teasingly, Dana squinted down at her and said, "You're not patronizing me now, are you?"

The Starbucks was a five-minute walk from their apartment. As always, the warmly lit ambience was instantly comforting. In tonight's case, though, the blaring reggae music seemed out of place, and the overcrowded seating shaved off a fraction of the comfort. The people behind the counter were bouncing up and down while they made drinks; clearly the music was a renegade staff selection.

"What do you want?" Gretchen asked, turning to Dana as they inched up in line.

"A caramel mochachino," she said.

Nodding, Gretchen said, "Go sit down. I'll get it for you."

"No. Thanks, but I have to tell him how to make it." Gretchen shot her a look, which Dana missed. "Excuse me, can I have a caramel mochachino—two parts mocha, two parts caramel, one part chino? Extra whipped cream. Thanks."

The heavily freckled server with blond dreadlocks just looked at her, scrunched his face, and reared his head back. "Whoooh!" he exclaimed, making a motion of waving his open palm across his nose. "Someone stinks like man's cologne! It that you?" he said, looking straight at Gretchen and still waving his dirty hand across his nose.

"No, of *course* not," Dana said indignantly, her haughtiness completely believable. She gave Gretchen a look that said *Where do they find these people?*

And Gretchen whispered, "One part chino? What's that?"

"That's the milk," Dana replied quietly. "I think he gets the point." She assumed so anyway, because he'd turned—with a skeptical look on his pruned-up face—to make her drink. He was clearly overwhelmed by the Tommy Girl. Dana's not-guilty act was flawless except for the fact that she edged back a good ten inches from the counter when he wasn't looking. "Sorry I smell," she whispered to her cousin.

"Forget him," Gretchen whispered back. "He has weird, ultra-sensitive olfactory glands or something."

"I reek," Dana stated with no room for argument.

Once they were sitting at a tiny table in the corner, complete with milk puddles and sticky patches of dried syrup, Dana made an important announcement. "So I got a callback!"

"Oh my God, Dana, that's great!" Gretchen enthused. "When is it for?"

"Tomorrow. I'm just gonna blow off work and go."

"Can you do that?" Gretchen asked, a bit concerned. If Dana wasn't careful, all her truancy was going to get her in trouble.

She obviously didn't think so. With a scoff, Dana waved her hand through the air. "No biggie. They'll never even notice."

"Okay, if you're sure . . ."

Dana sipped her drink, then made a face. "This is all wrong," she murmured with mild disappointment.

"I'm so excited for your callback! This is big news. I'm so proud of you!" Gretchen said with a smile. "Why didn't you tell me on the way over?"

"I wanted to hear about your day, and we're not done talking about it, by the way."

"We're not?"

"I still think you're crazy if you don't go to Romeo Ramero's party this weekend. God! Do you know how many people would kill to trade places with you? I mean, a personal invite from Romeo himself! What more do you want?"

"I don't know . . . I just wanted to stay in and relax this weekend . . ."

"You're telling me you'd rather stay home to watch me polish Marcia's silver and cry?"

"Why would you cry?" Gretchen asked, then realized the answer. Dana considered it a personal injury for Gretchen to miss the untouchable Romeo Ramero's party. She was counting on her to give her all the details. "Please," Gretchen said, rolling her eyes. "Don't act like I'm the guest of honor or something. He asked me only because I was standing there with his brother."

"Don't even get me started on the brother," Dana said with a shake of her head and took a sip of her drink. "I still cannot believe he's related to Romeo Ramero." When Gretchen had filled her in on the connection earlier that evening, she'd been appropriately shocked. "I'm telling you, if you're not careful, you guys'll probably end up getting married."

"What!" Gretchen yelped, stunned by the comment.

"I'm serious. The whole coincidence, running into him again—everything. It's just too weird. Like a *Sleepless in Seattle* kind of thing."

Skeptically, Gretchen wrinkled her face. "It's nothing like that," she said.

Dana shrugged. "Well, you know what I mean. Anyway, how can you not want to go to that party? Don't you want to see his house?"

"Not particularly. I don't know. I guess I don't just feel like being all sociable this weekend."

"You're too shy," Dana said matter-of-factly. "That's always been your problem."

"I'm not that shy," Gretchen argued.

"Well, not shy, but a hermit."

"Is that the best euphemism for shy that you can come up with?" Gretchen couldn't deny that she had been shy when she was younger. Her mom always said it was because she was "young for her grade," but in any case, it was only after Dana moved to Kaplan, Connecticut, that she'd come out of her shell. Dana had spent her senior year at the same high school where Gretchen was a sophomore, and having Dana there had made such a difference. Before Dana had moved close by, Gretchen had always spent her afternoons after school alone. Watching her favorite cooking show and experimenting with recipes, partly to dazzle her parents when they came home from their long, hectic jobs.

She'd had friends, of course, but the low-key kind you sat next to in honors classes and in the cafeteria, the kind you occasionally went to the movies with on Saturday. But on a day-to-day basis, the truth was . . . Gretchen was lonely. She hadn't really realized it until Dana came bursting onto the scene, into her life, making everything in Kaplan much more interesting. Even something simple like going to get frozen yogurt could turn into a minidrama with Dana—but in a good way. She always had some overblown story about something that had happened to her, or some scheme she was cooking up. And she'd pulled Gretchen into her bubbly world. After that, Gretchen had been more confident, in school and out. She'd even formed a "cooking club" during her junior year. Granted, nobody had signed up and she'd ended up alone again . . . but hey, at least she'd tried.

When she'd gotten to college, she had found a niche of friends. Unfortunately she'd lost touch with many of them between culinary school in Minnesota and then her move to California.

"This is Romeo Ramero we're talking about!" Dana was saying. "And you said yourself he looks pretty much the same in real life as he does on TV." For a moment Gretchen waited for the larger point, and then it became patently clear that that *was* the larger point. "He is so damn hot," Dana mused, dreamily holding her steaming cup by her mouth. "And who knows? You and he could end up hanging out. Talking, sharing a few drinks, etcetera, etcetera. Need I say more?"

With a brief laugh, Gretchen said, "I'm sure I'm not Romeo Ramero's type. And he's not mine, either. I know you're gonna find this hard to believe, but I'm actually not the least bit attracted to him."

Dana gasped.

"I know, it's an atrocity, but it's true."

"Really?" She seemed genuinely confounded. "Huh. This is like the time you said you didn't think Brad Pitt was cute."

"He's *okay* . . ."

Dana made a gruff sound of disbelief. "You're weird." After another sip of her coffee drink, she tapped her fingers on her paper cup and glanced more covertly at Gretchen. "So if you're not interested in him . . ."

"As soon as I get more comfortable at work—much more comfortable—I'll find a way to introduce you to him," Gretchen said with a smile. "I promise."

"Thanks!" Dana replied, beaming, then hastened to add, "But only because you don't want him for yourself."

No, Gretchen definitely didn't, which she'd like to attribute to the fact that she was older and wiser than she used to be—no longer vulnerable to the charms of flirtatious eye candy, too career oriented and levelheaded to go for the well-built player type again. But if that were true, why was she so damn attracted to Brett's brother, Rick?

It was a frustrating conundrum. And on top of Rick's impressive physical stature (which always spelled trouble) and his quiet arrogance, the guy obviously had problems. Really, hadn't she learned anything from her past mistakes? Why couldn't she like a nice nerdy guy?

Or better yet, she should push all romantic thoughts out of her mind, because for the time being, she couldn't afford to indulge them. How much more cautious could a girl be than to rule out men altogether?

She hadn't dated in high school—she'd been way too shy—and the relationships she'd had late in college and afterward never lasted; it seemed that Gretchen always got blown off after the second or third month of dating. Part of it, she realized, was the type of guy. No sticking power, all about the challenge. And with Gretchen showering him with affection and devotion, there was never much of a challenge. That, actually, was the second part of the problem: *her*.

She was embarrassed to think about the way she had acted with the guys she'd liked, always jumping in too fast, letting her infatuation fall out all over the place, never playing the game, too busy baking brownies and sending e-cards—and basically scaring the guy off completely. Well, scaring was too strong a word; really, she figured she'd bored most of them off.

Her last boyfriend, Tristan, had been her one serious relationship. They'd dated for a couple of years and had broken up about eight months ago. He was a new twist on an old favorite: a physical trainer at Deluxe Resort whom everyone on staff viewed as the cool guy with all the jokes. He was eye candy; he was Mr. Built Player. But here was the twist: He had a sensitive side. Too sensitive, sometimes. He cried to get himself out of a jam with her a few times. Once they'd started dating, Gretchen supposed she hadn't seen how little truly bonded them together. There was a physical attraction between them and a lot of laughs those first couple of months, but beyond that, there was nothing real, nothing with substance. Oh, how she'd *wanted* there to be substance, how she'd wanted this to be the one that lasted. And because Tristan was secretly more sensitive than the average guy, he'd become emotionally attached to her, as well. As disparate as they were as individuals, Tristan needed her.

Predictably, the boyfriend-girlfriend relationship they'd forged became harder and harder to maintain. Of course, Tristan's chronic flirting hadn't helped. But the more time that stretched on, the harder it became to let it all go.

Overall, Gretchen truly cared about him. He'd been more than just someone to make love with, to go to cute, romantic dessert shops with—even if he didn't eat white flour or sugar—or to hold hands with at the movies. But after two years, enough was enough. They had become more than tenuous; as a couple, they'd become threadbare. And just when Gretchen had been all revved up to end it, Tristan had gotten into a surfing accident, breaking one of his legs and both of his arms. Jeez, could his timing get any worse? Consumed by a fierce nurturing instinct she hadn't known she possessed, Gretchen had taken care of him. She'd caved when Tristan had told her that he felt so alone, so helpless, when he'd bawled about how he couldn't work, couldn't do anything for himself, how he needed her desperately. He'd counted on her and she couldn't desert him. She'd break up with him after he was recovered, she'd told herself.

But ultimately there had been no need to wait. A month into the nursemaid bit (which had been slowly driving her around the bend), she'd gotten a text message on her phone from Tristan—one that was not only filthy, but also clearly meant for someone else. That's when the truth began to unravel, leading to a tearstained confession on his part. The jerk had been *cheating* on her for months! Since before his accident. Okay, granted, before his accident, she'd been about to dump him, but still, *he* hadn't known that.

Did the asshole have no shame?

Looking at the bigger picture, though, Tristan was just one of Gretchen's poor choices. She'd always been drawn—much to her detriment—to guys who were more blatant in their physical appeal. Guys who were confident and charismatic—center-of-attention types who found her just as naturally and automatically as she found them. Well, she'd had it. That was it. She was through with this pattern. From now on, it was ugly, meek little dorks or nothing.

(She had her money on nothing.)

CHAPTER TEN

*T*wo nights later Rick lit a cigarette and blew smoke out the open window of his truck as he careened up a hilly road toward the Catskills. Sharp, cold wind hit his face. In general, if there was anywhere he didn't expect to find himself it was at his brother's annual ski weekend/birthday bash, which would be full of TV people and other quasicelebrities. But these were unusual circumstances. Brett hadn't gotten any more threats since that e-mail on Tuesday—so it had been three days with no threatening phone calls, no suspicious e-mails. Odds were better all the time that the whole thing had been a lame prank. At Brett's request, Rick had shadowed him for the rest of the week, but there had been no danger that either could detect. Now Rick's vacation from work was drawing to a close and he'd never made it up to Maine.

This weekend was out, too. Brett had begged him to come to his party. He swore it would be the last time, but he said he just didn't feel safe yet. He said he was about eighty percent sure that the threats had been harmless, but he still couldn't shake the feeling that someone from the network might have it in for him. If he could get through the party and the weekend with no problems, no threats, then he would dismiss it all.

Rick had agreed, figuring, as tedious as this night promised to be, it was better to be on the safe side. And Brett was obviously still scared. Inwardly, Rick was kind of shocked how much better Brett seemed to feel with him around. He acted like Rick was invincible—unless someone he knew came around them. Then he acted like Rick was a walking vegetable. Claimed it was so Rick would "blend in" and so no one would suspect his real purpose at the studio. Brett was such an egomaniac, though, Rick had to wonder . . .

But his fear seemed sincere, and that was what mattered. It was understandable; Brett had never dealt with anything like this. Rick supposed the level of his fame was just starting to sink in—for both of them. His brother's rise to stardom had been a quick one, and it was something based on personality and looks, not toughness or strength, so it made sense he'd been freaking out now. Despite his macho Brooklyn act for the camera, and despite his hardcore bodybuilding—or "sculpting" as he called it—he'd always been more of a pampered mama's boy. It was irritating on the one hand, but on the other, it made Rick even more protective of him.

They'd always had a rocky relationship, somewhat parallel to Rick's rocky relationship with his dad. God knew Rick had not been an easy kid. He hadn't been perfect growing up, always getting into trouble, drifting from one scrape to the next. Hell, when they were teenagers, the roles were as predictable as they were clear-cut. Rick was the family fuck-up and Brett was the golden boy. There were times when Rick had almost hated him. But Brett made it too hard to hate him. Their dad had made it easy, though. He'd always been so stern, so goddamn stubborn—and Rick had been unpredictable. That was a long time ago, too long to make amends now.

Now he turned off the main road, onto a long, winding side street, and took one last drag of his cigarette before he chucked it into the cup of old coffee that sat in his drink holder.

He'd been to Brett's house in the Catskills only twice. Now he'd be there, not to enjoy the party like everyone else, but to size up Brett's coworkers and anyone else who might strike him as having some hostility toward Brett—or even quite the opposite. Often people who stalked and threatened others actually believed they were in love with their victims. So he'd keep an eye out for lovesick weirdos, too, which would probably be the easiest part of the job. Nobody seemed to attract the lovesick like his brother.

He wondered if Gretchen would be there, too. Of course she would. If Brett had invited her, she'd be there, no doubt. She'd made that clear the other day. She'd seemed interested in getting to know Rick only after she'd found out about Brett. Then she'd been all smiles.

Luckily, Rick hadn't run into her again since that time in the food court. It was just as well. Considering that hot red dress . . . and that even hotter nightgown from the night they'd met . . . He had to wonder if she even possessed an outfit that wouldn't give him an erection.

Rick knew he wasn't a bad-looking guy, but he was hardly up there in Brett's pretty-boy league. Not that he had trouble meeting women, but still, Gretchen Darrow wasn't the first girl who'd tried to use him to get to his famous brother.

Sure, she worked for the same network as Brett, which was an "in," Rick supposed, but even at that, Gretchen was just one of the many girls at TCC who undoubtedly wanted to get close to him. She'd need some kind of edge and she knew it. Well, she could count Rick out. The sexy little opportunist would have to find some other way to get what she wanted.

Back in the city, Gretchen was preparing for the weekend, too, throwing a few wool sweaters into a suitcase.

"I'm so glad you decided to go after all," Dana said, sitting on Gretchen's bed, eyeing her open suitcase speculatively.

"I didn't decide. Susanna's making me. She said she needs me there. She begged me."

"Sounds kinda pathetic."

"It was." Gretchen had to admit, she liked her new boss, but she seemed a bit dependent on her after only one week. But then, she was starting to think that Susanna was a dichotomy of self-assuredness and vulnerability, ego and insecurity. Maybe she sensed someone she could relax around, someone she could trust, in Gretchen. Or maybe she was just bizarre.

"Is that all you're taking?" Dana asked, surprised.

"Yeah, why? You think I need more?"

"Well, either more . . . or less—of *that*," she said, pointing down at the thick olive-green sweater folded beside a nearly identical gray one.

"What? I love that sweater," Gretchen said, patting it gently. "It's snuggly—like me," she added with a grin.

"You are snuggly, I'll give you that. But where are the cute little ski outfits?" Dana asked.

"I can't ski."

"You can still wear the cute outfits, can't you?" Dana said. With a grimace, she picked up one of the undergarments folded and wedged in the side of the suitcase and waved it like a battered flag. "What is *this* savagery? Please tell me this is an accident."

"What?" Gretchen said, covering a giggle, and snatched the garment back.

Dana didn't appear amused. "Granny bra central," she said, clearly dismayed, and shook her head, as if to add, *Lose the orthopedic undies, will you?*

"You're so sweet," Gretchen said, grinning, "to think of me and my underwear like that. But really, nobody's gonna see them anyway."

"G, you *never* know—"

"Trust me, I know." She knew herself all too well. "The granny bras are in no danger of being torn in passion," she added lightly, but at the words, disappointment sank into her chest. *Where did that come from?*

Then another random thing happened. She thought about Brett's moody brother, Rick. Suddenly an image of *him* tearing her granny bra flashed into her mind. It didn't flash out nearly as quickly. Instead, she bit her lip and let herself contemplate it . . .

Not that it made any difference, but she still had to wonder: Would Rick be there this weekend?

Icy wind shuddered through Gretchen's chest, and snow crystals scattered through the air like silvery tacks. Standing on her front stoop, she ran her hands feverishly over her arms, trying to rub some heat into her bones as she waited for Susanna to pick her up and drive them both to Brett's house upstate. The sidewalk ahead had a pinkish glow from the streetlamp, and from this distance, the snow appeared to settle softly on the asphalt, like baby powder. When Gretchen stepped forward and turned to glance up at her own building, she looked at the windows to Marcia Rabe's apartment on the fifth floor, at the gauzy yellow light dappling against the curtains.

Suddenly her attention was diverted by a stretch limousine that came peeling down her street. When it slid to a stop next to the curb, a puddle of slush splashed up onto the sidewalk, reminding Gretchen that whether snow looked like sugar crystals or baby powder, it eventually turned to cold wet slop. Then it hit her—this was her ride!

Susanna had said she would have a car drive them both, but "a car" could mean many things; Gretchen ought to know. In her life "a car" had meant things like hatchback, Cutlass Sierra, and at one point, used-and-dented-twelve-year-old-Honda-to-buy-off-Mom, but never once had it been equated with such fabulous opulence.

The backseat door facing her building flew open. Susanna ducked her head out just a fraction and called out, "Gretchen, hi! Sorry we're late. Get in!"

So to repeat: a stretch limo? Gretchen was still taking it in.

But she acted casual about it, waving hello as she darted down the front stoop and crossed the slippery sidewalk to the sleek, black car with tinted windows. "You look great," Susanna said, as Gretchen crouched down to climb inside.

"Thanks," she said brightly. "So do you." Susanna's blond hair was tucked up into a French twist, and she wore chunky, shiny green earrings and a matching green-glass necklace with circular crystals. Underneath her open wool coat, she wore dress pants and a long brocade vest, which sparkled with green and gold embroidery and went past her knees.

Meanwhile Gretchen hoped she wasn't too underdressed. She'd opted for a simple red sweater, black pants, and black boots to add a couple of inches to her height. Over it she wore a caramel-colored acrylic coat that looked like super-shiny fur. With its soft, snuggly texture and its fluffy collar, wearing the coat itself was like wearing one big hug.

Once Gretchen slid across the bench seat, she saw there was someone else inside the car. It was Susanna's niece, Shawnee, the intern from the show who apparently brought her signature scowl along with her after hours. From what Gretchen had learned that week from some of the other crew members, Shawnee was visiting New York for a while and staying with Susanna for an unspecified amount of time. She'd taken a "break" from community college in Boston, where she lived with her mother, Susanna's younger sister, Wendy. It was hardly a secret that Shawnee had an attitude—and copped it often—but Susanna sucked it up for the most part. Everyone figured it was because Shawnee was family.

"Hi, Shawnee," Gretchen said, smiling.

Old Bulbous Nose absently grunted a hello while she cracked her knuckles and looked out the window. Briefly, Gretchen wondered how much of her social awkwardness was misanthropy and how much was insecurity.

The three of them rode in silence for less than thirty seconds and then Susanna turned toward Gretchen and said, "Well, let me give you the rundown on some of the people who'll be there this weekend. Just for your own information."

"Okay, great," Gretchen said agreeably.

"First off, whatever you do, don't bring up Ray Jarian's restaurant or his show. Both are defunct. I'm not sure if I mentioned it." Several times, in fact. It seemed that Susanna was just one of those people who went around prefacing things with, "I feel *so* bad—but have you heard about so-and-so's latest brush with ignominious decline?" (Well, Gretchen was paraphrasing.)

Also, the subject of Ray's show being cancelled had been raised but glossed over quickly at Wednesday's meeting, when Joel Green had cleared his perpetually congested throat, rattled some of the marbles around in there, and explained that Ray was moving on to "other opportunities." Sure, if you could call bankruptcy and the lack of a book deal opportunities.

"Right, Ray Jarian," Gretchen said, nodding. "What happened there anyway?" she asked, genuinely curious. It seemed like southwestern cuisine had been *everywhere* for the last five years, so why had Ray's show and restaurant become a flop?

Susanna shrugged. "I think people just wised up. Look, Ray's a nice enough guy, but he's no rocket scientist." True, Gretchen supposed, but why should he be? "I mean, look at what he's doing. The same old tired recipes, the same old tired twists on these same old tired recipes." Counting on her fingers, she rattled off some of the old and tired. "Tomatillos, chipotle, guac, pepper jelly, mango salsa, we've seen it all a hundred times. And if I have to watch him make margaritas one more time." She shook her head with blatant impatience, mild disgust. "My one-year-old nephew could make margaritas, for God's sake."

Shawnee grunted at that, which drew Gretchen's attention. Rolling her eyes with annoyance, she started biting her nails. Gretchen didn't know if it was the mention of her young half brother that bothered Shawnee, or just Susanna's penchant for exaggeration.

"The fact is, any of the other chefs at the network could do what Ray does," Susanna continued, "but unfortunately for him, he can't say the same." Gretchen nodded, but noncommittally, because she'd seen Ray's show, *Tex Mex Teddy,* only twice in her life. "And don't get me started on the heavy-handed cowpoke speak," Susanna added derisively. "It's outdated, desperate, and pathetic—kind of like his restaurant." Boy, was there anything this guy could do right? "Who knows which bombed first, the show or the restaurant; it's kind one of those chicken or egg things, you know?" She shrugged. "All I know is that one day Ray thinks he's a real big shot, having lunch with Misty and me, acting like he's Wyatt Earp, then—*poof.* Suddenly he's a laughingstock and Misty won't return his calls.

"Misty?" Gretchen said, then remembered. The black-haired, violet-eyed girl Gretchen had met in Susanna's dressing room—the one who'd given Gretchen no more than an appraising look before brushing her aside. "Oh, that's right, your agent."

"Ray's, too," Susanna qualified. "Or *was,* anyway. Now, to hear him tell it, she's dropped him cold. He makes it sound like she's an unfeeling bitch, but really . . . Misty's a sweetheart." There was a certain artifice to Susanna's voice, as though the sentiment, or at least the words behind it, were contrived. "Ray actually came to me about it a couple of weeks ago, wanted me to find out what was going on with her—to find out why she wasn't calling him back and what she thought of him. Can you believe that? Well, I'm not about to stick my nose in where it doesn't belong. Although . . . between you and me, if Misty's guilty of anything here it's good judgment. Ray's a dead-end loser—financially speaking. Why should she waste her time? Especially when she's *the* agent to have right now. She represents Brett, too, in fact."

"Really?" Gretchen asked, impressed. Personality aside, Misty

Allbright seemed pretty young to be this successful in her field. She must be a real shark. Again, it was oddly impressive.

"Are we almost there already?" Shawnee interrupted, her voice laden with impatience. "You know, I'm only going to this for the free booze."

"You're not old enough to drink," Susanna replied simply.

Shawnee snorted. "Whatever."

"And no one twisted your arm to come," Susanna added.

"Oh, like you wanted me alone in your apartment for the weekend? *Right.*"

"Ed's away on business," Susanna said to Gretchen, obviously feeling compelled to explain why her husband wouldn't be home.

"*Again,*" Shawnee muttered with deliberate insinuation. Susanna just ignored her. Smart move, if you asked Gretchen.

"So who else will be there?" she asked, anxious to cut the tension before it could develop. She watched the city lights disappear from view as the car careened into the darkness of the night beyond the invisible walls of New York City.

Susanna rattled off some names, most of which sounded familiar— people Gretchen had met briefly around the building or heard mentioned in passing. Included among them were Lila Mendal from HR and the main receptionist, Denise, both of whom Gretchen hadn't seen since her first day. "Oh, and Gretchen, perhaps you could ask Brett about that little thing we discussed the other day. You know, since you still haven't done it . . ."

Please. What a martyr. Gretchen had already explained that she hadn't seen Brett since Wednesday and hadn't gotten a chance yet to "spontaneously" suggest he invite Susanna for a guest appearance on his show. Jeez, if it weren't for Susanna's fragile ego, she could simply bring up the idea herself—if not to Brett, then to Abe. She could always ask Abe to suggest it to Brett or his producer. But no. Gretchen didn't know Susanna that well yet, but she could tell this much: She did not want anyone important at the network to know that she cared or ever worried about her ratings, her fan base, or the success of her upcoming prime-time show, *Dining Elegance.* That was reserved for peons like her set supervisor.

"Let's see, who else?" Susanna mused before her eyes popped

wide open. "Oh, I just realized! Misty and Abe will both be there. Together—but *not* together. Hmm, now *that* should be interesting . . ."

"What do you mean?"

"Misty and Abe were a hot item till a couple of months ago," Susanna explained, eyes gleaming. Gretchen recognized it as the conspiratorial glint that came with good gossip. "I introduced them. He's a good ten years older. Divorced. But they seemed to hit it off right away. They dated for, oh, I'd say three or four months."

"What happened?" Gretchen asked curiously. Honestly, it was hard to picture someone as charming and polite as Abe Santasierra with the snotty, aloof woman Gretchen had met.

"Well, according to what I *heard* . . . and I feel really bad repeating it, but . . ." She paused as if contemplating whether or not to share other people's misfortunes; it was easy to guess which way she'd lean. "Abe broke it off with her," she said finally, and it was all she needed to get the ball rolling. "I really don't know why specifically, since Abe's not the type to speak badly about anyone or to spread gossip, and Misty . . . well, Misty's certainly not the type to volunteer the fact that she got dumped." With a short but gleeful little laugh— one that betrayed just how "bad" Susanna felt about all this—she added, "It's probably the first time it's ever even happened to her."

"What, being dumped?" Gretchen asked incredulously, unable to disguise her shock and total, naked projection. Please, she'd been dumped so many times, she could do it in her sleep.

"But discreet as they might have tried to be about it," Susanna went on, "people talk. And I know that Abe did feel bad about hurting her. He indicated as much, without saying it expressly, of course . . ."

"I see." So, men didn't typically spit Misty out—she spit *them* out. Except this time. It wasn't Gretchen's place to judge, but still . . . a few more points jumped into Abe's column.

"Hey, is that fat chick gonna be there?" Shawnee asked, sounding tomboyish at best.

"Who? You mean Cady?" Susanna said.

"Yeah," Shawnee replied brashly, "the dessert lady."

"She's not fat," Gretchen blurted, not sure why she felt compelled to speak up in Cady's defense, except for the fact that

Shawnee's comment wasn't fair—it also threatened to descend the whole conversation into even lower depths of catty gossip.

Besides the fact, Shawnee, like Susanna and Gretchen herself, was hardly a waif.

"I'm sure Cady will come," Susanna said, clicking open her compact. Quickly, she touched up her face with a powder puff, then snapped the compact shut. "Poor Cady," she added, sliding Gretchen a sympathetic glance, as a distasteful grimace played at her lips. "I so wish she'd do something with herself."

Well, so much for Gretchen's attempts at deflection earlier; the conversation was a sinking ship.

"Her whole look—it's just depressing," Susanna continued. "Those dowdy clothes, that helmet hair, the pudgy, bloated face . . . I'm sorry. I feel so bad saying it. It's just . . . honestly, in this business, people expect a certain look. If you're going to tell people how to cook, you're also telling them how to entertain. Nobody wants to entertain looking like that—or looking *at* that." Really, that seemed ludicrously over-the-top, but Gretchen didn't have a chance to say so. "If you ask me, what Cady could use more than anything is a man. Or a woman," Susanna said, putting her palms up. "Hey, I don't judge." Gretchen had to force herself not to laugh at that one. "But she needs something. Her show's called *Sinful Temptations,* for God's sake. The title's practically selling sex, and let's face it: Cady's not getting any. I'm not trying to be mean, of course . . ."

Yet somehow she'd nailed it.

Minutes ticked by; Gretchen let the silence fall over the backseat. Her gaze moved to the window. As the car climbed the curve of the narrow mountain road, Gretchen's body tilted into the door and her fingers flexed on the door handle. Snow-capped evergreens seemed to move, as though on a conveyor belt, rushing past her in smooth, rapid succession.

Susanna pressed a button on the door panel and the tinted glass between them and the driver slid down, revealing the back of the driver's head. "Marshall," Susanna said, "turn up here; we're almost there." In a weird way, Gretchen felt overprepared.

They pulled into a semicircle drive that wrapped around a tall indecipherable statue covered with heaping piles of snow. Two tall columns ran parallel to the imposing front doors. "Stop here," Susanna said to her driver, who was in the process of doing that anyway. They all got out and took their bags.

Instantly, Susanna took Gretchen's arm, like she did at work; Gretchen still hadn't figured who was leading whom.

Once they'd crossed the stone driveway to the doors, which were shielded by an overhang, they rang the bell and waited. Brett answered the door himself, which was refreshingly unpretentious, and then he said, "Welcome to my little *dimora umile,*" and Gretchen thought, *Well, there goes that.*

He had them leave their bags in the entry foyer for his housekeeper and began leading them up the stairs.

It was then that Gretchen saw Rick. Something had drawn her gaze to the far depths of the entry foyer, and there he was. Near the stairs, but in the shadows. She sucked in a sharp breath and almost choked on it. It felt as though the bottom of her stomach had just dropped out. God, he had a maddening effect on her nerves.

She couldn't tell if he was watching her because his eyes were hooded by the dark, but still, she knew by the outline of his body that it was Rick.

With her breath coming up shorter, she forced herself to look away and follow Brett and Susanna as they continued up the stairs, making small talk.

"Gretchen, glad you could come," Brett remarked affably, glancing back just long enough to wink at her. Then he nodded at Shawnee, who was next to Gretchen, and said, "You, too." But no wink for her.

Suddenly she felt the prickling unease of self-consciousness. Had Rick told Brett about the night they'd met—the night of the fire? Well, why not? If he was as codependent as Brett had indicated, then surely he'd told his "idol" about meeting Gretchen before. Had he also mentioned what an overdefensive fool she'd made of herself?

Every time she thought back to their first meeting, she replayed that moment when Rick's eyes had dropped down to her half-exposed cleavage. It had lasted only a moment, but it was long enough; his expression had changed. His gaze had been focused and intense.

Intense . . . For some reason the word fit him too well.

And why was he downstairs alone, instead of enjoying the party with everyone else? Boy, was he weird or what?

Then she recalled what Brett had said about him. That lately he'd been having a tough time, that he "needed" Brett, that he didn't like to be social, he liked it to be just the two of them, and Gretchen decided whatever Rick's deal was, it was best not to bother trying to make sense of it. It was best not to dwell on him, period. Instead, she should try to enjoy the party. Susanna might have coerced her into coming, but now that she was here, she would make the most of it.

"I'm gonna find the booze," Shawnee informed Gretchen, as if she cared about her itinerary for the evening.

"Um, okay," Gretchen said with a nod when they reached the second floor. Hey, the girl was twenty; Gretchen wasn't about to monitor her liquor consumption—especially if her aunt wasn't bothering. As Shawnee veered off, Brett said a friendly "See ya later" because he was being summoned by someone, and Susanna reached back to link her arm through Gretchen's.

"Come on, we'll go mingle," she said and used her elbow to tug at Gretchen, who would have been kind of irritated by all the clinging, but she was preoccupied at the moment, struck by her surroundings. The second floor was huge and open with high ceilings and decorative white beams. The shiny hardwood floor stretched on endlessly and fantastically—like lacquered caramel. The party was in full swing. People sat on or meandered around the various pieces of bright white furniture, eating and drinking. Frail, skeletal plants stretched up each corner like freestanding vines, and on the far left side of the room was a wraparound wet bar lined with lights.

Right now the bartender was handing a pink drink to an orange-haired woman Gretchen didn't recognize. But that wasn't exactly news; she didn't recognize a lot of the people here.

"Hmm, where should we start?" Susanna mused aloud as she tugged Gretchen farther into the room, locking elbows even tighter. Come on, what was this? Gretchen preferred to be a free agent at parties—and all the time, actually—and she didn't want to give off the impression that she was Susanna's lackey. She'd had her job only a week; she still had yet to meet most of the people who worked at

TCC. It was bad enough that Susanna had already introduced Gretchen to several people as her "assist—um, set supervisor."

As they walked toward the clusters of people laughing and talking, Gretchen felt antsy. Inexplicably, all she wanted to do was glance behind her and see if Rick had come upstairs yet. Was he planning to? Or was Mr. Issues going to hang alone in the dark all night?

Forget it already.

One, you have no time to date. Two, dating a relative of a coworker would be too sticky even if you wanted to do it. Three, you don't want to do it—period. Oh, yeah, and finally: *Four, no one is asking.*

Plus . . . whenever she thought about his bizarre about-face at Terra Cottage the other day—the way he'd abruptly shifted his attitude, the way he'd just blown her off—well, enough said. It was pointless to even think about him.

CHAPTER ELEVEN

*A*fter making small talk with Cady Angle and her producer, Marjorie Bass, they found Abe—and Gretchen finally gave Susanna the slip. While Susanna talked shop with her producer, Gretchen ducked through the crowd, heading to the bar. On her way, she spotted Brett laughing it up with some girl—wait, it was that tall, orange-haired one with the pink drink again. As she made her way across the room, Gretchen's eyes wandered and suddenly fell on Rick again. So he'd joined the party. If you could call standing by himself with a beer in his hand "joining."

For some reason, he didn't look the least bit awkward, even though he wasn't talking to a soul. He definitely stood apart, though. With his tall, broad frame and the piercing coolness of his blue eyes . . . even from where she stood . . .

Quickly, she averted her gaze. She tried to act natural as she continued toward the bar. She stole a glance back and found him watching her—his expression serious, his eyes nearly smoldering her to the ground.

Her eyes darted away and she kept moving.

Even though she wasn't looking at him anymore, his image lingered powerfully in her mind. He was clean-shaven tonight, but his dark hair was almost rumpled, like he'd done little more than tumble out of bed before coming here. Honestly? It was cute as hell.

She couldn't help herself—she stole another peek, arching her back to see past Susanna, who was obstructing her view from this angle. Now Rick wasn't watching her. Brett had approached him and was introducing him to that orange-haired woman. Damn it, who *was* she? Gretchen hadn't given a flying fuck till this very moment.

She felt an irrational stab of jealousy. Was Brett setting them up? Trying to get a love connection going for his disturbed, overly dependent brother? *And why do I even care?* Gretchen thought angrily. This was absurd. Where were her standards? Was she into head cases now, too?

Why were her hormones reacting so unreasonably? Why were they clouding all her common sense, her good judgment? Granted, that was pretty much par for the course with hormones, but still.

The bartender was busy chatting with a group of people who were leaning against the bar. He'd set out two rows of martini glasses, each filled with a cinnamon-colored concoction that Brett had announced earlier as his very own "hottie toddy." Mildly curious, Gretchen reached for one and took a sip. *Whew.* The drink stung as it slid down her throat. But then a thoroughly relaxing wave of heat rolled through her chest. She sighed. Took another sip. She didn't even know what she wanted right now, but this was a good start, because she was suddenly feeling antsy and pissed off and slightly jittery, hell if she understood why.

"Having fun?"

She turned at the voice. *Gulp.* Rick was right in front of her, standing much taller than she, looking nowhere near as nervous. Inexplicably, her pulse started racing and her palms began to sweat. She surreptitiously wiped them on her black pants as she forced a casual smile.

Instead of smiling back, Rick eyed her for a long moment, his expression unreadable as his gaze raked down her body . . . then back up. Swallowing hard, Gretchen felt a warm fluttering between her legs. She nearly moaned when she caught a hint of his clean, masculine scent, but luckily, only a sigh slipped out. Her mind went fuzzy on what she wanted to say. Rick's presence just had a way of consuming the entire space between them, of stealing her breath, her ability to make good small talk.

Biting her lip, she found herself momentarily preoccupied with Rick's chest . . . strong and powerful . . . the way his navy sweater covered his thick upper body . . . his broad shoulders . . . his arms . . . his back . . .

"Hello?" he said, waving the beer bottle in his hand in front of her to break her trance.

"Oh . . . sorry, what?"

"I asked if you were having a good time," he said. His voice was deep and rough; it sent little shivers rolling across her skin.

"Yeah, it's great," she fibbed, and was about to ask him if he was having a good time or something equally innocuous except her attention got snagged by his hand, coming up from his side to scratch his jaw. Had he missed a spot shaving? Or maybe he'd shaved too close? The thought of him shaving brought other images to her mind—hey, it wasn't like she *enjoyed* being a slave to her imagination, but there it was. *Rick shaving, after his shower, his hair still wet and ruffled, with only a towel riding low on his waist, molding perfectly over his firm, round butt . . .*

She wondered if he had hair on his chest. But then, he was Italian—he had to have at least some, didn't he? With a gentle lick of her lips, she tried to do something about her dry mouth—she tried to remember where she was, what she'd been about to say. She tried to think clearly even as her lower body thrummed with heat.

She found her sudden fixation on Rick Pellucci's naked body to be bordering on a sickness. Well, an obsessive compulsion anyway. Because once she'd wandered down that path, she couldn't seem to find her way back. Now she had a horny girl's slide show going again. Rick naked, muscular, sweaty, aroused, in the throes of a hot, splintering climax . . . His back, his stomach, his . . .

Well, she could go on and on. But then she'd officially need professional help.

"That's the second time you've zoned out on me. I must be pretty bad at small talk," Rick said dryly. "Though you're not exactly great at it, either. After I ask if you're having fun, you're supposed to ask if I'm having fun, too."

"Oh . . ." She felt like an idiot. Shaking her head, resetting her mind, Gretchen rejoined the land of the lucid. She was a college graduate, for pete's sake; she should be able to act like one for five minutes. "Sorry," she said with a breathy little laugh. "Are you? Having fun, I mean?"

"Oh, I'm just thrilled," he replied in a deadpan tone. Hmm,

maybe Brett wasn't spending enough time with him? Brett had said once that being around other people often made Rick "skittish." Although . . . he seemed perfectly confident and at ease right now as he brought his bottle of beer to his lips and tipped it back to take a drink.

He had a good idea there; she drank more of her "hottie toddy," feeling the burn, which began moving from her chest, down her arms, into her belly, and lower.

"So what are you doing here anyway?" she said breezily, leaning her behind against the bar. "Don't you have some fires to put out?"

"Nope," he said, the corner of his mouth hitching up. "Unless you've done something I should know about."

"Oh, shoot!" she said, hitting her palm to her forehead. "I was making s'mores in my living room earlier and I just realized I forgot to put out the bonfire." She snapped her fingers. *"Crap."*

Rick smiled at her then, revealing some of his straight white teeth; she hadn't noticed those before. So he was scruffy but clean. And God, so adorable. How was it possible for him to be so ruggedly sexy, yet so boyishly cute at the same time? The smile, that was it. When he smiled, the fierce intensity about him seemed to melt away. When he smiled, he became all rumpled hair and cuteness.

She was surprised to find herself looking up into an empty glass. Where had it all gone? When she tipped it forward again, she glanced up at Rick, who raised his eyebrows. "Guess I drank it all," she said, stating the obvious.

With a grin, he stepped closer and leaned forward, reaching behind her to grab another glass off the bar. Her breath caught in her throat for a few alarming seconds when he was nearly up against her—but just as quickly, he was gone. After giving the drink to her, he stepped back to give her more space and she inched back a bit herself.

"So that's a pretty cool apartment you have," Rick said casually. "Who did you say you lived with again? Boyfriend?"

"Cousin," she said.

"That's right. Male or female?"

With a little crease in her forehead, Gretchen said, "Female," even as she was thinking, Did that really matter? It was her cousin, for pete's sake. Besides, if the person whose room caught on fire was male, Gretchen would say the frilly yellow curtains and phallic gold pillows with fringe would indicate that Rick had nothing to worry about there, either . . .

Wait. Why was he asking anyway? Was she getting some legitimate signals from him here? Searching his eyes, she felt a whimsical kind of appreciation for their iridescence, their blueness, their clarity, and she felt a silly kind of tilt of her mouth.

"What?" he asked.

"Nothing," she said, holding back a smile as she took her next sip. And the one after that. "So how long have you been a firefighter?" she asked afterward.

"Five years," he said.

"Oh . . . and you can take time away? I just mean . . . you know, because you've been visiting the network. I mean, I've seen you around the studio, and . . . now here you are."

"Well, I'm on vacation till Monday" was all he said by way of explanation.

Nodding, Gretchen silently digested that. So on Rick's vacations, he chose to hang around his famous brother, to go to work with him, to meander around the Cooking Channel, even though there were endless other places one could go. And on the weekend, he came to his brother's house in the Catskills. It all seemed to confirm what Brett had said about him—the dependency, the lack of his own life—but still, something was off. Studying him curiously, Gretchen tried to figure out what it was, but she couldn't. Rick became more of an enigma all the time. Too bad mysterious could be a bad thing just as easily as it could be intriguing.

"Do you like to cook?" Gretchen asked, twirling the stem of her glass in her fingers.

"Nope."

"Not at all?" she asked, surprised.

"I can't cook for shit," he stated bluntly.

Okay, there went that theory. She thought that perhaps Rick was hanging around Brett because they'd had the same dreams and he was trying to live those dreams vicariously. Oh well.

She sipped her drink again, and before she knew it, that one was gone, too.

Back to the matter at hand. So Rick couldn't cook (for shit). *Interesting . . . can't cook . . .* Briefly, Gretchen wondered if he had a girlfriend or wife who cooked for him. No ring plus no wife at the party equaled not married as far as she was concerned. But surely a girlfriend. And if not a girlfriend, then he was probably a pig. In fact, now that Gretchen thought about it, everyone knew the stereotype about firemen. They were players—*dogs,* to be technical—infamous for collecting girls on and off the job, for having groupies, even. He was probably juggling several girls already. She would be a fool to assume Rick was totally free and clear and available.

Then again . . .

Hadn't Brett indicated that at the staff meeting? Hadn't he said his brother was single? Now Gretchen racked her brain to recall his exact wording, but the more she tried to remember, the fuzzier her mind became. And dizzier.

"So where are you from?" Rick asked her now.

"Um . . . Connecticut. But I've been living in California till recently," she replied. "What about you? Oh, that's right. You and Brett are from Brooklyn, right?"

"Nope. Jersey."

"Oh. You mean . . . ?" She was confused.

"We're from Newark," he said. "Ever been there?"

Actually, she'd only *heard* about Newark—the White Castle and the assorted gang warfare, though so far she hadn't had the pleasure.

"We lived in Brooklyn for about five minutes," he added and took a swallow of beer. Then he motioned with his head toward her. "So what about you? How come you moved back to the East Coast?"

"Job opportunity. Working for Susanna Tate, you know . . . I couldn't pass that up . . ."

Unfortunately she couldn't think of anything more stimulating to say on that because the effects of her two hot toddies and Rick's potent presence already had her overstimulated. Lust stirred like hot lava bubbling in her veins, pooling down between her legs. She bit her lip and tried to act . . . what was it again? Oh, right—casual. Platonic. *Normal.*

"*You* should have your own show," he offered with a quirk of his mouth. "You're a chef; you've got the looks."

He was complimenting her, which made her want to smile, but she held it back. "Thanks, but I think I'll wait a few weeks before I start demanding my own show," she said wryly. "You never finished explaining to me, this block you have about cooking. I thought I'd read that Brett learned from your dad—didn't he teach you, too?"

Impassively, Rick shrugged. "Brett takes after him. Helped out at his restaurant since he was—Jesus, I don't even remember how far back."

"Your dad owns a restaurant?"

"Owned, yeah. *La Tavola Buona.*"

"Where is it? Newark?"

"Yeah, it was, but my dad sold the chain last year." Then he clarified. "He'd turned it into two restaurants by the time we were in high school. The other *Tavola Buona* was in Livingston—my parents moved there about ten years ago. My mom still lives there. Anyway, in answer to your question, yes, Brett learned how to cook from my dad."

"Wow," Gretchen said, nodding. "And what about your mom?" Only in that instant, when she heard her own words and felt a flutter of eagerness in her belly, did she realize that she was actively trying to stretch out their conversation and learn whatever she could about him.

"My mom helped, worked at the place, handled the books," Rick explained, then added, "but she can't cook for shit either. By the time my dad sold the business, though, I think she was just as happy to retire from it for a while—it had a good run, plus my dad was sick."

Suddenly Gretchen understood. Her chest tightened as the realization set in; it was like a fist gently squeezing her heart. Rick's dad had been sick . . . he'd sold the business he'd spent much of his adult life building . . . Rick hadn't mentioned him in the present tense even once. He'd said that his *mother* still lived in Livingston, not his *parents.* So his dad had died—and just this past year. *Wow.* That put a whole new slant on everything. (Of course, if she were sober, she'd be able to recall the old slant a little better.)

Now she opened her mouth to say something, but then thought better of it and pressed her lips together. Suddenly it made sense. *That* must have been explained what was going on—*that* must have been why things were so tough for Rick. He was the older son of the family and his dad had died and he wasn't himself. Surely that accounted for, or at least factored into, his various "issues."

Now Gretchen's lust turned into something different. Something more tender. More caring. Of course, she still wanted to throw Rick down—to peel his sweater off, run her tongue down his stomach, unzip his fly with her teeth, and work her tongue lower. Sure she wanted that, but now there was something else. She looked into his glimmering blue eyes and saw another human being, someone with real pain, with vulnerability and sadness, like anyone else.

Okay, now the alcohol was past the lust phase and into sappy sentimental phase. All she'd need now is for someone to put on some Joni Mitchell and she'd sink to the floor like a crumpled mess and start bawling. Why had she let herself drink too much?

She was hot and gooey like fresh rice pudding. All her emotional and sexual impulses hummed very close to the surface, waiting for the slightest provocation to go spilling into reality. The last thing she wanted or needed was to catch Susanna's eye across the room. Now Susanna mouthed something at her. Gretchen barely stifled an eye roll. Ugh, what did she want now?

Gretchen was finally feeling happy that she'd come to this soiree and there was Susanna to remind her she was still on call for any and all of the boss lady's neurotic requests. She mouthed the words again, whatever they were. Then Susanna started motioning to her, unsubtly jerking her head to the side and darting her eyes to the far left corner of her brain. Confused and irritated, Gretchen followed the direction of Susanna's eyeballs.

The orange-haired, pink drink woman again.

With a slight shrug, Gretchen raised her eyebrows questioningly at Susanna, who just jerked harder, really throwing her shoulders into it this time. *Ask him,* she mouthed more clearly now. *Go. Ask. Brett.*

Finally, Gretchen understood. Damn it all! Susanna was pestering her about this *now*?

"Gretchen?" Rick said, his smooth, deep voice like velvet caressing her skin. It was the first time she'd heard him say her name. She wanted to ask him to say it again because she loved how it had sounded.

"Uh . . . I'm sorry, it's just my boss . . ." Susanna's eyes were bugging out in panic now, like maybe she was afraid she'd been too subtle. *Brett,* she mouthed. *Go. Now.*

Holding back a sigh, Gretchen glanced around but she didn't see Brett anywhere. Susanna obviously wasn't going to relent. "I should go," she said suddenly, looking up at Rick with a half smile, trying to conceal her acute disappointment.

"Okay," he said simply.

"By the way, do you know where your brother went?" At that, Rick stiffened. When he didn't respond right away but eyed her suspiciously, Gretchen smiled sweetly and said, "I have to ask him something. It's important."

Standing up straighter, his eyes roved over her face, but his gaze was suddenly cool. Finally he gave her a derisive smile and said, "Just follow the smell of women." He seemed to be mocking her as he stepped aside to let her to pass.

Speechless, stunned—*what had just happened?*—Gretchen didn't have a chance to address Rick's mood shift, because she saw her boss twenty feet away, with her hand on her hip, craning her head to the side, doing her version of "I'm a little Teapot" (short and annoying). It was beyond time to go. Neutrally, Gretchen tried to smile goodbye, but Rick's face was blank, devoid of the friendliness that had just been there. She walked away anyway, confused and pissed. Was he jealous just because she'd asked to talk to his brother? Or was he just so close to Brett that he was overprotective to the point of incomprehensible?

Annoyance coiled in her gut. Damn him! He'd done it to her again—sucked her in, then become aloof, disinterested. Just like that. More proof that she needed to stay away from him. Yes, he turned her on—but he seemed to compel her to embarrassment at every turn.

Whatever. She'd go find Brett, who might be a phony, but after living in California for three years, at least phony was something she understood.

CHAPTER TWELVE

*R*egrettably, it flopped. When Gretchen found Brett he was sitting low in an armchair, but the omnipresent orange-haired girl standing beside it had been blocking Gretchen's view. So *that* was where Susanna had been motioning with her eyes. Just as Gretchen approached him, he stood to go work the room again. Quickly, she tapped him on the arm to get his attention. He turned and instantly flashed his winning smile. "Hey, Gretchen, you having fun?"

"Yes, definitely. Thanks again for inviting me—oh, and happy birthday."

"Thanks, thanks," he said, glancing over her shoulder, as though scanning the room for any interesting happenings other than her.

"Brett, who's this?" the girl said, coming closer and taking notice of Gretchen.

"Oh. Ellie, this is Gretchen. Gretchen, Ellie. Gretchen works on Susanna's show," he explained.

"Hi," Gretchen said amiably, getting a closer look at the woman who'd danced sporadically and distantly in her line of vision all night. She was tall, about five-seven, and slender; her hair was long and curly à la Nicole Kidman in *Days of Thunder*. She had that freshly scrubbed, freckled look of youth that set her at about twenty-five or twenty-six. She wore light blue jeans and a white turtleneck sweater.

"Ellie Galistette," the woman said with a pleasant enough smile and a brief handshake. "Sure, Susanna's with us, too. It's great to have you on her team."

Quizzically, Gretchen tilted her head. "What do you mean?"

"Susanna's one of our clients," she explained. "The Allbright Agency."

"Ellie is Misty's assistant," Brett explained, just as Ellie jumped in. "*Apprentice,* actually. I'm sure Susanna's mentioned me; I help her out whenever she has an issue that needs dealing with and Misty's unavailable."

"Oh, right, yeah, sounds familiar," Gretchen lied, because in the various pontifications and/or diatribes Gretchen could recall, Susanna had never mentioned Ellie. It seemed she relied totally on Misty. Speaking of Misty . . .

Gretchen just remembered what Susanna had told her in the limo—that Misty had been hot and heavy with Abe Santasierra until he'd broken it off with her a couple of months ago, and how they'd both be here tonight . . .

Briefly, Gretchen glanced around the room, but she didn't see Misty anywhere. She hadn't seen her all night. Could she have skipped the party altogether to avoid seeing Abe? Maybe the breakup was still a sore subject.

"Listen, Brett, I—"

"Excuse us," he said, still smiling. He genuinely didn't seem to realize that Gretchen was trying to talk to him. "Help yourself to another drink, or some food," he added with a wink that was more ostentatious than his usual, and led Ellie Galistette through the crowd with his palm flattened on her lower back.

He hadn't been gone two seconds before Gretchen felt Susanna's breath on her neck and her fingers close around her upper arm. "Well?" she said expectantly as Gretchen's face turned to make eye contact; Susanna's expression was eager, her eyes wide with hope. "So? Don't keep me in suspense? What did he say? Did he go for it?"

Jeez. If desperation were fabric, Susanna would be wearing a tweed-burlap blend right now. "To be honest, I really didn't have a chance to ask him," Gretchen told her.

With a melodramatic sigh, Susanna slumped a little into Gretchen's shoulder. Then she patted her arm and said, "Well, okay . . . at least you have all weekend."

Later that night Susanna introduced Gretchen to Ray Jarian—whom you had to admire for being able to hold his head high at a party full of TCC people, so soon after TCC had given him the ax. She recognized him right away. He was tall and lanky with silvery hair and a white-gray mustache. He wore a cowboy hat and a cowboy shirt (well, it was checked and Western looking, so it was at the very least a square-dancing shirt).

The Tex-Mex Teddy in the flesh.

Before Susanna had waved him over, she'd whispered, "Oh, there's Ray—listen, when you talk to him, just make sure you don't bring up how badly his life's going these days."

"Got it," Gretchen had said dryly.

Now as Susanna chatted with Ray, Gretchen stood in their circle of three, noticing the little details. Like the glob of mustard on Ray's tie; it was one of those brown twist-tie ribbons that looked terribly old-fashioned. His hands were tough and weathered, a combination of hot sun and hard living—or maybe it was all the limes he had to squeeze for his southwestern cuisine.

"Well, I know Gretchen and I will definitely miss your show," Susanna was saying now, jarring Gretchen back into focus. Huh? What happened to not mentioning Ray's failures?

He faltered for just a second, then tipped his hat, eyeing Gretchen. "Why thank ya, li'l lady. I surely do take that as the grandest a'compliments. And, ah, I hope I ain't talkin' outta school here, but . . ." He winked at Gretchen. (What, was it her? She was a wink magnet these days.) "Ya sure got yerself a purty assistant here, Suz. Purtier than a sunset over Albuquerque." Holding up his hands, he added, "No disrespect, a'course. Just that an old cowboy like me's bound to notice. After all, may've roped a lotta steer in my day, but I ain't dead yet!" He let out a hearty chuckle as he arched his neck back and took a swig of his drink. He wasn't drinking one of Brett's toddies but a glass full of amber liquid. It looked like flattened cream soda, but surely it was bourbon or whiskey or whatever cowboys drank.

Meanwhile Gretchen was totally taken off guard. That part about roping steers—was he being serious? She honestly didn't know; in fact, it just occurred to Gretchen that she really had no idea about Ray Jarian's background before coming to TCC. She knew something about all the other celebrity chefs, but not him. She hadn't noticed his professional bio up on the wall at work along with the other celebrities and hosts. Casually she wondered: What had Ray been doing before he'd abandoned his chuck wagon and headed up north?

"Come up to the mountains often?" Ray asked. Both Susanna and Gretchen said no. "Sure is purty, but dang it, the powder here's thicker than clover honey on a stack'a huckleberry flapjacks."

"Yes . . . that's true," Gretchen agreed with a bright smile. Eccentricity aside, she liked the fact that Ray's affable demeanor hadn't been affected by Susanna's reminder about his show.

As though thinking the same thing—and *not* liking it—Susanna spoke up. "So Ray . . . how have you been?" With a dramatic pause, she reached over to tap his hand sympathetically; then she dropped her voice, dragging it out as though he were a very slow child. "I know it's been hard on you. If there's anything I can do." Gretchen nearly winced at her boss's phoniness.

Still, Ray didn't damper. "Well, I tell ya, Suz, I been grand. Been spending a lotta time in Tennessee. Ever been to Tennessee?" He was looking at Gretchen.

She shook her head. "Ah, great country out there," he remarked, bringing his glass up in a "cheers" motion, which sloshed some liquid over the rim. Wait, was he tipsy? Good, then it wasn't just her. "But then why shouldn't I be grand?" he continued. "The world keeps on a'spinnin' and about as quick as a jackrabbit with a stolen carrot at a picnic lunch."

"Right, right," Susanna said, nodding, "but without your show and especially your restaurant to fall back on, I can't imagine it's been easy." She gave his hand another tap, the gesture brittle with false emotion. "If you ever need to talk . . ."

Then, what? She'd give him the number of the nearest suicide hotline? At this point, Gretchen was honestly afraid of what Susanna would say next. It almost seemed as though she needed to humble those around her to assert her own superiority. And the question was: Who was she really trying to convince?

Ray shrugged. "Can't do much 'bout it now, or 'bout the restaurant, neither. Gotta keep on goin'—like a merry-go-round in a doggone windstorm. Just gotta pick up your saddlebags and move on, I guess."

Gretchen almost laughed out loud. Ray's statement could be taken two ways; either the surface meaning that he would be moving on, or the hidden meaning that Susanna should pick up *her* saddle-bags, figuratively speaking, and move on to her next victim. *Ha!* It was too funny—had Susanna caught it? Looking at her now Gretchen would give that a resounding no.

"Well, are you gonna try to write a new book, or just put that aside for a while?" Susanna probed, thereby answering Gretchen's question.

Again Ray shrugged and hitched up his belt. A flash drew Gretchen's eyes toward the shiny gold plate of the buckle. "Who knows? Right now I'm 'bout as free as a turkey in July."

Okay, she didn't even get that one.

"So how about some skiing!"

It was Brett, standing on one of his ottoman squares in the middle of the room. People cheered at the suggestion. "Everyone, you know the drill—extra skis, jackets, and equipment are in the closet by the terrace." At that, he pointed toward the opposite side of the floor, where there were two sets of French glass doors. Apparently the back and side of Brett's house were vast and hilly and basically served as Brett's own private mountain.

"There's a hot chocolate bar set up outside, too, so even if you're not skiing, go outside and enjoy. Unfortunately, no snowboards this year because of what happened last year." The whole room chuckled. "And as far as the chairlift goes, let's keep it G-rated up there this year." Everyone erupted with laughter again, including Susanna, while Gretchen felt a bit like the oddball. Within minutes, people were swishing in their coats, clunking in their boots, diving into the cacophony of skis and poles, while others darted to the guest rooms on the third floor to change into their own gear. She saw Juan Mirando throw a shiny black parka over his I'M A BUTT MAN (PORK BUTT, THAT IS) sweatshirt. (God, did he have that hideousness embossed on every garment he owned?)

More coats, boots, skis clattering, and laughter. Then there was a mass exodus through the French doors, onto the snow-covered terrace and into the wintry, blue-black night.

The house was quiet. Where had Susanna gone? Gretchen had

fully expected to be called upon to help her boss into her designer snowsuit, to zip it up for her, to fit her boots on, but Susanna had shocked her by apparently slipping off to her guest room and doing it herself. Maybe she was private about changing—who knew?—but Gretchen wasn't going to question it.

And speaking of guest rooms, Susanna had mentioned on the ride over that she'd asked Brett to put them in adjacent rooms. Honestly, Gretchen felt a little strange about staying over at Brett's house because she barely knew him, and apparently only a handful of people got to stay at the house; the rest were staying down the street at the Brass Lion Inn. But still, she was grateful—she just hoped there was no "catch," like having to massage Susanna's feet before bed or assuage any four A.M. anxiety with cool cloths and pep talks.

It seemed like the only people left inside now were Gretchen and the bartender, who was cleaning up. If she thought Brett's second floor was airy and spacious before, now it was positively huge. And too airy, she noted, as the clinking of the glassware seemed to echo, reminding her that she was alone. Walking over to the French doors that were now closed, she thought for just a moment before turning to the adjacent coat closet and reaching for one of the extra jackets Brett had mentioned.

As soon as she pulled on the brass handle, the door flew open and she jumped back. Ice-cold wind smacked her in the face. It made her eyes water, swished through her ears, and sent shivers down her spine—even as it urged her closer.

Gretchen had walked partway down the mountain, sticking close to the dense thicket of towering evergreens that sealed in the whole property. She'd gotten tired of walking aimlessly, though, so she'd doubled back, changing her plan of action. No, she wasn't about to ski; she wasn't that stupid. She'd blown out her knee five years ago skiing in Minnesota, twisting her leg in a way that seemed inconceivable. Worst pain she'd ever experienced, and probably *would* experience—unless she had kids, of course, but that was a long time off.

Hot chocolate. That's what she'd do. She walked up the last incline, past the terrace, up to the hot-chocolate bar on her left. The bar was really just a long table, shielded from the snow by a wide freestanding umbrella awning. A couple of urns sat on the table with steam visibly shooting off their tops and up toward the clouds and their cords meandering over toward a shed about twenty feet away, intermittently disappearing in the snow. One portable outdoor light rose up from the ground on a tall metal spike. Beside the urns were two tall stacks of paper cups.

No one was at the hot chocolate bar now; they were all skiing and celebrating far down the hill. Gretchen wondered what the difference was between the two urns before taking a paper cup and filling it from the urn to her left. Then she headed toward that shed, the one that overlooked all the activity on the mountain. She'd go over there, relax, and just take it in the scenery.

On her way over, she took a long drink to warm herself up— *whoa.* So *that* was the difference between the urns. One was spiked, and it was obviously the one to the left. She knew she should probably dump it out right now, because she still hadn't eaten dinner and she'd had the two hot toddies before, but . . . oh, why not? The burn in her throat felt really good, especially when it melted into her chest, slid fluidly to her arms and legs. She took another drink, feeling warmer by the second, as her feet climbed over the snow, around the side of the shed. Breathing a heady sigh, she had the saturating sensation of utter, boneless relaxation. Just as she climbed around the side of the shed, some blustering flurries blew up with the wind and rushed in a scattered frenzy across her face. Only after her vision cleared did she spot a man she knew standing about five feet away. He was leaning against the shed, facing out, getting a bird's-eye view of the mountain, just as she had planned to do.

It was Rick. She froze in place, not wanting to take a step closer to him, not wanting him to notice her. Strange. Why was he standing alone in the dark? Why wasn't he skiing with everyone else? Then Gretchen realized: *She* was alone and not skiing, too, and hey, she was perfectly normal. Tasting the spiked cocoa on her tongue, she thought, *Drunk but normal.*

CHAPTER THIRTEEN

*R*ick shook his head, wondering why had he bothered talking to Gretchen tonight. She was obviously an opportunist, plain and simple. She'd blown hot and cold since the night they'd met, really warming up to him only after she'd found out who his brother was. Not a first for Rick—though not a regular occurrence, either—but this was the first time it had bothered him so much. And tonight she'd abruptly switched the direction of their conversation by asking about Brett. That fake sweet smile, too. *It's important.* Did she think he was an idiot? Hell, she wasn't even subtle about it.

But then, why should he be pissed off? He was the one who'd approached her, both times now. And if she liked Brett, hey, that was her snowball's chance in hell. Why let it bother him? He took another drag, savored it for a second before letting it out.

Sure, he was attracted to her, but she was obviously one of those girls looking to attach herself to Mr. Celebrity, not caring about his reputation with women, not caring what a goddamn prick he could be once he got bored with someone, which was almost immediately.

He still didn't know why the hell he'd gone up to talk to her tonight. But shadowing Brett had been pointless, not to mention goddamn boring. If someone still wanted his brother dead, he or she was being real low-key about it. No more calls or threatening e-mails and nothing awry at the party so far.

But when he'd seen Gretchen tonight and watched her with careful, speculative scrutiny, he hadn't been able to stay away. And she'd looked almost . . . lost. No one to talk to, her big dark eyes roving the room, and . . . Well, hell, it didn't matter why he'd gone up to her. Now he wished he hadn't bothered.

Rick had always been different from Brett when it came to women. He loved sex, but he didn't particularly feel the need to cut and run afterward. Even if a fling wasn't serious, there was no reason to be a dick about it. Brett, on the other hand, was a fuck-now, apologize-later guy. Or a bang-a-married-woman-now, hide-under-the-bed-from-her-husband-later guy, as the case may be.

Damn, sometimes his brother just got to him. Rick knew it wasn't right, but he couldn't help it. Their father had died proud of Brett. Yeah, he was proud of Rick, too, after he'd become a firefighter and found some purpose in his life, but still, it had taken way too long for Rick to get his shit straight. Way too long to make his dad proud, and now he was gone.

Rick tossed his cigarette into the snow just as he heard someone cry out, *"Ohh!"*

He whipped around and through the partially lit darkness saw a girl slip and fall flat on her back. Shit! Running to her, he went down the incline, toward the terrace where she was and then he saw who it was.

"Jesus Fucking Christmas—*you*," he said with disgust, reaching down to lift Gretchen up. She was flattened to the ground, looking more startled and confused than anything else, her breath coming up short. The impact of the fall had kicked up some of the snow, sending it onto her face and into her dark hair, which was fanned out around her. Dark liquid had seeped into the white, and for just a quick second, Rick's heart stopped—shit, was that blood? But then he saw the overturned paper cup and realized she'd dropped her cocoa. "Take my hand," he demanded when she failed to react.

She just blinked at him, then opened her mouth like she was about to say something, but it didn't make it out. With one hand, she reached behind her back and tried to push herself up. Maybe it was the weight of her snow-soaked jacket, but when she pushed up, her palm suddenly slid, sending her backward again.

"Here. Jesus," Rick muttered, leaning down to take her arm himself. As he pulled her up, he said, "What are you, the world's biggest klutz? I keep having to rescue you."

Her mouth pursed at that and she tried to jerk her arm away from him, but his grip was firm; he wasn't letting go until he was sure she was solidly on her feet. "I just slipped. I'm fine," she said and pulled her arm free just as he released it. The force of it made her wobble and nearly slip again. "Here—stop trying to do it yourself," Rick snapped. "Boy, I can't leave you alone for one second."

"Okaaay already," she said, frustrated and annoyed, plus her head was starting to spin. "Look. I know you're having a tough time of things lately, but you don't have to take it out on me," she insisted, even as she brought her free hand up to clutch at his jacket to steady herself.

"Tough time?" Rick repeated, confused. "What do you mean . . . ?"

"And just because you're hot," she added sloppily, "doesn't mean it's been ordained by the Oracle of Delphi that you also be an asshole!"

"Huh?"

"Oh, forget it," she yelped, wrinkling her forehead in frustration, struggling to get her breath. Her butt was soaked. And what time was it, anyway?

"The Orajel of wha—?" Rick said, as his mouth quirked up.

"I said forget it!" Gretchen snapped, pulling away from him. But he reached for her again, and she'd taken only one step before she hit a slippery patch, and it happened fast: She slid and took Rick down with her.

Omf!

The wind was knocked out of her—worse than the first time she'd fallen, because this time Rick was on top of her. With her heart pounding hard in her ears, she struggled to breathe, to think, as Rick shifted above her. He brought his hands alongside her shoulders and pushed himself up just enough to look into her face. Gretchen wanted nothing more than to shut her eyes. Not to face him or his scrutiny or his mocking, but instead she slid her gaze to his. She couldn't seem to help herself, and she bit her lip before she tried to speak. "Um . . ."

"God, you're clumsy," he said softly. His words were little more than a rough whisper, and whatever she was going to say drifted away before it got started. But their gazes held. His expression went from playful to serious as his eyes zeroed in on her mouth.

A moment stretched between them, charged with sexual tension, anticipation. Up this close, Rick smelled clean and fresh with faint traces of pine; he was masculine and sexy and Gretchen was afraid of making a fool of herself again. "And you're heavy," she finally whispered back. "You must weigh a ton."

With a husky laugh, he nodded, then shifted his body so the weight was more evenly distributed. *Mmm . . .*

Weight distribution, that was one way to put it. Another was: He'd aligned their bodies so she could feel him against her—intimately. Had he done that on purpose?

"So I'm hot, huh?" he said softly.

Yes, her mind chanted. *God, yes.* She sucked in a breath as he grew hard against her, his impressive erection pressing into the tender notch of her thighs. It felt too good. Against her better judgment (if she'd been using any judgment at all), she shifted her hips, trying to rub against him. Fluidly his hands skidded up her coat and gently squeezed the sides of her breasts. The heel of his hand seemed to rock purposefully against her thick jacket, his fingers fanning inward toward her nipples as his caresses became even bolder, stronger, more determined. Gretchen bit her lip and tried to catch her breath; she couldn't believe she was letting him touch her like this. But she couldn't seem to say anything to stop him or to question him. Her mouth was dry and her throat tight with desire. Her heart pounded like a frantic drum in her ears as her crotch inflamed with heat. To ease the burning, the ache, she shifted her hips again, this time rocking into Rick's pelvis, trying to fill herself with him even through their clothes, rolling her body against his, feeling the hard thrust of his cock between her legs with each stroke, each touch, and then Rick's blue eyes darkened. A gruff, smothered sound rumbled from his throat and he pushed back, pressing down as she lifted up. Barely holding back a moan, Gretchen let her eyes slide shut for just a moment. When she opened them, she saw Rick's mouth mere inches from her own. Her heart lurched into her throat as she realized then, without question, that he was going to kiss her. His warm breath mingled with hers as he came closer; she managed to lick her lips, waiting, anticipating the moment when he would—

Suddenly, he stopped moving closer . . . and started inching back. Huh? *What about my kiss?* she wondered hazily as Rick pulled away and climbed off of her.

Wait a second—where the hell was he going?

Before she knew it, he let out a heavy sigh and came to his feet, extending his arm down to lift her up. Confused and stunned, she took the hand he was offering and let him help her to her feet. Why had he pulled back like that? She'd been sure he was about to kiss her. Mortification suffused her cheeks like scalding fire, and she swallowed a lump of anger. It wouldn't have been so bad if she hadn't been practically puckering up, sliding her eyes shut, waiting for his kiss. And that was to say nothing of letting him fondle her breasts and start grinding against her. God, how humiliating!

Damn him! How many times would she let him mess with her head? This time she was steaming mad, more at herself than at him, but plenty at him still.

"Listen, are you gonna be okay?" he asked, his voice husky even though he'd decidedly broken the close, intimate moment they'd just been having.

"I'm fiiiine," she said, dragging out the word, sounding snotty even to herself. She hated her own immaturity right now, but she couldn't seem to stop it. "And I don't need you to rescue me. In fact, I would really prefer if you would just leave me the hell alone."

Once she was back inside the house, she went searching for a bathroom so she could dry off. She walked through the open room where the party had been before everyone had gone outside, then crept down a quiet hallway near the top of the stairs, and sure enough, at the end of the hall, through a door cracked halfway open, she spotted a sink and a mirror. When she pressed the door open, though, she quickly discovered that the bathroom was already occupied. By the light streaming in from the hall, she could see a man and woman wrapped in a passionate embrace, kissing. Startled, she gasped, but they were so into what they were doing, they didn't even notice. It took only a second for Gretchen to process the image before her. The woman was Ellie Galistette—those long springy orange curls again— and the man was Abe.

Quickly, Gretchen ducked away before they spotted her, but

froze when she heard Ellie moan, "Oh, Abe, was it like this with Misty?"

Morbidly curious, Gretchen loitered against the wall of the hallway, waiting to hear his answer. With a soft groan, he just kept kissing her, but then Ellie asked again. Abe's voice was gentle and caring when he responded. "*No*, sweetheart, you have absolutely nothing to feel insecure about. I'm crazy about you. Can't you see that?"

"Oh, Abe," Ellie murmured through kisses. "Yes, oh, yes. I don't know why I get so crazy sometimes . . ." At that point, groaning and suction noises took over for both of them.

Retracing her steps through the second floor, Gretchen found a short corridor that led to a stairwell. The guest rooms were supposed to be on the third floor. Forget the bathroom, she just wanted to strip her clothes and collapse into bed, under a swimming heap of covers, and sleep it off, not to mention push the latest unnerving exchange with Rick Pellucci out of her mind.

As she climbed the carpeted steps, she thought about Abe and Ellie and their clandestine rendezvous in the bathroom. So they were an item . . . *interesting*. Especially considering that Ellie worked for Misty Allbright—whom, according to Susanna, Abe had dumped a couple of months back. Whether her affair with Abe had started before or after the breakup, it was no wonder that they would keep the relationship low profile. It certainly couldn't be public knowledge or Susanna would've mentioned it. But did Misty have any idea?

Once Gretchen found her room—in fact there was a cream-colored card with her name in calligraphy on it hanging on a chain around the doorknob—she went inside, and under normal circumstances, would've been struck by what a beautiful, luxurious room it was. Would've really stopped to appreciate the embroidered drapery, the lovely lace canopy above the bed, the elegant, silk-covered settee by the window, but these weren't normal circumstances. She was suddenly bone tired and her head was pounding. She stripped down to her underwear, climbed under the covers, hit the lights, and sent her mind into darkness.

In the middle of the night Gretchen felt something pulling her out of her deep sleep. Reluctantly, she stirred awake, and as sleepy as she was, there was no denying what she felt beneath her covers. A large, warm hand running up her leg. It was rough and hot; it moved with strength and purpose. Gretchen opened her mouth to say something, to protest, to question, but all that came out was a breathy sigh of arousal—excitement.

Her room was so dark, it was impossible for her to see who had come in. She should be shocked, horrified, scared by this intrusion, but instead her head pushed deeper into the pillows and her eyes slid shut. Her lower body nearly quivered with need, as the strong, warm hand slid to her inner thigh. She wasn't scared because she knew who it was—it was Rick. Oh, God, why was she letting him come into her room and touch her like this after what had happened outside? But it felt so good . . .

His right hand ran up past her knees, sliding higher as Rick came closer, climbing up her bed, climbing onto her, bracing his weight with his left arm, and hazily, instinctively, Gretchen squirmed and reached down for his cock. *No, you shouldn't do this,* she thought. *Have some pride.* He was unpredictable; he was a prick. But she couldn't seem to stop herself, especially when the heat of his palm settled firmly between her legs.

Running her fingers up the back of his neck, she gave his hair a sharp little tug and used her other hand to fit between their bodies and stroke him through his pants. That was when she realized his zipper was already down, his erection already naked and probing. He was *that* confident. And suddenly, he was gloating—she could sense it. Still, she coiled her grasp around his hot, steel-hard shaft; she knew she shouldn't, but it was just so devastatingly irresistible. Then she heard his quiet laughter. His warm breath tickled her ear when he whispered, "I knew you wanted me."

His arrogance infuriated her, shattered the moment. Jolted out of her erotic haze, she tried to shove him away from her, but her arms were too heavy to move. So then she started kicking.

Only the more she kicked, the more she got herself all wrapped and twisted in her sheets. As her frustration skyrocketed, she opened her mouth to yell something.

Then her eyes flapped open.

Breathing hard and fast, it took her a moment to realize that it had been a dream; the only part that was real was how her legs were all twisted in her sheets now. She sat up and disentangled herself, resting her face in her hands for a second, shaking the last remainders of sleep and confusion from her head.

She could feel that the crotch of her panties was hot and damp and her heart was still rapping beneath her breasts. Wasn't it funny how sex dreams—unlike sex—only keyed you up, rather than relaxing you to sleep? (Funny in the miserable, unfortunate sense of the word, of course.) As soon as she climbed out of bed, she became acutely aware of her near nakedness. With a violent shiver, she darted to her suitcase and pulled out a wool sweater and a pair of fleece pants, which she threw on and shimmied into before venturing out into the hallway.

When she flicked the switch in the bathroom, she suddenly heard a low whistle. It was the wind picking up, blowing through the trees and sending branches swatting against the house. Then she heard something else—a definitive noise that imposed itself on the mellifluous swishing of the wind. Like a clack. She paused, then heard a thud. Had something dropped downstairs? But it sounded like the noises had come from outside.

She stepped out of the bathroom, into the dark hallway, and listened again. Now there was nothing except the ferocity of the wind, which had kicked up, knocking branches on the side of the house, rattling shutters. Maybe what she'd heard had been a couple of fallen tree branches.

Without giving it another thought, she went to pee, then rinsed her mouth with cold water and went back to her empty bed.

CHAPTER FOURTEEN

$\mathcal{T}$he next day, several people were enjoying brunch on the first floor, in the spacious area in the back of the house that opened up into a bright, airy sunroom. A buffet table extended along the wall, and Gretchen—mildly hungover and starving—made a beeline for it. She filled her plate with French toast, smoked bacon, and spaghetti omelet. Juggling that with a glass of orange juice, she also managed to snag an almond-ricotta muffin and balance it under her chin as she made her way over to join Susanna at a table by the windows. Susanna was sitting beside Cady, eagerly waving Gretchen over. "Hi, guys," Gretchen said, smiling as she took her seat. "How did you sleep?"

Susanna made a so-so motion with her hand, then said, "I never sleep well without my husband there."

"I slept great," Cady said cheerfully.

"Well, you're not married, so you don't understand," Susanna remarked casually, breaking into her brioche roll and spreading it with marmalade.

"The beds at the Brass Lion Inn are *really* comfortable," Cady said to Gretchen, ignoring Susanna's comment. "Didn't you think?"

"Oh, um, I don't know. Actually, I'm staying here," Gretchen said. Cady's face fell. And even after she resurrected a shell of a smile, Gretchen felt inexplicably guilty. Cady was probably thinking the same thing Gretchen herself had thought: Who is *she* to be among the select people staying at Brett's house? If only she could explain about Susanna's influence in this regard. How she'd asked Brett ahead of time if her "assist—um, set supervisor" could have an adjacent room. How the woman was a dichotomous mix of self-importance and paranoid insecurity, which was why she wanted Gretchen there in the first place. How Susanna spoke up a lot more than Cady, which was probably how she got things.

But Gretchen could hardly say any of this to Cady. Instead, she just smiled amiably, then focused on her food.

"Susanna, I didn't notice you out on the slopes too much," Cady remarked.

"Oh, sure, I was out there, zipping all around," Susanna said. "Gretchen, you went to bed early."

"Uh . . . yeah, I was tired." And drunk . . . and annoyed . . . and horny. Though not necessarily in that order.

"I'm surprised more people aren't up and about by now," Susanna said, glancing around the sparsely filled hall and sunroom. She shrugged. "I guess most of them are still down at the inn but will be back to ski early this afternoon. Cady, where's Marjorie?"

"She didn't stay overnight," Cady said, and Susanna snapped her fingers with recognition.

"Oh, that's right. I remember. Abe said he was giving Marjorie and that cameraman, Tom, a ride back to the city last night." At the mention of Abe, a memory of his bathroom make-out session with Ellie Galistette came into Gretchen's mind. "I forgot that Marjorie wasn't staying for the weekend. It's too bad, because I wanted to ask her something."

"What?" Cady asked curiously, and, if Gretchen wasn't mistaken, a bit warily.

Understandably, Cady was probably as possessive of her producer as Susanna was of hers. With a shrug Susanna replied, "It's nothing really. I just wanted to talk to her about possibly guest hosting your show sometime in the next couple of months."

"What?" Cady asked, crinkling her eyebrows, pursing her lips in confusion—or was it horror? "W-why would you want to do that?"

Dismissively, Susanna waved a hand through the air. "Oh, I thought it would be cute. You know, we'd have fun making your little desserts together and whatnot, and it would probably boost your ratings a bit." She made it sound altruistic, which obviously nobody was buying, and Susanna must have sensed that herself, because she admitted, "And hey, a little extra exposure with the prime-time audi-ence wouldn't hurt me since I'll have a prime-time show of my own this summer." She'd downplayed her agenda, as though it were merely an afterthought, but of course, Gretchen knew better. Inter-esting that Susanna felt comfortable enough to suggest the guest-spot idea to Cady herself, but when it came to Brett's show, she wanted to put it all on Gretchen. Obviously she was reluctant to look like she wanted—or needed—a favor from Brett.

The only conclusion Gretchen could reach was that Susanna didn't feel threatened by Cady—didn't view her as a viable competi-tor. Her show was "cute." She'd even said "guest host" rather than "guest star." Clearly, she considered herself superior in rank and didn't bother to camouflage it. Brett and Susanna were in a whole other class of celebrity than Cady, but still, Susanna worried about being outclassed. Whether it was Brett's youth, his looks, or his charisma that threatened Susanna most, Gretchen couldn't guess. Perhaps seeing an out-of-date relic like Ray Jarian fall out of favor with the network alarmed Susanna more than she let on. After all, Ray was only about ten years older than she. Star quality, everyone knew, was a tenuous commodity.

"But my show airs at noon," Cady protested mildly, bringing Gretchen's focus back to the conversation at hand. "My audience isn't prime time."

"I know," Susanna said, "but they air the reruns on Wednesday nights just to fill dead air."

More subtlety, Susanna style. Looking down, Gretchen felt the need to bury herself in her meal, anything to disassociate herself from this conversation.

"But . . ." Cady's voice trailed off, though Gretchen could sense her distress. She really didn't want Susanna guest hosting her show or having any part of it. It was obvious.

"Speaking of dead air, I wonder what will replace Ray's show—I mean permanently," Susanna said.

"Omigod, did you see Ray last night!" Cady said, eyes wide, a lit-tle grin curving her lips. Gretchen wanted to encourage her sunny mood since it was obvious Susanna had started pushing her buttons already.

"I met him briefly, why?" Gretchen asked, smiling.

"He was so drunk!" Cady exclaimed in a loud whisper. "In fact, has he come down yet . . . ?" She rose from her seat and glanced around but didn't see him. "When I saw him last night, he was stumbling around, knocking things over—"

"He really made a spectacle of himself," Susanna interjected. "It was after you went to bed, Gretchen. He was supposed to stay at the Brass Lion, too, but he passed out downstairs. Brett and his brother carried him up to one of the spare rooms."

With a laugh, Gretchen said, "Wow, I can't believe I missed that!"

As she drank her juice, the words "Brett and his brother" rolled through her mind. Especially the "brother" part. Yeah, speaking of a spectacle, her splat moment outside last night had been a good one. As fragments of her conversation with Rick came back to her, she cringed. Oracle of Delphi, God, had she actually *said* that?

"I guess he's still sleeping it off," Cady said with a giggle.

"He made such a fool of himself," Susanna went on, sounding disgusted. "And here I'm sure that Brett invited him just to be nice. He probably feels sorry for the guy—his life is pretty much in the pits right now."

"I don't know. He sounded pretty happy last night," Gretchen countered in Ray's defense. And it was true. He'd seemed genuinely at ease, talking about spending time in Tennessee, and that whole turkey in July metaphor—the guy had seemed content. Less than eloquent, but content.

"Let's just hope it's not too awkward when Misty gets here today," Susanna said, setting her fork down across her plate and dabbing her mouth with her napkin.

"Misty's coming?" Cady said, surprised. Gretchen was surprised herself—that Cady would know who Misty was. But maybe people in this biz just knew the big agents?

Susanna nodded. "I knew she wouldn't want to miss it. Misty *loves* Brett's cooking. She's always said that Brett's cooking is her weakness. And I'm sure you all know the story of how she signed him; she'd been dining at his restaurant on Fifty-third with a client, and the moment she tasted the lemon chicken, she asked to see the chef. Brett got wind of it and came to her table himself, and the rest is history."

"Wow, when was that?" Gretchen asked, silently wondering if it wounded Susanna's pride to know that another client's cooking was her agent's "weakness," rather than her own.

"A couple of years ago."

Though Susanna didn't say it, Gretchen knew that what followed shortly thereafter was Brett's gig on the Cooking Channel, which had exploded in popularity in the last year.

"I thought she'd be here last night," Susanna continued, "but then I asked Brett and he told me that she'd be coming today. Apparently she had important business to take care of."

Hmm . . . since Abe had already left last night, they would miss each other, which was probably a good thing. Maybe it was even part of the reason Abe hadn't stayed for the weekend—he hadn't wanted it to be awkward for Misty. He was a nice enough guy that that was a definite possibility.

Susanna still hadn't mentioned anything about Ellie and Abe dating now, so Gretchen was assuming she didn't know. If it was a well-kept secret, Gretchen wasn't about to be the person who blabbed it, so she kept quiet about what she'd seen in the bathroom last night.

"Is, uh . . . is Misty staying in the house, too?" Cady asked, acting blasé about the question.

"Of course," Susanna said emphatically. "I mean, I can only assume. She is Brett's agent. You've got to give her the royal treatment."

The doorbell rang then. Low-pitched chimes ricocheted through the walls of the house. In a way, it was a foreshadowing. Fate was delivering a dirge—a message—but of course no one knew it at the time.

When they got to the foyer, they found Misty exchanging ebullient pleasantries with Brett, who was in flirt mode—which Gretchen was starting to recognize as his main mode, but jeez, even with his *agent*? The guy was just too much.

Misty looked sharp in a straight-cut leather jacket, black cashmere sweater, black pants, and absurdly high heels. Her inky hair sprung just above her shoulders, coiled artfully to frame her rather pale face. Though her skin had a clear, creamy look to it, some color in her cheeks definitely wouldn't be a bad thing. She was slim and lithe—though maybe a little too thin (and no, that was *not* sour grapes because Gretchen had just put away three pieces of French toast, two strips of bacon, a mound of spaghetti omelet, and an almond-ricotta muffin—really).

Now Susanna flitted right over to encircle Misty in a bear hug, the petite girl nearly getting lost in Susanna's long, loose-fitting ensemble. Reluctantly, Gretchen came closer. "Hi," she said with a smile when Misty made eye contact with her. "We met briefly on the set the other day," she added by way of reintroduction. "I'm Gretchen."

Misty was no warmer the second time around. "Okay . . ." she replied with a brief, breathy little laugh, as if to say, *And you're telling me because . . . ?*

"Yes, Gretchen's my—" Susanna paused for a second, before finishing, "All-around dynamo." Hey, she'd take it. "We bonded instantly!" Susanna added, and Gretchen couldn't help but smile; the comment was oddly touching.

Clearly Misty wasn't concerned with the technicalities of Gretchen's position. She smiled kindly at Susanna before turning to Brett and saying, "I apologize. I know I just got here, but can you show me where my room is? I want to lie down and take a quick nap before I hit the slopes. I've had so much work this past week. I barely got any sleep last night and I'm exhausted after the drive."

Vaguely Gretchen noted Brett's response—namely to wink and beam a smile and say "no *prob*lem"—but in the forefront of her mind, Gretchen was more preoccupied with how she'd just been slapped in the face. Figuratively speaking. Why had Misty snubbed her? That was twice now. Swallowing a lump of discomfort, Gretchen felt warm color creep into her face. As dumb as it was, she was embarrassed. Sure, Misty was the one who'd been rude, but still . . . Gretchen had been openly dismissed in front of her boss and Brett.

Then, as Brett hoisted Misty's bags and Gretchen turned away, she realized that she'd been openly dismissed in front of someone else, as well. An elusive figure standing in the living room. Someone who didn't have the decency to look away—to pretend he hadn't just witnessed that. *Goddamn it!* Could she catch a break? It *so* figured that Rick would appear at this exact moment.

Averting her eyes, Gretchen started walking back toward the breakfast area, determined not to acknowledge him at all. But that required Rick to step back and let her pass comfortably since he was half shielding her path. Between his solid, imposing frame and the hard edge of the decorative oak table, Gretchen was left with only a narrow strip of space to walk through—which was why Rick should have automatically moved back or to the side, making sure his body didn't touch hers when she passed. But he didn't budge. He just stood there, eyeing her as she tried to shimmy by and avoid his searing gaze. Swallowing a lump of discomfort, Gretchen fought the surge of nervousness that swelled in her chest and forced her head and her eyes straight ahead, even as she could feel Rick looking down, watching her. But the space was so tight that she had to turn sideways to get by. So she did, giving Rick her back—but it didn't do anything to lessen her acute awareness of him. In fact, his presence and his closeness were visceral, overwhelming. As she tried to scoot by him, she could feel his strong thighs grazing against her bottom, and she sucked in a breath. In that moment she wanted the room to be empty except for him and her and for Rick to push up against her, slide his arms around her, take her breasts in his hands—

Damn the horny girl's slide show. Now was not the time.

Still, he didn't move. For pete's sake, this didn't even require Rick to be a gentleman—it was just common sense! Did he *want* her rubbing up on him? Was *that* it?

No, if that were the case, he wouldn't have dusted her last night, pulling away just as she'd been about to kiss the hell out of him.

"Ex*cuse* me," she murmured quietly but with unmistakable annoyance. Wordlessly, he finally stepped back—but barely.

Releasing a breath, Gretchen nearly crossed the threshold to the breakfast area when Ellie Galistette came flying past her, brushing shoulders with her as she jogged into the living room. Instinctively, Gretchen's head turned and her eyes followed Ellie's trail toward the foyer. "Misty!" she called, all but squealing with delight. "Yay! You got here!"

Overcompensate much? Add the big plastic grin to the fact that

Ellie was sleeping with Misty's ex, and you had a pretty disingenuous picture.

Misty froze momentarily on the stairs, casting her violet eyes downward—on a cautious slant—before starting to walk back down. Ellie had her arms outstretched, but Misty didn't hug her. Instead, she narrowed her eyes even more and twisted her mouth into a purse of . . . what? Disapproval? Anger? It was hard to say, but the sharp tone of her voice was unmistakable. "We need to talk," she stated. Her voice, as cool and as hard as steel, left no room for negotiation.

"Okay . . . uh . . . sure," Ellie said, still smiling, though, understandably, her expression had faltered. She either knew why Misty was pissed and she was scared, or she didn't know why Misty was pissed and she was scared. Either way, the two women went up the stairs together, as Brett led the way to Misty's guest room.

Later when Susanna would ask him what he'd overheard, Brett would just offer a lighthearted shrug and that affable smile he did so well.

Several hours later, the bluish glow of late afternoon covered the clouds like a gauzy blanket. Faint puddles of light spilled onto the snow.

Gretchen had gone inside to call Dana. She'd managed to avoid Rick all day, and now she sat cross-legged on the bed in her guest room, silver cell in hand, anxious to hear how the callback had gone. And, she supposed, she was eager to hear a friendly voice—to talk to someone who knew her as well as Dana did.

Just as she flipped open her phone, she heard a clattering in the hallway. Startled, Gretchen looked up. A second later, Ray Jarian creeped past her doorway, furtively looking from side to side, and the instant he spotted Gretchen sitting in her room, he nearly jumped. Flustered he stopped and paused. Then, tipping his cowboy hat, he said, "Oh—I, uh—well howdy, there, li'l lady. I reckon I overslept . . ." A smile briefly touched his lips, but it was clear from his expression that he was distracted.

"Hi, Ray," Gretchen said brightly. "I didn't realize you were still here. I thought someone mentioned that you'd left." Around noon, shortly after Misty Allbright's inauspicious arrival, Cady had told

Gretchen that she'd seen Ray through a window, crossing the side of Brett's house and heading up to the driveway where his car was parked. At the time, Cady had remarked that it was odd Ray hadn't left by the front door, nor had he said good-bye. Gretchen figured that perhaps he was embarrassed by how drunk he'd gotten the night before, or maybe he was just heading down to the Brass Lion Inn where he was staying to get cleaned up.

Seeing him now seemed to confirm that latter theory. Except . . . why was he acting like he just woke up?

"Well, ah . . . left?" he echoed, confused, then gave a hearty chuckle. "No, no . . . not at all. But if you'll 'scuse me, I'm just gonna grab my spurs and ride on outta here. Must be near time for sunset, and here I am just getting outta bed."

Just then Gretchen noticed the bulkiness of Ray's jacket, especially at his elbows. That was one lumpy coat. He must've seen her drop her gaze, because he hesitated uncomfortably, then said, "Actually . . . to tell the *truth* now . . ." He chuckled again—a raspy, artificial, desperate cough-laugh this time. "I had gone on my way earlier, but I just came back 'cause I forgot somethin', but I didn't want a make a fuss."

"Oh, I see," Gretchen said for lack of anything else. Hey, whatever. She didn't care what he did, but she didn't know why he was acting so weird about it. With another quick smile, she said, "Well, it was nice meeting you this weekend," then looked back down at her cell phone and started dialing Dana.

Out of the corner of her eye, she saw Ray's form disappear from sight.

Then she got the 411 from Dana: The callback went well; the casting director said they'd "be in touch" and she really liked "what was happening here." Dana was psyched and Gretchen was thrilled for her, though she had to admit it was hard to imagine her cousin on a soap opera, giving heavy-handed soliloquies with tinkling music in the background and not cracking up.

When Gretchen hopped off her bed, Susanna burst into her room. "Good, there you are!"

"Yeah, what's up? Do you need something?" Gretchen asked, going into helpful-and-efficient mode.

"I just talked to Ed. It turns out he's coming home from his business trip early. He'll be home tonight after all. But he has to fly out tomorrow again, so I want to get back now. What can I say? I miss my hubby. Do you mind?"

"Oh. No, not at all." Actually Gretchen was relieved; originally the plan had been Friday to Sunday, but it was Saturday and already this whole ski weekend was getting pretty played. Plus, Gretchen couldn't imagine twenty-four more hours of successfully avoiding Rick. As it was, whenever she caught a glimpse of him, her stomach started fluttering, her pulse started going crazy, and she had to fight to keep herself from going over to him and trying to "save face" or "get closure" or any of the other bullshit reasons a girl concocted to hang around a guy she lusted after. Basically . . . it was brutal.

But she was a little surprised that Susanna wanted to ditch the festivities a day early, especially since Gretchen still hadn't gotten to talk to Brett alone about "her" guest-spot idea. She'd looked for an opportunity, of course, but she hadn't been able to find Brett anywhere for the past two hours. "Let me just get my stuff together," Gretchen said, going for her half-packed bag that sat on the floor, across the room.

"Great! I'll just get Shawnee and we'll go," Susanna said, sounding almost urgent to haul ass out of there. Speaking of Shawnee, Gretchen hadn't seen her around for a while, too . . . In fact, the last time might have been the night before? She couldn't recall now . . .

Once Gretchen got to the entry foyer, she found Susanna waiting for her, tapping her foot restlessly, Louis Vuitton bags at her side. "Oh, good! Come on," she said, motioning with her head and leading the way to the front door. "Shawnee's outside already, waiting—"

"Oh, but I just realized, don't we have to call your driver?"

Shaking her head, Susanna struggled to drag both her bags; Gretchen quickly took one off her hands. "I called a taxi."

"We're going to take a taxi all the way to the city?" Gretchen said, surprised.

Susanna waved a hand through the air. "Sure. Ed will take care of it." Hmm . . . must be nice, Gretchen thought with a genuine flash of envy. Sure, Ed Tate might be a corporate mogul who was rarely home, but he was also loaded. But then, as quickly as she'd thought it, the words "rarely home" rolled through her mind again and the flash of envy was gone. It must be hard, and it would explain why Susanna was so anxious for whatever time she could spend with him.

Still . . . you'd expect her to grandstand a good-bye for everyone, but she was in too much of a rush. "There's the cab," she said, approaching the yellow taxi she'd already called. Shawnee tossed the cigarette she'd been smoking on the front steps, and suddenly Gretchen realized she didn't have her keys. She patted down her pockets again—nope, no keys. They must've dropped out of the front pocket of her suitcase.

"I'll be right back!" she said, turning back toward the house.

"Okay, hurry!" Susanna called from the backseat of the taxi.

Scurrying inside, Gretchen hopped up the steps, and as she reached the third-floor landing, she heard Brett say, "What's wrong? Are you okay?"

"I—I'll be okay," a woman replied. "I just, I'm sorry, Brett . . . I think I'll feel better if I'm home in my own place . . ."

Furrowing her brows, Gretchen curiously followed the voice. Misty, Brett, and Ellie were standing at the far end of the hallway; Ellie seemed to be helping Misty stand up, kind of propping her up for support as Brett patted her shoulder with concern. Misty had a dire look on her face, which Gretchen had noticed being pale before. Now it was more greenish. Well, yellow-green. She didn't look good, and she was holding her forehead, clutching it as though she could use her fingers to constrict her pain away. Dear God, what was wrong?

Gretchen recalled that Misty had gotten there late that morning, complaining about being exhausted. Maybe it was really a bad bug that she didn't know she had. In fact, that was exactly what it looked like. "I'm sorry," she repeated. "I've got to get home and . . . rest. It must be some bug I picked up; it's just hitting me now."

She leaned into Ellie a little, who pressed the back of her hand to Misty's forehead. "She's got a temperature," she said to Brett, speaking softly, almost as though Misty weren't right there between them.

"I don't understand," Brett said, sounding both confused and concerned. "What happened?"

"I just came to check on her, because, you know, she'd been lying down since she got here, but when I went to her room," Ellie said with a hapless shrug, "I found her burning up and in pain. She's just exhausted. You've been working too hard," Ellie said gently. At that, Misty tipped her head up and slanted a strange gaze at her assistant.

"Is there anything I can do?" Gretchen had blurted it before she'd thought about the futility of the words, but she couldn't help it. Brett looked over at her and managed a smile but shook his head.

"Thanks, Gretchen, but—"

"We've got it covered," Ellie said simply. Her tone wasn't rude, but it was dismissive. Misty said nothing to her, but nothing new there. When Ellie and Brett turned their focus back to Misty, Gretchen remembered that Susanna was waiting in the taxi. She'd better not keep her waiting too long. After retrieving her keys, left behind in her guest room, she darted back down the stairs. She wanted to tell Brett she was leaving and to thank him for a nice time, but it seemed gauche to interrupt them with trivial pleasantries when Misty was suffering.

Yet, as she stepped outside, Gretchen regretted it. Trivial or not, it was rude not to have said good-bye and thank you to Brett, who'd not only invited her but put her up in his home. Unfortunately she couldn't go back now. Susanna was motioning wildly, her arm this flailing thing sticking out of the open taxi door.

"Hurry!" she said.

As Gretchen slid in beside her, guilt niggled at her for skipping out. It wasn't that Brett or anyone else would notice or care that she'd left. It was just rude, that was all. Interestingly, Susanna didn't seem to have the same qualms. "Did you get to say good-bye to everyone?" Gretchen asked as the cab crunched along the hardened snow that had become encrusted on Brett's driveway.

She shook her head. "I couldn't find Brett" was all she said. She didn't mention trying to find Misty or anyone else for that matter. Clearly Susanna just couldn't get home fast enough.

CHAPTER FIFTEEN

*A*few days later, it was Wednesday and Gretchen was about to miss the elevator. But then the doors that had started to close miraculously sprung back open. Abe was inside the elevator already; he smiled at her. "Hi, I saw you coming," he said.

"Thanks!" she said brightly. The seldom done "door open" move—a remaining bit of chivalry, which, like all others, faced imminent decline.

They exchanged pleasantries as they rode up to the eighth floor. As soon as they stepped off the elevator a phone began to ring. It wasn't Gretchen's; Dana had teasingly changed that ring to the *I Dream of Jeannie* theme song to annoy her, and Gretchen hadn't changed it back yet. "Oh, excuse me," Abe said, taking his cell out of his suit pocket, glancing briefly at the number on the display screen before answering. "Hi." Then he gave a wave and turned to continue down the hall. But Gretchen was going in the same direction.

Tapping her fingers on her bag, Gretchen trailed behind Abe, acting oblivious even though you could always hear other people's conversations on their cell phones, and this one was no different. A woman was on the other end, talking loudly and frantically about Misty and how violently ill she was. It had to be Ellie. "Shh, calm down," Abe said gently. "Calm down. I'm sure she'll be okay. Has she been to the doctor?"

"Not since Monday, but she was getting better by then!" Ellie said. "Her fever had started to break and the doctor said it sounded like a bad flu, but . . . all of a sudden . . . I mean . . . she said she'd be in the office today, so when she didn't come in and didn't answer her phone, I went over to check on her. And I found her on the floor, Abe! She was burning up—she was delirious."

"Oh my God," Abe said, sounding genuinely stunned and worried. "Where is she now?"

"Lying down. I was able to help her up onto the sofa. I called the doctor. He's going to come over. I just don't understand what's wrong with her! She was getting better!" Ellie repeated, her voice bordering on hysterical. Obviously this was the point in a crisis at which Ellie became unglued; everyone had that point. Meanwhile Gretchen struggled to stay stone-faced, to act like she wasn't overhearing this whole alarming, disturbing conversation, as she walked two steps behind Abe. What was the etiquette in a situation like this? "I just don't know what to do."

"There's nothing you can do, sweetheart," he said softly. "You're doing everything you can for her." His voice had a calming effect, at least on Gretchen, who'd gone from tapping her bag restlessly to clutching it, digging her fingers into it. "But I do think you should take her to the emergency room instead of waiting for a house call," he added.

"Oh. The emergency room . . . I hadn't thought of that . . ." Gretchen heard Ellie say. What was she, an idiot? Sorry to be mean, but "emergency room" seemed redundant and obvious in the presence of an emergency.

"I just thought it was a bad flu or stomach virus or something!" Ellie shrilled, suddenly sounding defensive. "She was sick at Brett's party and then . . . but by Monday—I told you—her fever was breaking. The doctor said whatever it was, it was passing. And now—"

"Sweetheart," Abe said more firmly. "Don't waste time telling me this now. Take her to the emergency room. I'm sure it's just some kind of, I don't know, infection or something. But whatever it is, let them help her."

"O-okay," she said, "I will."

"I'll call you soon," he added and disconnected.

Uncomfortably, Gretchen glanced at him. She waited for some kind of encouragement to acknowledge what she'd just overheard, to ask if there was anything she could do (by the way, what was up with her compulsion to ask that question?), but when Abe glanced back, he offered a brief, polite smile, but said nothing. So he obviously didn't know about the whole loud cell phone thing.

Considering that he turned to make a pit stop at the men's room, now was apparently not the time to tell him.

Later that afternoon, during one of her tapings, Susanna stumbled over the cue cards again. Call it frazzled nerves, call it lack of concentration, call it being slightly nearsighted. Susanna preferred to call it illegible chicken scratch.

"Cut!" she yelled. "What the hell is *that* supposed to say?" she called out, over the homey facade of her kitchen to the director and crew. Gretchen stood on the side with her requisite clipboard, where she had a checked sheet of all the things that were supposed to be ready and done for the taping. When Susanna garbled her words it was very rarely the fault of the show's scriptwriters. Stepping forward, Gretchen angled her head so she could see the offending cue card in question. Depending on the show, TCC normally used a teleprompter or a large-screen flat monitor, but Susanna was old-school and that meant she liked things written in big black marker. (*Also* known as nearsighted.)

"Stop tape," Kit said, probably partly to retain some semblance of authority as director.

"Radio him? Wha—?" Susanna went on, squinting to make sense of the cue card. " 'It's like radio him'?" She let out a short humorless laugh and looked around the room. "Okay, it can't possibly just be *me* here . . ."

"*Radicchio,*" Shawnee corrected with a bored sigh. "Aunt Suz, can't you *read*?" Shawnee didn't just hold the cue cards, she also wrote them up, so she would know if Susanna were supposed to radio someone while making slaw.

Still, the girl was hardly a model intern.

This was an easy gig for her; Gretchen didn't know why she couldn't just enjoy it. But she seemed to prefer pushing her aunt's buttons. Surly and antisocial, yes, but Gretchen had a feeling the girl was also incredibly spoiled. Maybe now that her mom—Susanna's sister—was remarried and had a new baby, things were hard for her. In any event, Shawnee's attitude seemed to be here to stay. Now she flipped her hair, with the longer side of the lopsided mushroom do flopping away from her face, as she shifted her stance, her hefty men's shoes scuffing against the cement floor.

"Give me a break! That's totally illegible!" Susanna argued.

"It is *not*," Shawnee said. "Anyway, the radicchio's right there on the counter; you do the math."

Gretchen almost laughed at that, but she didn't dare. In fact, right now, you could hear a pin drop. Glaring her down, Susanna gave her the evil eye for a good thirty seconds before turning her attention to the director. "What's the point of this if I'm going to have to stop every two minutes because the cue cards are in Greek?"

Quickly Gretchen intervened. Might as well avoid a family feud, and with Shawnee being such an unapologetic brat, it could be a bloodbath. "You know what? I can go through the cards right now, if you want. I'll make sure they're all legible, no problem, okay?"

Susanna exhaled an overblown sigh of relief. "Thanks, Gretchen. I don't know what I'd do without you."

"That's five, everyone," Kit said, her voice weary with frustration, as though she'd been beaten down, as though she'd been promised more from life than this. (The tone was familiar by now.) On the sidelines, Abe offered her a sympathetic glance.

Gretchen went over and took the cue cards from Shawnee's hands. The girl didn't look happy, but nothing new there.

After reading through the rest of the cards, Gretchen fixed a few more sloppily scrawled words—God forbid Susanna pronounce fennel seed *tunnel sled*—and when she was done, Kit said, "Okay, are we about ready? Places . . . and . . . rolling!"

Taping resumed. Then several moments later, there was another crisis. As Susanna was chopping lettuce, something she'd done a gazillion times, she cut herself. "Ow!" she yelped.

"Cut!"

The cut was deep, too, with bright red blood welling up on the side of her index finger.

"Susanna, are you okay?" Abe asked. As usual, he was standing to the side, staying out of the fray unless absolutely necessary. (You had to respect that.)

"Oh . . . " she moaned, then looked up plaintively. "Gretchen . . .

I need you." Her eyebrows were cinched, her face pained dramatically; Gretchen crossed over, into the kitchen set, and went right to her side. "Here. Let me see," she said, taking Susanna's injured hand in her own. Leading her over to the sink, Gretchen ran cold water over the cut until blood stopped rising rapidly to the surface. Then she reached for the paper towels, tearing off one to dry Susanna's hand and another to wrap her finger tightly. Applying pressure, she spoke calmly. "Does it still hurt?" Weakly, Susanna nodded. "Okay, just leave this here for a few minutes, and press, okay?"

"Thanks, Gretchen," she said, her voice a little shaky.

"Sure. Just press," Gretchen said, then called to Kit, "Can we take another five?"

"Yeah, sure, whatever you need," she said quickly. The crew kept their eye rolling at bay, too. There was something about the sight of blood that made Susanna more forgivable to them right now, Gretchen supposed.

"Thank God you're here," Susanna said softly. "Nobody else knows what they're doing." Honestly, Gretchen couldn't think of anything more obvious than what she'd just done, but she accepted the compliment.

Smiling simply, she said, "Don't worry; you'll be fine." But she still had to wonder why Susanna seemed so damn nervous.

Just then, they heard the studio door open. Everyone turned. Denise, the receptionist from the main floor, entered, looking purposeful as she crossed the long distance of the room, toward the set, her high heels clicking more loudly the closer she came. She went to Abe, who pushed the earpiece of his headset back and leaned down to hear whatever she had to tell him.

Instantly, Abe looked stunned and sobered by Denise's news. She was shaking her head, looking just as stone-cold sober, and suddenly, Gretchen recalled the conversation she'd overheard that morning, the one about Misty Allbright, and she thought—

No, surely it wasn't that . . .

Eyes sliding shut for a moment, Abe shook his head. Denise exchanged a few more words with him that no one else could hear— but then Abe gave a nod, and Gretchen managed to read his mouth when he said, "Okay. I'll tell her."

When Denise turned to leave, Abe looked at Susanna—who looked back in confusion. "What is it?" she said.

Wordlessly, Abe walked onto the set, crossing over to her, and he spoke quietly. Gretchen heard the words, too, but Susanna was the one to echo them out loud. Her face crumpled, and she turned and threw her arms around Gretchen, slumping into her and hanging on tight. "Oh my God," she cried. "Misty's dead. Misty's *dead*!"

As Gretchen processed the words, she had no idea how they would eventually affect her—and how much her life would change before this was over.

Part Two

CHAPTER SIXTEEN

Rick woke up to the shrill of his ringing phone—at two o'clock in the fucking morning. After a long day that had stretched into the night, he hoped like hell there wasn't a four-alarm in need of backup.

"Hello?" he mumbled into the phone, his voice thick and gravelly with sleep even to his own ears.

"Brody. Thank God you're there."

"Jesus, it's two in the morning. Where the hell else would I be?" Slowly he pushed himself up in bed and rested his bare back against the headboard. Rubbing his eyes only revealed a mostly blackened bedroom; both windows had a view of a brick building adjacent to his own. But that suited him fine. And you know what else suited him fine at two o'clock in the morning? Some goddamn sleep.

"What's up? Is everything okay?" he asked.

"No . . . everything's so fucked up," Brett said. "I can't sleep . . . I . . . I don't know what to do."

"What is it?" Rick said, instantly becoming more alert. Had Brett started getting threats again? He thought they'd chalked up the few he had gotten over a week ago to pranks. But his brother was shaken up about something.

"Brody, I . . . I'm scared." Brett's voice cracked on the word "scared." Holy shit—was he *crying*?

"What is it?" Rick demanded. "Just tell me what's going on." Once his protective instincts kicked in, his gut tightened and he became short on patience.

Finally Brett sniffed and spoke again. "It's Misty—you know, my agent?"

"Yeah."

"She's dead."

"Oh . . . shit," Rick said, his mouth opened but momentarily speechless. He didn't know what to say. "I'm sorry, man," he said finally. "What happened?"

"It my fault," Brett murmured. "It's all my fault. It should've been me."

Upon hearing the words, Rick didn't know exactly what to make of them. He knew only that they were insincere. "How is it your fault?"

"Remember how Misty got sick at my house? And she left early?"

"Right."

"Well, she was *really* sick. Feverish and . . . we just figured it was the flu or something . . . but then . . ."

"Then *what*?" Rick pressed.

Brett explained. "Apparently, she'd been throwing up for days after she left my house. Her assistant, Ellie, took her to the doctor. They thought it might be food poisoning or something, but the doctor said it was impossible to tell at that point. But I guess her fever was breaking and he said to ride it out, because whatever it was seemed to be passing through her . . . but then . . ."

Rick waited, his fingers tightening around his phone as he leaned over to root around in the dark for the pack of cigarettes he'd left on his windowsill.

Brett sniffled again before continuing. "Ellie said she was gonna take her to the emergency room, but Misty was too weak to move, so Ellie called for an ambulance."

When Brett began to sob, Rick's chest constricted. He couldn't handle hearing his brother cry—hell, he couldn't handle hearing *anyone* cry. Unfortunately, because of his job, there were nights when he heard it a lot.

"She died on the way to the hospital," Brett finished. "She was just . . . dead. The doctors said it looks like kidney failure, but they don't understand it."

As his voice broke off, Rick expelled a shuddering sigh. *Jesus.* Food poisoning didn't cause kidney failure, that was for damn sure. "Did she mess with drugs? Anything?" he asked. "Maybe she had a genetic condition—"

"No, no way. She wasn't into drugs—she didn't even drink much. I'm telling you she was healthy." Brett's voice was strung tight as he tried to fight the very information he was reporting. Still, Rick didn't know how his brother could know for certain that Misty didn't have a bad kidney or some other infection or illness that the emergency room doctors just hadn't identified—yet.

Shoving his windowpane hard, Rick brought a cold front into his bedroom; he cupped his hand over the cigarette that was resting between his lips so he could light it. He exhaled slowly, then said, "But she said she wanted to go lie down as soon as she got there. So whatever it was, was starting to—"

"No, goddamn it, she was fine!" Brett snapped, then let out a long, unsteady breath. "I'm sorry, it's just . . . it should've been me. That's what I'm trying to tell you. It was meant for me!"

"What was? You're not making sense."

"Just listen. Misty was in her guest room. When I stopped in to check on her, she asked if there was anything to eat. She said she hadn't eaten since the afternoon before—said she was starving. So I boiled some pasta for her. Then I poured on some sauce that I'd made a couple days before—I had it stored in the fridge. She ate that and suddenly, an hour later, she's got abdominal pain, diarrhea, and she can barely stand on her own two feet. Don't you get it?" he cried, his voice thin and brittle, bordering on hysterical. "The food I gave her killed her!"

"Whoa, whoa," Rick said, shaking his head and squinting into the darkness. "Where do you get that? You still don't know if she had some kind of condition. You don't know if something she ate before she got to your house caused—"

"She said she was starving," Brett reminded him. "She said she hadn't eaten a thing. C'mon, Brody, you've gotta admit, this looks bad."

Wait, where had "looks" come from? Rick wondered. They were talking about reality here, about piecing together what had happened, not about how anything "looked."

"It was the sauce that killed her," Brett said. "It was something in the sauce, I just know it."

"But you said you made it yourself—wait a second. You're not saying . . . ?" *Shit.* Comprehension set in before Rick finished his question. Food poisoning wasn't likely to obliterate someone, but poison *in* the food was a whole different story.

"It fits with the death threats!" Brett exclaimed on a choking sob. "Someone must have slipped some kind of poison into my sauce in the fridge, thinking, just assuming, that I'd eat it, but instead . . . And they must've done it that weekend—it was someone at my party."

Wordlessly, Rick felt the impact of what his brother was saying like a hard punch to the chest. If poison really *was* involved, and if it was the sauce that was poisoned, then he had to admit, Brett's theory stood to reason. Especially if he'd made the sauce a day or two before the party and hadn't had anyone up to his house *until* the party . . .

But did someone really want Brett dead? Enough to come armed with *poison*—enough to execute an actual murder plot? Ironically, now that the possibility was so real, it seemed inconceivable.

Rick thought for a second, then said, "But if you had forty or fifty people at your house, anyone could've eaten something from your fridge. That would've been a stupid way to try to target you."

"No, but the sauce wasn't in my main kitchen. It was in my private kitchen. You know. I showed you."

"Yeah. I remember," Rick said, recalling the nook on the side of Brett's house with a narrow set of stairs that led up to his bedroom. It would be out of the way for any of the party guests, though. Who would even know about it?

They were just jumping to conclusions right now. They had no proof that Brett's sauce was poisoned or that the food he'd given Misty had in any way contributed to her mysterious death. They needed to talk more about this—but with a cooler focus. It was hard to talk to Brett when he was all emotional, and if he started crying again, Rick didn't think he could take that.

"You need to go to the police," Rick said.

"What! You're crazy. No way!"

"Why not?" Rick asked, scrunching his face in confusion.

"So then I can look all suspicious?" Brett began bawling heartily now as he protested the idea of police involvement. "I'm so fucking scared! And I'm not gonna call attention to myself! Especially since they don't know what made her sick. Yeah, I'm gonna walk in and be like, 'Hey, I'm the one who made her sick. Arrest me!' "

Rick rolled his eyes and stabbed out his cigarette. "Brett, why would they arrest you? If someone poisoned food in your house, they're not gonna assume you did it. Besides, what would be your motive? She was your agent. She was doing hot shit for your career. You can tell them about the threats you got, and—do you have any more of the sauce left?"

"Yeah . . ." Brett admitted reluctantly. "Just what Misty hadn't finished. I used it all up on her pasta, but she ate only half of it. I hadn't thought to get the bowl from her room until later."

"Good. The police lab can analyze it. Then at least you'll know for sure if you were the target or if what happened to your agent was just a tragic, unexplainable illness or something."

"No," Brett insisted. "I can't do it. Can you imagine the publicity if something like this leaked out? That I—*me*—famous for my cooking—the biggest freaking star on the Cooking Channel—might have killed someone with my *food*? It doesn't matter what the specifics are. That's all that will stick with people. I've got my reputation to think about, man—my image! Something like this could ruin me!"

Rick didn't respond right away. But now that he knew what Brett's tears were really for, they seemed more pathetic than before.

"I think I have an idea, though," Brett said in a wobbly voice that was in direct contrast to his macho image. "But I need your help, Brody. You're the only one who can get me out of this."

Torn between family loyalty and doing what was right—namely, going to the police—Rick agreed to meet him the following day. Of course he would; Brett was his brother. Nothing and no one, not even a murderer, was going to change that.

By the following evening, they'd struck an agreement. They'd met at a breakfast joint on Twenty-first Street, and the conversation had gone something like this:

"Brett, don't be stupid."

"I'm not. Going to the cops right now would be stupid. I don't even know for sure that the sauce was poisoned. I'd need to get it analyzed."

"I hear the police are doing that now," Rick said sarcastically.

"Yeah, and what if there's nothing in it at all? Nothing toxic, just sauce? Then what? Then I've called attention to myself for nothing. I don't want to be tied up with this, Brody. As far as everyone knows, Misty got to my house, went up to her room to take a nap, and then Ellie found her later, all sick and out of it. That's the story I'm sticking to—at least for now."

"But what if there *is* something in it?" Rick countered. "That plus those threats you got—I mean, think about it. This is about more than that girl's death, Brett. This is about your protection. How can the cops catch the guy if they don't have a legitimate lead? If Misty really was murdered, and *you* were the target, don't you think that fact is kind of crucial to their investigation?"

"Investigation?" Brett repeated, confused. "W-why would the police investigate if they don't even know how Misty died?"

"Uh, that *is* why," Rick said, stating the obvious.

"No, but . . . I mean, if they don't have any reason to think it's murder, then . . ."

"Are you kidding me?" Rick said incredulously. "A girl in, what, her twenties?"

"Thirty, I think."

"Fine. So a woman that young, who seems by all accounts perfectly healthy, completely destructs in a matter of days, and you don't think they're gonna investigate that? You can bet your ass they're gonna investigate."

"But if it was poison, they won't turn up anything because she barfed up all the evidence and then some."

"You're holding the evidence and you know it."

"Okay," Brett said, holding out his palms, "okay, fine. But this is what I'm thinking. Now, just hear me out."

"I'm listening."

"I need to know if the sauce is what did it. If we can find that out, and if we discover that it was poison and not just some bizarre coincidence, then I'll go to the cops. *But* . . . if we find out that there's nothing in it, then no harm done and I can just keep quiet and stick to the story. Misty arrived, went to take a nap, got sick, and left. Period."

Rick paused, thought about it, and agreed it was reasonable. Although, if there *was* foul play involved in all this, Brett would be putting himself in a suspicious light by waiting to come forward. When Rick tried to pose that to him, though, he'd predictably waved it off. Brett's mind was set. Now the only question was: How did Rick fit into this plan?

"A cop you're friends with," Brett explained. "Get him to find out for us—for you. But it has to be in strict confidence, of course, and it has to be someone you can trust." True, Rick had several acquaintances that were cops, but he ran the risk of attracting attention if he went to them, especially if the NYPD was investigating Misty's death and knew Brett's connection to her. But apparently Brett had already thought of that, because he had someone specific in mind.

"I'm thinking of that guy who used to play on your baseball team." Baseball team? That went back a few years, when Rick had played in a recreational league in Newark. "I can't remember his name, just that he was a cop. The short, fat guy who was going bald?" Brett said. So far it wasn't ringing a bell. "The one with the sweat stains and the pig nose?"

"Jimmy Yablonk?" Rick said, remembering.

"Yeah! Yablonk, that's it. Ask him. He'll have no clue what it's really about and he'll keep quiet about it."

With a sigh, Rick shook his head; he wasn't saying no, just thinking about the details. "I haven't talked to him in, what, four years?"

"He'll do it," Brett insisted. "The guy worshipped you."

"He-he-heyyy, what's up Pellucci?" Jimmy Yablonk said when Rick reached him at the Newark Police Department later that afternoon. "Put out any good fires lately?"

With a brief laugh, Rick said, "Just got back from vacation actually. So far it's been quiet."

"Damn, I can't believe how long it's been. When are you gonna ditch the city and come back to Jersey? Or you could at least join the team again—we could use a good hitter."

"I've been thinking about it," Rick said conversationally.

They talked for about fifteen minutes; Rick kept the conversation steered away from himself for the most part, but it wasn't difficult because Yablonk was a blowhard. Finally, Rick said, "Listen, I actually called to ask a favor."

"Sure, anything," Yablonk said eagerly. "You name it."

"I need to have something analyzed," Rick said, keeping his tone casual. "It's kind of a bet between me and a buddy of mine—well, it's a long story. I'll tell you all about it after I get the results." He made it sound like a fun thing—a game—but of course he had no idea what he'd tell Yablonk when the time came. He supposed it depended on the results.

Yablonk let out a squeal of a laugh. "That's funny! What is it?"

"Well, that's what I need you to tell me," Rick said, forcing a lighthearted chuckle into the phone, but still evading the question. "It's like . . . a liquid. Sort of." He needed to be as vague as possible, because if something peculiar *did* show up in Brett's sauce, the less Rick said now, the better. Also, the remaining sauce that had been swimming at the bottom of Misty's bowl had dried up some by now, though Brett had transferred it to a storage bag, so it was somewhere between liquid and solid. "Is there any way I could drop off a sample of it to you and you could get it analyzed for me? But keep it, you know, off the record? I know it sounds crazy, but—"

With a high-pitched giggle, Yablonk said, "No problem. It sounds like there's a great story behind this. Sure, drop it down to me later and I'll have my buddies in the lab take care of it for you. When do you need to know by?"

"As soon as you know," Rick said.

"No problem," Yablonk said again.

Well, that was easy. So far. Of course, if Yablonk's guys found poison, it was a whole other story. Then Rick would have to come up with some plausible explanation for where this "liquid" had come from and why he had it. But he'd deal with that later.

After making arrangements with Yablonk regarding when and where to drop the stuff off, Rick disconnected. And now he'd wait.

CHAPTER SEVENTEEN

"You heartless bastard."

"Uh . . ." Rick paused cautiously. "What do you mean?"

"I got the lab results," Yablonk said the next day when he phoned Rick at the firehouse. "I should've known you were up to no good."

Feeling anxious, Rick kept his tone even to disguise it. "Well, that was quick," he said casually, even as his gut tightened with anticipation, with dread.

"Of course it was quick, you asshole. It was tomato sauce!" Yablonk started cackling and said, "I could kill you—you made me look like a fucking idiot! I had my boys 'analyzing' goddamn tomato sauce. I'm the big joke around here now."

Rick blew out a sigh of relief. *Thank God.* So the sauce had been okay. It hadn't been part of some murder plot against his brother. A woman wasn't dead, indirectly, because of Brett.

"Let me guess," Yablonk continued jovially. "You were trying to figure out your brother's secret recipe, is that it? Mr. Big TV Star's not talking, so you come to me," Yablonk joked.

"Uh, yeah," Rick said with a chuckle. "Something like that. I'm sorry, man. I, uh . . . I was desperate."

"I'll say! Let's see what we've got here. Tomatoes, garlic, olive oil, salt, black pepper, butter, basil, onions, mushrooms, sugar, and rosemary—did I get it all?"

Nodding, Rick took out the list of ingredients Brett had given him yesterday morning and gave it a glance. Wait a second. "Mushrooms?"

"Yeah. 'Basidiomycota fungi,' " Yablonk said, clearly reading the lab report in front of him. "Also known as fucking mushrooms," he finished with a laugh. "You owe me for this, Pellucci."

"No, I know, I know. Listen, I'll take you out for a beer."

"Forget that. Just play baseball with us again. We start practicing in March."

"Okay, I'll think about it," Rick said, even as his mind was stuck thinking about something else: Brett's sauce recipe didn't call for mushrooms.

Rick's next two calls were trickier. The first one was to a high school science teacher—his ex-girlfriend, Amanda. Well, sort of ex-girlfriend. They'd dated for a couple of months, but broken things off after she'd introduced herself as his girlfriend one day, and hearing her say it made him realize it just didn't fit.

That was four or five months ago now; hopefully she wasn't still bitter. He dialed her cell.

"Hello?"

"Amanda," Rick said with familiarity that was probably out of place, "it's Rick."

There was a pause. Then she said, "Oh. Hi." Well, it was hard to tell if she was bitter, but she certainly wasn't thrilled.

"How are you?" he asked.

"Fine."

"How's school?"

"It's fine. I'm kind of surprised to hear from you," she stated bluntly. "I'm surprised you still remember my number." Bitter—definitely bitter.

"Well, I hope I'm not bothering you," he threw in warmly.

"No. It's fine, I guess." She paused and added, "I'm engaged, by the way."

"Whoa," Rick said, jerking his head back, surprised. "Engaged, huh? Who's the guy?"

"It's the man I was dating before you. Larry."

"Ohh," Rick said, nodding to himself as he remembered. Amanda had mentioned her ex-boyfriend a couple of times. Something about him being one of those dull, unexciting mama's boy types. And now they were engaged? Huh. You could never predict who'd end up together, but hey, as long as she was happy.

"Well, good," Rick said now, meaning it. "That's real good, Amanda."

"I'm very happy now," she said, obviously intent on making the point. And then Rick realized—he'd hurt her; she might be happy with Larry, but she was still pissed off with him.

"That's good," he said again. "Listen, to tell you the truth, I'm calling because I need to ask you some questions about mushrooms."

"Huh?"

"I know it's strange, but it's for this thing I'm working on," he explained vaguely. Normally, he might think it was jumping to conclusions to assume that the traces of mushroom found in Brett's sauce were ominous—*poisonous*—but considering the sauce was smooth, with no chunks in it, that meant that the mushrooms had been ground up finely—a deliberate act to conceal them—which was what made their presence very fucking ominous.

"I just need some information," he continued, "but I don't have a clue even where to begin looking. And I know you teach biology and you probably know everything there is to know about this stuff, so I thought I'd give you a call."

"I teach chemistry!" Amanda snapped. Now she was annoyed.

Chemistry! Rick scolded himself, making a fist. *That's right—did she tell me that?*

A moment passed before she softened her tone with a sigh. "Why, what do you need to know?"

"Well, I'm curious about mushrooms that are poisonous—you know, which ones are deadly and what they do and how someone could get his hands on them." Realizing how shady that must have sounded, Rick gave a brief laugh and qualified, "Obviously I'm not asking for *me*. But it's . . . it's kind of important."

"Hmm, that's really not my area," Amanda said. "But if you want . . . I guess I can put you in touch with the bio teacher here."

"Yeah?" Rick said, surprised and pleased. "That would be great. She won't mind?"

"He, and no. Jay lives for this stuff. He talks about bio all the time. He grows mold in his refrigerator. Last year he took the kids to Sandy Hook on a field trip; they saw a dead fish on the beach, and Jay cut its head open with his keys. He wanted to show them a real live fish brain. Two kids went home sick and he almost got fired."

"Wow," Rick said, furrowing his eyebrows. "Sounds like an interesting guy."

"He is when you're in the mood for it. Anyway, he knows practically everything about every organism ever; I'm sure he'll be happy to help you."

"Thanks, Amanda," Rick said. "I really appreciate it."

"Okay. Well, I'll ask him to call you. What time is it? Let's see . . . three thirty. Yeah, he should still be here. The bio club gets out at around three forty-five."

"Thanks again, Amanda. I owe you." She grumbled something under her breath, but Rick figured he was best not knowing what it was. Instead he said, "By the way—congratulations."

"Amanda told me you wanted to know about poisonous mushrooms." No hello, no small talk—Rick liked this guy already.

"Yes. Thanks for getting in touch with me so quickly. I . . . well, I'm trying to do some research on mushrooms, like you said, and I'm wondering what types are out there that are fatal?"

Jay Bernbaum chortled on the other end of the line, then let Rick in on the joke. "Sorry to laugh, but, uh, 'out there'? Out where? The country? The world? Because I must tell you, it's impossible to calculate. You can't prove a negative, of course."

"Um . . . what?" Rick said, squinting, partly in confusion and partly because he was walking to the subway and the afternoon rain had just turned into fat, pelting snow.

"Well, there are surely hundreds of species of mushrooms that have yet to be identified, so it's impossible to make sweeping statements, which would ultimately discount those nonidentified species that may or may not be poisonous, much less fatally so. An exercise in futility, speaking from a statistical standpoint. However, I suppose if you tell me the specific aim of your research, I could offer you a more finite answer—with my initial qualification standing, of course."

Rick paused to formulate an answer. He was never that great in school, so he might just be a dumb shit here, but wasn't Jay Bernbaum kind of talking in circles? "Right," Rick said finally, "well, I'd appreciate that. Basically, I'm curious about a mushroom that might make someone real sick. You know, vomiting, fever . . . kidney failure?" It probably sounded bizarre to jump from fever to kidney failure, but he figured he'd throw it all out there while he had the guy on the line.

"Kidney failure, now *that's* interesting. That would have to be quite a potent mushroom," Bernbaum said, then made a lip-smacking noise. "Gastrointestinal bleeding, as well?"

"Oh—I'm not sure." Whatever Rick knew about Misty Allbright's symptoms came from Brett, who'd gotten his sketchy details from Misty's assistant, Ellie. In fact, Ellie seemed to have been the only one who'd actually talked to the doctors.

"Coma?" Bernbaum asked.

"Yeah, I think so. Toward the end anyway." Catching himself, Rick qualified, "Hypothetically speaking, of course."

"What area?"

"What do you mean?"

"On the globe."

"Oh. America."

"Region?"

"Northeast," Rick said. "Basically, I'm thinking of a mushroom that might cause someone to get real sick, but then start to feel better. Fever breaks, it seems like the person's on the mend, and then *bam*. She—or he—is a mess again. Burning up, delirious and then—"

"Kidney failure," he supplied again.

"Ultimately, yeah," Rick said.

"The Destroying Angel," Bernbaum murmured with a touch of wonder in his voice. "That sounds like the one."

"Sorry?"

"The Destroying Angel," he repeated. "Its scientific name is *Amanita bisporigera*. There are other highly toxic mushrooms that, if ingested, can play out a similar course of symptoms, but they are typically harder to come by and of course there are variations. But what you just described seems dead-on," Bernbaum explained, then blew out a breath. "Wow, I haven't thought about the Destroying Angel in years."

Well, hell, why would he? "Can you tell me more about it?" Rick asked, feeling anxious, tense. This could very well be the poison that had come frighteningly close to killing his brother.

"As I said, it's an extremely toxic fungus," Bernbaum explained. "Sometimes called 'Death Angel,' which I've always found a little 'on the nose.' "

"And it grows in the Northeast?" Rick asked.

"No. But I suppose one could get it if one is determined."

"And it's fatal?"

"Extremely," he said again. "It's the incubation period that's tricky. Usually a person who has eaten a Destroying Angel mushroom—quite by accident, of course—will start to feel symptoms hours later. Sometimes it can take as long as a day for the symptoms to manifest. As you described, there is typically abdominal pain, vomiting, diarrhea, high fever."

"What if the symptoms show up sooner—like an hour or so after eating it?"

"No," Jay said. "That doesn't sound right. It takes at least five or six hours." Rick tucked that information away, as he recalled Brett's words: *An hour later, she's got abdominal pain, diarrhea, and she can barely stand on her own two feet.*

"Oh, I see," Rick said. "Go on."

Bernbaum seemed happy to oblige (and inwardly, Rick was grateful for people unlike himself—namely those who hadn't cut most of their bio classes in high school). "The tricky part, though, is—as you mentioned—that the symptoms wane. There is a short period of recovery. But it's only an illusion. A person will believe he is getting better, and then rapidly, the toxin takes hold, destroying him from the inside out, killing him before he can even realize the cause of his affliction. Kidney failure is just one of the possible effects."

"Jesus," Rick whispered, stunned, thoroughly disturbed by the horrible fate that Jay had just described so casually. Sucking in a breath, he asked, "So how would this Destroying Angel be identified

as the cause of death? In an autopsy? Sorry, this is probably out of your area of expertise, but—"

"No, it's a smart question. The truth is, unless someone consumed a particularly large quantity, by the time he died, he would have purged so much out of his system it would likely be impossible to find traces of the mushroom in his stomach contents. And as for toxin in his bloodstream, well, a medical examiner would have to know exactly what he was looking for to find it." Bernbaum paused to sneeze, blow his nose, then continued. "In cases of this kind of fatality—which is far from common, mind you—the cause of death has typically been identified by samples of the mushroom that were left behind."

"In other words, the remainders that the victim *didn't* eat," Rick filled in, thinking about Brett's leftover sauce and how that, then, would be the key to any investigation of Misty's death. As long as the police were unaware that Misty had eaten at Brett's house—especially something this toxic and this obscure—they would have no way of tracing or conjecturing the real cause of death. They would have no way to link her death on Wednesday morning to her brief appearance at Brett's house on Saturday. If Brett didn't go to the police with what he knew and the evidence he was holding, Misty Allbright's murder would likely go unsolved. And considering that the murderer was really after Brett, that left his brother still very much in danger.

Curiously, Rick asked, "So if a person realized that he'd accidentally eaten one of these mushrooms, what could he do to save himself?"

"Nothing, I'm afraid. There is no antidote for the Destroying Angel. In miniscule amounts it's not necessarily fatal, but when it's wolfed down by mistake, one's goose is as good as cooked. Or charbroiled, as it were."

On that grim note, Rick thanked Jay Bernbaum for his help and said good-bye.

That night, Rick was at Brett's apartment on Madison Avenue, discussing with his brother what he'd learned and what they needed to do. The two sat on opposing, but equally oversized leather couches that sucked a body down like quicksand.

Now that Rick had held up his end of the bargain, Brett was ready to renege on the deal like the sniveling coward he was. Okay, granted, he had a right to be scared; he had a killer after him, but did that mean he couldn't show an ounce of character?

"Please, *please,* Brody, just help me a little longer," he begged.

"What can I do?"

"Figure this mess out."

"Oh, is that all?" Rick said, his voice hard with sarcasm.

"Please," Brett pleaded.

"Look, we agreed—"

"I know, but I can't go to the cops now. And I know what you're thinking, that I'm just concerned about the bad publicity. But it's not just that, I swear. Okay, yes, that's a factor. A big factor—a huge factor—fine. But it's more than that."

Implacably, Rick crossed his arms over his chest and waited.

"I'm scared, Brody. Scared that I . . . that I'll somehow get this whole thing pinned on me." Suspiciously, Rick tilted his head and squinted at him, subjecting his brother to the scrutiny he was clearly trying to avoid. "Why would anyone pin it on you? Especially considering the death threats you got?"

"According to me," Brett countered. "But I have no proof. I didn't tape those two calls. And that e-mail—come on, a random Yahoo address, the cops could say I sent that to myself to avoid suspicion." Before Rick could interject, Brett pressed on. "If I come forward now, I'll link my name to this whole mess. I'll become front and center in the police's mind when they try to sort it out. There'll be a cloud of suspicion over me, and if the cops go looking for a fall guy, I'll be the first one to come to mind."

Rick sat back, assessing his brother. After a long pause, he said, "Why did you make pasta for Misty?"

"Huh?"

"Answer the question. There was a ton of food downstairs for the party. If she was hungry, why didn't you bring her some of that? Why did you make pasta?"

"Because I knew how much she liked my sauce," Brett said simply, then as if abruptly hearing his own words, his expression faltered.

"You were sleeping with her," Rick said flatly. "That's it, right?"

Brett didn't answer; he gulped, which was good enough. "That's why you're so scared of the police," Rick continued. "You're afraid if you call attention to yourself, they'll check you out. Find out you and Misty had more than a business relationship. And that, plus your connection to the food that killed her—"

"Yes! Don't you see?" Brett said anxiously, sitting forward and resting his elbows on his knees. He ducked his head down to plow his hands through his hair; when he looked back up at Rick, his eyes were troubled, terrified, his normally cheerful-puppy face was drawn and dark. "They'll try to pin this whole thing on me! They always pin it on the boyfriend."

Rick held back from pointing out that it usually *was* the boyfriend. That wouldn't make his brother feel any better. Instead, he sighed and rubbed his eyes. "So Misty was the one, huh?" he said finally, already tired of this whole mess even though it had only just begun.

"What one?" Brett asked, confused.

"The one you were telling me about last week. The, uh . . . casual thing."

Brett paused, obviously trying to remember the conversation Rick was referring to—the one in his dressing room when Rick had asked Brett if he was seeing anyone and he'd mentioned a woman he was "screwing" but wouldn't give her name.

Recalling now, Brett shook his head and said, "Oh, no. No, that was someone else."

"Someone else?"

"Yeah. That wasn't Misty. I mean, Misty and I were sleeping together, but that was more, you know, secondary to our business relationship. The, uh, casual thing is somebody else."

Angrily, Rick barked, "Jesus—how many people are you screwing, Brett?"

"Hey," Brett said sharply, somehow finding the balls to get pissed off and defensive in the midst of his whining and sniveling. "No judgments, man, all right?"

"No," Rick corrected, annoyed. "Judgments. A helluva lot of judgments. You're thirty years old, for chrissake. Do you have to sleep with every girl you meet?"

"Look, Brody, I'm having a really shitty night, okay! I just found out that someone is unquestionably trying to kill me and I'm holding the one piece of evidence that could either help the police find the guy, or make me the prime suspect. I don't need a lecture!"

Sucking in a breath, Rick paused and said, "Okay. Sorry." It wasn't any of his business who his brother slept with, he knew that, but another girl just added another complication to the case. Another person intimately invested in Brett's life was another person with access to details—like Brett's phone number, his e-mail address, and possibly his upcoming trip to Hawaii, which was mentioned in the threatening e-mail he'd received at work.

If Rick were honest with himself, he'd admit that his anger had little to do with Brett's flakiness or his shady track record with women. It came down to control. Rick was used to having it—approaching a problem with a clear, sharp focus—but this mess Brett had dumped on him was muddled and frustrating as hell.

Now he expelled a sigh and spoke more calmly. "So who's this other person?"

"Wha—why? Why does that even matter?" Brett asked uncomfortably. "She's not involved in any of this."

"Well, who knows? Maybe she is. Maybe she was more serious about you than you were about her. Maybe she knew about you and Misty and went around the bend—"

"No way," Brett said with a shake of his head. "She wouldn't do that."

"Fine. So who is it?"

Brett sighed with frustration. "Just forget it, man. I don't want to go there."

"Oh, you don't? Oh. Okay."

Relieved, Brett sank back in his leather couch. "Thanks, Brody. I knew you'd respect that."

"Sure, sure. No problem. Hey, let me know how it goes with the police." Rick stood to go.

"What! You mean—"

"I'm not helping you if you're not gonna be straight with me," Rick said, walking toward the door. "I don't need this kind of aggravation."

"Wait, Brody, please! I need your help!"

Rick paused and turned. He looked squarely at his brother, who seemed almost childlike, buried deep and small in his massive sofa. "I'm asking you a simple question. You ask for my help. You want me to try to find out who's after you. Well fine—"

"You mean you'll help?" Brett said, hopefully, desperately.

Rick held up his hand. "But it's gonna be on my terms, not yours." Given the sharp unyielding strength of his tone, Rick knew his brother would take it for the dead-serious ultimatum that it was.

A few beats passed.

Then Brett expelled an overblown sigh, undoubtedly for the effect. "Fine. But I'm telling you, you're way off base here."

"I just want her name, I'm not making any assumptions."

"She wasn't even at the damn party! This is stupid."

"I'm waiting."

Brett paused, stalling. "You know, you're gonna feel pretty silly when I tell you."

"I doubt that."

Another pause. Brett tightened his mouth into a hard line. Then, sulkily, he told Rick her name.

Rick furrowed his brows. "Kit Carmichael? Who's that?"

"She's the director of *Susanna's Kitchen*," Brett explained. "Look, I'm not proud of it, but it just happened, okay? Last month at the Christmas party, I was looking around for Misty toward the end of the night, but I couldn't find her anywhere. Then I ran into Kit in the coatroom. I barely knew her at the time, but she was suddenly all over me, man. I figured she was just one of those chicks who gets all lovey-dovey and clingy when they're drunk. The next thing I know, she's shoving her hand down my pants and grabbing my dick—well, what can I say?"

"Say no more," Rick said with a grimace. "I get the picture." But he didn't exactly need a play-by-play of his brother getting his cock jerked.

"Well, you asked!" Brett remarked petulantly.

"Fine, sorry."

"So you'll help me then? You'll try to figure this out—just a little longer? And if we still come up empty, then I'll go to the police. I swear."

"But what are you gonna do for protection in the meantime? I work for a living, in case you forgot. I can't watch your back indefinitely." Rick didn't say what else he was thinking, what he'd been feeling guilty about for the past two days: If he hadn't done such a piss-poor job of watching Brett's back up to now, a girl wouldn't be lying dead right now.

It didn't matter that by the time of the party, both he and Brett had pretty much dismissed the threats as pranks. Rick wasn't letting himself off on a technicality. Anguish stabbed at his chest, but he kept it to himself.

"I'll hire a bodyguard," Brett said, which was a damn good idea. "I'll just make up a reason for him being around me."

"And you're gonna need to tell me more about the people who were at your party. At this point, I'm assuming we can safely rule out Emeril," Rick said dryly.

With a faint smile, Brett said, "Yeah. I suppose."

"Fine. I'll try. But I'm not a trained investigator. If I come up empty, you go to the police. Agreed?"

"Agreed," Brett said, blatantly lying, something he thought he was good at.

"I do have a question, though." Brett waited to hear it. "If the thing with Kit Carmichael is no big deal, then why the big secret? Why didn't you just tell me?"

"Well . . . she's kinda old. And she's not exactly *hot*." He said it like the sentiment was so obvious, so clear, made so much sense.

Rick's grimace deepened; he shook his head, and when he spoke his tone was resigned. "You know something, Brett? You're just a dick."

CHAPTER EIGHTEEN

*S*usanna Tate was the key.

It was Saturday morning, and Rick was still nursing the thought over his second cup of coffee. He had the newspaper cast aside, still folded. He'd thrown on sweatpants and a sweater and gone to sit outside on his porch, which was only a little wider than a phone booth and overlooked the quiet street ten flights below. It was still early. The air was ice-cold and crisp; it helped him wake up, helped him think.

Susanna Tate. He'd been considering this possibility ever since he'd gotten home from Brett's last night. Susanna was the one who'd told Brett to check his corporate e-mail last week—directing him right to the death threat that was waiting in his in box. And with her extensive culinary training, she would know about all kinds of exotic mushrooms. Maybe it was a stab in the dark, but it was the only lead Rick had right now.

When he'd posed the idea to Brett, Brett hadn't resisted it, though he'd been unable to suggest any motive other than: *Maybe she's upset 'cause she can never have me?*

Rick had humored him with that one, then asked if Susanna Tate might view Brett as a professional rival—an obstacle, even. Reluctantly, Brett had agreed it was possible (though apparently not as possible as her being secretly in love with him).

Now there was one way Rick could think of offhand to find out more about Susanna Tate: befriending her assistant. Gretchen Darrow. Damn, he liked that name; it rolled easily through his mind, even as it drove him crazy.

She was sexy and voluptuous and clearly angling for a way to get to his brother. And at this point, why fight it? Especially now that Rick needed something from her, too.

He didn't have much choice. With Susanna Tate as his number one suspect right now, and Brett still too chickenshit to go to the police but still in danger, Rick had to try to figure this out.

On Monday, he'd stop over at TCC and see Gretchen. He didn't have to be at the firehouse till two, so he'd have some time to talk to her, to act interested. Fine, so he was a little interested—or attracted. *Fiercely* attracted. When he thought about the feel of her body under his when they'd fallen together on the snow . . .

It had been a perfect and erotic fit. Hot, sexy. She'd felt it, too. But then, she was drunk. Still, there was something about her. Gretchen just had a way of acting sweet . . . supple . . . kissable. Opportunistic as she was, though, the sweet thing was doubtful.

At least now he wouldn't worry about trying to make a good impression with her. It didn't matter if he was clean-shaven or even particularly charming; Gretchen would be sweet to him just as long as she thought it could get her closer to his famous brother. If he had to, Rick would even dangle that subtly in front of her. Gretchen was a big girl. She knew what she was doing.

She wanted to use him? Fine. Let her use him. In fact, it would be interesting to find out just how far she'd go.

Gretchen couldn't think of many worse ways to spend a Saturday night than at a funeral. She'd just gotten home from Misty Allbright's memorial service. There was no body; she wasn't sure if that made the whole affair more or less disturbing. Susanna had urged her to come with her, for "emotional support." The service had been held at an elegant funeral home on the Upper West Side; it had been organized by Ellie Galistette, who seemed appropriately contrite during the entire night (except for the time Gretchen noticed her slipping her business card to one of the mourners). On the way back, Susanna had given Gretchen a lift home in her limousine, and she'd passed along the gossip she'd heard: Misty's body was being held in the morgue, awaiting autopsy. Gretchen didn't know most of the people at the funeral, so if Misty's family was there, Gretchen didn't know who they were. Maybe they were the people in the front aisle, but none of those people seemed that personally upset—just appropriately solemn.

In any event, she was thrilled to be home now, turning the key to Marcia Rabe's luxurious sanctuary of an apartment.

"Hello?" she called, tossing her keys on the front table and proceeding down the hall.

"In here!" her cousin called from her bedroom.

Gretchen poked her head in and found Dana and her friends, Lolly and Chantal, sitting on the bed, watching Suzanne Somers peddle something age defying on HSN. Both Lolly and Chantal were still in their Medieval Faire uniforms, while Dana had changed into pajama pants and a long-sleeved T-shirt that read: BRUNETTES DO IT BETTER. (The shirt was Gretchen's—but it had been a gift from Dana.)

"Oh, hey, guys," she said, smiling weakly. She was suddenly exhausted; providing "emotional support" to Susanna was a tiring task. Her feet hurt, her eyes were drooping, and the most sinful, decadent fantasy she could conjure at the moment was of collapsing into bed.

"Hey!" Dana said enthusiastically, reaching for the remote to mute the TV. Her dark red hair was pulled up into a ponytail, making her look young and cute and like a quintessential cheerleader. To complete the overly simplistic high school metaphor, Chantal looked like a glamorous homecoming queen, and Lolly looked like a shy, pensive honors student. This was all from the neck up, of course. The medieval uniforms didn't exactly fit with the equation.

"How did it go?" Dana asked.

With a tired sigh, Gretchen gave the abridged version of her night—how nobody seemed to know how or why Misty had become so ill, and how the memorial was packed with people, most of whom were strangers to Gretchen—except for Susanna, Brett, Abe, and Ellie.

Though Ellie might as well have been a stranger; Gretchen had met her for only about five seconds at Brett's party.

Interestingly, Misty's disgruntled ex-client, Ray Jarian, hadn't attended the service. Susanna had pointed this out more than once, and "disgruntled" was her word. She seemed to use it repeatedly. Honestly? Ray hadn't seemed all that disgruntled to Gretchen.

But who was she to say? She barely knew any of these people.

"And it was just kind of weird," Gretchen said now. "Misty's clients were all saying how much they liked her, but here I didn't even *know* her and she was so cold to me. And not just once, but twice. I still can't figure it out . . . granted I never will at this point, but still . . ." She paused, pondering the mystery. "It was almost like she knew me somehow and really disliked me. Yet I *know* I've never seen her before in my life. I don't know. Does the name Misty Allbright mean anything to you, Dana?"

Dana shook her head. "No. It's not ringing any bells. Maybe she was just a bitch. But it's not like she's gonna be bitchy to her clients, right? That's probably all there was to it."

Reluctantly, Gretchen nodded. What other explanation could there be? Certainly none that she could think up while she was this damn tired. Slipping out of her heels, she yawned before she could stop herself; she quickly covered her mouth and needed two hands to do the job—not a good sign.

"Well, I hate to be a major dud, but I'm so tired, I'm going to bed," Gretchen said, bending down to scoop up her shoes.

All three said good night. As Gretchen drifted across the hall to her bedroom, she heard Dana and Chantal discussing the wonder of Suzanne Somers; Dana explained that she was a beautiful goddess, while Chantal maintained that she was a shill in a good wig.

Plunking down on her bed, Gretchen thought more about the memorial service. She couldn't get the night out of her head, as tired as she was. For some reason, Ellie's grief had seemed . . . almost insincere. There had been something posed about the whole affair. The cynic in Gretchen speculated that perhaps Ellie had intended it more as an opportunity to secure Misty's clients as her own than a memorial. As she'd said at Brett's party, she wasn't Misty's assistant, but her "apprentice."

But it wasn't just Ellie. There had been something stiff and unnatural about Susanna tonight. She'd been clinging and elbow strangling, per usual, but she'd seemed more nervous than she was sad. Gretchen wondered why.

On Monday morning, Gretchen was sitting in the office on the second floor that Susanna had bequeathed to her, doing paperwork, when the phone rang. It was Denise, telling her that there was some-one waiting in the reception area to see her. *Huh?* That was strange. Who on earth could it be? She hadn't had time to make any friends in New York yet. Oh, no! She hoped it wasn't Dana, tired of waiting for Gretchen to set her up with Brett. Was Dana taking matters into her own hands, showing up at TCC and demanding an introduction?

Nah—her cousin was ballsy, but she wasn't that ballsy.

When Gretchen went down to the first floor, she found Rick Pel-lucci sitting on one of the lime-green couches that lined the wall, per-pendicular to Denise's domed, silver desk.

Her jaw dropped. Her heart skipped a beat, as her mind buzzed, frantically wondering, *What the hell is he doing here?*

"Hi," he said, smiling as he came to his feet. As though it were normal for him to be (A) smiling, and (B) here.

It had been over a week since she'd seen him. The last time had been at Brett's house in the Catskills. Somehow the sight of him was like a blow to the chest—it stole her breath, knocked the wind right out of her.

"Hello . . ." she managed, brushing a strand of hair away from her eyes and studying him warily. "What did I do now?"

With a laugh, Rick said, "Absolutely nothing—*this* time."

She grinned in spite of her shock at seeing him and in spite of her residual annoyance with him for pulling away from their kiss. She'd succeeded in pushing memories of it from her mind, but it ob-viously didn't take much for the visceral longing, and subsequent dis-appointment, of that moment to flood her mind again. And her body, as she recalled the sexual thrill of his strong, heavy body on top of hers . . .

"Actually, I wanted to take you for a cup of coffee or something," he said. "Any chance you could get away for about twenty minutes? I'd ask you to lunch instead, but I have to be at the fire station by two." He glanced at his watch. "Well, it's eleven now, so it's almost lunchtime. What do you say?"

Whoa. Okay, this threw her. Just when she thought Rick couldn't be less interested in her, he did something to confuse her. And just when she'd finally muddled his face in her mind—his jaw, his eyes, his intensity—he appeared in front of her, he became real again.

Well, he could forget making a fool of her again! Not this time; she was weak, but she wasn't so weak as to keep playing games with him. She was done embarrassing herself over a guy whose own brother described him as a major oddball.

"Thanks for asking," Gretchen said, her tone even and polite, "but I can't."

"Oh," he said with a nod. "Other plans?"

She hesitated. It was only for a second, but it was enough to betray the fact that she had no plans other than catering to Susanna's wide array of neurotic needs. "I'm working," she said finally.

"So take an early lunch then," he suggested. He clearly wasn't flustered by her rejection—*that makes one of us*—but she held her ground.

"I'm sorry. I can't."

"What, they don't let you eat around here?" he joked, but instead of doing a pivot turn and skulking out of there (that was generally her move), he kept standing there, confident, assured, raking his blue gaze over her face, down to her mouth, and back to her eyes.

She swallowed. Damn, he was pushy—what did he want from her anyway?

"I really have too much work right now," she reiterated, then paused thoughtfully. "Um, let me think . . ." Her voice drifted off as she contemplated what to do. Part of her wanted to call him out for his behavior, to ask him why he blew hot and cold with her. Another part of her wanted to cut him off at the pass and just rudely walk away.

And yet another part of her was dying to go with him.

"Should I take a seat again?" he asked.

"Oh," she said, coming back into focus. A laugh slipped out then, in spite of everything. "No, I'm sorry. I was just . . . wondering something."

"What?" Rick asked, moving a step closer to her.

She sucked in a breath, forced herself not to reveal how much his closeness affected her. "Why are you here?" she blurted. There. She'd done it. "I mean . . . what's the catch?"

He stepped closer still, and her heart jumped into her throat. "The only catch," he said, his voice low and even, "is that you have to come." Nervously, she wet her lips. Was it just her, or did the word "come" conjure up some graphic images? At least it did when Rick said it. By the casual expression on his face, though, it was obvious that he hadn't intended it in a sexual way. "Listen, I feel like we've gotten off on the wrong foot, and I just want to make it up to you," he added. "No catch, really."

"I really don't think it's a good idea," she insisted. "You and me and coffee and . . . To be honest, you're not really my type." Yeah, right.

Unfazed by the comment, Rick took another step closer. "What type is that?"

"Forget I said that," Gretchen amended quickly, not wanting to open up an awkward conversation, especially at work and especially with Denise at the reception desk, pretending not to eavesdrop. "I just don't think it's gonna work," she said.

"It's coffee," Rick stated flatly. "How can that not work?"

Wow, he was really insistent. She couldn't help feeling flattered; he was really making an effort here. Had he meant what he'd said? That they'd simply gotten off on the wrong foot (four times now, but fine)?

"Gretchen." The way Rick said her name excited her. It was gruff, sexy. "I have no ulterior motive here. I just want to get to know you." A spark of excitement zipped through her.

Well, hell, if he was gonna sound all *sincere* about it . . .

How could she say no?

A smile broke across her face and she softened her stance. "Okay. That's . . . sweet. I guess I could get away for a *few* minutes. . . ."

"Great," he said, smiling, showing his straight white teeth. There was something wolfish about that smile, but inexplicably, she trusted him.

They left the reception area, stepping through the entrance doors of TCC, into the warm, stone interior of the main building. It stretched out to their left—housing shops, vendor carts, an elegant bakery, and a small café. The gray stone floor and the narrow, cozy ambience always made Gretchen think of a medieval castle. At this time of day, the sugary aroma of doughnuts and pastries seeped through the walls of the bakery. Adjacent to it was an espresso place.

They walked together in silence as Gretchen's mind softly warned her: *Don't get invested. Don't get excited. Focus on your career. Infatuation is pointless right now. And please, for the love of all common sense, don't get involved with a relative of the biggest celebrity at TCC.* You'd think this kind of incessant prattle would have some effect, but Gretchen just shooed it all away and led the way to the espresso place.

As he followed her, Rick eyed Gretchen's butt; it was round and curvy. Her hips swung from side to side when she walked—with purpose, with the kind of feminine sexuality that could bring him to his knees. Damn, he'd love to get his hands under that dress. Run them up her legs inside her panties . . . inside *her* . . .

She was wearing a simple black dress today—one that showed every curve of her body without actually being tight. As his eyes devoured her body, he had to jerk himself out of his trance and remind himself what she was really after.

When he'd come to see her today, he knew she'd eventually cave and go with him. He hadn't even had to mention Brett's name; it was this silent thing between them, the thing that would urge her on. Once they grabbed a table, Rick asked her what she wanted to drink.

"Um . . . an eggnog latte with skim milk. Please."

"You got it," he said, eyes sparkling, flashing her a smile before heading to the counter. Moments later, he returned. "So how did you get interested in cooking?" he asked, setting her latte down in front of her, then taking a seat. At this time of day, sun streamed through the tall wall of windows that expanded across one whole side of the food court.

"I started when I was younger," she replied. "In junior high, maybe. High school. I was bored a lot, I guess. Then I discovered this cooking show that I loved. The woman on it, I don't even remember her name now, was like a goddess. She was so cool, and she'd have her family come on the show, too. Her kids, and . . . I just wanted her life," she finished with a little laugh.

Studying her, Rick waited for her to continue. When she didn't, he said, "And?"

"And then I became a chef, and when I found out about the opportunity to work for the Cooking Channel, I couldn't pass it up. Not that I thought I'd get it, but here I am."

"How do you like it so far?" he asked, restlessly rotating his cup in his hands.

"I love it," she said on a sigh. "I mean, it can be extremely stressful, but mostly it's good. No, it's fascinating, honestly. I'm learning a lot. It's a whole new career path. God, I sound like one of those commercials for Barbizon," she said, just realizing.

He laughed. "Wow, now that takes me back."

Giggling, she said, "Yeah."

Still grinning at her, he raised his coffee to his lips. "So can you make key lime pie?" he asked.

She blinked at him. "Of course. Why?"

"That's my favorite."

"Dessert?"

"Meal," he said, and she laughed.

"Well, sure, I make killer key lime pie," Gretchen said, smiling. "It's actually really easy—like cheesecake."

Rick's eyes widened. "You can make cheesecake?" he said, sounding genuinely impressed.

Giggling, she said, "Yes, I'm a chef, jeez. Hey, you know what *else* I can do? I can make key lime cheesecake—can you handle it?"

He slapped his hand to his heart dramatically and dropped his mouth open in awe. "Wow," he said, smiling and shaking his head. "Jesus, I'm not sure."

Gretchen took a sip of her eggnog latte and felt its warmth and its sweet spice complement the moment. There was a certain easiness about Rick right now that made her want to smile.

"So how is working for Susanna Tate?" he asked casually.

Before Gretchen could answer his question, a girl appeared in front of their table; she had short brown hair and a doughy face. She looked vaguely familiar, and then Rick realized that he'd first seen her at Brett's party. "Hey, Gretchen," she said, smiling. Then she eyed Rick shyly, but didn't say anything to him.

"Oh, hi, Cady," Gretchen said brightly. "Have you met Brett's brother, Rick?"

"No, I haven't. Hi there."

"Hey, how are you doing?" he said, reaching out to shake her hand.

"Cady's the star of *Sinful Temptations*," Gretchen said by way of explanation.

"Right," he said, nodding amicably, even though he wished like hell she hadn't interrupted when he'd just been about to dig for information about Susanna. "Good show."

"I recognize you from Brett's party last weekend," she said, pushing a clump of her short hair behind her ears, but it flopped right back to almost instantly. "Um, you and Brett kind of look alike," she added, again fiddling with the hair that framed her face. Rick noticed that she wasn't making full eye contact with him, like she was nervous or something—Jesus, why did he make women nervous? He was a nice guy most of the time . . .

"Well, I saw you through the window, so I thought I'd come over and say hello. What are you guys talking about?" Cady asked eagerly, looking at Gretchen. Rick felt like saying, *Nothing—yet*.

"Just chatting," Gretchen replied.

"Mind if I join you?" she said, looking hopeful.

"Oh . . ." Gretchen fumbled. "No, not at all."

Rick concealed his irritation and held back an eye roll. Christ. There went his opportunity. He couldn't work Gretchen with an audience there. He wasn't going to take a chance that Cady would pick up on his curiosity about Susanna Tate, or suspect that he had any kind of agenda.

Hell, for all he knew, Cady could be the homicidal maniac he was looking for—but one suspect at a time.

They finished their coffees while Rick made small talk with both Cady and Gretchen. He tried subtly to find out what Cady thought of his brother, but he couldn't get a real sense. Every answer she gave him was generic. He tried even more subtly to find out about her personal life, but it seemed she didn't have one. (Given the motherly wardrobe and the monk hair Rick wasn't particularly floored.)

She'd mentioned something about a how she'd planned to be a nurse and even studied nursing in college, but then life had taken a turn and she'd become a chef instead. Apparently medicine was still her passion. Rick was struck by how bashful Cady seemed to be for someone who was on TV every day—maybe she was confident only when she was cooking?

When they got up to go, Rick managed to trail behind Cady enough to get Gretchen to fall in line with him. Touching her back, he got her attention. They both stopped in the middle of the food court; she turned and looked up at him. "Alone at last," he said, grinning.

She blushed, averted her eyes for just a second. "I should get back to work now," she said, sounding a little disappointed. "Susanna will wonder where I am. Plus, I need to go over some stuff with the choppers—that's the crew who cleans and cuts the food: dices, minces, you know, whatever to have it ready to use when Susanna tapes. But I don't want to give you too much excitement in one conversation, so I'll stop now."

Rick's grin spread into a smile; opportunist or not, she was damn adorable at times. "Would it be okay if I gave you a call sometime?" he asked. "Maybe we could grab dinner."

It didn't surprise him when she said yes. He was waiting for her usual "let's invite Brett" clause, or its equivalent, but she didn't dare. Rick supposed she was trying to play it a little cooler from now on. "Okay," she said with a trace of a smile. "That sounds fun."

Yes, it did. He didn't want it to, but it did.

CHAPTER NINETEEN

*R*ushing from work, Gretchen nearly slid on sleet three times, but eventually made it unscathed to June Bug's on Tenth Street. A red-upholstered restaurant with a muted glow and a wooden bar that wrapped around half the room, June Bug's was a cozy, warm reprieve from the cold. It was about halfway between TCC and Medieval Faire, which was why Dana had picked it.

"What's up?" Gretchen said on a breath as she approached the bar. "Sorry I'm late!"

"No problem. I got fired today," Dana said bluntly, then pulled out the stool beside her.

"What?"

"Fired," Dana repeated. "Canned, axed, dusted, call me soup-line girl."

"Okay. First of all, forget the soup lines," Gretchen said, putting her hand supportively on her cousin's shoulder, feeling a hint of sharp bone beneath her billowy faux-Medieval blouse. "I'll *make* you soup—anytime you want. Clam chowder, too."

"Really?" Dana said, perking up slightly. "Clam chowder? Manhattan or New England?"

"Whatever you want. And turkey chili, too," Gretchen said, offering another one of Dana's favorite comfort foods.

"And blondies with macadamia nuts?" Dana pressed. "And lobster thermidore?"

"Don't get greedy," Gretchen said, twisting her mouth into a wry smirk. "And you've never had lobster thermidore, so don't even." Grudgingly, Dana tried to smile, but it was halfhearted. Her elbow was resting on the bar, and the drink in front of her was barely touched. As she slumped her chin into her palm, Gretchen said, "Now, what happened?"

Shrugging, Dana straightened and said, "It's like this: some BS story about how I'm late too much and how I cut out too early, and I'm supposedly not"—mockingly, she made quotation marks with her fingers—" 'responsible.' Please! Don't they understand that of course I'd be more responsible if I didn't need to take into account auditions and casting calls and trying to have a real life?" She heaved a sigh. "The final straw was when I came late today."

"Oh, did Al go crazy?" Gretchen said sympathetically.

"What do you mean *go*?" Dana said with a look of disgust. Then she picked up her drink and took a big gulp. She'd never specifically said that she'd gotten passed up for that soap role, but Gretchen supposed it had been implied in the silences.

Once Dana set it down on the bar with a thud, she seemed to have found a new resolve. "Well, what can you do? These things happen," she declared. "It was just a job. It's not like this was my lifelong dream or something. It's not like when I was little I pictured myself serving 'wild boar'—also known as pork chops, by the way—to a bunch of tourists still hung up on the Middle Ages. And I'm *sorry*," she added, pressing a hand to her chest dramatically, "that I was unable to make the patrons feel 'transported in time.' " She was clearly quoting her boss, Al, here—though the nauseated grimace was distinctly Dana's. "What a failure I am as a human being. Really, I am so sorry. I failed as a 'serving wench.' I am just so. Fucking. Sorry."

"You definitely *sound* sorry," Gretchen said calmly, and finally Dana broke. Covering her face with her hands, she started to laugh. Supportively, Gretchen put her arm around her cousin's shoulder. "But like said, it was just a job, and not one you even liked." She gave her a gentle squeeze. "We'll just have find you a new job—a better one. Okay? I'll help you."

"How?" Dana mumbled, raising her eyebrows curiously—and then her eyes lit up and she smiled. "Oh, wait, you mean you'll get me hired as Romeo Ramero's personal masseuse? Something in that vein? Oh, thank you, G! Thank you!"

"Nice try. No, what I mean is I'll help you with your résumé and cover letters."

"Oh," Dana said, a little deflated.

"And I said *help*—not write them for you."

"Ohh."

Now she really sounded depressed. "Fine, I'll do *some* of the writing," Gretchen said, which cheered Dana right up. "And I'll circle ads in the paper if you want."

"Okay, thanks! Oh and I'll take care of the whole surfing-the-Internet portion."

"I had a feeling."

Smiling, Dana suggested some possible new jobs. "What about something exciting—like maybe a bank teller?"

Confused, Gretchen scrunched her face. "Since when is being a bank teller exciting?"

"You know, like when they uncover all those embezzlement schemes and stuff. 'Well, Mrs. Winston, we see you've withdrawn ten million dollars here—problem is, the account had only a thousand.' That kind of thing." Smiling feebly, Gretchen didn't know whether to laugh or humor her. "Or, no! Even *better,*" Dana said, eyes widening. "I could be a private eye like Davin," Dana said, referring to her older brother, who lived in Chicago and was always less than forthright about the kinds of cases he worked on. But Davin had always been the opposite of his sister in the discretion department. Gretchen remembered even when they were growing up, Davin was one of those people who measured his words; you never quite knew what he was thinking. For that fact alone, Gretchen couldn't picture Dana in the same line of work. "Or—oh, oh! I know—how about a professional cheerleader on those ESPN competitions?"

As if one could simply "be" that. "Well, if you're looking for job security, cheerleading might not be the field for you." But she had to give her cousin credit—she could be staggeringly optimistic, even on the cusp of dejection.

Dana mulled that one for a few seconds. "I guess you're right," she conceded. "You know what I'm thinking? As long as my acting career is floundering, I'm gonna need something with more stability and with benefits. Just to tide me over till I get that big break, you know? I think it might actually be time to do what I've tried to avoid for so long."

"You don't mean . . . ?"

"That's right," Dana said with deliberate seriousness. "Corporate America, sweetheart—the land of the cute boys with ties. Paperwork and water coolers. I think I'm finally ready."

But was *it* ready? That was the question.

It was eight o'clock that same night, after Gretchen had settled in for a night of sweats and slothdom, when her cell rang. She followed the less-than-soothing sounds of the *I Dream of Jeannie* theme song until she tracked her phone down inside her bag. "Hello?" she said, not recognizing the number.

"Gretchen." Her breath caught at the distinctively masculine voice. "It's Rick," he said—as if she didn't know.

"Hi," she said, managing to sound casual.

"Have you eaten?"

"Oh . . . actually I have," she said, thinking of the cheeseburger deluxes she and Dana had gotten at June Bug's.

Undeterred, Rick said, "Well, I know it's short notice, but any chance you'd be free for a drink later? Barring any unforeseen problems—you know, like girls with scented candles—I should be out of here by nine."

"Ha-ha," she said, grinning.

"I'll be in your neighborhood," he went on. "I'd love to see you."

It was that last part that did it. God, that voice. It just raked over her, teasing her skin and arousing her. With her pulse racing, she bit her lower lip, then agreed.

"Good. Oh and I have a set of wheels tonight, so I'll pick you up."

"Really?"

"Yeah, my neighbor's having family over tonight, so he begged me to free up my parking space for them. Well, begged me and paid me."

"Do you remember where I live?"

"Absolutely," he said. "If I forget, I'll follow the smoke."

Flirtatiously she said, "I know you *think* you're funny . . ." and Rick laughed. As anticipation fluttered in her belly, she smiled into the phone. "Just buzz me when you get here. Bye."

"Who was that?"

Startled, Gretchen jumped. Dana was standing in her open doorway, leaning against the doorjamb.

"It was Rick—that guy I told you about at dinner. He asked me out for a drink later." Then she glanced at the clock on her cell phone. Shoot, she had only an hour to get ready! Normally that would be doable, but because she was in sloth mode—which included a knot for a hairdo and a thin veneer of Clearasil—this would be trickier.

Then abruptly she realized something. "Wait, do you think I look too desperate? Just accepting at the last minute with no plans?"

"It's Monday," Dana said. "What plans are you supposed to have?"

"True. But still . . . maybe I should call him back and tell him I'm busy. That I just realized I'm booked."

"Yeah, he'll buy that," Dana said sarcastically, then made a fake phone call with her hand. "Hi, Rick? I realized I'm booked—pretending I'm busy, it's gonna take all night."

"Okay, okay," Gretchen said with a thready little laugh, her palms itching, her heart pounding, and her time slipping away.

When Rick climbed the steps of Gretchen's building, he'd had to remind himself, yet again, that he was on a mission. Helping his brother, protecting him. As serious as all that was, Rick seemed to lose his focus whenever he was around Gretchen. Christ, even their brief phone call earlier had stirred his excitement.

When he was on the job, he was always thorough, precise. But Gretchen had a way of distracting him—scattering his focus. She relaxed his guard when it needed to be up. *Pathetic,* he thought now as he knocked on her door.

When it swung open, he came face-to-face with a redhead who was smiling brightly at him. This must be her cousin. "Hi, come in," she said, ushering him in with her hand. Rick walked in, remembering the impressive place instantly. He still didn't understand how Gretchen could afford an apartment like this.

"Would you like to have a seat?" the redhead asked.

"No, thanks," he said.

"I'm Marcia. Marcia Rabe—as in broccoli? You probably don't recognize me."

Rick shook her hand and introduced himself. "Recognize you?" he said curiously.

"I know I look different in person. A little shorter, a little less blond, a little younger . . ." He just looked at her, confused. "Well, that was wasted on you," she said glibly, then crossed her arms. "So . . . you're really Romeo Ramero's brother, huh? Gretchen told me all about it."

"I'll bet she did," Rick said swiftly, grateful for the reminder that Gretchen was out for one thing—and right now so was Rick. Different agendas that both pertained to Brett.

"What's your brother's deal anyway? Is he single?"

"You'll have to excuse her."

Rick's head turned—and his mouth dropped. *Holy hell.* Arousal stirred in his groin as his eyes scanned down Gretchen's body. Her silky hair flowed over her shoulders, and her dark eyes were bright, inviting. She wore an electric blue dress that pulled tight over her full, heavy breasts and slid right over her curvy hips. His fingers itched to touch her, to run his hands over her hips and down over that round, sexy butt of hers. In an ideal world he'd go to her right now, haul her up against him, kiss her lips, lick inside her mouth, grip her hair, drive her back against the wall, grind against her, and bury his face in her breasts.

Damn it all—what was his mission again?

"Don't mind my cousin," Gretchen explained as she came closer. "She's got a huge crush on your brother. But then, who doesn't?"

Rick's gut tightened. "Yeah, it's definitely been known to happen." *Another reminder.*

When Gretchen grabbed her coat from the counter where she'd left it, Rick took it and slipped it over her shoulders. She turned back to thank him and noticed Dana giving her an ostentatious thumbs-up in the background.

Once they stepped outside, Rick said, "So Marcia's nice."

Marcia—? *Oh, Lord,* Gretchen thought, realizing but not bothering to try to explain her cousin's antics. "Yes, she is."

*   *   *

"So tell me something I don't know about you," Gretchen said when her glass of wine arrived and Rick's glass of beer was set down on the table with a clunk.

"Like what?" he said.

"I don't know . . . but this should be easy because I barely know anything about you."

"There's not much to know. I'm a pretty simple guy."

"Deceptively simple," she corrected with a smile.

With a soft laugh he asked, "What do you mean?"

She paused, squinted a little to appraise him. "I mean, ever since I met you I've been trying to figure out if you're a total enigma or just—" She stopped herself. God, what was she doing? She was at it again! Rushing into this, revealing too much of her crush on him, way too quickly. Here she'd already revealed how much she'd been thinking about him—about what was underneath his attractive but brooding surface.

She had to admit, she felt much more comfortable around Rick now. Nervous, yes, and excited, aroused, rattled . . . but at the same time, she felt like she could be herself more. Now that everything had been laid out between them, and Rick had said flat out that he wanted to get to know her, it really seemed to take the edge off their interactions.

She'd never felt one hundred percent herself with Tristan, but it really hadn't been his fault. At twenty-four, when she'd met him, Gretchen had still been getting to know herself in some ways. As time went on, it became apparent that she and Tristan weren't exactly drowning in common interests. Sure, he'd try to engage her in the age-old debate between burning fat and building mass, but it never really took off. And Gretchen was far from blameless. There had never been the deep connection with Tristan that she'd wanted there to be, but she hadn't figured it out—or hadn't let herself see it—until after she'd imagined herself in love with him and contrived him as "the one."

Eh. Whatever. Live and learn. Besides, who wanted to think about Tristan when Rick Pellucci was sitting right there?

"An enigma or a what?" he said now, expecting her to fill in the latter part of her sentence. Leaning back in his chair, he crossed his arms over his chest, looking expectant.

"Oh. Um. An enigma or a . . . straight shooter," she said, then immediately wished she hadn't. What a dorky save! Best to move on, so she leaned forward, resting the flat of her arms on the tabletop. "You and Brett seem so different," she remarked, tilting her head to study his face.

"We're definitely different," Rick said. When he didn't elaborate, Gretchen pressed for more. He shrugged. "Well, growing up he always took more interest in the family business . . ."

"Your dad's restaurant," Gretchen supplied.

"Yeah," he said, with a momentary look of surprise that she'd remembered that detail.

"What, you weren't interested in the restaurant? I mean, because you don't like to cook?"

"No, it wasn't that. I don't know. It just didn't do it for me," he said, slouching casually in his seat. "But I was a real punk as a kid. I was always getting into trouble—probably the last thing on my mind was working in the restaurant."

"Trouble?" she said curiously.

Again he shrugged. "Stupid stuff—fights, suspension, you know."

"Not really," she said, recalling what a good girl she was in the technical sense (but then, quiet, nonsmoking loners often were).

"I was definitely a punk," was all Rick said.

"You, really?" she said, eyes widening in surprise, though she didn't know why it should surprise her. He did have that kind of aloof I-shrug-all-authority-except-my-own way about him; his rebelliousness as a kid made sense.

"Why are you surprised?" he said, half grinning.

"I don't know . . . I guess I'm not. But you just seem so . . ." "Mellow" was the wrong word; he was way too intense to be called "mellow." "Guarded" would be a better way to describe him, but she wasn't going to say that, either. He might start to freak that she was trying to strip away his emotional male armor. (God, men were annoying with that.) So instead she said, "Reserved. Like you seemed to stay out of the fray, I guess." He was a loner of sorts, too, she realized then, which was the absolute antithesis of Brett.

Unless Brett's extroverted, outgoing nature belied a more serious, private side—one that couldn't possibly be detected through his showy veneer of charm and congeniality.

Nah . . .

"Yeah, well I'm older now—thank God," Rick said with deprecating humor, a simple kind of honesty. "There's not as much to prove. But I was always pulling sh—stunts . . . and then I ended up getting arrested when I was seventeen."

"What!" Gretchen almost knocked over her drink on that one. *Arrested?* Did he mean to tell her that she was sitting across the table from a real-life ex-con? Wow. Across the table from a felon and all she could seem to think about was slipping off her high heel and rubbing her stockinged foot between his legs, stroking his cock, making him rock hard, watching his expression change, darken, and his eyes hood with desire. (But if it wasn't broken in *Flashdance,* why fix it?)

Toying with her glass, she used her other hand to wave him on and to say, *Come on, details please.*

"Vandalism," he said by way of explanation. "It was so dumb. Me and my buddies thought it would be fucking hilarious to break into this locked-up area behind the post office—oh, forget it. Why am I telling you this?"

"Why not?" she said, afraid he'd stop when she was finally getting some more pieces to his puzzle.

He shrugged. "It's not exactly my best moment. And it was so long ago. I was just a dumb kid—really—I was dumb as hell."

"Well, how long did your rebellious period last?" she asked, realizing only after she'd said it that she sounded like a clinical social worker.

"Wait a minute now. Let's get to you. I take it by your shocked expression that you were a good girl, huh?"

There was something about the way Rick said it. Something flirtatious, suggestive. He leveled her with a smoky gaze, and she squirmed a little in her seat. Pressing her thighs together, Gretchen realized that Rick had just taken the conversation in a more sexual direction . . .

She sucked in a breath, thinking, *Yes,* because she'd definitely love to go there with him. It was well past time for both of them to be blatantly coming on to each other. (Meanwhile, she'd never realized she was this impatient, this savage, this ready to go to bed with a man she barely knew, but at this point she was sort of rolling with it.)

Struggling to keep a smile back, she took a sip of wine, let it slide warmly down her throat and burn soothingly in her chest.

"Well?" he said, pressing her with his low, rough voice and melting her bones with his blue gaze.

"Yes, I guess so" was all Gretchen could say on the good-girl topic. Well, sure, she wanted to keep flirting, but telling him about her puny sexual history wasn't exactly what she had in mind. She leaned across the table and touched his hand as though it were a casual gesture, but when his eyes dropped down to it, she knew he felt the thrum of heat between them, too. "So don't skirt around it," she said. "Come on, finish your story."

"What story was that again?" he said. With his free hand, he took a drink.

"The story of you," Gretchen said with a smile.

He looked at her for a few long moments; he seemed to be studying her in that maddening but thrilling way. What was he thinking? And what did he think about *her?*

"Okay, so let's see . . . the story of me . . . Growing up I—well I already told you—I was a punk. I thought I knew so much, but actually I didn't know shit—I mean, spit."

She giggled at that, and said, "It's okay, really. I grew up in Connecticut, not Walnut Grove."

"Okay. Sorry. Still, I'm gonna try to clean myself up around you."

"So you were the troublemaker type in high school?" she said. "I would've thought you were more the football player type."

With a faint smile, Rick shook his head. "Not at all."

"So go on."

"Anyway," he continued, "I used to fight with my old man a lot—all the time. He never thought I had my head on straight—especially after I got out of jail. I still had this big smart-ass attitude. Here I was, two months shy of my eighteenth birthday and my dad's wondering, what the hell's this kid gonna do with himself?"

That's right, jail, how could Gretchen have lost that thread a minute ago? Maybe she was drinking her wine too fast, or maybe she should've gone with Merlot instead of Shiraz. "How long were you in jail?" she asked now, suddenly getting a little wary of the idea. (Boy, her trip to the dark side hadn't lasted long, had it? But the thing was: The idea of Rick getting arrested *was* kind of sexy, but picturing the day-to-day realities of him in the orange jumpsuit . . . well . . . not so sexy.)

"It was the longest ten hours of my life," he said, and she let out a breath of relief. "Looking back, he should've let me sit there for at least another day," Rick added with a dry laugh.

She gave his hand a gentle squeeze before sliding her fingers back onto the table. He watched her hand the whole time, then looked right into her eyes like they both knew what was happening between them even if they weren't saying it.

"Well, that's not so bad," she said softly, referring to the ten hours, but not really thinking of much beyond the heat from their touch that still lingered. She licked her lips as she instinctively studied his mouth.

"Yeah . . ." he said, leaning forward and sliding his hand onto hers. Her breath hitched in her throat as hot shivers rolled through her lower body, pooling damply between her legs. Could she want him more? She could barely even concentrate on the rest of his story, she was so focused on rising, reaching across the table, pulling him forward by the back of his neck, and kissing him. "So my dad got me out," he continued, as his fingers strummed along her wrist. "There was a big fine, community service, all that shit—oh, sorry—and after that I pretty much cleaned up my act."

"How?" she asked, concentrating on the feel of his warm hand caressing her skin.

"I joined the Air Force," he said.

Her eyes widened at that. "Wow, and they scared you straight, huh?" she said.

"They got my ass in line, that's all."

"So does that mean you're a pilot?" This just kept getting hotter.

"No, actually, I was going through the police academy in there. It was something I kind of got thrown into after I joined, but it sounded good to me."

"Really? I didn't realize you could be a policeman in the Air

Force." Come to think of it, what did she really know about the Air Force or any kind of force anyway? And why was it suddenly now a completely fascinating area of interest?

"Oh, sure," he said, looking down at where they were connected, where they were still touching, and only then did Gretchen realized she'd shifted her hand so instead of lying flat on the table, it was curved into Rick's.

A little breathlessly, she cleared her throat. "So what happened?" she asked.

"I put in my four years, but by then I was burned on it."

"All that 'yes sir' stuff," she teased.

"Maybe," he said with a quirk of his lips, but she could tell he didn't mean it; he was teasing her right back.

"What did you do after you left the Air Force?"

"I went to work at a bunch of different things," Rick replied vaguely.

"Like . . . ?"

"Like driving an armored car for a while, working as a security guard for a federal bank, sh—stuff—like that," he finished with a shrug and took another drink. She had a feeling he'd had his fill of being in- terviewed about his job history. But she couldn't help it, she was curi- ous now how he'd eventually ended up doing one of the hardest jobs she could possibly imagine, fighting fires and in New York City of all places.

"So how'd you decide to be a firefighter?" she probed.

Reluctantly, he slid his hand from hers and sat back a fraction be- fore answering. "Honestly? After nine-eleven . . . I decided to do something with myself that was worth a damn." Offhandedly, he added, "It's funny. My dad used to say that one day I would piss away so many opportunities, all I'd have left is 'vague potential.' Nothing more than that. And then I'd have to figure out what the f—hell— to do with it. He was right." He tipped his glass back for a drink, then set it back down on the table.

"Well, wait then—"

"No, you wait," he said and took her hand firmly in his. This time he gave her a little tug as he leaned in closer. "How come I'm doing all the talking here?" he said, his voice a low purr. "Talking and drinking. What, are you trying to get me drunk?"

She figured it would take a lot more than a beer or two to get Rick drunk, but she just managed a smirk and said, "I thought I was going to get to know things I didn't know about you."

He let out a laugh. "That's what I've been telling you."

"I know, but I'm not done yet," she said, tilting her head at him as if to say: *I'm the boss of this conversation and isn't it cute?*

He seemed to agree, because he stuck his tongue in the inside of his cheek and appraised her with faint amusement. "Okay, but we're gonna do a new thing here. Everything you ask me, I expect you to tell me the same about yourself."

"Fine. So what are your best qualities? I'm nosy."

"Nosy, that's your best quality?"

"No! I meant . . . okay fine. Let's see, my best quality would be . . . hmm . . ."

"Should I get you another drink while you think about it?" he asked.

"No, no, I know what it is. It's gonna sound weird, but my ability to time red meat."

"Huh?" he asked, squinting at her, confused.

"You know, steaks, roast beef, filet mignon, all of it. Somehow I can always get it timed perfectly. Or that's what they told me in cooking school anyway." When he still looked skeptical, she said, "I swear, people always went on and on about it." Unfortunately the skill didn't do her much good at Deluxe Resort, where red meat was shunned even more than cheesecake. And perfectly timing a synthetic Tofurkey somehow lacked the same thrill.

He said, "So I take it you're not a vegetarian, then?"

"Oh, no! No way. I don't think you can be a chef and also be a vegetarian. No, I shouldn't say that. Of course you can," she qualified (well, she didn't want to look like a bigot on the first date). "I just can't imagine it, that's all. Probably the Italian in me . . ."

"You're Italian?" he said, raising his eyebrows, sounding intrigued.

"Part," she said. "The part with carnivorous impulses—well, you know how it is."

Raking his gaze over her, he said, "Yeah . . . I'm having some right now."

Even as she smiled, heat crawled up her neck and suffused her cheeks. She willed away her nervousness, but still her heart hammered away in her chest as her lower body ached with longing.

Rick watched her. She was only across the table, but it still was too far. He wanted her in his lap. He wanted her on top of him, wanted her underneath him, he was dying to kiss her, dying to fuck her. All the way across the table and he was as hard as a rock.

"By the way, how did you find that apartment?" he asked, absently tapping his thumb on the table. When she explained that it wasn't her place, or even her cousin's, but that it belonged to an actress named Marcia Rabe, Rick said, "Wait, I thought your cousin's name was Marcia."

"Oh, she was just impersonating Marcia. She's theatrical—don't ask," Gretchen said, holding her hand up. "Anyway, they have this arrangement worked out. Dana cleans her place, waters the plants, keeps up with the mail and the utilities, and she gets to live there for free while Marcia's away—which is all the time now that she's living in London filming a television show."

"Wow, that's a great setup," Rick said, nodding.

"Yeah, I know. I lucked in," Gretchen said. "What about you? Where do you live?" He gave her the streets, but she admitted that she still barely knew the city.

Rick found himself studying her face, and as much as he tried to get his mind back on track, Jesus, she made it hard. She was just too damn sweet, he almost had to catch his breath. Could he have been that wrong about her?

Something about the way that she was looking at him right now . . . like there was nowhere in the world she'd rather be, including with Brett himself.

"So tell me . . . California, what was that like?" he asked.

"Eh, it was okay," she said. "If you like it bright and sunny all the time."

With a scoff he said, "Hell, that sucks," and she laughed. "Did you have a boyfriend there?" he asked.

"Yes," she said, feeling the conversation might get sexual again.

"When did you guys break up?"

"About eight or nine months ago."

Rick didn't ask her anything else, but his intent gaze was enough to make her slump in her seat. Swallowing hard, Gretchen took another sip of her wine. She wondered if he was thinking the same thoughts as she.

As desire throbbed between her legs, she suddenly felt it had been way too long since she'd had sex. The wine spread heat through her chest, sent it pouring through her veins, her body felt on fire, and she could feel that her panties were getting wet. A fantasy about her and Rick in his truck, him putting his big hand down there, up her skirt, underneath her panties, and up her—

"What do you look for in a guy anyway?" he asked, but he had a cocky kind of grin when he said it, which ruled out her replying, "Got a mirror?" (The ultimate cheesy reply, no matter how true.)

Saved by the cocktail waitress. She approached the table asking if they wanted another drink. Gretchen didn't speak, but Rick seemed to read her mind; another drink and she'd be lost. As it was, it was hard enough to act civilly, casually, with the thick, choking arousal that smothered the air around them. "Just the check," he said, not taking his eyes off Gretchen. She had a feeling she was in over her head, but tonight she was going to be like Dana and act like she wasn't.

CHAPTER TWENTY

*W*ordlessly Rick drove Gretchen back to her apartment. He didn't know what to say anyway. She seemed to suck the air out of him, and the more time he spent in her company, the less plausible his own theory seemed about her using him to get to Brett. It was possible, he supposed, but she'd barely mentioned Brett all night. She'd been much more interested in learning about him, and he felt the same way about her—or would under other circumstances. Right now it was all he could do to focus on the road.

As the silence stretched on, his mind ran rampant with thoughts of sex, of sliding his cock inside her from every angle and riding her hard. Thoughts of her ripe, luscious lips closing over his dick, sucking him, taking him in as deeply as she could. *Damn.* He was hardly in a position to make idle conversation—with his cock hard and straining against his fly, anything that came out of his mouth right now would probably be dripping with innuendo.

Gretchen was quiet, too. She'd put the radio on, flipped the stations a few times, then shut it off, and now she was looking out the window. She was like a sexual magnet for him. He just wanted to reach over, squeeze her knee, run his hand up her leg . . .

No, too soon with her.

Rick slowed to a stop in front of her building. As he double-parked, Gretchen turned to him. "Okay, just one question."

"One question? You had your one question about eighty-nine questions ago."

Smiling, she said, "This'll be quick. I promise. And by the way, I never did find out your best quality, so you still owe me on that."

"Okay, okay. What?"

Unbuckling her seat belt, she turned all the way in her seat so she was facing him. She hesitated a moment before asking her question. "What did you think of me when we first met? I mean, the night you put out that fire in my apartment?"

"Oh, that's easy," Rick answered. He cut the engine and looked at her. "I thought you were a sweetheart." Not exactly the truth, but he was pretty sure he thought it now. He wanted to kiss her—hell, what was he waiting for? "Why, what'd you think of me?" he said, searching her face, always coming back to her lips.

With an almost shy grin, she inched a little closer; she seemed to be considering her answer. "I thought you were the big bad wolf," she said finally, then held up her finger. "Only bigger—and not so bad."

He kept looking at her, noticing the way her mouth opened slightly, the way she took in a breath and held it before biting her lip and releasing it. Almost imperceptibly, he moved closer. "One more question," she said softly.

"No more questions," he said.

"Wait, just one more. I promise." He waited, his eyes flickering over her mouth, and she said, "Why were you so mean to me at Brett's party last weekend?"

"Ah, hell," he murmured, reaching for her just as Gretchen leaned over, pulled on his shoulders, and kissed him.

Her lips landed too hard at first, almost smashing his, but he pulled back enough to give them each a breath, and in the next second, their mouths folded into each other. The kiss picked up heat instantly. He wrapped his arms around her and nearly crushed her chest to his, and when their lips parted for just a second, she heard her own soft, breathy pants and tried to get her bearings. Rick took her chin in his hand and slanted his open mouth on hers again. Even deeper than before, his scalding-hot tongue aroused her beyond belief. Clinging to his shoulders, Gretchen hung on tight as the electric sensations reached a fever pitch, and she moaned and dug her fingers into the fabric of his coat.

When they finally pulled apart, Rick's breathing was ragged, and Gretchen was still dazed, bleary-eyed, panting, her lips open and wet. Tipping her head down for a moment, she tried to think of something to say. But her mind drew a blank. Reaching inside Rick's open coat, she rubbed the solid wall of his chest, feeling the muscled strength beneath his sweater.

"Wow . . . you're a *really* good kisser," she blurted (and couldn't help thinking that she'd just uncovered his best quality, after all).

Grinning, he said, "Thank you," and his voice was low and evocative and masculine enough to make her want to collapse against him. But if she leaned in for more, she wasn't gonna be pulling back for a while.

"Um . . ." She licked her lips, glanced down at his shirt collar, trying to get her mind back. Then she looked back up into his face, at one shaft of light cutting across it. "Maybe we could go out again sometime . . ." she said, and it came out more like a question.

Rick pulled her even closer, holding her snugly at the waist. "You had me at Italian carnivore," he joked softly, and she could feel his breath on her lips.

A laugh bubbled out of her, and then swiftly, he ran his hand behind her neck and pulled her closer, taking her mouth again in a carnal, hungry kiss that sent hot ripples of pleasure down between her legs.

"Mmm . . ." she moaned, clutching his coat again, surrendering to the kiss, melding her mouth with his, climbing up and leaning over. She set her right knee on Rick's seat, right between his thighs. Greedily, she slid her body down until she was pressed firmly against him. He groaned with raw arousal as she rode his thigh and slid her tongue in and out of his mouth.

Rick gripped her hair and slid his other hand to her butt, balling up a fistful of her dress, dragging it up, and then, abruptly, he broke the kiss.

His breathing was ragged. With hooded eyes, he spoke huskily. "I think we'd better stop." He sounded as frustrated about it as she felt.

But of course he was right. It was getting out of control, fast. Where could it go right now with Rick double-parked and Gretchen, flustered and reckless but on her way inside?

Wow, talk about straying from her no-kissing-on-the-first-date rule! Ridiculous! But in her defense . . . he was *really* good.

They said good-bye and once Gretchen was safely inside her building, she peeked through the narrow window beside the front door to watch Rick's car go, then smiled to herself.

This isn't going well.

Rick's thought exactly before he'd spoken to Brett the following day. Christ, when he thought back to his date with Gretchen—screw mission; it had turned into a date the minute he'd seen her in that blue dress—and how he hadn't bothered to find out one damn thing about Susanna Tate. Where was his head?

If only he'd thought to ask Gretchen one question remotely relevant to the case last night. Where was his focus? It didn't take much for him to still feel her fingers clinging to his shirt, then his collar, the warmth of them seeping into his neck, those thready little moans she'd made when she was kissing him back.

Expelling a frustrated sigh, Rick rubbed his eyes; shit, he needed to get on track.

Rick's guilt was moderately appeased when he called his brother. Brett was in great spirits. Still no new threats, which was good . . . but at the same time seemed bizarre since, presumably, the killer had missed his target. But apparently things had been quiet for Brett since his agent's death, and his new bodyguard helped to ease his mind.

Still, why wasn't Brett more worried? In general, he wasn't exactly a brave guy. On the other hand, he *was* a charmed guy. Things had a way of working out for him, so maybe he figured this would, too.

"Dude, I *am* worried," Brett insisted when Rick asked him about it over the phone. "Would I have hired Epau if I wasn't? I've got him with me all the time, and his boys are downstairs watching the lobby and the elevators. I feel safe with them."

"Who are Epau's boys?" Rick asked.

"His cousins from Hawaii or something. I didn't catch the details. But they're all huge."

"Well, that's good. Someone's most likely still trying to kill you; remember that."

"Jesus! What are you trying to do, freak me out just when I tell you I'm feeling better about everything?" Brett whined.

"You'll feel better when you go to the police," Rick stated bluntly. "The longer you wait, the worse it's gonna be."

"Yeah . . . I guess . . . but hey, I was thinking, if we figure out who's out to get me without having to go to the police about the whole Misty thing . . ."

"We? What are you doing?"

"What are *you* doing?"

Valid point. "Not much yet," Rick admitted. "Although . . . last night I went out with that Gretchen to see if I could find out anything."

Brett snorted. "Gretchen? Please, what could she know? She just started. Anyway, I'm sure she's too busy wiping Susanna's ass after she shits to notice much else."

"Hey," Rick said sharply, "a little respect." His tone was forceful even to his own ears.

"What? I'm insulting Susanna really, not Gretchen."

"Whatever, just don't speak about her like that. In fact, don't speak about her period. How's that?"

"Where's this coming from?" Brett said, sounding confused. "Oh, wait, did you and she . . . ?"

"No," Rick said quickly. "No, nothing like that." Rick had only *thought* about having sex with Gretchen—until they were both were sweaty, wrung dry, and could barely move—but he had yet to actually do it. "We just talked. But unfortunately, not much about the case."

"Then what *did* you talk about?" Brett asked, sounding totally bewildered as to what two people could possibly talk about that didn't involve him.

"Just our backgrounds. My life . . . I don't know, whatever, that's not the point," Rick said stopping abruptly, realizing he was zoning off the subject.

"Well, what are you telling me? You like her now or something?"

"It was a good time" was all Rick said.

"Fine, so great, you like her, she's a great girl, but right now we have bigger issues," Brett said.

"That's what I've been telling you. By the way, have you seen that woman, Kit, lately?" Rick asked, afraid of the answer.

"Nah," Brett replied, which was a relief. The less complicated his life was, the fewer people he gave access to his world, the better off he'd be. "Normally, I'm the one who calls her, but lately, I just haven't been in the mood to get together. You know, with Misty and everything . . ." He paused, then said, "So, do you still think it might be Susanna?"

"I don't know," Rick said. "I want to find out more about her and the other people who work with you, too, but you don't seem to know much about anyone else"—which kind of came with being self-absorbed—"and I can't exactly show up at your workplace asking lots of questions. Don't forget, you've already introduced me to everyone as your brother. How exactly do you expect me to crack this? You can't even name one person who might want to kill you."

"No, that's not true," Brett said. "I guess Susanna might. She's big, but not as big as she used to be. She's getting old and she knows it. Sure, she's only in her late forties, but it's like anything, you know? Old talent fears young talent."

That gave Rick pause. "What about that older guy who was at your house? The one with the cowboy hat?"

"Ray?" Brett said, then waved his hand as if Ray wasn't a person worth any consideration. "Nah, he's harmless. Besides, he's got nothing against me—*and,* from what I hear, he left New York this week."

"Left to go where? And for how long?" Rick asked curiously.

Brett shrugged. "I don't know. I just heard people saying something about him going away for a while, to Tennessee, I think—that's where he's from—but I don't know if he's moved back there or if it's just a long vacation. The point is, if he were trying to kill me, don't you think he'd stick around? Oh! Wait, I just realized! That was a great idea you had about hanging out with Gretchen. You can totally bullshit her into letting you go backstage and scope out Susanna's dressing room—"

"What else?" Rick interrupted, feeling the uncomfortable coiling of guilt in his stomach. Was lying to Gretchen about his motives, was using her, okay as long as he really did like her?

"Let me think now . . ." Brett said. "Have you considered that it's a crazy obsessed fan? A girl who thinks she's, like, in love with me? Or maybe it's a *guy* who's in love with me."

Rolling his eyes, Rick struggled to keep his tone even. "But it had to be someone at your party. You said yourself that's the only time someone could've poisoned your sauce."

"Oh, that's true. I forgot. Unless . . . maybe someone crashed the party and I just didn't notice. There were so many people there, it's possible . . ."

"But how would a fan know about the Hawaii trip? You said that was still in the works and hadn't been officially announced yet."

"Right, right," Brett mumbled.

"Also, this isn't exactly stereotypical crazy-fan behavior," Rick said, thinking about it more himself. "Or the behavior of someone who thinks they're in love with you. If someone were obsessed with you, they'd want to get your attention, to string you along longer, to make you notice her—or *him*," he threw in to appease Brett. "It just doesn't make sense. Why call you twice and send you a one-line e-mail and then nothing else after that?"

Brett paused and thought about it. "What about this possibility? Those threats were just to torment me. Whoever's behind them wanted to, I don't know, mess with my head—shake my confidence, throw me off my game. Probably planned to drag it out a lot longer, like you said, but then an opportunity came up. A chance to get rid of me instead of waiting for me to self-destruct."

Huh. Brett actually made good sense. The opportunity that had come up was Brett's party. And considering how virtually untraceable the Destroying Angel mushroom was once it destroyed its victim, it had probably seemed like a clean and perfect crime.

Rick remembered what Jay Bernbaum had said about how the Destroying Angel mushroom didn't grow in the Northeast but was accessible to anyone who was determined to get it. Misty Allbright's murderer had certainly been determined.

"By the way, since we've ruled out obsessive love as the motive," Brett said, "I don't expect you to care about this—but you said you want to know about the people I work with." Rick waited. "Cady Angle, you know that chubby chick with the dessert show? She totally wants me. And I've always wondered if she was still a virgin. Just throwing that out there."

*   *   *

Between tapings, Gretchen was on her way to Susanna's dressing room when her cell phone rang, and she was pleasantly surprised when she saw the number.

"Hi, Mom," she said when she answered it. She was starting to think with the success of their dentist mystery novel series, her parents had forgotten her entirely, that maybe at their swanky book parties when people asked how many children they had, they reflexively answered, "One—Dr. Culpepper."

"Why haven't you called me?" Gretchen blurted, which was a terrible move. Why make her mom defensive, especially when she knew exactly what she'd say?

"The phone works both ways," she said. Yup, that was it. Florence Darrow didn't buy into that whole guilt and maternal obligation thing that other mothers did.

"I know," Gretchen admitted. "It's just . . . Nothing, never mind." It was just that she'd hoped her parents would think of calling on their own now that they were all in the same time zone . . . and maybe they'd want to check on her new place, her new job, her new city. Basically, she'd wished her parents gave a damn, were more like Dana's parents. Uncle Dane, who Dana was named after, was as successful in his career as his younger brother, Wil, but he also was jovial, gregarious, and warm. Even though they moved around a lot because of Uncle Dane's job, Dana's family was very close—with Uncle Dane and Aunt Mary still the nucleus, even now with all three kids grown. Unlike Wil, Florence, and Gretchen, who were more of a cellular mutation. They were a unit, but at times it seemed like their connection was more of a technicality.

"Is something wrong?" her mom asked, sounding confused by Gretchen's silence.

"No, I just missed you guys, that's all. How's the book tour going?"

"Oh, it's crazy," she replied and went on to detail some ego-boosting incidents that had happened at Culpepper-crazy bookstores. While her mother talked, Gretchen's mind wandered. She didn't mean to do it but . . . Rick again. She kept thinking back to their date last night. How passionate he was, how warm, how wrong she'd been about him.

Like a drug, he made her crave more and more and more . . .

"Gretchen?" Oh! She snapped back into the conversation, feeling like a total hypocrite. Here she'd wanted her mother to call, and then as soon as she did, Gretchen was zoning out to fantasize about Rick. "I asked if you're enjoying your new job."

As soon as she started to tell her mom about her work, she heard clicking keys on the other end. So her mother was typing something while Gretchen was talking to her. They were both terrible at this. "Mmm-hmm," she was saying, "mmm-hmm. By the way, have you worn the new suit your father and I got for you?"

"Um, no, not yet."

"Why not?" When Gretchen hesitated for just a second, her mom said, "It's a very expensive suit, you know."

"I know. I really like it," Gretchen lied. "I'm saving it for a special occasion." Like maybe a masquerade ball where Gretchen went as a set of shoulder pads.

"Mmm-hmm. Any interesting men at work? Oh, have you met Romeo Ramero yet? He's supposed to be quite the eligible bachelor, right? I know his last cookbook was twenty-two spots higher than your father's and mine on the *USA Today* list."

"Sure, I've met him. I went to his house in the Catskills last weekend." Her mother gasped at that one, showing uncharacteristic emotion. "But actually, I went on a date last night—with his brother!" She couldn't help gushing a little.

"His brother? That sounds promising," Florence said cautiously. "What does he do?"

"He's a fireman." At that, Florence made a noise, basically the grumbling equivalent of "ick." "Actually that's how we met, it was funny—" Gretchen started to tell the story when her mother interjected.

"Wait, do you mean a volunteer fireman, as in it's something he does to help out in the community, in addition to his real career?"

"That *is* his real career," Gretchen said, feeling defensiveness surge in her chest. "This is New York City, Mom. They have a paid force." *Please, who doesn't know that?*

"Oh." There was a pause, during which Gretchen sucked in a breath and waited. "Well, where did he go to college?"

"Um . . . he didn't. He joined the Air Force instead." After a stint in jail—but why bore her with the details?

"What? No college degree?" Florence said, appalled. "Oh, forget him."

That did it. Normally Gretchen had an even temper with her parents—a simmering restraint—but her mom was pissing her off now. Yes, of course, her parents deeply valued education; Wil was a dentist and Florence was a PhD, and yes, of course, Gretchen valued it, too. But still, there was nothing remotely inferior about Rick as far as she could see.

Besides that, her mom was wrong. Gretchen couldn't forget him even if she wanted to, and she did *not* want to.

"Don't be such a snob," Gretchen argued. "He's really smart. And I like him—a lot."

"*Great.* Out of the two brothers, leave it to you to pick the one who's going nowhere," Florence muttered.

"What are you talking about? He doesn't *have* to go anywhere—*you* couldn't do his job!"

"And if he's a pilot, let me tell you, he's got a girl in every port. You'll end up being sorry in the end."

"Oh, as opposed to dating a womanizing TV star, which is always considered a good idea," Gretchen fumed. "And he's not a pilot."

"I'm not going to fight with you. Do what you want," Florence said coolly. "You will anyway."

Gretchen thought how untrue that would've been when she was growing up, when she'd tried so hard to please her parents, even tried to use cooking to impress them, to give them a reason to be excited when they got home. But now, she knew with certainty, her mother was right.

The call-waiting beeped, so Gretchen took it as her opportunity to end the call. "I've got to go, Mom. I'll call you next week or something."

When she clicked over, her breath caught at the sound of her name. "Gretchen."

"Hi," she said, smiling into the phone.

"Hey," Rick said. "I can't talk long, but any chance you're free later?"

"For what?"

"For whatever."

"Okay, why don't you come over," she said. Somewhere in the back of her mind, she warned herself not to make the same mistakes she'd made with the various guys she'd liked in the past. *Don't be so available. Play the game; act aloof.* But, for better or worse, her instincts won out. "How's nine o'clock?"

"Good. You're probably getting sick of me by now, huh?" he added lightly.

"Extremely," she lied. "Don't be late."

CHAPTER TWENTY-ONE

*T*hat night Dana was out with Chantal and another girl from work; Gretchen had come home to a note saying she wouldn't be back till late. Perfect—she'd have Rick over for a romantic evening.

Initially she'd been extremely tempted to make a key lime pie, which Rick had said was his favorite, but she didn't dare. She wouldn't jump in too fast this time, which was always her fatal mistake. Besides, Dana had warned her to wait at least four months before baking for a guy. According to Dana, guys had to earn that kind of gesture (with affection, consideration, devotion, take your pick), or they'd simply take it for granted. Gretchen had to agree—it was only logical. Anything in the cake, cookie, or brownie vein this early in the game reeked of desperation. After all, she barely knew Rick; he could still turn out to be a jerk.

The stage was set for tonight. Thanks to Dana's housekeeping, the apartment was clean—though Gretchen couldn't say the same for her mind, filled with explicit thoughts of sweat and nakedness and Rick, of course.

He hated feeling guilty. Right now that, more than anything, was why he needed to see Gretchen. He felt shitty having gone into this thing with the intention of using her for information, of playing with her, because he'd cast her as some shallow opportunist.

When she opened the door, a warm smile broke across her face. She wore a dark red sweater that dipped low, teasingly close to her line of cleavage. Her cheeks were bright and flushed pink, and all he wanted to do was grab her and hug her. And then pull the sweater off.

"Come in," she said, leading him in, and he handed her a bottle of wine; as she walked to the counter to set it down, Rick watched her move, that sexy swing of her hips. When she turned around to face him, he was still all the way across the room, so she urged him closer. "I'll take your coat," she said.

"No, that's okay," he said, feeling a little on edge. He wanted to clear the air with her and get it out of the way. Maybe it was dumb as hell, but the truth was, he trusted her.

"Want something to eat?" she asked, walking closer, and he crossed the room, coming closer, too, but carefully. "I have some homemade sourdough bread," she said, motioning toward the plate she'd set out, "and crab dip baking in the oven. It's almost ready." (Okay, technically she *had* baked but it didn't count against the four-month rule because this was real food, and hey, *she* had to eat.)

"No, no, that's okay. I mean, it sounds great. I'll get to it, but uh . . ." He looked around, his chest tight. He wanted to get this over with, but it was tough with her looking at him like that. Blinking sweetly, innocently, openly . . . "Listen, there's something I wanna tell you."

"What?" she said, still smiling at him. Then she sat down on the couch and patted the cushion next to her for him to join her. He knew if he sat there he might forget his purpose again and fall under her spell, get pulled to her like a magnet, led by his dick, by the sensual lure of her scent. She smelled like apple pie or something. He couldn't put his finger on it, but it was her skin, it was *her*. Christ, it was the way she was looking at him.

When he didn't sit right away, when he faltered, her expression did, too. She got this crease in her forehead and he could tell she was about to ask what was wrong.

"Look, the truth is . . ." he began, and went on to tell her about his real motive for asking her out and for taking her for coffee. How his brother was supposed to die, not his agent, how whoever was responsible most likely worked for TCC and was still out there, hating Brett. How Brett wouldn't go to the police because he was too chickenshit (Rick had paraphrased that), and how he'd asked Rick to help him sort it out.

Rick left out the part about Brett's sexual relationship with
Misty. He did trust Gretchen, but still . . . she didn't need to know
that, and no matter what, he was still protective of Brett.

He couldn't believe he trusted her as much as he did, because he
didn't trust people easily, but there it was.

When he finished, Gretchen let out a breath and sat back against
the couch. Now he sat down beside her, shrugging off his coat, but
sitting forward with his hands resting on his knees. "So you really
think Brett's in danger? That someone from work would want
him . . . *dead*? *Wow.* And Misty . . . murdered." She shuddered. "I
can't believe it. Susanna told me that Misty's death had been ruled a
mystery. Or whatever they call it when the medical examiners can't
figure out what caused it and the police have got a thousand other
cases that require their attention, so they close this one for the time
being or at least put it on the shelf."

"How does Susanna know all this?" Rick asked speculatively.

Gretchen shrugged. "She's a gossipmonger. It's like a way of life.
You'd be surprised what she knows about people. Anyway, it seems
like people at work have just moved on from what happened. Like
Misty died from some bizarre illness that no one even understands,
but once that fact sank in, everyone who worked with her just went
back to business. Like, 'Okay, she's gone. Show's over; nothing to see
here.' It's kind of sad how people can do that," she added wistfully,
more to herself. "But now you're telling me that it wasn't even a
bizarre illness—it was *poison*? And that it could be someone from the
network. Wow." With another shiver, she let the notion settle in her
mind.

Rick touched her knee, letting his hand rest firmly on it, soaking
up the heat from her leg into his palm. "I just thought if I got closer
to you maybe you could be my in—you know, my access to the people at the network." Chewing her lip, Gretchen looked thoroughly
distressed by what he was saying to her. He gave her knee a squeeze,
and added, "But now . . . I like you."

After a pause, she covered his hand on her knee with her own.
Automatically they threaded their fingers together.

"Wait," she said, looking wide-eyed at him, "you said you
wanted to get close to me so you could—omigod, do you suspect Su-

sanna?" He hesitated and she said, "That's it, isn't it?" She tightened her hold on his hand. "You can trust me."

"It crossed my mind," he admitted.

"Rick, no. I can't see that. Susanna's neurotic, yes, but she wouldn't kill anyone. And why hurt Brett? She's been dying to guest star on his show—oh."

"What?"

Waving her hand, she said, "No, it's nothing. Just that I think the reason she's dying to be on his show is because of his ratings. She's at a point in her career where she's not the top dog—"

"And Brett is."

"Yeah. But I still can't see it."

"Well, were you with her all weekend at Brett's place?" Rick asked. "Was there any point at which she could've slipped away and planted the poison?"

Gretchen shrugged. "Sure, I guess. But we didn't even stay the weekend. Susanna wanted to get home on Saturday afternoon. She was rushing us all home, actually, because apparently her husband, Ed, was getting back early from his business trip and she wanted to see him."

Rick mulled that for a moment. Then Gretchen told him that Brett should just go to the police and Rick said he agreed; she told him that *he* should just go if Brett wouldn't, and Rick said he couldn't sell out his brother like that.

"You're so brave to try to protect him the way you have."

Rick was too struck by her words to smile, to respond even. He just looked down at their interlocked hands and ran his thumb over her soft skin. "So you only asked me out to get information, huh?" she said softly. "What a shame. I thought you liked me; I thought you might want to get down and dirty with me. But that's okay, we can just be friends."

His eyes shot up to hers, and she was suppressing a smile. "Like hell," he said gruffly and brought his other hand up to run behind her neck. Just as he pulled her to him for a kiss, a loud beep from inside his coat pocket startled both of them and blew the moment.

It was his cell phone/pager. "Shit, that's the firehouse. Hold on." He stood and reached inside his jacket pocket, which was on the chair. "Yeah," he said into the phone, then two seconds later, "Okay, I'm heading over."

"What's wrong?" Gretchen said, coming to her feet. "Is everything okay?"

"I'm sorry—there's a four-alarm on Songtree. They need extra hands," he said, setting his phone on the table and shrugging on his coat. "I gotta go."

"Songtree, what's that?"

"A street," he said, "in Harlem."

Gulp. Call her sheltered, but so far what she'd heard about Harlem hadn't been particularly warm and fuzzy. Worry prickled through her as Rick leaned down to give her a quick kiss. "I'm gonna stop by the station and grab my shit. I'll call you later, though," he said hurriedly, and headed toward the door.

"Okay . . . but please call me," she said her voice wobbly with concern, and Rick looked back at her.

"Don't worry. I'll be fine," he said swiftly. "And save the food for me. I'll have it next time. I'm really sorry about tonight."

"It's okay, but . . . will you be back?"

"No, I don't want you to wait. I don't know how long this'll take. Lock this behind me," he added before he left. It was only when she plopped back down on the couch that she realized he'd left his cell phone there.

About an hour after Rick left, Dana called Gretchen to say she wouldn't be home that night but would just crash at Chantal's place. Apparently she, Chantal, and Lolly were still waiting to get seated at Bonsai, and the longer the wait dragged on, the more resolved Dana became to, quote, never say die.

Calling from the loud waiting area of the restaurant, Dana had to compete with the din of the background noise. "So he just left?" she said after Gretchen recapped her encounter with Rick.

"Yes, he had to," Gretchen replied as she shimmied out of her tight black pants and pulled a nightgown from her drawer. Too keyed up to sleep, she was going to slip under a mountainous heap of covers and finally catch up on some reading. She had three novels to choose from, which had been lying in wait since she'd moved. "He left his cell phone here, though," she added, then dropped the phone for just a moment to whip off her sweater and bra and throw on her nightie.

When she snatched the phone off the bed, she realized her cousin was talking.

"Wait, what did you say?" Gretchen asked.

"I said, 'left his cell phone there? That changes everything.' He'll have to come back and get it, right?"

"I doubt he'll come back tonight for it. He told me not to wait for him."

"I think he'll be back," Dana said.

After she got off the phone, a shiver rippled over Gretchen's flesh. Cold in her slinky nightgown, she peeled back her covers, but just as she was about to slip into bed, she had a thought. What if Dana was right? What if Rick *did* come back for his phone tonight?

Hmm . . .

Wouldn't Gretchen like to be ready when he did?

So she hit the bathroom, did a quick freshening—spritzed some perfume between her breasts, rubbed lotion all the way up her legs, across her belly, and down her arms, did a second toothbrushing, then donned some black-cherry lip balm to give her mouth a dark pink glow. Then she tossed her head down, spilling her hair over her head, shaking it loose from its loopy bun. When she flew back up, her hair tumbled down wildly over her shoulders. Still wavy from her bun, it looked chaotic and tousled. Hopefully sexy.

She double-checked the nightgown. It was a long, form-fitting, navy blue silk gown with a lacy bodice. This should work. Next she went to Dana's room, searching for some scented candles.

Nearly two hours later, she'd given up hope. The candles she'd placed all around the living room and along the kitchen counter were burned down like melted mounds of plastic caving in on themselves, flickering rather than flaming.

Just as she was climbing off the couch with a tired sigh to blow out the candles, there was a knock on the door. Her heart jumped. Could it be him? Darting to the door, she looked through the peephole and just like that, her pulse kicked up and her palms began to sweat.

*   *   *

The door swung open more quickly than Rick expected. He figured Gretchen would be dead asleep by now. She seemed to be awake, though the apartment was dark. And she was barely dressed, he happened to notice.

"Hi, I'm sorry to come so late," he said, keeping his voice low.

"Come in," she said, pulling him in. He had to pry his eyes off her immediately because he didn't think she'd appreciate if he yanked her nightgown right down, which was basically what he felt like doing. As soon as he stepped in, he noticed she had candles lit all over the place. The apartment reeked like too much pudding or something. "What is this?" he joked, going to the coffee table where he'd left his phone. "I thought I'd catch you asleep, not having a séance."

The cell wasn't there, so he glanced around the area. "Sorry to get you out of bed, but I left my phone here," he explained, as he looked behind the throw pillows on the couch. Then he felt between the cushions. "And I knew I'd need it early tomorrow. By the way," he added, turning and roving his eyes around the room, to all those mounds of melting wax. "I'd tell you this is a fire hazard, but I wouldn't wanna look like I was showing off."

Gretchen didn't laugh or even smile at that.

Hmm. Was she pissed at him for coming over without calling? She was still standing about ten feet away from him, her mouth was curved into a small O, her expression unreadable.

Even in the dim glow of the candles, goddamn, she was hot in that nightgown. Her long, dark hair was floating over her shoulders, with one wisp veering off, half covering her right eye.

As if reading his mind, she blew it back—and just looked at him.

Still trying to brighten her mood, get some kind of friendly reaction, he sniffed the air. "Man, those candles are pretty strong, huh? Is this like one of those girlie incense rituals, or do you just polish your furniture with vanilla extract?"

No reaction. Jesus, he was only teasing.

As he headed over to the kitchen counter, she slowly walked closer, following him from a distance of a few feet. "Damn, I can't figure out where I left that thing . . ." Rick was muttering, as

Gretchen just stared at him, her blood boiling, irrational as it might have been. Here she'd set the scene for romance, and then not only does he come back, he doesn't even get it. He'd barely even noticed her nightgown! He'd even made fun of her candles!

She felt like an idiot—hurt and undesirable. Irritably, and silently, she went from candle to candle, blowing each out with a quick, sharp puff.

"Hey, you don't have to blow them out on my account," Rick said. Casting her eyes off to the side, she muttered something indecipherable. "What?"

"Forget it."

"Well . . . do you want me to turn on the lights?"

"No, really, it's fine," she replied tightly, partly wanting to cry.

"What, you're just gonna stand here in the dark?" he said with a laugh and came over to her. Wordlessly, she grabbed his phone off the shelf she'd set it on earlier. "Here," she said, and slapped it into his palm.

"Oh, there it is, thanks," he said, looking at the phone, then looking up at her questioningly. "Is something wrong?"

"No. Not at all."

"Well, you seem kinda testy. Are you pissed at me 'cause I woke you up?"

"I wasn't asleep," she said with a touch of exasperation. Granted she'd forgotten to put on the sexy music, but did she need to draw him a road map? Couldn't he at least have kissed her when he'd come through the door?

"Well, that's good. At least you didn't fall asleep with all the candles going again. We wouldn't want a replay of that," he said, grinning.

Rolling her eyes, she slapped her hands on her sides and blurted, "For God's sake! I was trying to seduce you, you jerk!"

Rick's face darkened, going from playful to serious in less than a second, and in one step, he bridged the gap between them.

Then he was right there, barely an inch away, and up this close, Gretchen could feel the heat of his body, feel his strength. He towered over her, nearly a foot taller than she was in her bare feet. Her eyes traveled up his chest, his neck, to his face, and even in the darkness, she could see the naked arousal in his gaze. There was blatant, carnal desire in the way his eyes devoured her.

She swallowed a gulp as her heart pounded in her ears, her breath coming up shorter. Instinctively she rose on her feet, just barely resisting the urge to slide into him, to fall into him, to drag them both down to the floor in a heap.

Wordlessly, Rick reached up, slid his hand behind her neck, and cupped the nape, the burning heat of his palm seeping into her skin. Instinctively, her head tipped back, and he pulled her closer, lowering his mouth to hers, and just before their lips met, he said, "Why didn't you just say so?" And then he kissed her. It was warm and gentle, just lingering there, his soft lips working over hers with sensual skill, with patience, and it took only seconds for her to become frustrated with arousal, wanting more from him—needing it—and the longer it went on, the less she could take.

So she tried to take more of him, gripping her hands on the front of his jacket, trying to pull him in. But he kept her mouth at enough of a distance that he had complete control and kept their kisses breathy and soft until Gretchen was moaning in frustration, tugging hard on his coat. Her fingers crunched the fabric and then her hands peeled the coat apart.

That seemed to step things up. With a grunt, Rick tightened his hold on the back of her neck, slanted his head, and finally slid his tongue inside her mouth. Instantly her knees buckled. Kissing him back, she pushed his coat over his broad shoulders and all the way off, then heard it hit the floor. With a soft, low moan, she savored the scalding wet heat of his tongue as it snaked against hers, and she practically climbed up him—wrapping her arms around his neck, clinging to him, rubbing up against his body, trying to feel him huge and hard like she'd done the night before.

Restlessly, she dropped one hand down, reached down for him, rubbed her palm hard against his arousal, squeezed him, stroked him through his pants, made him groan.

He gripped her hair. Then he slid his other hand off her waist, down to her bottom, and squeezed her there. When she dug her nails into his shoulders, he practically growled; it was a gruff, savage sound that only drove her hunger more. He started walking her backward until finally her back hit a wall and Rick pushed into her. Pressed up against each other, she could feel him solid and thick and fully aroused. He dragged her up just enough to feel him right between her legs and then dipped his head and ran his tongue down her throat. The sensations shocked her. His steel-hard erection stabbing her tender, aching crotch, the scorching wetness between her legs, the flimsiness of her thong, Rick's mouth sucking the curve of her neck—they set her whole body on fire.

They kissed hungrily, with Rick grinding his pelvis into hers, almost hurting her but turning her on so much at the same time, and then his hand reached down low and his fingers moved to drag the nightgown up inch by inch. Gretchen could feel the coolness of air on her bare leg as it became more and more exposed. Nearly panting, she rocked her lower body against his, needing to feel more of him, needing him sliding inside her, filling her up, feeding her savage hunger. She needed him to be devastating, urgent, untamed.

Suddenly his hand was completely under her nightie, which was bunched up around her hips. He slid both palms over her near-naked bottom, squeezing it, pulling her even harder against him. She cried out as he held her butt tightly, keeping her plastered to him, and he thrust his cock against her over and over. Growling deep in his throat, he dug his way between their bodies and fingered the slim strip of silk of her underwear, running it back and forth over and over. "Oh, God . . ." she whispered, barely recognizing the cracked voice as her own. "Deeper," she urged before she could stop herself.

But he didn't go deeper. Instead, still fingering the damp fabric of her thong, he tugged on her hair again, arching her neck, and dragged his open mouth up her throat. He spoke right into her ear, his voice gruff and his breath warm. "Let's go to the bedroom," he said. "I want to touch you more . . ."

More? God, at the thought she nearly wilted to the floor, but he pulled her closer, harder, catching her before she could fall, holding her up between the wall and the strength of his body, and then, before she could process it, he scooped her up off her feet, straddling her legs around his hips, and turned to walk them from the living room to the hall.

"First room to your right," she whispered, coiling her arms

around his neck, squeezing her legs tight, practically vibrating with anticipation. He pushed the half-opened door all the way open with his foot and carried her inside. She thought he'd set her down on the bed and fall on top of her, but that wasn't what happened.

Her light was on and she briefly contemplated shutting it off but didn't get a chance to suggest it.

Instead of setting her on the bed, Rick let her slide off him with maddening slowness, forcing her to ride down his powerful body and the vee of her legs to slide against his thick, hard erection as she went. When her feet landed flat on the floor, her legs felt weak. They stood there for a few seconds, looking at each other, before Rick brought his hands up and ran a finger underneath both straps of her nightgown. Gretchen sucked in a breath and waited. Confidently he pulled the straps down over her shoulders and sent the silky nightgown sliding to the floor in one swift motion.

She gasped, standing in the lit room in just her flimsy underwear, so aroused she couldn't speak, as she watched Rick's eyes glaze over at the sight of her naked breasts. He scanned down her body with stark hunger, his chest rising and falling, the faint flare of his nostrils, the almost dangerous arousal marked on his face. "Holy Jesus," he whispered molding his hands over her breasts, shutting his eyes as if unable to help himself. Then sharply he stepped back just an inch; he whipped off his shirt and tossed it.

Her mouth dropped. He was everything she could ever dream up—powerfully built but with plenty of flesh for her to hug. No chiseled piece of cold hard slate here, but more what Dana would call the "teddy bear type." He had a tattoo high on his left arm, but she couldn't tell what it depicted. Biting her lip, she couldn't help but stare at his corded muscle and the dark hair that fanned across his chest and trailed down his stomach.

As her gaze drifted lower, she sucked in a breath when she got to the pronounced bulge in his pants. Staring at it, Gretchen licked her lips, still unable to speak, feeling the hot, soaking wetness between her legs. Rick moved forward, closed his hands over her bottom, and she ended up flat on her back.

They were on the bed now and he was on top of her. She opened her legs, spread them around him, rocked up to feel some of him, all of him. She thought she would die if she didn't get some satisfaction soon, and he was breathing hard, slid his hands up her naked belly, giving her shivers and chills before they closed over her breasts. "Oh, man . . ." he said roughly, and groaned as he massaged them, ran his thumbs over her hardened nipples. "You're so beautiful," he whispered huskily. Burying his head in the crook of her neck, he mumbled something unintelligible. It sounded like "apple," but that couldn't be right. Who could think straight at a time like this?

Gently squeezing her breasts together, Rick lowered his head, pressing his face against her cleavage. Fondling one breast while he sucked the other one deep into his mouth, he let his free hand trail lazily down her belly to her side. His fingers lingered at the edge of her thong but didn't go any farther.

Moaning, Gretchen kept rocking her pelvis, tilting her hips off the bed, and the more he aroused her, the more she scratched her nails against the smooth, hot flesh of his back, the harder she grasped his shoulders, the more she bucked her lower body against his. She wanted to run her hands over his butt, but she couldn't reach that far. He was too big, and she wanted to beg him to touch her where she needed him to touch her, wanted to tell him how she ached—the ecstasy and wanting both so acute—but instead, her head rolled restlessly on the comforter and her eyes slid closed as Rick suckled her other breast.

Finally, her clawing and moaning got to him, broke his leisurely pace. He started tugging at her thong. She lifted her hips up to help him, but he was too impatient; he yanked it down past her knees and then cupped her crotch with his big, warm palm.

For a few seconds he stayed just like that, breathing raggedly, as though trying to regain his control. Then gently—so gently—he ran his finger over her opening, moving so slowly, so thoroughly, she felt like she could die from the pleasure. The more he stroked her, the more wet heat that seeped between her legs. Vaguely she wondered if she should be embarrassed; she'd never been this turned on in her entire life. Still it seemed impossible to be embarrassed when Rick was spreading liquid fire through her lower body, when he was on the verge of going deeper, when she was dying to come and even close to doing it.

"Please . . . please . . ." she said.

"Don't worry, I'll please you, baby, believe me," he murmured thickly, and in such a husky, confident voice, she bit her lip and waited.

He slid a finger inside her, slowly and gently, and she sighed blissfully. He withdrew and did it again, and just as he got an intoxicating rhythm going, he slid two in. The sensation was so acute, so electric, she cried out—then panted harder, waiting for more. Boy, he was right. He *did* know how to please her—*very* well, and they'd barely begun. Fluidly, he continued to touch her, making her body quiver, until she nearly shook with hot, rippling tremors, and biting her lower lip hard, she struggled, on the verge of convulsing.

"Yes," she moaned as he licked the shell of her ear. *"More . . ."*

Distantly she heard the jingling of keys. Then the front door opened and closed. Gretchen jerked in surprise, and Rick stopped what he was doing, his hand stilled between her thighs, his other still cupping her breast, and in the silence over their heavy breathing was the sound of someone dropping her clanging keys down on the front table, then walking closer, down the hall, and oh—*damn it*—why was Dana home?

Shimmying quickly, Gretchen tried to move fast enough out from under Rick, who rolled off her, but the damage was done. There wasn't time to hide. Gretchen was stark naked with her bedroom door wide open, and Rick had his shirt off—hey, when had he opened his pants? In any event, like all good humiliations, this one happened fast.

"Gretchen, are you still awake—oh!" Dana yelped, slapping her palm over her mouth, her eyes growing huge with surprise. "Oh, I'm so sorry! I didn't realize—um, bye!" she said, turning to go, then doubled back to grab the doorknob and close Gretchen's door behind her.

"Oh my God," Gretchen croaked as flaming heat suffused her cheeks, and she could barely swallow the hard lump of emotion that clogged her throat. Shaking her head, she brought her hands to her hot, flushed face and said, "I'm so embarrassed. My cousin just saw me naked."

With a soft laugh, Rick reached for her, hugged her to his chest. "It's okay," he said, stroking her back as she buried herself against him.

A moment or two passed before she looked up at him. He seemed to be waiting for her decision: to continue or wait till next time?

"Maybe we should call it a night," she said, because she was too self-conscious with Dana home now, and anyway, her shameless exhibitionism had kind of killed the mood.

"Okay," he said, brushing a gentle kiss across her lips. He wasn't pressing the issue, though when he stood to zip up, she saw that his erection was straining hugely against his pants. "I'll get going," he said, grabbing his sweater off the floor. While he was at it, he tossed her her nightgown.

When she went to walk him out, they realized that his coat was still in the living room. "Sorry about tonight," Gretchen said when they finally reached the door.

"Don't be," Rick said and leaned down to kiss her again. It was a tender, lingering kiss, one that made her almost change her mind about him staying. "You know what they say about firemen . . ." he added. Shifting over, he nipped her ear and practically purred right into it, " 'We find 'em hot—and leave 'em wet.' "

He winked at her and left. With a shaky breath, Gretchen slumped against the door.

CHAPTER TWENTY-TWO

The next day was Wednesday and Susanna was her usual frazzled diva with a dependent twist. "What do you think of my new skirt?" she asked Gretchen, who was sitting on the settee in the dressing room, rubbing a coffee spill out of the cloaklike jacket that went with Susanna's skirt. (She'd offered to do it since her boss was easily stressed out by such debacles.)

Now she glanced up and smiled. "It's pretty," she said simply. What more could you say about something teal, linen, and floor-length? The less said, the better. The jacket that matched was cream colored with teal trim on the sleeves and a Nehru collar.

"How's that spot coming?" Susanna asked, crossing over to sit at her vanity.

"I've almost got it all out," Gretchen said.

"After that, I was thinking of trying something different with my hair. Some kind of updo. Could you help me?"

"Sure . . . You mean for your taping this afternoon? Because the studio hairstylists will do whatever you want. You know that."

With a scoff, Susanna started brushing her hair, making eye contact with Gretchen through her reflection in the mirror. "They annoy me," she said distastefully.

As always, Susanna's frilly pink dressing room was heavily perfumed with fresh flowers. The arc of lights that framed the mirror imbued Susanna's reflection with a soft, muted glow and made her seem almost delicate.

There was a light knock on the door. "Yes?"

Abe ducked his head in. "Susanna—oh, hi, Gretchen, how are you?"

She smiled. "Hi. Fine."

He looked at Susanna again, who'd spun in her chair to face the door. "Listen, I ran that idea by Joel—about you guest starring on Brett's show in May? He said they're planning to spend May plugging the upcoming Hawaii special, so thematically, the month is blocked off. However, Joel mentioned the possibility of you doing something sooner."

"How much sooner?" she asked, eyes wide, sitting forward on her seat, anticipating.

"I'm not sure. Joel wants to come to the set tomorrow and talk to me more about it. Between you and me, I think he wants to check out your taping firsthand to get more of a sense of how you work and how your physical style in the kitchen will mesh with Brett's. Still, it's looking good. I just wanted to give you an update."

"Thanks, Abe," she said. "As I'd said to you, it was really *Gretchen's* idea, but she didn't feel comfortable bringing it up to you herself, and while I'm casual either way, I have to admit it couldn't hurt to get a little extra exposure."

What a phony! Gretchen forced a poker face in the light of such blatant pretense. But admittedly, Gretchen had dropped the ball on that particular errand, and she had to hand it to her boss: When Susanna wanted something, she found a way to get it.

Abe turned to go, but Susanna vaulted out of her chair. "Wait! Abe, can I talk to you for a second?"

"Sure," he said, stepping into her dressing room and shutting the door.

"It's kind of . . . personal. About you." Trying to be subtle, Gretchen rose to go, but Susanna said, "No, stay, Gretchen. I might need you to help me with my pantyhose in a minute." Huh? What did that even mean? Help her on with it, or off? And why, dear God, why?

"What is it?" Abe asked, with confusion tingeing his otherwise calm and honeyed voice.

"Well, there's been talk. It's just vicious gossip, but I thought you should know about it." Ugh. Why wasn't Gretchen surprised? "There's been some rumor that you have been . . . well, *seen* with Ellie Galistette. Of course, I'm sure it's all business, but you know how people are—they turn everything into something sordid and ugly."

"Uh . . ." Abe glanced down for just a moment. "To tell you the truth, Susanna, the rumors are correct. Although I must say, I'm surprised my relationship with Ellie even ranks up there as newsworthy with the gossip circuit."

"R-relationship?" Susanna echoed, clearly stunned. "You mean it's *true*? You and Ellie are—an item?"

"Yes, it's true. I apologize for not telling you sooner." This guy was a priceless testament to diplomacy; he was willing to apologize to Susanna for neglecting to tell her something that was never any of her business to begin with. "We wanted to keep it discreet because of . . . well, my previous relationship with Misty. We didn't want it to affect Ellie's job. I guess now we're ready to be more open . . ."

Gretchen bit her lip, the implication of what Abe had said sinking in instantly. Now that Misty was dead, he didn't have to worry about upsetting her—didn't have to worry about her finding out that he was dating her assistant. Or "apprentice," as Ellie had said.

"I hope this won't affect how you feel about Ellie," Abe added with mild concern. "I assume she's representing you now." Again it went unsaid: now that Misty was dead.

"Well, yes . . . yes she is," Susanna said, clearly far from recovered by the unexpected turn the conversation had taken. As far as Gretchen could tell, Susanna had been trying to earn some kind of gratitude from her producer for alerting him to false rumors. She loved being in the know and she'd ended up being the clueless one.

Politely, Abe excused himself and left. When he was gone, Susanna murmured, "Well, I'll be damned." (No comment.)

All this talk about Misty got Gretchen thinking about the murder and what Rick had confided to her—that it was really part of a plot against Brett that had gone awry. She thought about Rick's suspicion of Susanna, and though the idea seemed so far-fetched, Gretchen still pondered it . . .

What could Susanna gain from Brett's demise? Yes, she'd be the top dog at TCC again in terms of ratings, but Susanna was a grown woman—surely she had adult perspective here. Surely she realized that there could always be another Brett around the corner.

"Hey, Susanna, I was thinking," Gretchen said, rising to bring her cleaned jacket to her. Right away, Susanna turned around, giving Gretchen her back, and held her hands out wide, waiting to have the jacket slipped on for her. "We should really do a show about mushrooms," Casually, Gretchen tilted her head so she could see Susanna's profile and gauge her reaction.

Confused, Susanna said, "What do you mean?"

Was it really that complicated? They usually featured a particular ingredient as a theme for an entire episode.

"Mushrooms," Gretchen repeated. "All kinds. Exotic ones, too. We could even have you give a spiel about the types to avoid. Or you know, what mushrooms go best with beef, fish, chicken. Which mushrooms make the best stock—um, which mushrooms are . . . poisonous."

She still wasn't seeing a reaction, but then, abruptly, Susanna did an about-face. "Well, how do I look?"

It was all Gretchen could do not to roll her eyes and say, *Get over the teal linen drapes, honey, we've got bigger issues!*

"Great. So what do you think about my idea?"

"Um . . . to be honest, I'm not terribly interested in mushrooms. They've never had a central place in my oeuvre—so I'll have to pass on that one. Come on. Let's go back to the set."

When she swung open the door, Cady Angle was scurrying away from it, but she hadn't moved quickly enough. "Cady! What are you doing?"

"Oh," she said, freezing on the cusp of the short stairwell that led up to Susanna's set. Glancing over her shoulder, Cady said, "I was just . . . I was wondering if you'd seen Marjorie."

"No, I haven't."

"I haven't either," Gretchen spoke up quickly to help deflect Cady's embarrassment about being so blatantly caught in the act of eavesdropping. Maybe she really had come to ask Susanna about Marjorie, but it seemed doubtful—why would Susanna know where Cady's producer was? And why scurry guiltily away when the door opened? She'd obviously come after Abe had left, so you had to wonder what she'd been listening in on that she'd find remotely interesting. Just Gretchen subtly asking Susanna about mushrooms (okay, maybe not so subtly).

"Well, thanks anyway," Cady said, smiling congenially, and turned to continue on her way, cutting through Susanna's set. (The only way to get to Susanna's dressing room was through Stage C; however, there was a fire exit at the end of the short corridor. Apparently Cady wasn't so flustered as to try to escape that way, which was good.)

"Why would I know where Marjorie is?" Susanna challenged, not letting the girl off that easy. If Cady were going to scramble away pusillanimously, she wasn't going to do it with dignity.

"She said she was running up to the eighth floor," Cady explained, inching up the steps as she answered. "That was about an hour ago, so I just wondered . . ."

"Susanna, we should go," Gretchen said, reminding her boss of the time. Cady used the distraction as her ticket out, waving and disappearing from sight. It was obvious that Susanna put her on edge, but that was hardly an atypical reaction.

They left, but an hour later, Gretchen was back. She couldn't shake the feeling that Susanna had been less than honest with her earlier on the mushroom question. Once she slipped inside the dressing room, Gretchen went right to the bookshelf that stretched across the wall, above the settee. This was where Susanna had all her cookbooks lined up, including the several from the beginning of her career that were now out of print.

After several minutes of flipping through tables of contents, Gretchen came up empty. Besides the expected array of recipes for standard dishes like chicken and veal marsala, stroganoff, and stuffed mushrooms, it appeared that Susanna had been telling the truth—she wasn't big into mushrooms.

The door opened, and Gretchen jumped, snapping the book in her hands closed. "What are you doing in here?" Susanna asked, dark blond eyebrows arched in surprise.

"Oh . . . Susanna . . . um, hi." Kneeling on the settee, facing the wall and floundering, Gretchen couldn't have appeared guiltier. "I was just looking at your old cookbooks," she explained, holding one up to make the point. "I wanted to see about your mushroom recipes, because I'm telling you, I really think we've got a show there!" she said cheerfully.

With a dramatic look of incredulity, Susanna said, "Gretchen, you have to stop with this obsession you have with mushrooms. Now, I'm not interested in that idea, and I'd appreciate it if you'd get back to your work!"

"Right," Gretchen said feebly, sliding the book back in its place on the shelf. "Of course. No problem. Totally understand." She started to go, assuming Susanna meant work as in paperwork, order forms, supply sheets, etc., and she *did* have plenty of that waiting for her in her office on the second floor. But that wasn't what Susanna meant.

It involved pantyhose. Don't even ask.

That evening, after most people had left for the night, Gretchen was walking around the curved hallway on the eighth floor when she heard whistling in the near distance.

The whistling got louder, until Gretchen turned and saw Brett Pellucci rounding the bend behind her, alongside a big hulking man with a brown complexion and an exotic-looking face. When their eyes met, Brett stopped the whistling to flash a smile. Dwarfed by his companion, Brett looked much shorter than usual—almost child-like. It was an inadvertently diminishing moment for him (think Jason Priestley on the beach in *Calendar Girl*—if you dared).

"Hey, Gretchen," he said, coming closer. "What are you still doing here?" The Massive One followed. He had hoop earrings in both ears, hair slicked back from his face, and deeply indented pock-marks on his cheeks and chin. "By the way, this is Epau—Epau, Gretchen," Brett said. Gretchen said a friendly hello, which Epau met with a stoic nod.

"He's, uh, my cousin from Hawaii," Brett elaborated. "He wanted a grand tour of TCC, and . . ." Standing on his toes, he managed to clap Epau on the shoulder. "Well, how could I refuse my own flesh and blood, right?"

"Right," she said amiably. "Well, that's great, have fun." She motioned toward the door to Stage C, several yards from where they stood. "I just have a couple more things to take care off before I can head home. Nice meeting you," she added, looking at Epau, who nodded again.

"Have a good one," Brett enthused with a wink, then looked buoyantly into Epau's chin. "C'mon, Cuz!"

When Gretchen entered Stage C, she crossed over to the kitchen set and was surprised to find Kit there. "Oh, hey, Gretchen. How's it going, honey?"

"Good. I didn't think anyone would be here."

"I think I left my keys here before," Kit explained, patting the many zippered pockets of her khaki vest as she went around looking under chairs and behind cameras.

"Oh, I'll help you look," Gretchen said, setting down her bag. "By the way, did you see Brett's cousin?"

With a nod, Kit said, "Yeah, I can't remember his name now, but I ran into them on the elevator earlier—oh! Here they are!" She bent down and apparently retrieved her keys from beneath the craft table, which during tapings was filled with sandwiches and snacks for the crew.

"Except for the hair, I don't see a resemblance," Gretchen remarked offhandedly. Brett definitely had his flaws, but looking like a man-eating giant wasn't one of them. "But then, they're cousins," she added, realizing there shouldn't necessarily be any resemblance between them.

"Yeah. Brett said the guy worships him." Wait . . . why did that sound familiar? "I guess Brett enjoys humoring his family and taking them around a *real TV studio—oooh*!" Kit said mockingly. "He had his brother hanging around here two weeks ago, remember? I mean, what is this? Bring Your Starstruck Relatives to Work Month?" There was a trace of bitterness in Kit's sarcasm that Gretchen couldn't define, and with that, Kit saluted a good-bye and wished Gretchen a good night.

His brother . . . The words echoed in Gretchen's head, though these days thoughts of Rick were never far from her mind. Especially after last night, from which she was still recovering. The whole steamy encounter had ignited her, *inflamed* her—but at the same time, depleted her, left her limp, enervated . . . aching for more.

And the gentle, utterly seductive way Rick had left things. He must have known the devastating effect he was having. Thinking about his intense arousal now aroused her even more.

Maybe Rick was moodier than Brett—well, no maybe about it—but he seemed much more honest. No, he wasn't unfailingly upbeat, but he wasn't habitually winking either. And he certainly didn't crave the kind of attention and fame that Brett reveled in, despite what Brett had said about him initially. In fact, now that Gretchen knew the real reason Rick had been hanging around TCC, Brett's portrayal of him as some desperate hanger-on seemed especially ludicrous.

Alone on the set now, Gretchen went to do her routine check of the appliances that Susanna would be using for tomorrow's taping. She usually saved this until the end of the day, after she'd finished her other work, because it didn't take long.

Gretchen wondered what expectations would be placed on her when Susanna began filming her prime-time show, *Dining Elegance*. It was set to start taping in March and would air June through August. Granted, in theory, it shouldn't affect Gretchen; *Dining Elegance* would have its own set and crew. But would Susanna's reliance on her carry over to the new stresses and issues brought on by the new show?

As she reached to test the food processor to make sure it was in perfect working order, she was only half focused on the blades and how precisely they moved with their various settings. With all Gretchen's culinary training, this kind of thing was pretty much second nature to her now. She could tell by looking at or even just listening to a kitchen device, how well it would get the job done. And Rick was still lingering in that hazy place between memory and lurid imagination.

Next thing to check was the blender—only that wasn't plugged in. She reached for the cord and stuck it in the socket.

Hisssss! Zzzzz!

Gretchen let out a shriek of surprise, as sparks flew before her eyes and exploded loudly in the air. *Snap! Pop!*

Her heart jumped through her chest as a sharp zing pierced through her hand and shot straight up her arm.

She managed to drop the cord and jump back—her heart racing frantically, the terror and shock of what had just happened still startling her. Breathing hard, she waited to get her bearings. *What the hell just happened?*

After a few moments, she pressed a hand to her chest, feeling relaxed—relieved—and she leaned in closer to the socket. First of all, the blender had already been set to "on" when she'd plugged it in. But second—and far more important—there was a tiny patch of frayed cord at the very back of the blender, completely out of view.

CHAPTER TWENTY-THREE

The following afternoon, Gretchen was babysitting Shawnee—or "keeping her busy" as Susanna had put it when she'd tried to make it sound less odious than it really was. Intent on making the best impression on Joel when he stopped by today's taping, Susanna was willing to sacrifice Gretchen's presence on the set if it meant Shawnee wouldn't be there to screw things up with her borderline competence and her lip.

Over the time that Gretchen had been working at TCC, she'd come to sense an aspect of Susanna and Shawnee's relationship that was undoubtedly unbeknownst to Shawnee herself—Susanna felt sorry for her. Gretchen didn't know much about Susanna's family history, but she knew her boss well enough to see that she cared about her niece. Enough to take her in when her sister had begged her to, enough to give Shawnee a job at the network that might give her some direction, some purpose.

Hey, Susanna couldn't control if Shawnee didn't seize the opportunity, but the fact was, Shawnee was so obviously insecure (well, it was obvious to Gretchen, anyway), and Susanna was, too, in her own way. Maybe on some level, she sympathized with her niece or even identified with her at that age. Actually, it would all be touchingly bittersweet . . . if Gretchen didn't have to deal with it.

But she did.

And the little worker bee that Shawnee *wasn't*, she wasn't about to argue when she was given a free pass on her work, even if it meant accepting Gretchen's invitation to lunch at the food court. Susanna acted as though she weren't the puppet master behind it all—told them that it was fine, that they didn't have to be on the set today, no problem. Kit, Abe, and the assorted cameramen must've have gotten it, because they didn't question it.

Now Gretchen and Shawnee were sitting at an isolated table in Terra Cottage. It was past two by now, so much of the lunch rush had passed. Gretchen had asked Shawnee about herself, her life in Massachusetts, and it had kick-started quite a tale. Shawnee talked about her high jinks in high school—how she'd been suspended three times, how she'd gotten in trouble for "stealing" her mother's car, how she'd really "stuck it" to the assistant principal once during in-school suspension ("Little did he know I'd poured chocolate milk on his chair—when he jumped up and turned around, it looked like he'd taken a big juicy crap right in his pants!")

Then she moved on to the post-high-school years, all two of them. "Yeah, I was gonna work at a gas station, but my mom said I'd embarrass her. As if working at a gas station was somehow 'beneath' our family. She's such a bitch, you know?"

What was Gretchen supposed to say to that? With a vague, non-committal mumble, she buried her mouth in her Greek pita.

Then Shawnee railed against her suburban malaise—how her mother had begged Susanna to let Shawnee stay with her for a while, and how Shawnee had been thrilled to come, thinking that New York City would be a thousand times more exciting than what she had going at home (which included a 1.0 GPA at community college). But now, Shawnee grumbled, she was stuck with Aunt Suz, who wouldn't let her have any "real fun," whatever that meant.

Boy, once you got the surly thing talking, she was a real chatterbox.

"Uh-huh," Gretchen managed, intermittently nodding, chewing, and sipping her diet soda. "Mmm-hmm, mmm-hmm, that's interesting . . ."

Surreptitiously, she checked her watch. Jeez, was the taping almost done? When could she ditch this girl? Even if she enjoyed Shawnee's company—which she didn't, of course—her time would be better spent doing work than listening to angst-ridden stories of teenage rebellion (*Pump Up the Volume* once was enough, thank you). Not to mention, Shawnee was twenty—wasn't she a little old for this crap?

"Hey, did I tell you that I used to work at Dick's Last Resort?" she said now.

"Um, no, what's that?"

"You *never* heard of Dick's Last Resort?"

"I work too much, what can I say," Gretchen remarked blandly. Shawnee went on to explain that Dick's Last Resort was a restaurant where the waitstaff's gimmick was being rude to the customers. Definitely sounded like Shawnee's calling. "So people pay to get treated badly?" Gretchen asked, mildly confused, though nothing shocked her about the general public these days.

"Yeah, but the food's good, and it's not big-deal stuff—just like funny stuff, you know? Like the waitress will eat fries off a customer's plate or when someone asks, 'Can I get another soda?' the waitress will be like, 'No, you can't,' but eventually she'll bring it anyway. It's supposed to be funny." The humor eluded Gretchen, but she nodded along.

"But, like, *I* was the only one who had the balls to take it to the next level," Shawnee said. "Like people would say, 'Hey, can I have another coke?' and I'd be like, 'I think you've had enough, lard butt!' And the funny thing was: I'd say it even if the person wasn't fat!"

Gretchen frowned. "Shawnee, that sounds kind of mean." She knew it wasn't her place to reprimand the girl, but the lines were pretty blurred at this point, and besides, it was *very* mean.

"Hey, you get what you pay for," Shawnee stated unapologetically. "But my manager felt like you, I guess, because he fired me. Claimed it was 'cause I was late a few times, but really I think customers complained about me because they're big babies." Then Shawnee's face puckered with mischievous glee and she ducked in closer. "And you know what else?" *Oh, dear God—what?* The night I got fired, I'd been waiting on this guy and his girlfriend. So I'd been doing the usual—eating fries off their plate, giving attitude; then I made a comment about his chrome dome. I know he must've complained because, oh, suddenly I'm 'late too much.' So you know what I did? I waited for the guy and his girlfriend to leave; then, just as they stepped out onto the sidewalk, I egged them!"

"*What?*" Gretchen asked incredulously, horrified.

"Yeah, took some eggs from the kitchen when I packed my shit up." She *heh-heh-heh*ed before adding, "Hey, I was just doing my job. They knew when they came that their waitress was gonna be shitty to them, so, fired or not, they were on my shit list for the rest of the night."

Gretchen sat slack jawed, her forehead creased, her brows cinching together, deeply troubled.

"And I kinda got revenge on my manager, too," Shawnee continued proudly. "When the couple was running away from me, I kept throwing more eggs and I yelled, 'You ever come back here, I'll rip you a new one!'" With a gleeful cackle, she noted, "There's two customers he'll never see again."

Gretchen didn't know where to go with this conversation. She did know that she'd lost her appetite. (The thought of two people being bludgeoned with eggs could do that to a girl.) Setting her pita down, she inhaled a breath and tried to rediscover that elusive something called banal small talk. "So, how do you like New York? Have you seen Times Square yet?"

"Times Square? Big fucking whoop," Shawnee replied. "New York sucks. Aunt Suz is a stiff. But it's either this or go back home to my mom and that tool she married and their son—the kid's *such* a loser."

"How can a baby be a loser?" Gretchen asked, confounded by that.

With a shrug, Shawnee didn't bother to explain the specific failings of her one-year-old brother. Instead, she expounded on the failings of her aunt. "All I kept hearing from my mom was, 'Oh, visit your Aunt Suz in New York. She rides around in a limo. You can flip the bird outta the sunroof,' the whole bit. But I've been here for almost two months already and we've only used the limo service a few times. And she never lets me open any of the windows. She's a total control freak! Especially when you're in *her* home, oh, boy, you better do *exactly* what she says. She even makes Uncle Ed wipe his feet whenever he comes in the door!"

"Well, that doesn't seem unreasonable," Gretchen remarked curiously.

"After he's already taken off his shoes? She makes him take off his shoes out in the hallway and then wipe his socks on a welcome mat."

"Oh," Gretchen said.

"You know, it's probably stuff like that that made him . . ." Her voice drifted off and she raised her brows suggestively.

"Made him what?" Gretchen asked. She probably shouldn't pry, but what the hell else was there to talk about? The taping wouldn't be over for another half hour, and Shawnee still had a mass of mutilated chimichanga to get through.

"Maybe I shouldn't say anything, but . . . well . . . Uncle Ed cheated on Aunt Suz once." Gretchen's eyes widened, her mouth curved into an O of surprise. "Once that we know of, anyway. Hell, he's probably done it, like, a million times. Probably boffed all his secretaries. He's one of those CEO Big-Shot Boff-the-Secretary types, you know? But there was this *one* time . . ."

Shamelessly Gretchen waited to hear the gossip instead of telling Shawnee that the conversation was inappropriate. She rationalized it this way: Shawnee had already subjected her to so much that was inappropriate, why stop her now that she was actually about to say something interesting? "You know her agent, Misty? The one who kicked it?"

"Yes," Gretchen replied.

"*Bingo,*" Shawnee said smugly. "That's who Uncle Ed cheated with! I heard them fighting about it. Apparently he boffed Misty's brains out at the Christmas party this year." (If Gretchen hadn't been so blown away by the information, she might have had to declare a moratorium on the word "boff.") How could Susanna have continued such a friendly rapport with Misty? Was she that good of an agent that Susanna was able to sweep a betrayal of that magnitude under the rug so quickly? Assuming the Christmas party was in December, and it was presently the end of January . . . the wounds had to be painfully fresh.

"I don't know how Suz found out about it. Maybe Ed confessed out of guilt, or maybe she just suspected—'cuz from what I've heard Aunt Suz say, Misty was a real slut."

Gee, that didn't sound like the usual praise Susanna had had for her agent. Had all of that gushing been an act? A facade?

Of course. This was show business. No, scratch that. It was business, period. Staying in her agent's good favor had obviously been more important to Susanna—and more financially advantageous—than confronting what Misty had done.

"I'll tell you, if that were me," Shawnee added, "I'd have gotten revenge."

The comment left Gretchen pensive. If what Shawnee said about Misty was true, it only seemed to confirm what Gretchen had suspected both times she'd met her: She wasn't a very nice person. And if Rick was right—that her death had been accidental—the result of a botched attempt on *Brett's* life—then whoever was behind it had indirectly given Susanna the revenge she may or may not have been seeking.

That night, Gretchen was walking around the eighth floor hallway on her way to the elevators, after having done her routine check of Susanna's set. She was glad to see that the new blender she'd sent for had been delivered. The one that had nearly electrocuted her yesterday had been chucked and Susanna had apologized, explaining that it had been her own blender, which held sentimental value. It had hardly seemed old enough to have sentimental value *or* a frayed cord, but whatever—Gretchen was just glad to have the thing gone.

She'd put in another long day, catching up on paperwork mostly, making up for the time that was lost when she'd been enduring Shawnee's company that afternoon. Now it was nearly nine o'clock; the hallway was deserted and quiet—until Gretchen suddenly heard giggling. Pausing, she followed the sound a few steps to Brett's studio. The door was ajar, allowing the lilting, almost tinny sound of giggles to escape. Then Gretchen heard a deeper voice murmur something. More giggles. Curiously, Gretchen inched the door open a bit more and peeked inside. From this angle, all she could see was the counter and the backdrop of Brett's lighted kitchen set. Then Brett moved into her line of vision, pulling a petite Hispanic girl along by the hand. She was laughing and pretending to follow reluctantly; Brett was beaming from ear to ear.

Wait, Gretchen recognized that girl . . . She was a PA who'd worked on *Tex-Mex Teddy,* but now that it was defunct, was working on Juan Mirando's show. Susanna had pointed her out once. What was her name again? Lupe Rodriguez—that was it.

Lupe was in her early twenties, pretty, wide-eyed, and if she was with Brett, Gretchen would also venture that she dug winking. Captivated by the scene, though she didn't know why, Gretchen watched. Brett brought Lupe around the counter, giving Gretchen his back. Lupe was smiling coyly at him. "Now, where are you from again, little Lupe?" he was saying.

"Mexico," she replied, pronouncing the word "Meh-hee-co" in a tinny, delicate accent.

"Oh, that's right," Brett said, his voice silky and suggestive. "Well, it seems we've got a little something in common. Or should I say a *big* something . . ."

"What's that?" she asked and giggled again.

"Hmm, what is that?" he murmured playfully, then shrugged one shoulder. "Feels like an enchilada to me. Maybe you oughta go south of the border and check it out," he finished. (At least Gretchen *hoped* he was finished.)

She bit her knuckles to keep from gasping, from laughing. What a cheeseball! So *this* was the legendary Romeo Ramero at work? If Dana ever got lines like this she would absolutely destroy the guy. In fact, this might shatter all illusions Dana had about him. Vain and flirtatious she could work with—but dud one-liners as foreplay? Her cousin wouldn't be having it.

At the same time, Gretchen was thoroughly aware that she should not be eavesdropping on this. But like a movie about killer ants the size of boats, she just couldn't look away.

Meanwhile, Lupe giggled and said, *"Otra vez?"* Another time. Did she mean let's go "south of the border" another time, or did it mean she'd already tended to his throbbing enchilada once and now he wanted her to do it again?

Brett dipped his head and kissed her. It took a matter of two seconds for them to erupt into a wild, obscene frenzy of ravenous mouths—lips smacking, tongues flapping out, swiping up cheeks and down chins. They rotated their bodies again and again, giving Gretchen every angle.

God, what did Lupe see in Brett anyway? Maybe it was the perfectly sculpted body, or his smoothly handsome face. Okay, admittedly, that was a good start. And maybe it was his fame and the way that people gravitated toward him, and the way he seemed to thrive on that—

Then it hit her. How stupid she was not to see it! Here she'd been anxious about getting involved with Rick, worried that maybe he was that same type she always went for, the type that never lasted. But Rick was nothing like her usual type—*Brett* was her usual type! *Brett* was the too-shallow, too-cocky, too-needing-to-be-the-center-of-attention guy, not Rick. Rick was nothing like him. The thought made her smile . . . but her reverie was broken when she heard Brett say, "I've got a little latex sombrero here in my back pocket. Why don't we try it on?"

Rolling her eyes, Gretchen made gagging gestures to no one and hurried away from the door. When she got to the elevator, she stopped short, startled. Brett's cousin, whom she'd met yesterday, was standing there with his back to the wall, his arms crossed and his expression serious and purposeful. He appeared to be watching the elevators, but why would anyone do that?

Then she realized: Epau was merely biding his time until his cousin finished having sex with a production assistant down the hall.

Okay, Brett just got a million times lower.

As she approached the elevators, Epau whipped his head to the side and gave her a fierce, scrutinizing assessment. Feebly, Gretchen smiled hello and moved past him to hit the button. Anxiously, she tapped her foot. She was uncomfortably aware of Epau's eyes still on her and his overwhelming physical presence. Finally the doors sprung open and she hopped inside.

On her way to the ground floor, she recalled what Rick had told her about Brett and his poisoned sauce and how someone was out to get him and she couldn't help thinking: He wasn't acting like someone who was afraid. Judging from tonight's antics, Brett didn't behave like a person who was watching his back. Here he'd left the studio door ajar and when Gretchen had pushed it open, he'd been more preoccupied with Taco Bell–esque dirty talk than his safety.

Something was off here. And she just didn't trust him.

CHAPTER TWENTY-FOUR

*L*ater that night Gretchen discovered the truth about Misty All-bright. But first, she lay in bed, thinking about the whole messed-up situation.

She couldn't get past what Shawnee had told her yesterday about Misty's tryst with Ed Tate, Susanna's husband. Based on various things she'd said, Susanna was obviously into her husband. It just seemed inconceivable that the idea of her agent sleeping with him was water under the bridge, especially so soon after it had happened. Also, Gretchen couldn't help thinking that when you added up that behavior with the way Misty had dropped Ray Jarian cold the moment he hit a rough patch in his career, it seemed much more logical that she would be the target of a homicide, not Brett.

It just didn't make sense. Who would want to kill him? After tonight, it was safe to say the guy was a sleaze—and undoubtedly a womanizer—but even in that, he was so damn affable. It was nearly impossible to picture someone having such a severe, icy hatred for him, such an unforgiving grudge against him, as to actually try to murder him. It didn't make for convincing reality. Or, she should say, it didn't seem nearly as realistic as someone loathing and wanting to off Misty. Was it possible that she really had been the target all along? Could Rick have been wrong about Brett being in danger? *Think about it . . .*

All he really had was Brett's word for all of this.

Maybe whoever killed Misty had found a way to poison the food Brett had brought to her. But who had access to her guest room?

Susanna had been standing there in the foyer with Gretchen

when Misty had announced that she was going to lie down, so she knew where she'd be. Gretchen had lost track of her boss until that afternoon when she'd come looking for her, hustling her to go back to the city. She'd been in such a mad rush to leave Brett's . . . which had seemed strange, even at the time. She'd said it was so she could get home to Ed, but could she have been fleeing the scene? Could she have wanted to dart away before Misty began showing signs of discomfort?

Gretchen thought back. At breakfast that morning, Susanna had said that she'd expected to see Misty the night before, but that she'd asked Brett and he'd told her Misty would be arriving that day. Maybe she'd been waiting for the perfect opportunity to slip the Destroying Angel into her agent's food. She'd said that Brett's cooking was Misty's weakness, so she'd known, without a doubt, that if Misty came, she would eventually eat at some point. Susanna could've stopped up in Misty's room, seen the food Brett had brought for her, and the second Misty was distracted or her back was turned, slipped the poison mushroom powder into the bowl.

Still, it was ludicrously far-fetched.

Wasn't it?

It was so hard to picture Susanna—neurotic and almost childlike at times in her need for validation—hatching a murder scheme, and even harder to picture her going through with it. As for the fevered exodus from Brett's house, well, Gretchen supposed it made sense in a way. If Misty had slept with Ed, who knew the kind of problems Susanna and her husband were having? It stood to reason that upon hearing that Ed would be home from his business trip early Susanna would want to spend as much time as possible with him—to heal their marriage, to hold on to him. Besides, as Gretchen discovered when she'd been caught riffling through her boss's old cookbooks: Susanna was hardly a mushroom enthusiast.

Okay, not that you had to be one to commit murder—it probably just took some research—but still, it was too difficult to fathom Susanna as the killer.

Yet . . .

The more Gretchen mulled it over, the more she became convinced that Misty was the intended victim all along. No one else.

Whoever had poisoned her had set out to do so. So again she considered who'd had access to her room—to her food.

Like a neon pink flashing vacancy sign (well, you get the point), it blinked in front of her. Ellie Galistette. *Of* course! Ellie had been the one to find Misty sick in the first place; Ellie had been the one to "take care" of her in the days that followed. Ellie had been the one with Misty right up until the time she died.

And when Misty had arrived at Brett's on Saturday morning, she'd been distinctly annoyed with Ellie—angry even—and Ellie had followed her upstairs "to talk." Could Misty have found out what Gretchen stumbled upon herself the night before—that Ellie had taken up with Abe, who'd broken things off with Misty just a couple of months ago?

Remembering that night more clearly, Gretchen thought back to Abe and Ellie's make-out session. She recalled Ellie's insecurity, the way she'd been fishing for Abe's reassurance, basically asking him if she were as passionate as Misty. There was obviously an inferiority issue there, which probably stemmed from their work relationship. Misty was the powerhouse, the shark, the beautiful agent who made eight-figure deals for a living. And Ellie was her "apprentice," but how quickly she was actually going to advance to Misty's level was another issue.

Suddenly the poised, polished way that Ellie had carried herself at Misty's memorial service seemed so contrived, so purposeful. She was there, more than anything, to establish herself as Misty's replacement—to take much of Misty's client list as her own and to make it seem like an effortless, logical transition.

Ellie had everything to gain by her boss's death. Personally, she'd get her competition out of the way. Even though Abe had lost interest in Misty, Ellie had still been intimidated by her. More important, with Misty dead, Ellie could go public with her and Abe's relationship without fear of reprisal. And professionally, she won again. Now Ellie was representing Susanna Tate, and God knew how many more of Misty's clients had become her own. The transition was complete.

Gretchen needed to talk to Rick about all this. She felt certain that he was going down the wrong track if he thought this was about Brett.

Brett—damn that little weasel! Sorry, but she was peeved, now more than ever, that he was too cowardly, too intent on avoiding bad publicity, to go to the police. Only four people knew the real cause of death: Brett, Rick, Gretchen, and the destroying angel himself.

The police had put Misty's death on the shelf, probably written if off as "kidney failure brought on by unknown medical complications" or something equally vague. If only they had more information, maybe they could begin to solve the crime.

But if Brett wasn't talking, what could she do? Rick wasn't going to sell out his brother, and Gretchen certainly wasn't going to break Rick's confidence. But still, she wanted to protect him . . . only she didn't know exactly from what.

Just then she heard Dana come in the front door, and within seconds, she knocked on Gretchen's bedroom door. "Yeah, come in," Gretchen said, glancing over. The light from the hallway shone into the room and cut a diagonal shaft across the bed.

"Hey! Sorry, did I wake you?"

"No, I was awake."

"Oh, good. Listen, I've got something to tell you."

"What? Where were you, anyway?" Sitting up more, Gretchen climbed backward to put her weight on her elbows. Then she shivered, her bare arms chilled by the sudden loss of heat from the covers. Quickly, she sank back down and waited.

Meanwhile Dana came over and sat on the bed. "I was at Lolly's, looking for jobs because our Internet's not working," she explained. "I was kind of putzing around, wasting time, when I remembered what you'd said the other day. And since I was bored and felt like procrastinating anyway, I did some searching. It didn't even take that long, but the point is—I figured it out."

"Figured what out?" Gretchen said, confused.

"Misty Allbright," Dana replied, her face bubbling over, exuding warmth, life, a revelation. "Aka Melissa Borg," she added emphatically. "Aka *Missy Borg*."

She looked expectantly at Gretchen, who just shook her head, baffled. "Missy Borg?"

"From high school!" At that, Gretchen shot up in bed. Bare arms be damned; she was too stunned, too confused. "She was in my grade," Dana went on, "which would make her two years older than you." Dana's family had lived in Kaplan, Connecticut, for only one year, when Gretchen was a sophomore in high school and Dana was a senior. Because of Dana's friendship and effervescence—because of the days Gretchen spent hanging out at her cousin's house with Aunt Mary, Uncle Dane, Dana, and her brothers—that year was important to her. It was inexorably memorable—but Missy Borg was not.

"I found this picture," Dana continued, pulling a folded piece of paper out of her coat pocket. "I printed it off of oldyearbooks.com. You tell me. Did that agent look anything like this?" she said, unfolding the printout and holding it in front of Gretchen's face.

Anxiously, Gretchen leaned over to switch on her bedside lamp, then practically snatched the sheet of paper from her cousin's hand. Studying the grainy black-and-white but mostly black picture (damn inkjet printers), Gretchen saw a girl with short dark hair and a familiar face. Yes, this *could* be Misty . . . if Misty had gotten even skinnier over the years, and grew out her hair, and curled it. Then Gretchen eyed the caption below: "Missy Borg, Kaplan Class of '94."

That was Dana's graduating class, all right. But this was just too bizarre!

As Gretchen's eyes raced over the page, she said, "Omigod, this is incredible. Could it really be—I mean, how on earth did you make the connection?"

"It was actually pretty easy. I just typed in 'Misty Allbright' and did a general search. There were tons of entries that came up, linking her name with Romeo Ramero, Susanna Tate, Ray somebody, and a few other TV personalities I can't remember right now. I know one of them was a talk-show host or something. Anyway, I just kept hitting next until I was on, like, the eightieth page of entries for Misty Allbright and I saw this link to some low-budget message board. When I clicked on it, I realized it was part of Kevin Pepper's personal Web site—do you remember him?"

"No."

"He was in my class, too. That blond wrestler, remember? Loud and annoying? Not funny but thought he was? Major nasal voice? Well anyway, apparently he's an accountant now, but he keeps this personal Web site. It has a bunch of stuff, including photos of Kevin

from various swimming competitions and marathons. Well"—she
took a breath, then blew it out—"I had to scroll and scroll, but I finally found where Misty Allbright's name was mentioned."

Eagerly, Gretchen waited.

"A couple of people had posted messages about the Kaplan High
reunion this past fall, and this girl, Lisa Spence—I remember her, she
was lame—wrote that Missy Borg hadn't attended, but apparently
Lisa had run into Missy in New York City several months back and
found out she was going by Misty Allbright now and running her
own talent agency."

"Wow," Gretchen said, shaking her head, still taking it all in.
"That's incredible."

"And the thing is, once I heard the name it hit me like a ton of
bricks. I totally remember her!" Dana said, pressing her palms flat on
the bed. "She was kind of awkward and bizarre. I remember she had
long hair in the beginning of the year and then hacked it all off to
make some sort of statement. She always seemed kind of . . . I don't
know . . . desperate for an identity, maybe."

Looking at the picture again, studying the grainy face, she said,
"You're right. It's definitely her."

"Wow!" Dana exclaimed. "My first official case solved as a free-
lance private detective!"

"The key word being *free,*" Gretchen remarked dryly, with a grin
curving her mouth even as the surprise of what she'd learned still settled. "I hope you don't think I'm gonna pay you."

With a giggle, Dana acquiesced. "Okay, fine. But the point is,
that explains why Misty was snubbing you. You said it was as if she
knew you somehow and didn't like you. Well, she *did* know you!"

"No, but . . . it still doesn't make sense," Gretchen countered,
pondering it. "Why would she be a jerk to me? I didn't know her personally. We weren't even in the same grade."

"Oh, come on. It's too coincidental that she would single you out
to give the brush-off. She must have recognized you as someone from
her past. Maybe she was one of those people who wanted to erase her
past. Think about it: Why else would she change her name? I told
you, the girl always seemed hurting for an identity. And here, once

she carves a cool one out for herself, someone from high school was ruining it for her."

Could it be? Had Misty remembered Gretchen, who, admittedly, hadn't changed all that much in the last twelve years? Her body was about fifteen pounds heavier, her hair was longer, her teeth were straighter (braces in college), but otherwise, she was more or less the same. Unlike Misty, who'd made quite a transformation.

"Maybe you're right," Gretchen said, slapping her palm to her covers with affirmation. "Maybe Misty just couldn't face me—a reminder of her teenage angst or something."

"Yes," Dana said, nodding, "exactly. That was it . . . um, probably was it . . . I'm sure it was . . ."

Then Gretchen noticed that her cousin's eyes were darting guiltily to the side, and she couldn't seem to stop nodding. "Dana?"

"Hmm?" she said, her tone high-pitched, her voice lilting with innocence, her eyes still darting around, avoiding contact.

Narrowing her eyes with suspicion, Gretchen spoke slowly. "What did you do?"

"Nothing!" Dana yelped, but when Gretchen continued squinting at her, she sucked in a breath. "Weeelll . . . I'm sure that was definitely *one* reason Misty didn't like you." Then she made a clicking sound with her tongue and shrugged. As Gretchen eyed her speculatively, Dana added, "But there might"—she held up her hands and pushed forward, as if to say, *Bear with me here*—"just possibly have been another reason . . . that could—*technically*—have to do with me."

"What do you mean?"

"See . . . another thing I remembered . . . I kind of—ever so *slightly*—made out with Missy's boyfriend at the prom."

"*What!*" Gretchen nearly shrieked, eyes wide, jaw dropped open.

Haplessly, Dana held up her hands as her innocent act crumpled and guilt contorted her features. "Like I said, when I saw her name and her picture, it all came back to me . . ."

"I can't believe this . . . Talk about a small world."

"Okay, I just want to say, in my defense, they were broken up at the time. At least, he *said* they were. But . . . they weren't."

Gretchen slumped back against her headboard. After a pause of contemplation, she said, "But you know what? It still doesn't make sense. Even if you *were* a major hoochie at the prom—"

"Hey! I thought they were broken up! I was young and stupid!"

"Fine, well, regardless—I still don't see why Misty should dislike *me*. I was nice. I never made out with anyone's boyfriends." (Or anyone at all, until her second year of college.)

"Oh, come on, we're cousins," Dana said, like the explanation should be obvious. "It's all in the family."

Grinning, Gretchen sank back into her pillows and teasingly muttered, "Don't remind me."

Gretchen could barely look Lupe Rodriguez in the eye the next day when they rode the elevator together. Vivid memories of Lupe and Brett's erotic encounter still played in Gretchen's head like cheesy sax music in a B movie. Luckily, Lupe got off on the sixth floor, where Juan Mirando's studio was; Gretchen coasted on to eight to get an early start on today's kowtowing.

During the taping, Susanna noticed that her wedding ring had slipped off. After getting Kit to "take five," she asked Gretchen to run to her dressing room and find it for her. Apparently, Susanna didn't trust anyone else with the huge, glittering rock Ed had given her. In hushed tones, she explained that if she sent one of the crew members to get it, they could pocket it and claim they couldn't find it. Shawnee, Susanna's own flesh and blood, was implicitly lumped with the potential thieves.

Sometimes efficiency was a bad thing. Gretchen moved so efficiently that she hadn't thought to watch where she was walking. She went through the door that led to the stairwell and barely made it past the first of the four steps when her heel slipped out from under her.

With a keening cry, she slid, slamming hard on her butt and banging her back on the sharp metal edge of each step as she went, *Clunk, clunk, clunk*. Then her sore body thudded on the floor below. Panting and bleary-eyed, she found herself staring up into a light fixture that looked like a big breast. It was a round translucent dome with a pointy brass nipple in the center.

A few seconds passed before her breathing returned to normal and the panic and shock of what had just happened finally subsided.

Still shaken, she climbed to her feet. Rubbing her backside, she reached for the door to Susanna's dressing room.

It was only when she gave a cursory glance back at the stairs that she noticed something. Liquid streaked heavily down the first two steps. Abruptly, Gretchen dropped her hand off the doorknob and walked closer. She bent to touch whatever it was, finding it wet and greasy. Then she sniffed it. *I'll be damned . . .*

Olive oil?

"Good, you're still here! We have dinner plans." Susanna swept into Gretchen's office—or rather, the one she'd given her. Like everything else, it came with a price.

"We do?" Gretchen said, glancing up from this week's supply sheets, pencil in hand. "I mean . . . thanks for asking me, but I actually have plans."

"Oh, I'm sorry," Susanna said with dramatic emotion, "but I'm going to need you to cancel them. We've got a *crucial* dinner meeting with Brett tonight."

"What do you mean 'we'?" Gretchen said with a slight edge to her voice. It was past five o'clock; she was tired and irritable and her back still ached from her tumble on the stairs.

Susanna stepped closer. A gleeful smile curved her lips into a half-moon, and she lowered her voice. "I'm *this* close to getting the guest spot on Brett's show! Abe said that Joel was impressed with the taping the other day and the way I move fluidly through the kitchen. He thought it would be a wonderful counterbalance to Brett's kind of fiery energy."

"Really?" Gretchen said a little skeptically. Raspy, abrasive Joel Green had used the words "move fluidly" and "wonderful counter-balance"? Please. Now if Susanna had said he'd hacked out a wheez-ing cough of approval, *that* Gretchen would believe.

"Don't you *see*?" Susanna went on with a doe-eyed mix of naïveté and enthusiasm. "I'm on the cusp of getting what I want. And a few minutes ago, I *happened* to overhear Brett mention to his cousin that he's free for dinner tonight and that they should grab a bite later. I need to seize this opportunity! I know if Brett and I spend more time together, he'll realize how great we'd be as cohosts!"

Whoa, whoa, whoa—*cohosts*? What happened to a couple of guest spots? Hmm . . . sounded like Susanna had been dreaming bigger than that the whole time but was only now revealing it.

If Gretchen still believed that Brett was the target of a murder plot, this latest information would only confirm that Susanna had no reason to want him dead. Speaking of Misty's murder . . . tonight Gretchen planned to tell Rick all about her revelations—how Misty had likely been the intended victim after all, and how Ellie Galistette was sitting at the top of the list of suspects.

Now, on another note, Brett's cousin was here again? Jeez, the guy needed to get a life. Abruptly she realized she was starting to sound as bitter and judgmental as Kit. Oh well, she was tired and moody, so too fucking bad.

"I need you there," Susanna begged now. "Please, Gretchen, please! If you're there, it'll seem more natural. Plus, you can keep Epau busy while I talk to Brett."

Oh, Jesus. Okay, the truth was: Gretchen hadn't made dinner plans yet. That had been an exaggeration, but a hopeful one. She'd talked to Rick earlier and they'd discussed getting together later, but he'd had to run, so he'd told her he'd call her when he got out of work. Now Susanna was looking more pathetic than ever, begging to the point of clasping her hands prayer style, and as usual, the woman seemed convinced they were Siamese in a former life.

Finally, Gretchen agreed, but with a stipulation. "All right, I'll go—but I have to be home by eight tonight."

"Eight o'clock?" Susanna echoed doubtfully. "That's too early. I was thinking we'd meet him at the restaurant around seven thirty and—"

"At eight, I have to leave," Gretchen said firmly. "Sorry, like I said, I have plans tonight."

Apparently Susanna knew when it was futile to keep pressing. So she accepted those terms, but said she would have to take care of a few things first and she'd meet Gretchen and Brett at the restaurant at seven thirty. Then she said that maybe it was better this way. Gretchen would be there to "warm Brett up" and then she could leave by eight, from which point Susanna would "close the deal." (By the way, had Gretchen mentioned that Susanna hadn't even invited

Brett and his goon cousin yet? That this was all presumption on her part?)

After giving the name and address of the restaurant, she flitted off. Gretchen blew out a sigh. She was tired and she wanted to relax with Rick tonight, not his pretty-boy brother.

But then again . . .

This might be her one chance to talk to Brett about Misty's death. She didn't know if Rick had told him what he'd confided to her, so she couldn't be too direct about it. But maybe she could fish around . . .

Picking up the phone on her desk, she dialed Rick's cell number to tell him about her newest work obligations and that she would be free around nine. His phone rang a few times and then clicked to dead air—it didn't go to voice mail. She tried again, but the same thing happened. Great, now she couldn't even leave him a message. Oh, well, she'd just have to try him later.

CHAPTER TWENTY-FIVE

*A*n hour later, Gretchen was sitting alone at a linen-covered table, waiting for Brett and Epau to show. Finally, after twenty more minutes of waiting, they strutted in. Well, Brett strutted. Epau moved more like a tank—powerful, stiff, unyielding, and in no rush.

As he winked at several of the women he passed, Brett even made a point to angle his head back and ogle a waitress's butt. Discreetly rolling her eyes, Gretchen thought: *Hurry, Susanna—please.*

"Hey, Gretchen," he said as he approached the table, knocked twice on it, winked, and then looked up at his cousin. "Epau—*Cuz*—remember Gretchen? You met her the other day?"

The stoic nod seemed to indicate either that he remembered or didn't give a fuck.

"Hi, guys, how are you?" Gretchen said brightly.

"Great to see you," he said, leaning down to plant a kiss on her cheek. She held back a grimace, recalling the way he'd kissed Lupe on the cheek the night before—or should she say *licked*.

"You, too. Um, Susanna should be here anytime now. . . ."

"So what's up with you and my brother?" Brett asked bluntly after he took a seat across from her. That definitely caught her off guard.

She wasn't sure why she was surprised. Surely if Rick and Brett talked to each other on a regular enough basis, Rick might've mentioned that he and Gretchen had started dating.

"Oh, well . . ." she said, feeling a warm blush wash over her cheeks. Before she could flounder, though, Brett's cell phone rang inside his jacket. It loudly crooned a loungey beat so as to draw as much attention as possible.

"Oh, excuse me," he said, pulling it out of his pocket, glancing at the number. "Yo," he said. From across the table, she could only hear a low-pitched murmur on the other end. "I'm okay. Yup, he's here with me." Brett paused, then said, "Gretchen? What a coincidence. I'm with her right now. Yeah, *right,*" he said, clearly imitating the caller, "it's true. What are we doing? What do you think? We're having dinner together."

Gretchen squirmed uncomfortably. Was that Rick on the phone? And why was Brett making it sound like they were on some kind of date?

"Oh, you don't believe me?" he said. "Here she is." Then he passed the phone across the table. Gretchen took it with a questioning look, and as she brought it up toward her mouth, she asked Brett who it was, even though she knew, and then she spoke into the phone.

"Hello? Hello?" But the line was dead.

It was a dank and dreary night and the air was raw. Rick walked down the sidewalk, still thinking about the conversation he'd had with his brother only ten minutes before. Thinking about the sound of Gretchen's voice coming through the line. Irritably, he reached for a cigarette out of his inside coat pocket but then realized he was out. Fuck it. He kept walking, still trying to grasp how life had just flipped upside down and knocked him on his ass.

Gretchen was out with Brett? At a restaurant—having dinner, for chrissake? She was supposed to be hanging out with him tonight. They'd even discussed it before, when Rick had said he would call her once he got out of work. So why was she out with Brett? And when the hell had they made these plans?

Saved him another call, that was for sure. After checking in with his brother the shithead, he'd been planning to call her to figure out what she wanted to do tonight. There went that.

As he walked, he blocked out the noises of the honking cars and the blaring music from the pizza place to his right. The more he played back the conversation with Brett just now, the more anger that swam in front of his eyes.

Brett hadn't been apologetic about it, even though he must have figured out by their previous conversation that Rick had a thing for Gretchen.

His brother was a jackass—plain and simple—and Rick wasn't gonna forget it. But he was far more disappointed in Gretchen. His gut twisted and his jaw tightened as he thought about it. Jesus, had she been bullshitting him this whole time? Had his earlier impression been correct—that she was after his brother?

Sure, Brett was rich and famous and outgoing, but at the core he was a selfish bastard. What could a girl like Gretchen possibly have in common with him, besides cooking? She was deeper than that. Someone as shallow as Brett couldn't make her happy—couldn't she see that?

Goddamn it! Why should he care if she made herself miserable trying to chase Brett, who'd never been faithful to a girl in his life? She didn't deserve it—she'd been trying to work it both ways. Sex with Rick for the thrill of it, but the whole time, she'd had her eyes on the prize.

Rick knew Gretchen was attracted to him; he knew how turned on she'd been the last time they saw each other. He remembered how wet she'd been—practically trembling in his arms, her body strung tight but on the verge of collapse, pleading with him to touch her more, moaning in his ear, gripping his arms, bucking her hips, rubbing hungrily against his cock . . .

There was no doubt in his mind, they'd been halfway to a long, steamy fuck when they'd been interrupted.

So that was it, then. That was the extent. She'd finally gotten Brett's attention, and Rick would be damned if he'd let her play both angles.

Traffic moved around him like a flood of lights, ants treading water, the street flickering with all kinds of colors, but mostly he just saw red.

"Who was that?" Gretchen said again after Brett finished making small talk with the manager who'd come to the table. Followed by four people who'd wanted autographs.

"What?" he said absently, reaching for his glass of carrot juice that the waitress had just set down. It was garnished with a celery stalk, which looked equally as appealing as the juice itself.

"Who was on the phone?" Gretchen said, getting very irritated now.

"Oh. That was Brody, uh, Rick, actually," he said, just as Susanna approached the table.

"I made it here early!" she declared, taking a seat beside Gretchen. "Hi, Brett—hi, uh . . ."

"Epau," Brett said by way of introduction.

Before Susanna could start prattling, Gretchen balled her fists under the table and pressed on. "Um, you said that was Rick on the phone? But there was no one there when I answered." Brett just shrugged. "Well, his cell phone wasn't working right earlier when I tried to call him . . . so maybe it just died on him now when I got on the line?"

"Probably" was all Brett said.

Well, that hadn't exactly been reassuring. She needed to get in touch with Rick and explain about why she hadn't waited to make dinner plans with him, and why she'd been out with Brett instead. Surely he would understand, but she still needed to let him know. "Will you excuse me? I want to go make a phone call . . ."

Susanna just nodded and said, "Okay, but hurry back." (God, what had this woman done before Gretchen came to work for her? Oh, yeah, fire everyone else.)

She scurried to the ladies' room, where she pulled her cell phone out of her bag and checked for missed calls. None from Rick. She dialed him, but got no answer. This time, though, his voice mail picked up, so she left him a message—explaining that she'd tried to call him a few times, but something had been wrong with his cell phone service because his voice mail hadn't been picking up, and that she'd been roped into a dinner with Susanna and Brett, but she'd be free around nine so she would call him then.

Snapping the phone closed, she reminded herself: *Just make it to eight o'clock. Then Susanna can start "closing the deal" and I can get the hell out of here. And by then, Rick will have called.*

The next day was Saturday and by late afternoon, Gretchen still hadn't heard from Rick, though she'd left two messages, the final one saying, "So I guess we'll get together another night . . . but call me." And he still hadn't called! Nothing! It was unreal—what a jerk!

Foolishly she tried to figure out what he was thinking and why he was being distant all of a sudden. (Always a waste of a girl's time, but what the hell?)

Even if it had sounded strange to Rick when Brett had told him that he was out to dinner with Gretchen, why would Rick suddenly blow her off? Wasn't it obvious that it had to be a work thing, and if he wanted clarification, why hadn't he called her back for it?

Why hadn't he picked up his phone last night? Obviously he'd seen it was her number calling, but he still hadn't picked up.

Maybe she was overreacting, paranoid about getting blown off. After all, Rick was embroiled in a lot of stuff these days, between his job and his brother's whole so-called life-threatening situation.

God, what if something bad had happened . . . ?

No, she was making excuses for him, slipping into the old maybe-he's-lying-in-a-ditch-somewhere line of thinking, when in fact he simply wasn't calling her back. Swallowing down a lump of anxiety, she told herself to stop worrying so much, to focus on her job—for pete's sake, hadn't that been her vow to herself when she'd taken the position at TCC? *Focus on the career. Dating can wait.*

Stop worrying, she scolded herself again. Rick was special. He was straightforward and reasonable and he wasn't a player . . . was he?

No—surely he would call soon.

If only it wasn't for that niggling doubt in the back of Gretchen's mind that told her: *You've done it to yourself again.*

Late that night, Gretchen was sitting cross-legged on one of the kitchen counters, with the glass cabinet door open above her and half of Marcia Rabe's spices in her lap. She was channeling her frustration—her annoyance, her all around man hate—into something productive: organizing the spices by their nuances of compatibility. (Hey, it beat eating a pie.)

She was sitting with her hair half up in a spiky messy bun, wearing green fleece pants and a T-shirt from Dana's days at Rutgers. It was pale pink with silver cursive that read: JERSEY GIRLS RULE.

Just then Dana emerged, bounding into the living room and flapping a sheet of paper in her hand. "Okay, how's this?" she said, flattening the paper down on the counter opposite from Gretchen and hopping up on a stool herself.

Surprised, Gretchen stopped juggling ten bottles of spices and set them down. "I thought you were asleep," she said.

"No, that was just a power nap. Something to help me unwind."

Grinning, Gretchen commented, "You know, you're the only person I know who needs to unwind from unwinding." Then she hopped off the counter she was perched on, crossed the kitchen to look at the paper Dana had laid out for her.

"No, really. Unemployment is not as restful as it's cracked up to be," Dana said. "I looked for jobs online so long my eyes actually started to burn."

Gently, Gretchen gave her a sympathetic look. Dana really was trying to find her niche. Even if no "big break" ever came, hopefully she'd find it.

"So that's my updated résumé," Dana explained, as Gretchen started to read it. "The other one didn't seem to be getting lots of replies. So I just made a few . . . tweaks. Now, give me your honest opinion. Don't hold anything back."

As Gretchen's eyes scanned the page, a wisp of laughter slipped from her lips. "Dana," she said, tilting her face, leveling her cousin with a be-wildered, quizzically amused glance, even though her tone had been flat.

"Yes?" Dana said, looking expectant.

Pausing for just a moment, Gretchen bit her lip, then said, "Um . . . this is okay, but . . . maybe a little unprofessional." *Maybe* being hugely generous.

"Meaning?" Now it was Dana's turn to tilt her head and fold her arms across her chest.

"Well, first of all, what is *this*?" Gretchen pointed to the middle of the page. "Under 'skills' you list Microsoft Word, Excel, Access, and Pilates."

"All true," she said, "though I see what you mean, it's confusing, Microsoft doesn't have anything to do with Pilates . . ." Tilting her head, Gretchen gave her a knowing smirk. "Too much?" Dana said, scrunching her eyebrows, then explained. "I was going for some lev-ity there. You know, something to make my résumé pop?"

Smiling speculatively, Gretchen said, "Yeah, I could be wrong, but I don't think potential employers are big on levity. Or sarcasm. At least on paper—in an interview it'll come off better."

"Fine, so what are they 'into' on paper?" Dana asked, quoting with her fingers. "Bland formality and blatant suck-up-ness?"

"It's a start. And what's this? Under your reason for leaving your last job you have a two-paragraph rant about your struggle to preserve your personal integrity in a man's world."

"No good?"

"No."

"Well, it works better with manic hand gestures."

Gretchen drew a big X through the whole thing. "Moving on . . ." Her eyes wandered down the page. "Now this part's my favorite. Under salary requirements, you have, 'Fifty K and a private jet—negotiable—but not on the jet, ha-ha.' "

"Oh, well, I can fix that," Dana said, taking the résumé from Gretchen's hand and pulling her pen out from behind her ear to scratch it out and write something else in its place. "There," she said, passing the résumé back.

Gretchen read it back. " 'Fifty K and Flexible—just ask my exboyfriend, ha-ha." She laughed in spite of herself, then said, "You're really into this whole 'ha-ha' thing, huh?"

A frustrated but still lighthearted sigh dissolved from Dana's lips. "Oh, what's the point? I can't do the uptight bit, even in a résumé."

Leaning her forearms on the counter, Gretchen let the résumé slip from her fingers and nearly float away. "May I make an observation?"

"Sure."

"I'm getting the feeling that maybe you don't really want an office job."

"What do you mean? Of course I do. I need it. Corporate America, desks, staplers, health benefits, we discussed this. Besides, someone's gotta bring home the turkey bacon—"

"*Dana . . .*"

"Besides you, of course," she amended quickly, but Gretchen just leveled her with a kind but assessing glance. Looking guiltily around the room, Dana finally blew out a breath, which sent some of her reddish brown wisps fluttering. "I know. You're right." She sank her chin into her hands. This blows. Remember the days when you could be a sloth and still make a cool G?"

"No. Now, listen, nobody said you had to work in an office. What ad are you answering here anyway?"

"Executive assistant at a mutual funds company," Dana replied.

Grimacing, Gretchen said, "Dana, that isn't you! Look, I know you need a steady paycheck and all that, but . . . what about what Chantal suggested? About you working with kids?"

"Yeah, but doing what?" she said, slumping her face farther down till her cheeks were nearly level with her wrists.

"How about teaching a drama class—for kids? At a school, or an after-school program? A community theater thing? Hey, that would be fun! Or . . . you could work at one of those youth centers or something. Anything with kids would be great because you have all that energy. You're youthful, optimistic, peppy—"

"And I do like to nap . . ." Dana offered, considering this.

"Exactly," Gretchen said, smiling.

"Okay, I'll think about it. I mean think about it for real." Smiling sincerely, she said, "Thanks, G. You're like my sister," and then headed back to her room. The words clutched Gretchen's heart even after Dana was gone; Dana had brothers and Gretchen was an only child, but ultimately, they had both always longed for a sister.

Again she focused on the spice rack, because she was still too keyed up to sleep. Damn it, why hadn't Rick called her back? She knew she shouldn't keep obsessing about it, but she couldn't help it. Why was he suddenly pulling the distant guy routine? What had made him lose interest just like that? Even if he was put off by her being out to dinner when they'd made plans to see each other, it still didn't make sense that he wouldn't call her to clear it up, especially when she'd left him two voice mails.

Granted, it had been only a day and so, by all reasonable standards, she was being totally paranoid. But tell that to the all-too-familiar sinking feeling in her stomach. Her gut was telling her, *You're getting ditched,* and her gut never lied when it came to Matters of Ditching. Maybe she was simply getting too old to date. It was always so damn disappointing.

CHAPTER TWENTY-SIX

*T*wo nights later, Gretchen found herself at TCC, helping Susanna get ready for her guest appearance on Brett's show. It had been a power play, pure and simple. Whether it was Joel or Brett's idea was anyone's guess, but Susanna had finally been offered a spot—though the offer had come with next to no notice. If she took it she would have to scramble, betraying how eager she was for Brett's exposure and all but admitting to a decided pecking order at the network. If she passed on it . . . Well, there was no way she would pass and she hadn't.

Throughout the evening, Susanna has still tried to act as though she were blasé about this, like it had all been Abe's idea, like she hadn't been salivating over it for weeks.

The taping was wrapping up. Outside the high partitioned walls that closed off the set, Gretchen paced the cement floor of Brett's studio with her clipboard in hand. She heard more boisterous applause from Brett's live audience, and then Brett's voice call out, "Now Susanna's gonna finish the mousse cake off for us—give it up for Susanna!" More applause.

Irrepressibly, she smiled. As much of a handful as her boss was at times, she'd done a great job tonight and Gretchen was proud of her. Strangely, Susanna's dependency on her was a little contagious; at times Gretchen almost felt like she needed to take care of her, to protect her, because she had so few true allies. Of course, in this business who did?

Tonight, Brett's audience responded well to Susanna, and surprisingly, she hadn't pulled any of her diva nonsense to slow down the taping.

Any good news was a boost for Gretchen's mood, too, considering that today had been a terrible day at work, and it had had nothing to do with Monday blues. First thing this morning, when she'd sat down at her desk, her chair tilted over and she'd swiftly lost her balance and toppled over, with the chair crashing down beside her. Once she'd crawled off the floor and taken a look, she'd seen the problem. There had been a loose wheel that rolled right off the leg of the chair when Gretchen had taken a seat. After that mini debacle, she went about her work, only to find more bad luck waiting.

When she'd been on the *Susanna's Kitchen* set checking the ingredients for that afternoon's show, she'd opened the fridge and pulled out the bowl of prepared custard only to find an ugly brown spider perched right on top of it. With a startled scream, she'd plunked the bowl back on the shelf and called for someone to come over. She knew she was a big baby, but bugs freaked her out. One of the crew members, a sweet guy named Jeff, heard her and rushed right over.

Nervously, Gretchen had jumped back a few feet and pointed at the refrigerator. "There's a spider—will you kill it?" Jeff grabbed a piece of paper towel, opened the fridge, and Gretchen hadn't bothered to ask him what kind of spider it was or anything other than, "Is it dead? Is it dead yet?" He told her yes and not to be so scared, and truly, she felt like a foolish cliché with her skittish behavior. When she thanked Jeff, he told her "No problem," then added, "but that fucker was nasty."

No, this definitely had not been her day. But now, looking at her watch, she saw it was quarter to eight, so the day was nearly done.

To keep busy while the taping finished up, she straightened some of the items on the craft table. It was filled with antipasto platters, cookies, water bottles, and cans of soda. At the far end of the table were two metal urns for coffee and hot water, and a basket overflowing with tea bags, instant cocoa packs, and sweeteners.

She eyed the shiny metal coffee urn for a long moment, contemplating a cup, when her train of thought was interrupted by footsteps. When she glanced over her shoulder, she gasped before she could stop herself. Mouth curved open, her heart sped up, and she meant to look away—she *wanted* to look away—but couldn't manage to drag her gaze off his. More than anything, she wanted to smack him. Maybe this was her day after all.

As Rick's eyes locked with Gretchen's, his chest tightened. Damn, seeing her up close, in person, it sucked the breath right out of his lungs. She was so damn pretty, so warm looking, so inviting, so frustratingly big-eyed and sweet.

He missed her already, everything about her, especially that cute giggle of hers. Kissing her soft, wet mouth, and feeling her hands on him.

Abruptly, she turned her back on him. So she was pissed. He could hardly blame her. Until this moment, he'd thought he was, too.

Ever since Friday night, he'd been pushing her out of his mind, or trying to but never having much luck with it. He had wondered if he'd overreacted, and now, seeing her stiffly tending to the food table, he knew that he had. There'd been a flash of hurt and anger in her eyes before she'd turned away from him.

His jealousy about her and Brett had made him crazy, made him lose the cool, sharp focus he was known for at work, that he prided himself on. Just the thought of Gretchen with his brother had sent rage pumping through his blood; he hadn't been able to stay detached, to stay in control. Which was why he hadn't called her. Sure he'd heard her messages giving her excuses, but he'd still been so put off that he hadn't even wanted to deal with her anymore. It had been a blow to his pride, but it had been a helluva lot more than that.

Even when Brett had called him yesterday vaguely apologizing for the "misunderstanding" and offering a truce with tickets for the VIP section, Rick had remained aloof. He hadn't even considered going until Brett mentioned that Susanna Tate was guest hosting the show. Correctly, Rick had figured that Gretchen might be there, too. He'd told himself he was done with her, but he'd still been dying to see her.

And here she was. Testily straightening platters and napkins, and he knew without a doubt: He wanted her.

She seemed intent on ignoring him. He'd managed to screw this whole thing up, and now there was only one thing he could do—go after her.

"Hello," he said casually, approaching the table. Gretchen's shoulders straightened a bit at his voice. Rick scanned down her body, eyeing her cute round butt and the mouthwatering curve of her plump breasts pushing against her white T-shirt before he came around the other side of the table so she had to face him.

"Hello," she said crisply, barely sparing him a glance. "I didn't expect to see you here." Her voice was flat, uninterested, as she reached over to adjust the napkins. She was taking some from one stack and moving it to another stack, making the stacks equal.

"So, how have you been?" he asked casually.

"Just peachy," she replied icily, avoiding eye contact. "Of course, if you were really curious, you could've called."

Ah. There it was. She'd opened the door. There was still hope.

Instead of addressing her comment, Rick deflected it, which would probably work better to his advantage. "It was a good show in there," he said, scanning the table. "Made me hungry."

With a puff of breath, Gretchen gawked at him, as if to say: *How can you talk about food, you dick?*

Rick acted oblivious. The fact was, he might want to grab her and kiss her and say, "Let's start over," and have that be the end of it, but it was never that easy with women. If he wanted her to come around, he would have to needle her a little. To get a reaction, to strike a match to her temper and stoke her fire.

"Have you been hanging around out here the whole time? Don't they let you sit inside and watch the show?" he asked.

"The crew works behind the scenes" was all she said.

"Want to know what they were making tonight? It looked pretty good."

"I *know* what they were making. I'm Susanna's assistant—I mean, set supervisor," she amended quickly, then gave a frustrated shake of her head. Turning away, she walked to the end of the table to grab a paper cup off the mile-high stack.

"Oh, that's right," he said conversationally as he followed her direction, walking down his side of the table. Talking to her like they were buddies was bound to irritate the hell out of her. Clearly she was waiting for him to bring up what happened, the fact that he'd blown off their plans to hang out on Friday night as well as her messages, and at the very least, to apologize for not calling her. But he didn't do any of that—yet.

"Look, I'm working now, okay?" she said curtly, as she filled her paper cup with coffee.

"Hey, don't let me stop you," Rick said, holding back a grin. She was damn cute when she was as tense as a knot. "I can see you're working hard," he added dryly, which earned him a glare. After a pause, he said, "So what's up with that outfit?"

Confused, she said, "What about my outfit?" Then with an edge of defensiveness, added, "The whole crew is dressed casually. It's not like *we're* on camera. Why, what's wrong with what I'm wearing?"

Crossing his arms over his chest, Rick shrugged. "Nothing's wrong. Just that you look like someone kids come up to for dope, that's all. What's that, your father's undershirt?"

"What!" she yelped. He managed to keep a straight face at her flustered, appalled reaction, but it wasn't easy. Sucking in a breath, she said, "First of all, this is a woman's casual tee. And I was wearing a sweater over it before, but I got hot." Briskly, she grabbed a sugar packet and started tapping it against her finger.

"Okay, okay," he said, holding his hands up. After a pause, he added, "I guess I shouldn't even ask what's up with the Army fatigues, huh?"

She looked down at her loose-fitting green pants, then back at him, like he was an idiot. "They're cargo pants! Don't you know *anything*?" Then, pressing her lips together like she was holding in an outburst, Gretchen shook her head and said, "Look, just don't even speak to me, all right? I'm not going to discuss my clothes or anything else with you."

Again he held up his hands. "Fine with me."

Then Rick proceeded to actually *not* speak to her. *Huh?* What planet was this guy living on? Gretchen wondered. Clearly the least he could do was come up with some half-assed excuse for not calling and then beg her forgiveness. What was difficult about this?

Just then Ellie Galistette emerged from the set, walking out the same side exit that Rick had a few moments ago. She flashed a smile at Gretchen when they made eye contact, and she came over to the craft table. "Oh, are you guarding the food?" she said in a "kidding" voice. "Fabulous show tonight!" she added, reaching for a cracker. "Both my stars really shined up there. They make a great team."

Assessing her, Gretchen felt the same suspicion she had been feeling for the past three days. Her heavy orange hair was pulled back from her face with a headband and her smile was pleasant and benign . . . yet vaguely smug. Gretchen still considered Ellie the prime suspect in Misty's murder—she'd clearly had the most to gain. In fact, if Rick hadn't been such an asshole about everything, Gretchen would've had a chance to talk it over with him.

Speaking of Rick . . . Suddenly Gretchen realized that if she made polite conversation with Ellie, it would help her look oblivious to him. He was still lingering around the table, rattling her nerves. She was too aware of him . . . too cognizant of how much she still liked him even though she didn't want to. She longed to climb up on him, to bury herself in his arms, but she couldn't.

Basically? It sucked.

"Listen, Gretchen," Ellie said, breaking her train of thought, "I just wanted you to know . . . I'm sorry. About Misty. It must be weird for you. You know, because you went to high school with her."

Surprised, Gretchen furrowed her brows. "How did you know that?" Perhaps Misty had simply told her . . . though it didn't seem likely considering that she'd avoided acknowledging the connection herself each time she'd seen Gretchen. Either Misty hadn't remembered Gretchen either, in which case she couldn't have told Ellie, or more likely, she *had* remembered and hadn't wanted to deal with high school memories of any kind—in which case, she *also* wouldn't have told Ellie. But then, maybe Ellie had snooped through Misty's old yearbooks when she'd been playing nursemaid to her at her apartment, in those days right before she died.

In any event, Gretchen wasn't sure how to respond to the awkward choice of small talk. "I mean, it's none of my business what kind of issues you guys had," Ellie pressed on. "It's just an interesting coincidence."

"Whoa, wait, we didn't have any *issues*. I didn't even know Misty in high school."

Looking skeptical, Ellie remarked, "Well, it was pretty clear she didn't like you—no offense. Anyone could see that, right? I just assumed it was mutual . . ."

Caught off guard by the whole topic, Gretchen went to rest her palm on the tabletop and accidentally knocked over her own cup of coffee. "Oh!" she yelped, quickly righting the cup, but all of the coffee had spilled, soaking the tablecloth and dripping heavily onto the cement floor. "Oh, shoot," she mumbled, reaching over to grab a bunch of napkins. Her face flamed with embarrassment because Rick was still there, watching. Though he'd already moved down toward the other end of the table, so she wasn't sure if he'd heard the conversation.

"Oh, Gretchen, are you all right?" Ellie said with over-the-top concern. "Did you burn yourself?"

"No, no, I'm fine. Just clumsy," she threw in halfheartedly.

"You should really be more careful," Ellie said, speaking deliberately, looking right into Gretchen's eyes. "Sometimes accidents can be dangerous."

With that, she turned. Catching sight of Abe at the other end of the floor, talking to Joel and some network executives, Ellie said, "See you later," then scurried over to join him. Just then Gretchen noticed that beyond Abe and several other people was Marjorie Bass, Cady's producer. Huh—when had she arrived? And what was she doing here? Perhaps she'd been working late and simply stopped up?

As Ellie flitted over to Abe and the others, her words reverberated in Gretchen's mind. *Sometimes accidents can be dangerous.* The comment was oddly unsettling . . .

Now it was just Rick and Gretchen at the table again, but by the sound of the cued music inside the set, the floor would soon be flooded with people who would be scrupulously herded out of the studio, down the corridor, and into the public elevator.

Frustrated, Gretchen didn't feel like being there anymore; Rick had put her too much on edge. Tonight he was clean-shaven and breathtakingly handsome. She still didn't understand what he was doing there—since when did he go to Brett's show? But she didn't dare ask. If she asked, it only showed that she still cared.

"So you still haven't explained the Army fatigues," he said gently. His voice was softer, not mocking like before. And he wasn't looking at her pants—he was looking into her face with his damn unreadable expression.

"They're cargo pants," she repeated feebly, lacking any of her former zeal on the subject.

"So . . ." he began, walking around the table to her side. "I'm sorry our date never happened the other night."

What exactly was he sorry for—that he hadn't called to cancel or that he hadn't called ever again?

"Me, too, but I got over it," she lied, just as the music inside the set kicked up even louder, and she knew she had to make her escape now before Susanna or anyone else accosted her. This was sensory overload; she couldn't possibly keep a level head with the endless, neurotic demands that Susanna would inevitably place on her following the show. She had to get out of there!

Turning on her heel, she left Rick standing there, walked briskly across the floor and out the door. Once she was in the hall, she picked up speed, scurrying around the bend, determined to avoid a confrontation with him, her boss, or anybody tonight. Enough was enough. She was tired and frazzled. She needed to think. She didn't know what to make of Rick's disappearing act and she didn't want to be steered wrong again by their undeniable attraction to each other.

"Wait up. Where are you going so fast?" Rick called, jogging lightly to catch up with her at the elevators.

"I'm going home," she said simply, jamming her fingers on the button several times.

"Listen, about what you said, you know, about how you're over everything? Well, I just wanted to tell you that I'm not surprised." Suspiciously—cautiously—she tipped her face up and studied him. "Hell, you've probably got some other guy by now, huh?"

"It's been three days!"

The elevator dinged and she hopped on. Unsurprisingly, Rick followed. He seemed intent to make up with her, to try to act like nothing had happened, but something *had* happened—and she was still damn mad about it!

Once the doors sealed shut, Rick turned to face her. "Then you haven't forgotten me yet," he said, coming closer. Soon he was standing only inches away, enveloping the space between them in his heat.

Looking up at him levelly, she forced herself not to show how flustered his nearness made her . . . how excited. "What do you want?"

"I want you," he said softly, gruffly, flickering his blue eyes down to her mouth.

The admission sent her pulse skittering wildly. No, she couldn't get sucked into this again, no way. "Let me explain how dating works," she said, inching back to put more distance between them. "A man asks a woman out, a man is lucky to go out with that woman to begin with, I might add . . ." Rick nodded along like this was a great education, all the while matching each step she took backward with another one forward. "And after a nice evening together, they say good night, and if the man says he'll call her, he actually *does* call her."

Okay, so it was an *idealistic* view of dating, but it was the story she was sticking to.

"Wait. Back up," Rick said, trespassing on more of her personal space until her butt nudged against the back wall of the elevator. There was nowhere left to go—she was trapped between the wall and Rick and right now, she didn't know which was stronger. Her breath hitched in her throat and her mouth ran dry as Rick put both hands on the wall, bracketing her in with his arms. Then he looked down at her and silkily he said, "You skipped over the best part."

"W-what?" she mumbled, having momentarily forgotten the conversation leading up to their intimately close quarters.

"Best part of the date," he said, his voice low and purring. "The part where they say good night. And they kiss." He brought his body up even more snugly against hers. "And sometimes . . . they get naked."

Swallowing hard, Gretchen licked her lips and struggled to get her breath back. "N-no. No kissing on the first date."

She was about to add "generally speaking," when he injected, "We kissed. In my car, remember?"

"That was technically our second date," she said, counting the espresso place near TCC as the first.

"And on our next one, we got naked. Remember?" Grinning wolfishly, he let out a whistle and murmured, "Now *that* was hot."

Her heart was pounding in her ears; her palms were starting to sweat. "Those were special circumstances," she said in her own defense.

"So it was special, huh?" he challenged. "Well, if it was special, then how could you have moved on already?" He pressed himself against her and she nearly melted. Suddenly her chest was so tight she could barely breathe. White-hot lust and attraction all but crackled between them.

Flattened against him, she was overwhelmed by his height, his strength, his muscle, and heat and bone, his power to seduce her so easily.

"I meant it was special in the moment," she said, even as she traitorously rose up on her toes to try to feel Rick's thick, engorged shaft against her crotch, "and now the moment's passed."

"So it's not special anymore? Well, if it's not special, then what is it?"

"It's . . . crap," she replied, trying to think of some way to salvage the tough act, but it was a pathetic attempt and he wasn't deterred.

Lowering his head, Rick ran his hands down the wall until, just like that, he jerked her lower body against his. Suddenly he had his hands snaked around her waist and her head angled back, her face tipped up, her lips waiting for a kiss, even as she whispered, "The moment's gone. We can never get it back."

His voice was rough and sexy when he said, "It feels like we're kind of having one right now." And then he purred hotly in her ear, "God, you're so warm. . . ." She could barely balance on her toes, but she didn't have to because Rick's body was pressed fully and firmly against hers, sandwiching her between him and the wall so she couldn't slip if she tried. They were flattened together, his groin hard and hers aching; heat soaked her panties and sweat broke out on her back and neck. "You know, you can kiss me if you want."

"No," she whispered stubbornly. Rick pushed his hips forward, driving his arousal hard against her. She bit back a moan . . . and tilted her hips and pushed back.

"Just a kiss, apple girl," he said, his voice little more than a thick rasp. The sweetness of the words, whatever they meant, stole her breath. As he dragged his lips against her cheek, then down to her neck, blood raged in her veins. Sexual heat choked the air like a humid cloud sucking up all the oxygen. *"Kiss me,"* he urged.

"No . . ." she whispered.

"Okay, no tongue," he bargained softly. "How about that?"

"No tongue?" she repeated incredulously. "Then what's the point?"

He chuckled at that and she gave up fighting him. "C'mere, baby," he murmured and covered her mouth with his.

At first the kiss was slow and wet and searching, his tongue tangling seductively with hers, slicking inside her mouth and licking flames up between her legs. Her fingers slid up the front of his shirt, underneath his suit jacket, and up to his broad, solid shoulders. He groaned, uttering something imperceptible, before one hand tightened on her waist and the other came up to cup her neck, massaging it as he deepened the kiss, making love to her mouth.

Lust roared through her. With a moan, she kissed him back and writhed against him to get more, to get even closer. She ran her fingers over his cock, which was impossibly hard and full inside his pants. When she tried to stroke him, Rick grunted his arousal and pushed his hips into hers again. She nearly cried out from the sensation—for things to come. And before she knew it, Rick's hands had moved down to her bottom, cupping it possessively, squeezing it.

They kissed aggressively. Hungrily. It was a blurred frenzy of carnal desire, and Gretchen didn't stop to question how much time had passed or her own savage behavior.

Her eyes slid closed as Rick bit her neck lightly, then traced a hot wet line down her throat. Greedily, Gretchen gripped Rick's hair, wordlessly urging him to do it again. As he worked his open, scalding-hot mouth on her neck, he fondled her breasts through her T-shirt. Fluidly, his hands slipped underneath her shirt and bra, and his warm, roughened palms cupped her bare breasts, her nipples. When he started to rub them, she moaned weakly, feeling too aroused to stand up for much longer. She was nearly limp with arousal, wanting to sag against the floor and have him just take her there.

Then his fingers were pulling down her fly and sliding right inside her underwear, and she broke the kiss to gasp, to catch her breath, and in doing so, gave him access to her cheek. He kissed his way across it, moving her hair out of the way so he could run his tongue along the rim of her ear, and ran his fingertip lightly over her opening. A hot ripple ran through her as she tried to rock against his finger, which only teased her with its gentle strokes. Sweltering and sticky, her body trembling, she would've begged him to go deeper if she'd had the strength, if she could form the words, but she couldn't seem to manage it, so she just rubbed his cock harder with her hand, more urgently.

With a guttural sound of desire, Rick slid his finger inside her, making her gasp again, loll her head restlessly against the wall of the elevator, waiting for more. But he didn't give her more; he withdrew and then only teased her opening. Running his finger back and forth over it, gently, breathtakingly. Gretchen thought she could die of the anticipation, the arousal.

She buried her frustration in another searing kiss. Her fingers gripped his shoulders, her body arched against his, as their mouths continued to assail each other, their kisses becoming rougher, wetter, more desperate, more frenzied, and it was too much, it had to stop. If they didn't, they'd end up doing it right there—on the elevator!— and it would be unbelievably reckless and irresponsible. She *worked* here, for pete's sake!

But just when she was about to put a halt to all this madness, Rick moved his hand to palm her whole crotch, heat from his hand seeping into her sensitive flesh. Her knees almost buckled. She brought a hand down to his wrist to still him before he took this any further, but it was too late. In an instant, he sank to his knees, and she hadn't had a chance to question him before he stripped her pants and thong down in one motion. "No, we can't," she whispered, then groaned shamelessly when Rick gave her a thorough, open-mouthed kiss between her legs. No, he couldn't—not *here*—this was insanity now.

But he did. Ardently, he pulled her baggy pants and her underwear off of her entirely and left them pooled on the floor. Then he gripped the back of her thighs, lifting her and bringing her legs around, to rest on his shoulders. As he caressed her bottom, he continued to kiss and lick her intimately, until he angled to suck her hottest spot. She ran her fingers through his hair, telling herself that she'd pull his head away, but it felt so good, she didn't stop him. Instead, she found herself clutching him to her, all but pulling his hair; the closer she got to that elusive climax, the harder she pulled.

What had happened to her? She'd always been a nice girl up until now. Now she was out of control, desperate for more.

"Wait," she breathed. "Rick . . . we have to stop."

Raggedly, he muttered, "I want to make you come," then sucked on that sweet spot again before sliding two fingers inside her. Just like that, she erupted in a shuddering orgasm that took her completely by surprise.

"*Ohh* . . ." she groaned, savoring the rippling sensations that poured up her body as Rick rode them out with his fingers. "Oh . . . *God* . . ."

Murmuring to her, he pressed suctioning kisses to her belly while still stroking her with his hand. Then he soothed her thighs as he lifted her off of him, set her feet on the floor, and rose up off his knees. Sliding his fingers into her hair, he pressed his forehead to hers. His eyes looked dazed with passion. "I'm so turned on right now," he rasped.

Speechless and suddenly emotional, Gretchen hugged him. Rick folded her into him, holding her close. When she finally spoke she said, "I'm so embarrassed."

He pulled back, concerned. "Why?"

"Because we're in an elevator," she said softly, her lips against his shirt. "And because I work here." Abruptly, she realized her precarious position and bent to pick up her pants and thong. "Just look at me," she mumbled, more to herself.

"Believe me, I am," Rick said with blatant sexuality.

"I'm serious," she said, even as a hot blush crept up her neck and into her cheeks. Once she'd shimmied back into her clothes, she didn't feel as vulnerable.

"Oh, hell," Rick said and stroked her cheek. "I'm sorry. I got carried away."

He got carried away?

"First things first," he added, and pressed the "door open" button. Sometime when they'd been making out they'd made it to the ground floor. Had the doors sprung open and they hadn't even realized it? They must have; opened and then after a few moments idle, closed again. How could she have been so lost in passion, so overwhelmed by desire, that she'd been so oblivious to her surroundings? Yet . . . the thought that Rick had been, too, was *extremely* exciting.

He backed away from her and wiped the back of his hand along his mouth lightly. "Let's get out of here," he said, taking her hand.

The lobby was dark and deserted. "Oh, damn!" Gretchen said, as they passed the reception desk.

"What's the matter?" he said, slipping his fingers through hers, interlocking them in an affectionate lover's gesture.

"I just remembered I left my sweater and jacket upstairs."

"Here," he said, taking off his jacket and draping it over her shoulders; it was huge on her, which for some reason made her smile. She was melting, falling into it again. *Oh, please let this be the right thing to do . . .* "C'mon," he said, leading the way, then abruptly, he stopped. Quizzically, she looked up at him, and here, by the glass doors, there was shadowy darkness, but she could make out his face better. Not that it mattered because his expression was unreadable.

Gently, he tugged on her hand, bringing her down with him to sit on the lime-green sofa that lined the wall.

"Okay. Listen up," he said, his voice firm and authoritative, and she found herself mesmerized by him right now, by his potency, his commanding, powerful presence, and she thought: *God, what's happened to me? Since when was 'authoritative' a turn-on?*

"I'm sorry," he said. "I fucked up." *Valid*—boy, this night was getting better and better. "But you have to understand, a lot of women are really into Brett. Well, not *him* necessarily, but his whole image. They wanna be on his arm at all the parties and big events and . . ."

What was he getting at? Gretchen wondered. She knew all this already.

"I misunderstood what happened that night. I guess from the beginning I didn't know how to read you, if you were interested in Brett or not. Like you yourself said the other night, most girls have a crush on him. I wondered if maybe you were using me to get to him."

"What?" she said, genuinely shocked by this. Then she realized how loud she'd just been and dropped her voice. "Are you *serious*?"

"It's happened from time to time," Rick stated, but Gretchen was still flummoxed. Using *Rick* to get to *Brett*? Please! Rick was twice the man his brother was, and she didn't just mean his height. The last things Gretchen fantasized about at the end of the day were celebrity parties and the paparazzi. She was too busy fantasizing about having enough time for a long, hot bubble bath.

Didn't he realize that about her?

"Me? Interested in Brett?" she said. "Instead of *you*? You must be insane!"

Grinning, Rick said, "Okay, you sold me."

Whoops! She supposed she *had* sounded kind of emphatic there. Well, there went playing it cool. But they were beyond that now. Biting her lip, she said, "No, I just meant . . ."

"That's okay. Keep it as it is." With that, he reached over. Cupping her face in one hand, he leaned in to kiss her. The instant their lips met heat rose between them and her chest swelled with longing. Rick slowly licked inside her mouth, kissing her softly but passionately, letting his lips linger on hers as his arm wrapped around her waist and urged her closer.

"We . . . we should go . . ." she managed, her voice breathless even to her own her ears.

"All right," he said, taking her hand and tugging her to her feet. "Let's get out of here." A taxi ride later, they were in Rick's apartment.

CHAPTER TWENTY-SEVEN

*H*e didn't bother to give her the tour. The place was pitch-dark, with only a hint of light streaming from a partially opened door. "What's that?" Gretchen asked, suddenly feeling nervous. Rick came up behind her, wrapping an arm around her waist and pulling her against him.

"What's what?" he murmured against her skin as he pushed her hair to the side and placed suctioning kisses down her neck. Then he must've realized she meant the light, and he said, "Oh, that's my bedroom." She swallowed, shutting her eyes, dropping her head back as he ran his tongue along her ear.

His bedroom. What she'd experienced so far of Rick's ability to please a woman was enough to make her legs wobbly, her knees weak, and a breathy sigh spill from her lips.

He tunneled his fingers through her hair, gripped her tight, and used his other hand to spin her around. Then his mouth claimed hers with a kiss that was wet and feral, blatantly sexual, and she responded with a keening moan and clawed his shirt to hold her upright—or to tear it off—to have more of him. And just like that, he pushed his jacket off her shoulders—vaguely she heard it hitting the floor—and he hitched her up, pulling her legs apart to straddle his body as he walked them toward the light.

Feverishly, she clung to him, kissing his lips, his cheek, his jaw, his throat, anywhere she could. He moved quickly, and before she could notice much about the room, she ended up flat on her back— on his bed, the rumpled, unmade covers bunching underneath her.

They rolled around until they'd stripped each other completely and only after Rick landed on top of her, completely naked, did Gretchen have a realization. "Wait!" she said, the weight of what she was about to do hitting her.

That startled him. He looked up from between her breasts, panting, his hair already messy, and his shoulders tight. In that moment, he was just such a beautiful, powerful animal—it was the sexiest thing she'd ever seen.

"What's wrong?" he asked, his voice thick and gravelly with arousal.

"Nothing . . . it's just . . ." Squirming, she tried to move out from under him; he pushed up on his arm to give her room, and she managed to shimmy up toward the headboard, until Rick's face was more at her knees. In kind, he sat up more, or knelt, and her eyes went straight to his erection, which was huge and mouthwatering. For a few moments, she couldn't drag her gaze away. Instinctively, her mouth curved open. She was hungry for him, craving him— fearing him because he was so hung she didn't see how she could take it when he—

"Oh, come here," he groaned, pulling her down as he brought himself up. Now they were lying snugly alongside each other, and he was stroking her spine with his fingertips.

Um . . . what was she going to say again?

Raising his eyebrows questioningly at her, he waited, but when she didn't say anything else, when she leaned over and crushed her mouth on his, he rolled back on top of her, kissing her with unrestrained hunger. She was lost, drowning in disarmingly erotic sensations, and the only thing that snapped her back into focus was the feel of his thick shaft between her legs.

He wasn't pushing inside her, just letting his cock rub her, over and over, making her moan and break their kiss, and whisper brokenly, "Wait . . . God . . . I remembered what I was going to say . . ." She gave a light shove to his chest to get his attention; he pushed up on his arms and looked into her eyes. "I'm not on birth control," she said, still catching her breath, "and I—"

"Don't worry," Rick rasped huskily against her cheek. Trailing soft, slow kisses along her throat and down to her collarbone, he said, "I'm not going anywhere yet." He paused; then she got his meaning.

"I've got condoms," he added—and it was a relief, because she sure as hell didn't carry any around with her.

Why didn't it surprise her that Rick had some on hand? Not that he was some kind of sex fiend; he was just a man who was pre-pared . . . bringing her to the heart of her next point. "Rick, wait," she said gently, flattening her palms to his chest to stay him, to keep their eye contact. "This . . . this is moving really fast for me. Can we maybe slow it down a little?"

"Yeah," he said suddenly, rolling to the side to free her, to give her space. She could finally breathe easily again, but she wanted him back on top of her anyway. "I'm sorry, I didn't realize—"

"No, no, it's okay," she interjected, turning to face him. They were lying side by side, and she gave him a faint, shy smile.

"What's wrong?" he said again, speaking gently to her as he brought his hand up to smooth her hair away from her face, caress-ing her cheek as he did it.

"Well . . . this just isn't my usual. I know you probably can't tell by what happened in the elevator and . . . stuff," she added, thinking about the other time in her apartment and their torrid, untamed first kiss in his truck. "But the truth is, I don't have that much experience, and—"

"Shh, don't worry," he coaxed. "We won't do anything you don't want to do."

Don't *want* to do? No, that was hardly the problem. She wanted to—and planned to—but she had to know some stuff first. "I want to, Rick," she said, "but it's been a while for me."

"Okay," he said tentatively, like he wasn't sure what her point was. Truly, what *was* her point? This was sex, not leaving out your pierced earrings too long. She was still a functioning female with a higher sex drive than she had even realized she possessed. She was frantic for him, sweaty and shaken, and right now, even the *thought* of Rick making love to her was enough to make her writhe on the bed, spread her legs, moan, beg . . .

And it really hadn't been that long when you considered how long Gretchen had waited to have sex in the first place. But "it's been a while" just seemed like the thing to say when you were about to in-troduce the next, more delicate topic.

"Uh . . . how many partners have you had?" she asked cautiously, afraid of the answer. Not like the number itself would tell her much, but it seemed like good information to have. She braced herself for something terrible. This was where it would all fall apart; this is where he'd say something like "two hundred" and she'd have to bolt.

Or what if he said something even worse, like: *I lost count?*

Dear Lord. There couldn't possibly be a respectable number when it came to a guy as hot as Rick. He was so confident with her, especially when he touched her, kissed her—surely that expertise came from somewhere. Cringing, Gretchen waited for his answer.

He thought for just a second, then answered, "Nine."

"Nine?" she echoed, horrified. *"Nine different women?* Oh my God!"

"What?" he said with a surprised kind of laugh. "Is that bad?"

"It's just . . . so *many,*" she said with a touch of disgust.

Though in truth it was better than what she'd feared. He was thirty-two years old after all, and unbelievably sexy. With his dark, dangerous looks and his simmering intensity, Rick had probably started having sex in high school, and in light of that, was nine so terrible?

Still . . . it was nine times as many as her.

"I'm sorry," he said sincerely, looking eager to please. That alone touched her heart. Then he said, "Oh, wait, you know what? That number's wrong." *No, don't lie,* she thought fretfully, *Don't reduce the number just to keep me from changing my mind.* "It wasn't nine," he said. "It was eleven."

Her jaw dropped. Her eyes bugged out of her head. Her dismay was ludicrously apparent. "Eleven!" she yelped. "Holy cow, I can't be-lieve it—*eleven?*" Clutching her neck, she murmured, "Oh, I feel faint . . ."

"Jesus, would you calm down?" Rick said. "I just forgot about these two girls in the Air Force for a second, that's all."

"Two girls . . . oh, no," she said, getting a little panicky again. "You mean . . . two as in . . . ?"

"As in *what?*" he asked, clearly confused. (Jeez, he was kind of slow at times, wasn't he?) Then Rick let out a bark of laughter, getting it. "What, you mean two *at once?* No—Jesus! Two different girls I dated, that's all. What do you think I am, anyway?"

Heaving a dramatic sigh of relief, Gretchen pressed her head back into the pillows, gulping in a breath of air before looking back up at him. She could see the traces of amusement in his face. Explaining herself, she began, "Well, I know a lot of guys fantasize about—"

"Sure, a fantasy's one thing," he interrupted, rolling closer, cupping her cheek with his palm. His blue gaze burned a path from her eyes to her mouth. His playful expression was gone, replaced by a look of raw, smoldering desire. She breathed in, waiting for him, and then he kissed her. Gently working his lips across her cheek, he sucked on her earlobe before whispering into her ear, "But I'm all about one man on one woman." Her pulse quickened. *Yes.* She hoped he meant that literally; she might have limited experience, but for her, sex was at its finest when the man was on top, doing most of the work. "Grinding against each other, kissing and licking every inch of her body," he added thickly. "And I like to concentrate." Then he slid his tongue inside her ear, making her tremble and clutch at him. "Mmm . . . like with you and me . . . I have a feeling you'll be more than I can handle—almost."

"I doubt that," Gretchen managed weakly. More like the other way around. In fact, would she even be able to walk after this?

Her words gave him pause. Pulling back, he scanned her face and quirked his mouth. "Why, how many people have *you* been with?" he said.

"Um . . ." She supposed she "had" to tell him since he'd told her and it was the "right" thing to do. (*Don't you just hate that?*) But she felt a little silly saying it, even though she shouldn't.

Gretchen hesitated for a long moment and Rick arched his eyebrows expectantly. Finally, she copped to it. "One," she said and waited for the requisite shock, confusion, and questions that would follow.

"One," he repeated, nodding, taking it in; then he squinted at her and tilted his head. "Wait a second," he said, and rolled over her, pushing himself all the way up on his hands, so he was bracketing her in, looking down into her eyes. She couldn't help but noticing the way his biceps flexed as they took his weight.

"You broke up with your ex-boyfriend how long ago?"

"Almost a year," she said.

"And how long were you two together?"

"Two years."

"So then . . . do you mean to tell me . . ." Jeez, how long did they have to drag this out? "You're telling me you lost your virginity at, what, twenty-*three*?"

So he wasn't great at math; he was still cute.

Unless maybe he forgot and thought she was twenty-six instead of twenty-seven. Either way, no sense in correcting him. "Yeah, I guess," she hedged. "What's wrong with that?"

"Nothing . . . Nothing at all. I'm just shocked."

Here it came. She'd had the "I'm shocked" conversation with Tristan, too, only then the answer had been zero.

Rick seemed still to be absorbing the information. Gretchen couldn't help wondering why guys made a big deal about it. But then she supposed they could ask her the same thing. Why had it been a big deal to her? Why had she waited?

"Well, you don't have to have a moment of silence about it," she threw in, and he chuckled.

"I'm sorry. I just never saw that coming. But it's nice. Different."

"All right already, I'm not an exhibit at the zoo."

Now he laughed. "I'm sorry, baby," he said, and her whole chest warmed at the way he'd said that. "It's just, you're such a fox, that's all. I mean I'm really dying to know—"

"Twenty-three's not so long to wait," she said quietly, running her hands up his arms, over his smooth, sleek triceps.

"You're right," he conceded.

"I was waiting for my soul mate," she added by way of explanation.

"Oh, and how'd that work out for you?" he quipped.

With a breath of laughter, she shoved at his shoulders and said, "Oh, shut up, will you."

And then he was on top of her again. Kissing her thoroughly, aligning their bodies perfectly. Squirming beneath him, she adjusted to his weight and moaned softly at the feel of his naked body on hers. The heat that radiated off him seeped into her bones. When he spoke, his smooth, rich voice seemed to caress her skin. "You set the pace," he said, and the words warmed her body like a blanket, sent waves of both longing and tenderness rolling through her.

Her breasts were like flattened pillows against the wall of his chest, and her legs like a vise around his hips; she glided one bare foot down the back of his leg, then the other, slowly and softly, and after another moment, she pulled his head closer for a kiss.

One kiss turned into many and throughout, his hands ran over her body with blatant possession. She felt every inch of him, listened to his breathing, his grunts, all his sexy words—and she honed in the movements of his body, the flexing of his muscles, the heat that rose like steam off hot pavement. Nearly choking, Gretchen finally felt Rick's fingers sliding inside her, and spearing white heat right between her legs. Rocking on the bed, she rode his hand, never able to get enough, feeling how wet he was making her, how frustrated. On a thick groan, she said, "I want you so much . . ."

"I want you, too," he replied huskily, withdrawing his fingers and thrusting again. "God, you drive me crazy . . ."

"And you said you have a condom . . . ?" she gasped, reminding him because she didn't know how much more she could take. His foreplay had her so turned on that her body was quivering. She wanted to tell him, *Just fuck me—please,* but she'd never said anything like that before, and she was too shy to say it now.

Quickly, Rick reached over, which pressed his weight on her even more, would've crushed her if she didn't love the feel of him too much to care; when he pulled back he had a condom in his hand and he was paused to tear the packet open with his teeth.

"Thanks," she breathed with a faint smile.

"No, problem. I'm used to wearing rubber," he said, grinning, and a second later, he slid inside her. It hurt and she winced; he was so big and she automatically tensed up, maybe from lack of practice— but there were searing sparks of pleasure on the fringes of the pain. He withdrew and drove into her again. Gretchen gasped.

All hints of pain burned into hot, seeping pleasure. As he rocked his hips in gentle motions to warm her body to his, he lit flames of erotic sensation through her, arousing her to the point of urgency. She gripped his back and urged him on with her hands, her sighs, her undulating hips. Again and again, he thrust himself inside her.

They rode together—both of them panting, sweating, clinging to each other, and it seemed to go on endlessly, each stroke of Rick's cock heightening Gretchen's arousal, driving her toward ecstasy. Rick's hand moved down to where their bodies were joined and with two fingers he started rubbing her. Gretchen was stunned. For some reason it had never occurred to her to be touched like this during sex—to have both. It certainly wasn't one of Tristan's moves.

Her excitement climbed as the sensual sensations he stirred in her spiraled higher. The harder he rubbed, the closer she was to—

She started to come. Thrilling shocks of fire raged between her legs. With her blood ringing in her ears, her heart thundering in her chest, her back arched, her muscles tight, she buried her head deep into the mess of Rick's covers, and tried to express how good this felt, but her throat was too dry and the climax was too strong. All she could do was moan and ride it out, as contractions rolled through her, making her body throb to achieve satisfaction.

Breathing hard, Rick rose up higher, balancing on his arms again. He jerked his hips, thrusting harder, faster, hammering into her until he climaxed, and a long, hoarse cry ripped from his throat.

Moments later, he rolled off her, his chest rising and falling. He slung his arm across his eyes with an exhausted sigh.

Gretchen would've laughed or agreed or said *something* if only she'd had the strength, but her eyes were already drifting shut. She rolled over, curling into Rick's side, and drifted to sleep. Soon after, she was cradled against him with his warm sweaty body faintly sticking to hers and the blanket pulled up over her hips—something Rick must've done before he'd fallen asleep himself.

A few hours later, Gretchen woke up to an empty bed. The room was dark and she was alone. Then she heard noises in the apartment, outside the bedroom. "Rick?" she said. He didn't answer; then she heard another noise, like a cabinet slamming closed. She shot up in bed, covering her bare breasts with Rick's blanket as unease coiled in her stomach.

Then the bedroom door opened, and Rick came in, carrying a brown bag and two cans of soda under his arm. He stopped to hit the light switch with his elbow.

"Oh, good, it's you," she said, smiling.

"Who else?" he said with a questioning grin. He wore a pair of sweatpants and no shirt, his strong, hairy chest a thoroughly arousing image to wake up to. "I'm glad you're awake. I'm starving," he said, and sat down on the bed, dropping the sodas down, too.

"Hi there," Gretchen said softly, stretching sleepily, then leaning up and over to kiss his cheek. His arms snaked around her bare back and hugged her tightly; heat and comfort spread through her chest like a warm drink of cocoa or flannel sheets on bare skin. Rick was here with her and this night was real, not one of her fantasies, and on top of everything that was already wonderful, it smelled like Chinese.

"Are you hungry?" he said.

"Yes, starving." She hadn't even realized it till right this second.

"Good," he said, unrolling the bag. "I didn't want to wake you so I took a chance. Sweet and sour chicken, rice, egg rolls."

"*Yum,*" she said eagerly and reached for some napkins and a plastic fork. "When did you get this?"

"The delivery guy came about ten minutes ago, but you were asleep."

"Wow, where did you find a place to deliver in the middle of the night?"

"Middle of the night? It's only eleven thirty."

"It *is*?" she said, surprised.

"Yeah," he said, biting a chunk out of his egg roll. "We cut out of TCC around eight. And by the time we got back here you were pretty anxious to get in my pants. But I guess I don't have to tell you that part."

"Oh, right, I remember now—*smarty,*" she said with a smirk, then climbed up on her knees, keeping one hand on her breasts to secure the blanket and wrapping the other around his neck. She kissed his cheek and let her lips linger there. "And *wow,*" she breathed, "was it worth *not* waiting for."

He let out a laugh, his face creasing into a smile against her lips. "Thank you. I tried real hard, ma'am."

Gretchen giggled, then suddenly had a thought. "Hey, I just remembered something," she said, pulling back a fraction to look at him. "It *was* you, wasn't it? You were the one who left the fire extinguisher at my apartment that day."

"Oh. That." With a brief nod, he said simply, "Yup. Why, how many times have you used it so far?"

"None," she replied with her hand on her hip, smiling sardonically at him. "I totally forgot about that until just now." Tenderly she added, "That was sweet."

Their lips met for a soft, supple kiss; then Rick ducked his head to go lower. When he had kissed his way across her chest, he nudged at the blanket with his fingers to pull it down.

She squirmed back, so he tugged harder. She grasped his wrist to still his hand.

"Why are you so shy all of a sudden?" he asked.

"Not all of a sudden. I am shy."

"You weren't shy when you were jumping my bones tonight," he teased, his blue eyes sparkling with mischief. "Hey, remember that night when I came back to your place to get my phone and you were all mad at me?"

"I wasn't mad. I was just upset." *And all mad.* "It seemed like you just came in and barely even noticed me at all—"

With a bark of laughter, he said, "Are you kidding me? Of course I noticed. But what was I gonna do? Grab you and start copping a feel right there in the doorway?" She weighed that in her mind; hey, she would've gone with it (but only because it was Rick). "I didn't want you to think I was a jerk," he added like this should have all been pretty obvious.

Then he put down his half-eaten egg roll and leaned over. "It's not like I didn't want to touch you," he said and kissed her bare shoulder, "and rip your nightgown off." He dragged his mouth up to suck the curve of her neck, drawing a sigh from her lips. "It's not like I didn't want to kiss you right here," he whispered, nuzzling the same spot he'd just sucked, "right here where you smell like a little apple."

Sighing again, she thought, *Apple . . . now I see,* and combed her fingers through his hair.

When he looked at her face, he smiled and said, "Hey, you're blushing. Don't get all embarrassed on me now."

"I can't help it," she mumbled and hugged him.

Rick urged Gretchen backward, shoving the food and unopened cans of soda out of the way, and they ended up lying on their sides, bodies entangled. Now the blanket was well on its way past covering any part of her and she wasn't so embarrassed from this angle. Strumming his fingers along her arm, Rick said, "What I want to know is how the *hell* you lost your virginity at twenty-three. That's what I want to talk about."

Rolling her eyes, Gretchen groaned. "Not this again, please."

"Sorry, but I just have to know. I mean . . ." He looked down at her naked breasts and shook his head as if in amazement, then trailed his hand down to her hip and looked even lower. *"Damn."*

"Stop. You're embarrassing me again," she said lightly, and shimmied a little closer. "I don't know how to explain it," she added, stroking his chest lovingly. "I just always wanted to wait. For the right person, you know. The right moment."

"So what was so great about *that* guy?" Rick asked with a slight edge to his voice. Holy cow, was he jealous?

"Looking back, not that much really," she admitted. "I thought I loved him—or I wanted it to be love, I guess. Not that I had any frame of reference, but . . ." Smiling coyly, she threw in, "I still have a lot to learn about men."

"I'm definitely not complaining," he murmured, and kissed her. "Mmm . . . you have soft lips," he whispered between kisses. "Soft, pretty lips . . ."

As their mouths clung to each other, Rick snaked his tongue against hers and rolled them both over so she was on top of him and his hands were tightened on her back. He reached all the way over to his nightstand and pulled out a condom.

Gretchen moaned as he entered her. With her neck arching and her eyes sliding closed, she got lost in the moment, moving rhythmically up and down, rubbing her nipples, vaguely hearing Rick's husky words of encouragement. Gripping her hips, he helped guide her until the tension became white-hot.

Then, swiftly, he rolled them again, spinning her over like she

weighed nothing, taking control, and riding her with relentless
passion.

He was so confident in bed, so commanding, yet so warm and
so tender. It almost made her cry now for no reason. There was no
reason to cry, but still, emotion overwhelmed her. Suddenly he
seemed invincible to her. The whole idea was illusory, but in that
moment, it gripped her. She'd never felt such passion and unrestrained desire in her life, and she wanted more of it, much more.
Undulating against him, she gasped and held on tight. "Teach
me . . ." she whispered.

"Teach you what?" he rasped.

"Everything," she sighed, and then he began.

CHAPTER TWENTY-EIGHT

"*W*ow, this is so beautiful," Gretchen said as she and Rick stepped inside his late father's cabin in Maine. He'd said it was a cabin, but to her a "cabin" was a tiny, rustic pile of logs, two rooms, maybe three, and a fireplace with a big black pot hanging inside it. But this place was impressive. A tall white house with black shutters, it was a breathtaking contrast to the dark green pine trees that cloaked its back.

Closing the door behind them, Rick thanked her for the compliment and gave her the tour. The house exuded a cozy kind of warmth, with its woodsy décor and brick accents, but it was spacious at the same time, with high ceilings, four large bedrooms, and a long, winding old-fashioned kitchen that looked like a stone cave—one with copper pots and recessed lighting.

After what happened between them on Monday night, they'd spent nearly every night that week together, except for when Rick had to work. Gretchen had told him her theory about Misty Allbright's murder—how Misty had actually been the intended victim. She'd managed to convince him that since there had been no more attempts on Brett's life or even threats since it happened, it stood to reason that the killer had, in fact, gotten the right person after all. Otherwise, why not find a way to finish the job?

When Gretchen learned that the hulking Hawaiian was Brett's bodyguard and not his idolizing cousin, she felt like an idiot. How could she not have put that together herself? It seemed so obvious! Rick said that Brett had found Epau through one of his "discreet celebrity friends" (Brett's words). And Rick admitted to her that even

Brett didn't seem that worried these days; he'd started to believe that somehow the sauce was poisoned after it was brought to Misty, and not beforehand, so Brett was back to being full of himself, fat and happy minus the fat part.

So that seemed to be that. Except . . .

Even though Misty Allbright wasn't the nicest girl in the world, Gretchen didn't feel right about just letting her murder go like it didn't matter. Brett should go to the police and tell them about the mushrooms and the sauce, and then the police could try to retrace everyone's whereabouts during the party and find the point at which someone slipped in and poisoned her food. The biggest suspect was Ellie; Gretchen was willing to bet anything that she'd done it and would eventually crack if someone applied the right pressure. She'd filled Rick in on all Ellie had had to gain by her boss's demise, not to mention the off-putting conversation she'd initiated with Gretchen at the craft table the other night, putting her on the spot about going to high school with Misty and implying that the two of them had had "issues." There was something fundamentally sneaky about the girl.

Again, police intervention was what was needed here. But with Brett deciding to let the whole matter go so he could stay out of the line of fire, that was never going to happen.

There was only so much that Rick could do about it. The fact was, the two brothers weren't close. Rick wanted to help him, but Gretchen knew that he couldn't enforce a specific sense of ethics on Brett if he weren't the least bit inclined toward it. So Gretchen was trying to let it go in her own mind. She didn't know why she couldn't. Misty treated her shabbily, and apparently she hadn't been too stellar to some other people in her life—Susanna coming prominently to mind—but there just seemed something fundamentally wrong about turning a blind eye to her murder.

Now it was Friday. Rick and Gretchen were spending the weekend away from the city in a secluded house that was half shielded from the world by a thick arc of snow-capped pine trees. It had been a long drive; they'd left at five that afternoon and now it was nearly one.

It was a dark, clear night; Gretchen had thought it was cold in

New York, but it was colder than ice in Maine. Yet there was something about the quality of the air when she breathed it into her lungs—starkly cold but also startlingly clean.

The last stop on the cursory tour around the house was the kitchen. With his hand still resting on her lower back, Rick looked down at her and said, "I'm starving—you?"

"Oh, no, I'm okay," she said. She'd packed food for the car, leftovers from the set, including a frozen-solid steak that would've defrosted in the car if it hadn't been so damn cold outside. She didn't feel much like eating at the moment, but Rick had an appetite like an ox. (Did oxen eat a lot? Well, in any event, the boy could eat.) "But I'll fix you something," she offered because so far she had yet to use her greatest talent to her advantage in this relationship. A whole week together and Rick still hadn't tried her cooking. Every night, food was always a distant afterthought to sex; it was takeout, followed by more sex. But now, Gretchen was revved up to use the stove. Rick had mentioned once that he couldn't cook, so this would work out just fine.

"Really? You're not too tired?" he said now, running his hand gently over her back.

"I'm not tired at all," she replied. His eyes, on the other hand, looked a little sleepy, but he was willing to hold it together for a steak. She told him to sit down and she'd get started. He sat at the table, pulling out the heavy wooden chair and sliding into it with a sigh. "Man," he said and set his head on the table as she started to cook.

Several minutes later, she went over and stood behind him as he rested his head on the table. "*Man,*" he said again, this time with a yawn. "I guess I'm more tired than I thought."

"You should be tired," she said warmly as she rubbed his shoulders gently at first, then circled her thumbs against the skin of his neck. Groaning, he urged her to continue.

A minute later, she had to return to the stove. She slid his steak on a plate and poured a glass of beer for him from the six-pack she had in the cooler. When she brought it to him, she approached tentatively, quietly, because she couldn't tell if he'd fallen asleep. He looked so boyishly adorable right now, his dark hair rumpled, one lock curling over his forehead and his eyes shut. "Rick?" she said so quietly she barely heard herself.

Nothing.

She went to put the steak back on the counter when suddenly he grabbed her waist and pulled her to him, which gave her a start. "Oh! You startled me!" she said, putting a hand to her heart, smiling down at him.

With his eyes peering open, he smiled sleepily at her. "Where do you think you're going with that?" he asked.

Smiling, she replied, "Nowhere, silly," and set it down in front of him. He sat up fully in his seat and went about eating, but before that said, "You're sure you're not hungry?"

"Nope."

"Okay, I'll be quick."

"Take your time," she said, sliding into the chair next to his.

"And tomorrow we'll go to the market down the road to pick up some groceries for the weekend and stuff," he added, before setting his first bite of steak into his mouth.

It only took two seconds for his eyes to come more alive. "Holy shit," he said with a touch of wonder in his voice. "This is the best steak I've ever had."

Happily, she said, "Really?"

Chewing heartily, he dove right into it, his second and third bite, saying, "*Damn*, this is good," until finally he asked, "What's your secret?"

"Honestly? A really hot pan," Gretchen said simply.

"That's it?" he said, surprised.

Not quite, but for the most part. "That's it."

"So when do I get my key lime pie?" he asked with a sexy yet boyish grin.

"When you've earned it," she replied teasingly—though, little did Rick know, she meant it.

After he was done, she took his plate, set it in the sink; then they headed upstairs to his bedroom. Though she was tired, she wanted him. She'd been fantasizing about making love with him the whole ride up, and now, watching him move as he locked up the house, feeling him close by her side as they walked up the stairs . . . it was all she could do not to turn and jump on top of him. Maybe he'd be too tired for sex—she should be prepared for that possibility.

As they walked into the dark room, tension thickened between them. As usual, Gretchen's lust for Rick overpowered her body, her mind. She couldn't seem to get enough of him. She didn't know if she ever would, and it scared her. Agitated her . . . excited her . . .

Rick didn't bother turning on a light; he just shut the door. There wasn't even a stream of moonlight in the room. She turned, knowing he was right behind her, but she couldn't see him. Then she felt his hands on her. Wordlessly he snaked his arms around her waist and pulled her to him. She felt his arousal against her body and it made her moan, knowing too well the thrill of his thick, swollen cock inside her . . .

Her arms coiled around his neck as she folded into a passionate, drugging kiss with Rick. It only heightened the tension between them. Instantly, there was an upsurge of heat that sexually charged the air, igniting the already explosive attraction between them. Running her fingers through his hair, Gretchen kissed Rick even harder, which sent him into action. Aggressively, he spun them around and backed her up against the closed door.

She gasped.

Restlessly, she rocked her body, rubbing her hips against his, rising up as he bent down, so he could grind against her, driving his steel-hard erection into her damp, aching center over and over, and each time he did it, she let out a punctuating little moan. It was so intoxicating, so good, that she wanted it to go on and on, even as she longed for relief from the torment of so much arousal. He held her bottom in his hands, keeping her pressed tightly to him with each movement. Hazily, she reached for him, cupping his stiff cock through his pants, squeezing him. He grunted and thrust into her hand. She squeezed harder and they gasped together.

A gruff sound tore from his throat as one of his strong hands went to her waist, popping open the button on her jeans, shoving the zipper down, yanking her jeans and panties down her thighs in one motion.

"Ohhh . . ." she gasped again and reached for him, fumbling with his fly. But her fingers were too clumsy. He tore his pants open with one hand and used the other to stroke her, rubbing her clitoris. She could almost hear the sluicing sounds when his fingers went inside her—in and out, stimulating her almost to the point of discomfort, working her into a frenzy. She gripped the hair at the nape of his neck with one hand and his muscular biceps with the other, and tried to steady herself, but she couldn't quite do it.

Sweating, panting beyond embarrassment, with both hands she reached up to his shirt and started to claw at it to drag it up and off of him. He pulled back to whip it off, and crazily, she began running her hands all over his chest, his sleek shoulders, combing her fingers through his chest hair, and he descended again, shoving her panties and jeans all the way to the floor, then sliding his hands behind her naked thighs and scooping her off the floor.

He spread her legs around his hips. Sandwiched between Rick and the door, Gretchen felt secure, protected, but still, a little out of control. When she felt him finger her opening again, she said, "Wait, what about a . . . ?"

"I got it," he said hoarsely, his voice strained. Somehow he got a condom on in seconds, from who knows where, and vaguely Gretchen thought, *There's something to be said for experience,* as she tightened her grip on his biceps, waiting for him to enter her. And just like that—

It was a hard sharp thrust up her body, with a shock of pain that burned into hot, seeping pleasure. He drove into her again and she cried out, her legs bracketing his hips, her thighs starting to ache, but she was barely aware of it. Eyes closed, she bit her lip and savored every move Rick made that pushed her closer to ecstasy.

"Yes," he whispered in her ear. "Oh . . . *yeah* . . ." And then he went off, mumbling a string of incoherent things she couldn't make out, but after endless moments, she found herself urging him on even more.

"Harder . . ." she whispered almost tentatively, because it was plenty hard as it was, but still she wanted more of him.

With a harsh grunt, Rick increased the pressure of his thrusts until they were relentless, almost animalistic, and Gretchen's body was thumping against the door over and over. Her neck arched, her head dropped back, and she let out a strangled cry as her orgasm took hold and vibrated through her in hot, rippling contractions. The sensations were overpowering and new to her; it had never been like this before. It seemed like she was always reaching new heights with Rick. Logically she knew that all things eventually leveled off, and sex would become saner between them, but that itself was a sweet and precious thought. She looked forward to comfort with Rick just as much as she savored the chaos. Now, dazed and still catching her breath, she felt she could almost drift off on a cloud.

The muscles in Rick's back tightened as he moved faster still, in a frenzied rush to the end, thrusting wildly until his orgasm rumbled through him. His shoulders nearly shook from the force, and his groans of pleasure were deep and long.

Seconds later, she heard him thunk his forehead on the door and mutter, "Jesus Christ." Her neck slumped forward, bringing her cheek to rest on Rick's shoulder; his skin was hot and faintly sweaty. Depleted by exhaustion and satiation, Gretchen barely registered it when Rick carried her to the bed and when, only seconds after, she conked out on top of him.

A few hours later, Gretchen rolled over on the softest, most comfortable bed she could ever imagine. Something flickered, so she opened her eyes. Blinking sleepily, she saw a small crackling fire before her eyes. And then she realized she wasn't in Rick's bed anymore. She had a vague memory of him carrying her downstairs, but she'd been too zonked out to process it really. Now she was in the family room, she realized, lying beside Rick on an unbelievably thick, luxurious white rug. Was this one of those bearskin rugs? (Because if so, she'd rethink using the word "cabin.")

The fire bathed the room in an orange glow. They were both snuggled under a flannel blanket, and she was naked—even though she hadn't recalled taking off her sweater before she'd fallen asleep upstairs. Wait, she did remember. It had been in the darkness of the bedroom. It could've been minutes or hours after their first time; sleepily, she'd turned in to him, curled against him, and he'd rolled over, peeled her sweater off, and climbed on top of her. She'd held on to him as he'd made love to her slowly, sensually, both of them gliding against each other in a deep, almost drugging haze of arousal, until Rick eventually brought her to an intense, scorching climax that left her throbbing.

Now he was lying flat on his back with one arm draped over his eyes as his chest rose and fell deeply. Gretchen smiled to herself and inhaled a deep, satisfied breath, then rolled in to Rick till their bare bodies touched. He shifted in his sleep, pressing closer. Then he started to snore lightly in her ear, and for some reason, she smiled at that, too.

Rick's truck crunched through the snow as he drove them to the Corner Store. Today he was going to show her the Crests, a snowy set of mountainous hills that overlooked the frosty bay below. Gretchen had bundled up to the hilt for this; it was a cold day, but the sky was a sunny bright blue.

"So I liked that rug we slept on," she said now.

"Yeah?"

"Yes, was it a bearskin rug?"

"Yup. My dad got it about ten years ago, I think." At the mention of his dad, his voice was flat, didn't seem to want to elaborate. "They sold a bunch after a big bear hunt."

"Your dad hunted bears?" she said, surprised and a little put off; she was a huge hater of hunting for sport but didn't think now was the appropriate time to debate the point.

"No, no," Rick corrected her. "I mean, the bear population in this area got to be too much, so they had an organized hunt to reduce the population. My dad didn't personally have a part in it, though." After a brief pause, he said, "I know you probably think that's terrible, huh?"

"Yeah, kind of," she admitted. He didn't bother trying to sell her on the concept of organized bear hunts, which she appreciated. "I don't even remember you putting me there," she remarked.

"Yeah, you were pretty tired," Rick replied, then slanted her a look. He grinned at her, and she lifted her brows and said, "What?" and he just shook his head, still grinning. "Nothing," he said and refocused on the road.

As he turned into a small wooden shop, he didn't bother trying to find a parking space, but just parked kind of perpendicular to the place. It appeared to be what the other customers had done, as well. Come to think of it—where *were* the parking spaces?

"All right," he said, leaning over to brush a kiss across her lips. "Be back in a minute."

Suddenly she thought about the bears in the area and how there seemed to be nothing for miles around this little shop, and she said, "Wait, I'm coming with you!" and hopped out of the car. Reaching back, Rick put his arm around her shoulders, gave her an affectionate squeeze, and another kiss, this time on her cheek.

When they ducked through the door, a little bell jingled over their heads and they stepped inside a wood-paneled shop lined with shelves full of food and cans. There were only two small aisles, but they were filled with every kind of supply, snack, or thing you could want. "We can stop back for groceries for dinner later if you want," he said.

"Sure," she said. "I'll cook again."

"No, you don't have to," he said.

"I know; I like it."

Rick went about getting some items for their day, and Gretchen browsed, loving the charming quality of this rustic little place. Light music tingled in their ears, and the sun streamed through windows with homemade-looking green-and-white floral curtains. "Hiya, Brody! How have you been?" the old lady behind the counter said, lighting up when Rick went up to pay.

"Hey, Alice, how are ya?"

"Good, good. I haven't seen you or your brother up here in a while. Ever since . . ." Her voice trailed off, and Gretchen wondered if she was about to mention Rick's dad. Maybe she hadn't seen Rick since before his father had died.

And Rick said, "I've been here, just never for too long at a time, with work and everything in the city." He handed her money and set his wallet into the back pocket of his jeans.

"Heyuh," Alice said, looking over at Gretchen, who was across the store. She lowered her voice, though Gretchen could still hear her. "Who's that? Your girlfriend?'

"Yup."

Gretchen froze in the aisle, having heard that. Her heart kicked up and she smiled to herself.

"Pretty," Alice said.

"Yup," Rick said again. "I know it. Listen, take care Alice. We'll be back later today."

"Okay, Brody. It sure is great seeing you again."

"You, too. Ready?" he said when he met up with Gretchen at the door. He held it open for her, his other arm filled with the bags.

"Hey, you never told me why people call you Brody," she said, recalling that was what Brett called him, too.

"I didn't? Oh, it's a nickname, that's all."

"For?"

"For Broderick, that's my real name—and don't laugh."

"Why would I laugh?" she said, hopping up into her seat.

Rick slammed her car door, then went around to hop in his side. "I'm named after my grandfather," he added. "Broderick O'Meara. Alice has known my family for years."

Impulsively Gretchen leaned over in her seat and pulled him down for a kiss. He wasted no time sliding his tongue in her mouth. "So . . . I'm your girlfriend now, huh?" she said sweetly when their lips broke apart.

"Yeah, baby," he said, grinning with confidence, then started up the engine.

Meanwhile Gretchen's heart swelled in her chest. "I like that," she said casually. "So what should I call you? What do you like better—Honey Pie or Sugar Cookie? Or I know! How about Little Ricky?"

With a laugh, Rick said, "Yeah, that works."

"Done," Gretchen said, smiling. When they turned the corner, sunlight blared through the windshield; squinting, she angled her head to avoid the sting of it but had trouble blocking it out of her line of vision. She pushed down her visor, but it didn't do much good. The visor on the driver's side seemed to get it done for Rick, but then, he was much taller than she.

"I think there're some sunglasses in the glove compartment," he offered, noticing her discomfort (not that she'd been all that subtle,

squeezing her eyes closed and ducking her head in awkward, unnatural ways).

"Oh, thanks," she said brightly and popped the glove compartment open. It was stuffed with junk, paperwork, wrappers, and she
was feeling around for sunglasses when she felt something else.

"You smoke?" she blurted, surprised, as she pulled out a pack of
Marlboros.

"Oh." With a brief pause, Rick shrugged. "Yeah, a little."

"I didn't know you smoked. You don't smell," she said, then realized how it sounded.

Slanting her a wry glance, he said, "Thank you."

"No, no, I mean—you know what I mean."

"Yeah, I do," he admitted. "I've cut back a lot over the last few
years."

"Oh," she said, nodding, setting the pack back in the glove compartment. "Well, that's good," she added supportively but casually,
because she didn't want him to think she was going to start nagging
him about it. "I'm trying to quit, actually," he threw in. His eyes
stayed focused on the road, but she could tell he was deliberately
making the point. And he hadn't smoked at all in the time they'd
spent together, so he'd clearly not wanted her to know. He must have
considered it a weakness, or if nothing else, a turn-off. She didn't
know why, but that made her smile.

"How long have you been trying to quit?" she asked neutrally.

He shrugged and slid his gaze at her before refocusing on the
road. "I don't know, recently."

Biting her lip, she smiled again.

A few hours later, they'd plowed the hilly roads up to the Crests,
walked the wintry trail, and built a fire. Now Gretchen was showing
Rick how to make perfect s'mores. "The trick is in being patient. A
golden brown, evenly toasted marshmallow actually has better flavor
than a charred one, but most people don't know that because they
don't want to put in the time." Skeptically, he cast her a sideways
glance. "Seriously. You just have to be patient, methodical. Hold
your stick just the way you are, but make sure to keep it steady, about
two inches above the flame for the first minute, then—"

"Screw that," Rick said, and shoved his stick with his marshmallow into the fire, setting it ablaze. He pulled it right out, blew out the flame, leaving a blackened, wholly charred square shriveled at the end of his stick.

"Or that's another way to do it," she said dryly.

He grinned mischievously at her and fed her half of the gooey marshmallow. "What can I say? When I want something I'm not a patient man."

With a smile, Gretchen nestled closer to him and sighed. "God, I really love it up here. It's so serene." From here they could see a lighthouse down below, quite a distance away, and waves rolling toward it. "So is that house yours now?" she asked delicately, not wanting to tread too hard on the subject of his dad.

"Sort of. Brett and I both inherited it. I want to keep it, but unsurprisingly, Brett wants to sell." That struck Gretchen as odd since Brett had been so much closer to their father growing up than Rick—but then, maybe that was why it made perfect sense. Rick was the one who was rife with regrets. To Brett it was a piece of property, but to Rick it was a piece of their dad.

"Won't Brett just sell his half to you?" she suggested.

"Yeah, but not for anything I can afford."

"You and he seem so different," she remarked.

"We are, believe me."

Curiously, she asked, "Has Brett ever been in love?"

"Sure," Rick said. "Oh, you mean with another person? Then, no."

Gretchen couldn't help but laugh. "Have *you*?" she probed.

"Ever been in love?" he said, his voice warmer. "Yes . . . I think so."

Suddenly there was a loud crash. Startled, Gretchen sat straight up and said, "Rick! What was that?"

"I don't know. I'll go take a look," he said, coming to his feet, leaving their blanket draped loosely around Gretchen's shoulders.

"Wait, don't leave me here!" she said, scrambling to get up from the log she was on.

"Don't worry, baby," he said. "I'm just gonna look over the bluff. I'm not going far. Stay warm by the fire."

"Hell no!" she yelped, jumping to her feet. "What if a bear comes over?"

"Won't happen."

"But what if? Seriously, we should have a plan in general in case that happens. What *should* I do if I see a bear?"

"Well, whatever you do, don't run," he said, though he didn't sound like he was taking this conversation that seriously.

"Don't run," Gretchen repeated, crouching close to Rick's side as she glanced around. "Okay, so should I just stand there and hope for the best?"

"No, that doesn't sound too good, either."

"I guess I could run up a tree . . ." she mused.

"Okay, but bears can climb trees."

"Oh, right . . . and I can't—well, there goes that."

Hitching the corner of his mouth, Rick leaned down to kiss her cheek and said, "You worry too much."

Then he crossed to the bluff with Gretchen close behind him. He surveyed the ground below and saw nothing—except a large branch had fallen off one of the trees and come crashing down. "Must have frozen and cracked off," Rick said, pointing it out for her. "It happens." Then he noticed her forehead pinched with tension. "What's the matter?" he asked, concerned, and slid his arm around her shoulders.

"Nothing. Sorry, I guess I'm just a little . . . skittish lately." She hadn't even realized it till just now. But she supposed all of the jarring, bizarre incidents that had happened at work lately—the frayed blender cord, the olive oil on the stairs, the broken chair in her office . . .

The creepy brown spider.

She shuddered. "Baby, what is it?" he asked gently, giving her shoulder a gentle squeeze.

At first, she shook her head to brush off her own silliness. She'd always been a little klutzy—Rick had even teased her about it once. Surely most of what happened could be attributed to that. Well, half of it . . . she supposed . . .

Still, it was weird. Her luck had never been that bad.

"Well," she began, leaning into him, "it's going to sound silly, but . . ."

After she'd told Rick about her various "accidents," she insisted that each one was no big deal, but apparently he wasn't prepared to be as dismissive as she was.

"Each one separately, no," he said, an edge of concern in his voice. "But all together, in a matter of what, a week?" He shook his head firmly. "I don't like it."

After a deliberating pause, she said, "Do you think . . . It will probably sound crazy, but . . ."

"What?"

Swallowing, she measured her words in her own mind, thinking that they weren't all that far-fetched after all. "Maybe it's related to Misty's murder? Maybe someone knows that I . . . that I know something. Or that I've been asking questions—"

"*What?* What do you mean you've been asking questions?" he said, eyeing her sharply.

"Just to Susanna," she replied in her defense. "Just about mushrooms." As defenses went, it was probably pretty feeble. "Hey! Do you think maybe she mentioned it to Ellie? If Ellie's the killer and she thinks that I know or even suspect that Misty was poisoned by mushrooms, then maybe she's afraid I'll somehow illuminate the police about that fact, causing them to reopen the investigation into Misty's death!"

With a sigh, Rick ran his hand over his eyes and said, "Gretchen, Jesus, I don't want you doing that. I never wanted you to put yourself in any kind of danger with this. I told you what I told you because I wanted to be honest with you. But I never wanted you to try to get involved in some kind of . . . investigation, for chrissake."

"I know, but I just thought I'd feel Susanna out, that's all. But she didn't seem to have a clue what I was talking about, anyway. And come to think of it, unless she's in on the whole murder scheme with Ellie, Susanna seems too self-absorbed to recall some inane conversation I had with her about mushrooms, or to think it important enough to mention to anyone else."

"Baby, you have no basis to think Ellie murdered Misty," Rick reminded her. "What about what you told me, how Misty was bang-ing Susanna's husband? That seems like a helluva motive."

"True," she said, ignoring the crassness of the term "banging." (They'd work on that later.) "But it just seems like Ellie's life has sky-rocketed since Misty's death."

"Granted, it sounds like she had a lot to gain and *if* the poison was slipped into Misty's food sometime after Brett brought it up to her, then yes, Ellie definitely had the opportunity," Rick said. "But we still don't know she's the one."

"I know, but—wait! What about that comment she made to me at the taping on Monday night? About how I should be 'more care-ful,' that 'accidents can be dangerous'? Considering the stuff that's been happening to me lately, was it just a coincidence?" she asked rhetorically. Then, thinking out loud, she added, "Now I'm not so sure . . ."

After a speculative pause, Rick said, "Was anyone else there when you were asking Susanna about mushrooms?"

"No," Gretchen replied slowly, shaking her head before she re-membered. "Oh, wait. Cady Angle was there. Sort of. I mean, we caught her kind of loitering around Susanna's dressing room. I guess she could've overheard it. But it's not like she has a connection to Ellie—or to Misty. That I know of, anyway."

"Cady Angle? Right," Rick said with a nod of recognition. "Brett mentioned that she always had a crush on him."

Ugh. So what else was new? What was wrong with these women? Did everyone in the world have a crush on Brett? Gretchen won-dered. *God, why?* So he had a picture-perfect face, so he was rich and famous—he was also a class-A pig, not to mention, a major cheese-ball. And if that wasn't enough persuasion, he was also a shellacked-gel-head.

Well, whatever. They had more important issues at hand.

"But even if my 'accidents' lately have been, well, less than acci-dental, what's the point? It's not like a fall off my chair is gonna put me out of commission or something," Gretchen said with an incred-ulous wisp of laughter. But then her words drifted off and her humor faded. No, a tumble from a broken chair might not kill her, but get-ting electrocuted by a frayed cord or bashing her head on a spill down the stairs certainly could. And she'd never bothered to find out what kind of creepy brown spider that was, anyway . . .

"Gretchen, promise me you'll be extra careful," Rick said now, his expression darkening, his hug possessive. "I don't want anything to happen to you."

"Me, either," she said lightly, trying to eschew the sense of doom that threatened to impose on her weekend with Rick. She kept it at arm's length and that was good enough for now.

CHAPTER TWENTY-NINE

*W*hen they returned to New York City, the shit hit the fan. "Brett's been *arrested*?"

Rick expelled a sigh and sat back in his chair. It was an old leather thing that creaked as it gave. "Jesus, this is such a mess," he muttered, running his hand over his eyes.

Incredulously, Gretchen said, "But how? Why?"

She was sitting across from him on his sofa. They'd gotten back from Maine less than an hour before and found a frantic message from Brett telling Rick that he was in jail. He said that he'd called his lawyer but hadn't been able to get ahold of him yet, and that he was freaked out and needed Rick there. He was really blubbering and carrying on, which kind of surprised her. Hey, if she was in jail, she'd be wailing, too, but she supposed it just sounded odd coming from a guy as "macho" as Brett. Rick hadn't seem fazed by his brother's blubbering, though, just the desperation itself—the fact that Brett, for all his faults, was in jail and scared out of his mind.

Now Rick hung up the phone, after getting some sketchy details on Brett's arrest from a cop, who was an acquaintance of his and a buddy of one of the firemen in Rick's squad. Turning his head to meet Gretchen's concerned, curious gaze, Rick relayed what little he knew. "Apparently they found a stash of a 'toxic mushroom powder' in Brett's dressing room at TCC," he explained to Gretchen now. "Someone called the police with an anonymous tip about it, said that Brett was bragging about how he killed a girl with it."

"What?" Gretchen said in a state of total disbelief. It was just too bizarre!

"I guess when the cops did a little following up on the tip, they made the connection between Brett and Misty Allbright, whose death still remained mystery. I'm guessing *that,* plus the fact that Brett was sleeping with her—"

"What?" Gretchen said again, though she didn't know why she was surprised. "You didn't tell me that!"

"Oh. Yeah, I'm sorry," Rick said, appearing genuinely contrite. He didn't explain any further, though Gretchen suspected he'd been trying to protect some of his brother's privacy, after telling her so much of what was going on already.

"So the police know about their relationship?" she asked.

With a shrug he said, "I don't know, but my hunch is, if they apply even the slightest pressure, he'll break down bawling. Good thing his lawyer's there. Still, to arrest him the police have got to have something to go on besides traces of poisonous mushrooms—"

"Which were obviously planted," she injected. "His dressing room, that could be anyone at the network! Well . . . except they'd have to have a key. Unless Brett doesn't keep it locked . . ."

With his expression unreadable, Rick seemed to be assessing the facts in his own mind, so Gretchen decided to assess them out loud. "We need to think who could be behind this," she said, coming closer, setting her hand gently on his shoulder.

He covered it with his other hand, then angled his chair so he could pull her on his lap. Inwardly, she smiled at the affectionate gesture; even though he had a taciturn, solitary way of dealing with things, he wasn't shutting her out. Which made it that much more important for her to help him. "Goddamn it," he muttered. "I want to have a clue what's going on before I go down to see him. I don't want to just show up empty-handed." Then he slanted an apologetic glance at her. "Sorry."

"I don't care if you curse," she said with mild exasperation. She was flattered he was trying to be a better person for her, but right now she needed to focus. Draping her arms loosely around his neck, she started to contemplate. "The first thing is this—why come out of the woodwork now? As far as anyone knows, Misty's death isn't being investigated at this point. Why try to frame Brett for it? Why call attention to something that people were pretty much starting to forget about? Oh! Unless, whoever it was knew that *we* knew about the real cause of death and wanted to get the jump on us before we could go to the police about it! Which goes back to my theory that maybe someone overheard me asking Susanna about poisonous mushrooms, or maybe Brett told someone."

Firmly, Rick shook his head. "Brett wouldn't tell anyone. He was too terrified of bad publicity. But it's a good question. Why bother to frame Brett for Misty's murder? What's the point? Unless whoever's behind it wanted to get rid of Misty *and* Brett all along."

"Well, then, it can't be Ellie," Gretchen remarked with regret. (Ellie had been her best suspect up till now.) "Brett's her biggest meal ticket. It just wouldn't make sense. But who else?"

They reconsidered Susanna, who might have had a reason to want Misty dead, but with her hopes for more cohosting gigs, her incentive to bring Brett down went from unlikely to nil. Then they went through several different suspects—if you could call them that, since each smacked of more implausibility than the next. First, they pondered Abe Santasierra, who'd dated Misty a couple of months back, but they were hard-pressed to find a motive. *He'd* broken up with *her.* Plus, he'd left Brett's house on Friday night and given Marjorie Bass and some camera guy named Tom a ride back to the city with him. Misty hadn't arrived until Saturday. So when would Abe have had the opportunity to poison her food, or even known she was going to be coming the next day?

Along the same lines, they had to dismiss Marjorie Bass, too, and the camera guy, whoever he was. Next they considered Kit. (That is, after Gretchen forcibly lifted her jaw off the floor, where it had plummeted upon learning that Kit and Brett were sleeping together.) According to Rick, Brett had been blowing Kit off for a couple of weeks now. Maybe she'd killed Misty because she'd known about her affair with Brett, and then when Brett started acting aloof, Kit framed *him* for the murder to get back at him. Actually, Gretchen had to admit . . . that one wasn't all that implausible.

The only specter of doubt was that—according to Brett—Kit hadn't been at the party.

Next they waded through various crew members of *Brooklyn Boy Makes Good . . . Food,* but Brett didn't seem close enough with any of them to warrant a grudge, much less to gain them access to his agent. They considered his producer, Joel Green, but that made no sense for obvious reasons. Like Ellie, Joel had everything to gain financially from Brett's success. Then Gretchen said, "What about Juan Mirando? He was at Brett's party."

"Who?" Rick said curiously.

"You know, the desperate guy with the pork butt sweatshirt?"

"Oh," Rick said after a momentary pause. "Right, I remember." (Since Gretchen was still adjusting to the idea of dating Rick, who seemed too good to be true, she braced herself for him to add, "Pork butt sweatshirt—damn, I gotta get me one of those!" Or something else that would ruin her bliss. Happily, it didn't happen.)

Continuing on, she told Rick about how she'd "stumbled upon" Brett and Lupe Rodriguez making out. "Lupe works for Juan Mirando's show. Maybe *he* likes her—I mean, he's obviously desperate to be the big Latin lover."

"That's obvious?" Rick said, grimacing skeptically. Hey, she never said Juan Mirando was *good* at it, but you had to read between the lines here.

"God, I don't know. None of this makes sense!" Gretchen said, slumping against Rick with frustration. "It all happened so fast."

"Yeah . . ." he said, suddenly distracted.

"What is it?" she said after a long moment.

"It all *did* happen fast," he said, "too fast." What had? She'd just been throwing a good cliché out there. Rick sat up straighter, still keeping her balanced in his lap. "Brett said that he brought Misty her food and an hour later, she was sick. An hour." Gretchen waited, eyes wide, searching. "Jay Bernbaum said that it takes five or six hours for the symptoms to show. He was emphatic about it. He said with the Destroying Angel, it could take anywhere from six hours to a day—so how did Misty get sick so fast?"

Mouth curved open, Gretchen thought quickly. "Maybe because it was such a concentrated amount of the mushroom. You said yourself it was ground up finely—like powder. Right?"

"Yeah . . ." He still seemed troubled. But then, why wouldn't he be? His younger brother was in jail. The irony of this was that if only Brett had gone to the police earlier he could've avoided all this, or at the very least, looked far less suspicious now. But instead, he'd said nothing, had not come forward with what he'd known about Misty's death, and now . . .

If they exhumed the body, and this time knew what to look for, it wasn't going to look great for him to have had a stash of the obscure poisoned mushroom that killed her.

Poor Rick. She knew it was Brett she should feel sorry for, but looking at Rick's face, drawn with concern, his cheeks clenched, his shoulders tense, Gretchen wished she could make him feel better somehow.

Soon after, he left. He said he'd try to get ahold of Brett's lawyer again on his way down to the police station. Then he told Gretchen to stay at his place and get some sleep, since it was nearly midnight, and when he kissed her softly he told her not to worry.

But she *did* worry. She cared deeply about Rick, and she wanted this to all go away for him. She wanted his brother, slimy pimp lothario that he might be, out of jail and safe again. She wanted Misty's killer brought to justice. Maybe she was overflowing with clichéd wants and needs right now, but they drove her onward and firmed her resolve to learn all she could about the Destroying Angel. She'd been so focused on *who* might want to harm Misty and Brett that she hadn't paid enough attention to the *means*.

Tomorrow she would discover that it had been the key all along. Tomorrow she would see the light just as she was plunged into darkness.

The following evening, Gretchen was working late in her office. Now that Susanna and most other people had gone home for the night, Gretchen could finally get back to the Internet search she'd started at lunch that day. If only it wasn't for all her damn "real" work, she could've gotten further by now. Rick had gone to talk to Brett again that morning. Apparently, the bail hearing wasn't for two days, so until then, Gretchen assumed Brett would pretty much be stuck in his holding cell. She hadn't been in touch with Rick since earlier today; she thought he still planned to go to the firehouse that night, but she wasn't positive. She would call him in a minute, but right now, she had to get back to her search results for "Destroying Angel."

Much of what she found was repetitive and general, each link bringing her to the same basic information as the next: Its scientific name was *Amanita virosa* or *Amanita bisporigera,* its origin was North Carolina, its location was varied, its appearance was fairly generic— a white cap and a white or tan stalk—and it predominantly grew in forested areas. If ingested, it could be fatally poisonous. It wreaked havoc on the body, with a false recovery period between the first and final rash of symptoms. And, as Rick had said, it had an incubation period of several hours before symptoms occurred.

She shook her head and scrolled farther with her mouse. It didn't make sense. Why had Misty gotten sick so fast?

She searched for another hour, reading through online environmental journals, agricultural bulletins, botanical publications, and a slew of blogs, all of which she found when searching for "poisonous mushroom" and "kidney failure." Most of what she pored over was useless, with her keywords actually quite disconnected in the text. But then—finally—she found something.

It was a link at the bottom of an article she'd skimmed about the Destroying Angel. That particular article had imparted the same factual information she already had—but the link was much more provocative. It read: *The Destroying Angel Builds a Family,* and it led to another article in *The Tennessee Wildlife Ledger & Guide.*

As Gretchen read, her heart sped up; she chewed her lip, thinking: *This is it!* The piece was brief, but shattering. It detailed the recent discovery of a new mushroom that appeared to be so closely related to the Destroying Angel, scientists debated whether it was a hybrid or the result of a mutation that had evolved and spawned over time. This fungus, dubbed the Gabriel mushroom, had a shorter stalk and a narrower cap than its predecessor but possessed the same devastating effects once ingested. The big difference was: Its initial attack on the body happened at an accelerated rate. *Misty was sick an hour later. An hour.*

This was it!

As Gretchen's eyes scanned wildly over the screen, she read the rest of the article, detailing the discovery of small bunches of Gabriel mushrooms that were popping up in various parts of Tennessee. And then the other shoe dropped.

Tennessee.

Where Ray Jarian spent much of his time. She recalled the way he'd talked about it at Brett's party, saying he'd been there recently. Of course—Ray was the killer! Why hadn't she seen it sooner?

It all made sense now. His whole "drunk" bit had been an act! He'd probably acted drunk at Brett's party and made quite a show of it to be sure that whenever Misty showed up, he would have the perfect "alibi." He could pretend he was passed out drunk, when really, he would find his opportunity to slip the poisonous mushroom powder into her food. Gretchen recalled what Susanna had said, that Misty loved Brett's cooking, that she made a thing about how it was her "weakness." So Ray knew that when Misty was there, she would eat—and he would be lurking, waiting for an opportunity. He'd done his homework. He'd either read about the Gabriel or heard locals talking about it when he'd been in Tennessee last, but surely after learning about it, it hadn't been hard for him to get. All it took was a little research and determination—and a taste for revenge. So Susanna had been right after all. For all his good-ol'-boy act, Ray was disgruntled and bitter—filled with fury for the young woman who'd dropped him as a client so callously, who'd tossed him like he was trash the minute his career started to sink. Or maybe, Misty was the tip of the iceberg. He'd lost his restaurant, his show, he couldn't get a new cookbook contract, and then his agent dumped him cold. He must've wanted to make her suffer, to destroy her as he'd been destroyed by the vicissitudes of his career.

Gretchen remembered now that he'd been lurking in the hallway on Saturday afternoon—after some others had mentioned that he'd left Brett's already. He must've left, then upon seeing Misty drive up, turned around and come back. When she hadn't come Friday night, he must've figured she wasn't coming to the party, but then he saw his opportunity and returned.

When he'd been lurking in the hall, he must've been coming from her room. How had he gotten in and gotten access to her food? Maybe he begged her just to listen to him; maybe when she was distracted for a moment, he slipped the poison in—who knew? The point was, Ray Jarian got his revenge. And he *almost* got away with it!

Frantically, Gretchen seized the receiver of the phone on her desk and dialed Rick's cell. It went right to voice mail. "Rick, it's me. Oh, God, I figured it out! It was Ray! Ray's the one! It's a long story of how I realized it, but the point is, he got the mushrooms last time he was in Tennessee—and it wasn't the Destroying Angel exactly. It was this kind of spin-off called the Gabriel. Anyway, call me when you get this. We need to go to the police and tell them!"

Suddenly she heard a noise and she paused. It was like a clunk, right outside her office. She waited, but there was nothing. "Okay," she said, resuming her message, "well, I'll talk to you soon, but call me. And I miss you. And I hope everything's going okay. Bye."

Whew. What a relief! She finally found the answer—then the lights cut out.

CHAPTER THIRTY

*W*ith her heart in her throat, Gretchen froze. A moment ticked by before she had the courage to speak. "Hello?" she said tentatively, feeling like a horror movie cliché. "Hello . . ." Her voice trailed off; no, she would *not* be that girl. It was probably just the bulb on the ceiling fixture. *Don't panic,* she told herself. *If you panic, it'll be something.*

Then her eyes adjusted to the light, which came solely from her monitor, so for the most part, the room was still cloaked in black. Still, she didn't see anyone, no silhouettes coming closer, and she heard no sounds.

Slowly, she pushed out her chair, rolling the wheels silently on the carpet. She made her way toward the door; each careful, creeping step treaded through and cleared away more of the muted darkness, until she finally reached the door. And that's when she realized it wasn't shut all the way. It was ajar about half an inch. If someone had deliberately cut the lights, all they would've had to do is reach their hand in and hit the switch on the wall.

Quickly, Gretchen yanked open the door, flooding her eyes with light from the hall. She stepped out into it, knowing that on either side of her and farther down would be the empty offices of network executives who'd gone home, but the common area where the administrative assistants' desks and filing cabinets were was well lit.

Gretchen looked one way, then the other. No one was there. She was alone. Until she heard shuffling and some kind of swishing noise behind her. Whipping around, she saw a dark figure disappear past

her before she could make out who or what it was. Curiosity un-
bound, she took off after it, chasing some amorphous darkness.

The shuffling got louder. Whoever it was, was running *from* her.
He was afraid. That kicked up her confidence. "Come back here!"
she called. "Who is that?"

When she rounded the bend, she heard a loud thump. Undeterred, she followed the direction of the sound, running until she saw
Shawnee lying facedown on the floor. "Aww," she groaned, then
rolled over and flopped gracelessly onto her back like a beached
whale. "Look what you made me do."

"What *I* made you do?" Gretchen echoed incredulously.
"Shawnee, what are you doing here so late? Why were you running
away from me?" She extended her hand to help her up.

"Aww . . ." she groaned again, slowly sitting up, then begrudg-
ingly took Gretchen's hand. When she was on her feet again, but off
balance, Gretchen realized what she'd "done" to Shawnee. When
Shawnee had tripped she'd twisted her ankle. Served the freak right.

"What were you doing?" Gretchen demanded again. "Did you
turn the light out in my office?" Shawnee mumbled something incoherent and Gretchen tipped her ear toward her combatively. "*Excuse*
me? What was that?"

"It was just a joke," she mumbled. "What's the big deal?"

Wrinkling her face in confusion, Gretchen said, "But why would
you play a joke on *me*?" And then she realized. With a gasp she said,
"It was you!" Shawnee flipped her head, rolling her eyes like
Gretchen was crazy, but Gretchen pressed on. "You're the one who's
been doing all that mean stuff to me! You put the olive oil on the
steps and frayed the blender cord. You loosened the wheel on my
desk chair and put the spider in the refrigerator!"

"Spider?" Shawnee said, flaring the nostrils of her bulbous nose
as she insisted, "Gross. I didn't put a spider anywhere."

Oh. Well . . . Gretchen supposed it could've just been in the fridge
on its own. The point was, Shawnee hadn't denied the rest of the charges.

"Why? Why would you do that to me?" Gretchen demanded.

Shawnee shrugged. "I was bored. And I don't like you."

Mildly affronted, Gretchen softened her tone and said, "Well,
why not?" *I'm damn likable!*

"You're a kiss-ass."

Oh. Interesting. Gretchen preferred to think of it as reserved, quietly efficient, easygoing, adept at navigating diva-infested waters—

"Gretchen?"

Both she and Shawnee turned and saw Abe approaching them. "Oh, hi, Shawnee." He held out an envelope in his hand. "This came to my office by mistake." Gretchen took it from him; it was an invoice addressed to her, something she'd ordered for Susanna.

"Thanks," she said, smiling warmly even as the shock of her confrontation with Shawnee still rattled her.

"Sure. And—I'm not sure what you're doing now, but do you have a minute?"

"Yes, absolutely," she replied, then eyed Shawnee warningly and added, "but you wait right here."

"*Fat chance,*" Shawnee mumbled when Gretchen turned to Abe. And when she looked back, Gretchen saw Shawnee's ample behind getting farther and farther away. She'd never seen the girl move so fast—and with a limp, no less—but here she was, in the face of confrontation, rushing for an escape. *What a coward!*

"Shawnee!" Gretchen cried, starting after her. "Stop—we're not done here!"

Hobbling quickly, Shawnee cast a frantic glance over her shoulder after she'd shoved through the glass doors that led to the elevators and pounded a beefy fist against the button on the wall. Just as Gretchen reached for the door handle, she saw the elevator to Shawnee's right spring open and Shawnee hop inside.

With her hand frozen on the cool metal of the handle, Gretchen watched through the glass as Shawnee smiled smugly and the elevator slid closed. Rolling her eyes, Gretchen puffed out a sigh of exasperation. What was she going to do, follow her down to the main floor and then chase her through the building? What would be the point? Just to yell at her some more? Forget it. She'd just deal with her tomorrow. Or better yet, she'd go straight to Susanna and tell her about all of Shawnee's "pranks." Gretchen had never been a tattletale, but enough was enough; obviously Shawnee had been excused and humored for far too long. It was time she took some responsibility for something that she did.

Besides, to go after her now would be absurd; she was so unimportant in the scheme of things, and here was Abe, someone who *was* important at TCC (and a helluva lot nicer of a person), and he was waiting for her. As it was, he was probably supremely confused by the spectacle that was Shawnee's exodus.

Turning back to face him now, Gretchen gave a brief, somewhat resigned smile. "Sorry about that," she said, waving off any questions before he could ask them. "It's a long story."

On their way to Abe's office, he explained, "Listen, I don't know if she mentioned it, but Susanna's birthday's coming up. I'd love to do something nice for her, you know, a surprise with everyone. Well, I had some ideas I wanted to run by you . . ."

"Sure," Gretchen said, following him.

He held his hand out for her to go first; once he crossed the threshold, he quietly clicked the door closed behind him. She went to take a seat at the chair beside his desk when he said, "No, that won't be necessary."

Curiously, she turned around. There was something different about Abe's expression. It was still a veneer of civility, but it seemed . . . colder somehow. Calmly, he walked closer to her. "Gretchen, I want you to know that I really like you. You're bright, you're highly capable, and you seem to be the only person who can work well with Susanna, calm her nerves, and give her some"—he paused to choose his word—"stability."

"Thank you," she said, a little tentatively because she didn't understand why he was walking closer and why he'd told her not to sit down. But she didn't want to be all weird about it by backing up. Biting her lip, she said, "Speaking of Susanna, I didn't realize her birthday was coming up . . ."

"It's not," he said simply. "I just said that to get you here." A lump formed in her throat. Oh, no—was he making a *pass* at her? No, Abe was too much of a gentleman for that. And what about Ellie?

"I—I don't understand," she said, forcing a pleasant if faint smile.

"Gretchen, I think you're wonderful," he said, his voice flat as though it were filled with resignation. Like he didn't want to feel this way . . .

Dear God. He'd fallen for her! How awkward. (Yet totally ego boosting—who said she needed to lose ten pounds?)

"Abe . . . um . . . what about Ellie?" she said, forming the words delicately, not wanting to presume too much, but not wanting to dance around it, either.

"Ellie?" he repeated, his lips curling slightly and not in a good way. "What about her?"

"Well, don't you and she have something going?"

Abe's lips slanted distastefully in a response that was both automatic and fleeting. Flatly, he said, "Ellie's just another amoral city girl—nothing special there."

"But—"

"Ellie's irrelevant," he interrupted sharply, then murmured, "and that's putting it mildly." Gretchen's mouth dropped. Even though his words were jarring, his tone was bland. It was the first time she'd heard Abe's mild, honeyed Southern accent lose its sweet curvature. Now it flirted with a bitter edge. And she couldn't help thinking, *Where is Abe? Considerate and polite—polished and diplomatic?* The man standing before her wasn't him.

"The point is, I don't want to do what I'm about to do, but I don't have a choice." He looked up and around as if grappling to find some meaning. "I suppose I feel guilty. I know it will pass, and maybe it doesn't even make a difference, since you're going to die anyway, but—"

Die? I'm going to die? Her pulse raced as he walked closer; now she started to back up. Suddenly she could barely breathe. Her chest was too tight and she had a golf ball in her throat. Thoughtfully, Abe said, "I'd like some way to ease my conscience about this."

"I—I don't understand," Gretchen said again, but this time tried to skirt around him. It didn't work; he grabbed her arm, digging his fingers into it painfully. "W-why—"

"Because you obviously aren't going to let it drop. I heard you talking in your office about the Gabriel mushroom. I don't know why you're intent on getting involved with any of this, but now that the police have been led to believe that Brett is their prime suspect, I can't have some busybody continually butting in and trying to lead them in a different direction. I don't want to give them any reason to dig deeper or look where they wouldn't normally look."

The words took a moment to sink in and then Gretchen realized: *Abe* was the one who'd called the police with the "anonymous tip." *Abe* was the one who'd planted the poisonous mushroom powder in Brett's dressing room.

But why on earth?

"If you want to ease your conscience," she managed, "please . . . at least tell me *why*."

A glaze came over his eyes, as though he was suddenly emotional, but he kept it at bay. "It was a terrible, terrible accident. It was meant for Brett, but somehow, through some fluke, Misty ended up eating the sauce that I'd poisoned."

Gretchen struggled to breathe as her heart pounded hard and furiously in her ears. She didn't want to die! Maybe if she kept him talking he'd unconsciously loosen his hold on her arm—but Abe wasn't a fool.

Again Gretchen tried to run, but his grip tightened painfully. What could she do? Abe was a shrewd man, but running wasn't working. Talking was all Gretchen had. "But why would you want to kill Brett?" she asked, her voice quavering.

"Brett's always been a cocky man, but I never had a problem with him—until I found out that Misty was sleeping with him while she was involved with me."

"Ohh . . . and that's why you broke up with her?" Gretchen asked.

He let out a sharp, humorless laugh. "No, I didn't figure out about her and Brett until after *she* dumped *me*."

"But I thought . . ."

"You thought what I led everyone to think—that I'd broken up with her. Obviously Misty never made it a point to correct it. Besides, with the exception of Susanna, Misty and I didn't travel in the same social circles anyway. Ellie knew, but it didn't matter. She'd always had a crush on me when I was dating Misty; I could tell. After Misty dumped me, I tried to get her to change her mind. I even reduced myself to begging—but I saw that it only made her recoil more."

"So you never really liked Ellie?" Gretchen asked curiously, though she must have sounded thick in the head; he'd pretty much said that a few times by now.

Again, Abe grimaced. "Dating her was the only way I could think of to keep tabs on Misty and what she was doing." So he wasn't over Misty after all, Gretchen thought, scrambling to learn more. And he'd been fixated on her enough to use her assistant to spy on her! "Ellie told me that Misty was sleeping with Brett," Abe continued. "I'm sure she thought it would put Misty in a bad light—Ellie was always so damn intimidated by her—but all it did was infuriate me. Just the idea that Misty would prefer *him* over *me*?" He physically shuddered at the thought. "The man's a cartoon—a parody of himself! Big muscles, tight shirts, the 'old neighborhood' act. Why do people *like* him?"

Haplessly, Gretchen shrugged. "Got me. I can't stand him."

Abe must've known she was telling the truth because he laughed. A genuine, quiet chuckle that reminded her of his charming facade, the one she'd come to know and like so much. He obviously found it refreshing that when it came to Brett, they were of like minds. And Gretchen deftly took advantage of the moment of solidarity.

"Abe . . ." she said gently, calmly. "Can I just ask you one question?" She tilted her head at him so sincerely, so pensively, and Abe raised his eyebrows, poised for the question.

Suddenly, in a split second, she kicked him hard, right in the kneecap. Her heels were sharp, and instantly, his leg buckled and he let out a cry of pain. His hand dropped off her arm and she pushed past him. When she yanked on the handle, his door flew open so hard it hit the wall, and she sprinted out, running down the hall with her adrenaline propelling her forward.

Rick arrived at TCC only to find out that at this hour he couldn't get in without a pass. He called Gretchen's cell a few times, but for some reason she wasn't answering. She'd left him some crazy message about that guy Ray and now Rick just wanted to make sure she was okay. Ever since she'd told him about the "accidents" at work, he'd felt more possessive of her than ever—more than he had a right to feel, but, screw it. She was his. Fiercely protective of her, Rick didn't bother to analyze why he felt such an intense level of emotion for her already—he just did. Gretchen was important to him.

Back in Maine, when Alice had asked if Gretchen was Rick's girl-friend, it hadn't occurred to him for one second to say no. He wanted her all to himself—and most of all, he wanted her safe.

After trying her cell again, he cursed softly and stuck his phone back in his pocket. If only she'd answer, he could ask her to come downstairs and let him in. If she was done working, he'd see her home; if not, he'd wait until she was done. He didn't want to leave her alone. But then again, maybe she'd left work already. She'd told him that morning that she'd call him when she finished, but so far he'd gotten the Ray call and that was it.

Pulling out his cell again, he checked the time. It was after eight o'clock. Why would she be working this late? She must've left. Maybe he'd be able to track her down at her apartment—and on his way, he'd try her cell again.

Gretchen kept running. She knew Abe was following her, but she didn't dare look back to see how close behind he was. *If you look back, he'll be right there. Just keep going.*

Frenzied and scared, she couldn't chance waiting for the eleva-tor, so she cut down the hallway and body slammed the door to the stairwell. As she ran down the steps, she heard her own ragged breath, as fear choked her, made her gasp for air. Vaguely she felt the cool metal of the railing beneath her clammy palm as she gripped it in spurts and told herself, *Faster, faster.* It was only two flights—

The door on the level above her flew open. *Shit!* She panicked; she'd been so close to an escape but now it seemed impossible.

Then, in a flash, she hit the ground floor and reached out for the door handle. Slamming it open, she bolted out into the carpeted hallway and kept running. She raced through the reception area to-ward the main entrance. With her blood ringing in her ears, she could barely hear the footsteps behind her, but they were there, and she was almost running blindly when finally she looked back. Just as her body shoved on the glass doors and careened through, Gretchen flew right into a huge hard monstrosity—one that grabbed her by the arms and held her up before she landed on the floor in a bruised, defeated heap.

"Gretchen!"

Dear God, it was Rick! He was here, he was right here. How could he be? Breathing hard, she tried to explain, but she could barely speak, her throat ached or maybe she was still too shaken to form the words, but she finally managed to say something.

"He's after me," she croaked just as Abe charged to the entrance. Abruptly, he froze when he saw Rick—but Rick didn't hesitate. He lurched forward and dropped Abe to the floor with one hard punch that cracked like lightning—or maybe a jaw.

CHAPTER THIRTY-ONE

A week later, Rick and Gretchen were soaking in his tub, and he had his arms wrapped tightly around her. She'd been dreaming of a long, hot bubble bath since she'd moved to New York, but so far, she hadn't been able to find the time. Had she mentioned that to him? How else could he have known?

"One thing we need to do is get you a new cell phone."

"I know. My cell service is shitty," Rick admitted, and that was putting it mildly. The going-straight-to-voice-mail-without-ringing thing had been more than a nuisance—it had nearly been a matter of life and death. It had been only a week, but it seemed like longer since Gretchen's whole showdown with Abe, when Rick had saved her life. Thank goodness he'd checked his voice mail and discovered her message—and thank *God* he'd come to see her at work and hadn't left by the time she'd found him.

But in the week since it all happened, she'd managed to clear up a few important questions. She'd found out why Ray Jarian had been lurking around the third floor of Brett's house the day Misty had arrived. Her initial conclusion had been *half* right: He'd left on Saturday morning, but when he'd seen Misty driving up, he'd turned around and decided to come back. But it wasn't to kill her. It was to talk to her, to beg her to represent him again, to give him more time to get his career back on track. She wouldn't return his calls, she wouldn't make lunch dates or take meetings with him; cornering her at Brett's became his last chance to reason with her, and he couldn't pass it up. When he'd heard she'd gone upstairs to her guest room, he'd been creeping around to figure out which one was hers. If it hadn't been for him dropping his keys, Gretchen wouldn't have even heard him or realized he was there. Apparently, though, when he knocked on Misty's door, there was no answer. And when he'd cracked it to take a peek, she was sleeping. He couldn't just enter and wake her up—even a good-ol'-boy like Ray knew that would be an invasion and way too weird, so he'd simply left.

Interestingly, Gretchen learned all this from Ray himself, when she'd spotted him at the network this week, saying a final good-bye to various crew members and employees, and gathering the last of his personal belongings. He'd been forthcoming, too, apparently ready to put the dark period of his desperation behind him and looking forward to getting back to "Tennessee," where life was simpler. Hey, it was hard to find a flaw in that.

There were things she'd probably never know. She'd never officially figured out why Cady had been eavesdropping that day at Susanna's dressing room door, but she'd subsequently spotted her eavesdropping in a stall in the ladies' room when the receptionist had been talking on her cell phone while peeing. When Gretchen had walked in on that, she'd decided to chalk up Cady's eavesdropping to a habit, at best—and a deviant pathology, at worst. Either way, for the moment it seemed harmless.

She'd also never know what Misty was annoyed with Ellie about the morning she arrived at Brett's. It could've been anything, but it wasn't likely to have involved Abe. As far as anyone knew, Misty had no idea that Ellie was involved with Abe, and even if she did, she wouldn't have had much reason to be angry, since she'd dumped him.

Which brought Gretchen to the final piece of the puzzle: Abe, of course. It was still such an incredible disappointment to accept the menace that belied his charming civility, his wholly likable persona. It almost made a girl question if anyone who seemed simply polite could be taken at face value. Clearly the answer was no. But at least he'd made a confession. Apparently, he'd placed the threatening calls and sent the e-mail to Brett just to torment him, never thinking of killing him until he was home in North Carolina visiting relatives and got the idea. With the Destroying Angel local to the area maybe all it took was a passing comment or an item in the paper for Abe to learn of the mushroom and its highly toxic nature.

Gretchen could perfectly recall the conversation at the staff meeting weeks back, the day she'd first met Abe, when he'd mentioned recently returning from a vacation to North Carolina. Yet, even when she'd been researching the Destroying Angel online and come across North Carolina as its origin, she still hadn't made the connection. If she had, she might have also realized that if the Destroying Angel grew in North Carolina, it stood to reason that its hybridized variety, the Gabriel mushroom, would grow there, too—and Abe would have access to both.

Apparently, when he'd set about to find the Destroying Angel, he'd unwittingly found its "cousin," the Gabriel. After having it very discreetly—and expensively—analyzed, and discovering what it was and how closely it mirrored the fatal effects of the Destroying Angel, he knew it would serve his purpose equally well. Then he headed back to New York City and set his plan in motion.

All he needed was the opportunity to slip it to Brett; the poison would be undetectable, death would be torturous and inevitable.

He'd planned to leave the party early to make himself an even more unlikely suspect if Brett's death were ever traced to the night of his party. Abe had no way of knowing what item he'd slip the poison into or when Brett would eat it; he planned to figure it out when he got there. Before he'd left Brett's house that night to drive back to the city, he'd tried to find an opportunity to plant the poison in something in Brett's private kitchen. He'd known about the private kitchen from the tours of the house Brett had given partygoers in past years. But there never seemed to be a time when he could slip away from Ellie long enough to accomplish his goal. So he'd driven Marjorie and that cameraman back to the city, and then later, he'd driven back to the Catskills. When Gretchen heard a noise in the middle of the night, it had been Abe sneaking back into Brett's house to plant the poison in the sauce. Apparently—and this was genius—he'd improvised before he'd left that night, sticking a wad of chewed gum on the inside of the lock on a side entrance to the house. That way, he was able to block the lock from clicking into place when the door was closed, which had made it easy for him to sneak back in and accomplish his mission. The sad twist was that Misty—the woman he'd convinced himself he was in love with, obsessed with, couldn't live without—had ended up consuming the poison.

When Abe had realized the mistake that had been made, he'd been too shocked and appalled to do anything else. He wasn't about to make another attempt on Brett's life when he'd already wasted the perfect murder on the wrong person. He couldn't very well do it again without drawing attention. One person's mysterious fatal illness was one thing, two was something else. The police would never let that go. It would be too risky. And yet, any other murder plot against Brett was simply too risky.

So then he'd finally figured out what he wanted to do. He would get his revenge on Brett another way—by framing him for Misty's murder.

"So how is it?" Rick asked now as he kissed her shoulder.

"Nice," she breathed and sank her back deeper into his chest. She hadn't had a bubble bath since she'd worked at Deluxe Resort, and that hadn't been too great because it'd been in the same tub that the spa used for mud baths and avocado soaks. Remarkably hard to get out the residue with those . . . and speaking of mud and residue . . .

"How did you get your tub so clean?" she asked.

"I scrubbed for two hours while you were sleeping. What are you saying? I'm a pig or something?" he said, reaching for their drink. Earlier, he'd poured a tall glass of ice-cold Sam Adams for them to share, and set it down on the bathmat beside the tub.

"No, but . . . well, you are a little messy, you have to admit," she said, grinning up at him, tilting her head back. "You're pretty messy."

"You didn't seem to mind the last time you were over," he said with a smug quirk of his lips.

"Well, you were distracting me . . ."

"I'll distract you again. Don't worry," he assured her and began massaging the back of her neck with one hand. With a blissful sigh, she snuggled in, savoring the hard strength of his chest . . . and some other hardness that was thickening against her bottom. "Besides, think of my good points," he murmured. "Like my killer personality. My ability to move furniture—" She laughed at that. "How I always pull you out of trouble. And of course, let's not forget how we burn up the sheets together."

"And who's going to distract me from how cocky you are?" Gretchen teased.

"*Moi?* Cocky?"

"You are cocky as *hell*," she said with a laugh.

He pretended to weigh that, then feigned confusion. "You know, I don't see it." As he pulled her in tighter, his full erection rubbed against her opening through the warm water. She sighed breathlessly and tilted her hips back to press against him, felt herself begin to pulse, to throb. "Is this what you meant by cocky?" he said, whispering the words right in her ear, sending whorls of heat fluttering between her legs.

"Tell me my bad points," Rick said softly. "You know, since we've already covered my good ones." On the face of it, he was teasing, but there seemed to be seriousness underlying his words. As if he didn't want to blow this—that this was somehow too good, but he'd hold on anyway—which was funny, because that was exactly how she felt.

But he was wrong about one thing: They hadn't remotely covered his good points. He had so many that went beyond the surface, that were hard for her even to put into words, but that she simply felt whenever she was with him.

Still . . . he'd asked a question, so she might as well take advantage of the opportunity. "Well . . . you can be kind of sexist," she offered tentatively, sitting forward so she could turn her head and look at him.

"Me? Sexist?" he said, surprised. "Really? Doesn't sound like me."

"Oh, you know," she explained, "with your 'girlie' this and 'girlie' that."

"Ohh," he said, nodding. "Okay. I'll work on that. What else?" Biting her lip, Gretchen had trouble suppressing a smile; he was just so damn cute. "C'mere," he said—commanded really—his voice low and serious, as he slid his arms around her belly and pulled her close again. A thrill shivered through her even as she was reminded of another point.

"You're a little bossy, too," she noted, then smiled sweetly. "And stubborn."

"Right, strong. We've covered that."

"We have?"

"The whole furniture-moving thing?"

"Oh," she said with a wisp of a laugh. "True, but strong and stubborn are not the same thing," she argued.

He shrugged. "It's all in the same ballpark."

"Fine, but *bossy* is in a different ballpark," she maintained.

"Okay, I'm kinda bossy," he conceded. "Is that all? Anything else?" He said it like he just wanted to make sure he was getting it— all of it—like he was clarifying.

"Actually, I don't even mind it," Gretchen admitted with a warm smile. "Though I have a feeling I'm gonna have to keep you in line."

"Oh, you'll definitely have to keep me in line," he said with a rough laugh. Like he was thinking: Jeez, is *that* all?

As Gretchen leaned in to kiss him, she thought of one more thing. "And the kind of, uh, blunt expressions you use at times— maybe you could soften those a bit?"

"Boy, you're just full of grievances tonight," he said, eyeing her mischievously, and she giggled. Then he covered her mouth with his, kissing her softly, tenderly.

When they finally pulled apart, Gretchen's lips moved to the curve of his neck and she sighed against his skin. "Oh, Rick . . . I didn't mean any of it. I don't want you to change a thing."

He ran a hand up her back, then into her hair, urging her to look up at him. When her eyes met his, their gaze held. As he studied her, his expression darkened. He looked pensive, romantic, and then slowly it changed. An amused sparkle appeared in his eyes. Curving his mouth into a sexy grin, he said, "Thanks, I'm glad to hear that. So what now—should we bang?"

With a startled laugh, Gretchen shoved his chest in exasperation. He knew damn well that bang was one of his "uh, blunt expressions" that needed work.

Rick burst out laughing and pulled her tighter. "Oh, I'm just messing with you, baby," he said, his voice low again, but gentle now—so she turned her body, rose up, wrapped her arms around his shoulders, and straddled him. He looked so boyishly cute, almost in- nocent the way a lock of his black hair was dipping onto his forehead, the rest messy and half wet, and his dark eyes glittering as they searched hers.

"And in answer to your question," she said, and pressed her hips down, almost sliding him inside her. *"Yes."* With a groan, he pulled her tighter, and she sighed and melded her mouth with his, and both of them tried not to drown.

EPILOGUE

*T*wo months later Rick and Gretchen were at Rick's house in Maine. Brett had relinquished his half, selling it to Rick at a much lower price than Rick had expected. It was a kind of thanks for all that Rick had done and maybe an unspoken truce between them. Rick always said it was the second-best thing he'd gotten that year—Gretchen was the first. (He was so sweet like that.)

Things weren't quite as peachy for Brett these days. Though he tried to twist the publicity from his arrest into a good thing, rumors of his salacious relationship with Misty and the notion that he'd withheld information from the police regarding her death had tarnished his image. His shadiness lost him a lot of fans . . . but gained him a slew of new ones. (People were such sick fucks.)

But for all intents and purposes, Brett was still on top. He still had his Madison Avenue apartment and his Hawaiian bodyguard, who kept the paparazzi and gossip columnists at bay. Soon it would die down. Like every other kind of chaos, it would eventually level out.

Just like work—which was consuming these days, but better now that Shawnee had returned to Massachusetts. Meanwhile Susanna was more anxious than ever with her new show, *Dining Elegance,* going into production, so she still leaned heavily on Gretchen, but it was all just part of the job—a job she loved. Dana had been lucky, too, landing a position at a beautiful day care center on the West Side, with her weekends and nights still free for auditions.

"Holy Christ, is this damn thing done yet?" Rick said now, waving his stick in the air. He was lying on his back on the bearskin rug right by the fire, while they made s'mores indoors. A favorite pastime of Gretchen's when she was growing up, it was so much better when she shared it with someone. "I can't believe it's April and we're sitting by a fire," he added.

"But it's fun, right?"

He quirked his mouth. "Yeah, it's fun." Bit by bit, Rick was acquiescing, trying her way of patience with determination when it came to cooking his marshmallows, but it was *killing* him. She could tell he was still just dying to char it black and then slap it on a graham cracker.

"A little patience, please," she said now, smiling sweetly, knowing it would only frustrate him more. Then she leaned down to place soft kisses on his cheek. "Good, you're learning," she murmured teasingly. "Soon you'll have it . . ."

His arm came up and slid from her neck, down her back, to her waist—and suddenly she was pulled forward and rolled over onto her back, and Rick was kissing her deeply, passionately, with a savage appetite. She moaned softly and melded into the kiss, folding her mouth over his, gently sucking his tongue, which slid in and out with lazy sensuality. What happened to his marshmallow stick? He must've dropped it. But neither of them really cared as they rolled again, and Gretchen was lying on top of him, looking into his flickering blue eyes. Straddling him, she could feel him hard beneath his jeans and she pressed into him. "C'mere," he said huskily, reaching up to cup her neck and pulling her down for another kiss. It was soft and gentle—lingering—and his breath brushed against her lips when he said, "I love you."

Her heart jumped at the words. She'd thought she'd heard him mumble them a few times during sex, but neither of them had ever addressed it. But now Rick was telling her straight out and she knew with every ounce of her soul—

"I love you, too," she whispered, and he kissed her again.

A breathy, blissful sigh spilled from her, feathered his lips, and she wrapped her fingers around his wrist and held on, freezing this moment, savoring it. It hadn't been the requisite four months yet, but . . . maybe he'd get his key lime pie a little early. She couldn't help it; when it came right down to it she was just a softie.

His kisses went on slowly, tenderly, like he was luxuriating in and absorbing the feel of her, the taste of her—but in his arms, she was combustible.

She slid her tongue down his neck, running her mouth over his bare chest and lower, until she got to his fly. Teasingly, she rubbed her cheek against the hard bulge in his pants, until he groaned, "Unzip me," and she did. He wrapped her hair through his fingers, holding her in place. There was something arousing in his grip, the intensity, the authority, because it was Rick and she knew how kind and gentle his heart was. And the sight of him naked and erect, jutting before her, so close to her mouth, undid her.

Leaning forward a fraction, she wrapped her lips around his cock, and when she sucked it deep into her mouth, she ran her tongue around, stroking him as he was inside her. With a deep groan, he tightened his hands in her hair. But she pulled back, and succulently, she kissed the tip. Holding him tightly in her hand, she kept on kissing until he nearly growled—then she slid him back inside her mouth as far as he could go. She could feel him full and throbbing, ready to burst. Gruffly he urged her, *"Keep sucking,"* and the rough sound of need, together with his power, his maleness, his hunger, sent her over the edge. She sucked him even harder and, with his hand gripped in her hair, he exploded in her mouth. She took in all of him, aroused by the rush and the taste of him, and when she finally climbed back up to look into her eyes, he was drowsily looking back at her.

"Holy Jesus Christ Mary Mother of God . . ." he said in a string of religious words that, given the context, would offend good Catholics everywhere.

Later, when they were hugging sleepily on the bearskin rug, watching the glowing embers, she said, "Isn't it funny how the first night we met, you—"

"Saved you from a fire," he supplied.

"I was gonna say yelled at me."

"Oh, right . . . but why's that funny?"

"Because here we are. And putting out a fire. Okay, you're right about that. And then I saw you again and you were helping me at Terra Cottage when I dropped my stuff everywhere—and Susanna's lunch, too—and then I saw you *again* at Brett's house and you were being all enigmatic and hard to read, because you thought I liked your brother . . ."

"Oh, that's right . . ." he said casually, acting like his jealousy were mild, now that it had passed. Snuggling in closer, Gretchen rested her cheek in the crook of Rick's neck for a moment and sighed. "And don't forget how I helped you up when you fell in the snow," he put in.

Smiling softly, she said, "Yes. That was sweet . . . but then you were a jerk again, of course."

"Was that before or after you seduced me?"

"I seduced you?" she echoed incredulously. "Ha! You seduced me."

"No, I'm pretty sure you who seduced *me*," he insisted, but she wasn't buying it. By the gleam in his eye, she wasn't sure that he was, either. "And then I saved you from a murderer," he added. With a shake of his head, Rick clicked his tongue and said, "A lot of saving your cute butt going on in this relationship." Comments like this that might have seemed sexist if she didn't know him better—but she did know him. And besides being sweet and caring, when he was feeling mischievous, he loved to tease her.

Curving her mouth, Gretchen concluded, "Well, I have to say, in light of everything you've laid out here, you *are* pretty wonderful."

"Thanks," Rick said with a satisfied grin.

"I'd better get my hooks in fast."

"You already have. Let's monogram the towels right now."

Laughing, Gretchen said, "Okay. And let's carve our names in the nearest wooden surface. Oh! And let's get matching T-shirts that say ENDLESS LOVE."

Doubtfully, Rick slanted her a look. "We'll start with the towels and see how far we get." Then he leaned in closer with that wolfish grin of his, and she knew what came next. Sliding his warm, strong hand up her neck, he kissed her deeply, drugging her with the slow, sensual glide of his tongue, until she was clutching the fabric of his shirt, nearly breathless. As he strummed his fingers along her skin, he murmured, "*Rick plus Gretchen,* that's simple enough."

"For what, the carving, the T-shirts, or the towels?" she asked playfully, knowing that none of the above was actually going to happen.

"Take your pick," he replied, kissing her cheek.

"Hmm," she sighed. "It's nice . . . but I think I know something even better."

"What?"

Grinning, she ran her palm over his roughened cheek and looked into his crystal-blue eyes. *"Little apple and the wolf."*

Well, he could hardly argue with that.

Jill Winters realized that she preferred fiction to term papers when she wrote her first novel, *Plum Girl,* instead of her master's dissertation. Coincidentally, this was around the same time she became a sleep-deprived, ruminating coffee junkie. A Phi Beta Kappa, summa cum laude graduate of Boston College with a degree in history, Jill has taught women's studies as well as numerous workshops for aspiring writers. She is the author of *Just Peachy, Raspberry Crush, Blushing Pink,* and *Plum Girl,* which was a finalist for the Dorothy Parker Award of Excellence. *Lime Ricky* is her fifth book.

You can visit her online at www.jillwinters.com.